With a debut novel, Alex Bertea has written *The Speed Merchant* with a keen eye to strong research, strong character development, and strong narrative. For sure, his technical knowledge of airplanes and flying in general, is unsurpassed. With years of experience in aviation, Alex brings to his pages a compelling plot and authentic characters that will keep the reader up well past midnight. The settings are authentic and well-cast making the reader feel as if he is right there. And don't forget to buckle up. Because the same applies to the flying scenes with the reader in the cockpit for every kick of the rudder pedal and touch on the stick. Not since the days of Ernest K. Gann (*The High and the Mighty*) will readers be so well satisfied.

—John J. Gobbell,
Author of *The Last Lieutenant*, the Todd Ingram series, and other novels of the Pacific War

THE SPEED MERCHANT

To Kristen,
Clear skies & tailwinds!
A Bertea

ALEX BERTEA

ISBN: 978-1-64184-592-2 (Hardback)
ISBN: 978-1-64184-593-9 (Paperback)
ISBN: 978-1-64184-594-6 (Ebook)

DEDICATION

To my father, who taught me everything worth
knowing about life, and flying.

ACKNOWLEDGEMENTS

First off, I would like to thank my father, Capt. Richard Bertea, USMCR, Ret., for introducing me to the world of the airman, his unstinting support, advice, and suggestions, and the several read-throughs which helped improve the story. I would also like to thank Ed W. Hennings for his insight into the commercial aviation industry in all its facets, and former C-130 pilot LCDR Sharon Hennings, USNR, Ret., the first female Navy aircraft commander in Antarctica, for her supportive technical guidance. Heartfelt thanks to John J. 'Jack' Gobbell, for his invaluable insights, extensive comments on my manuscript, and tips on the publishing industry in general. Also, special thanks to Dale Brown for his sage thoughts on where to go next. Many thanks to retired FBI Special Agent Mike Comella, LtCol USMCR, Ret., for his suggestions on federal law enforcement procedures, and to John Muszala of Pacific Fighters who greatly helped me understand the inner workings of warbird aircraft. And grateful thanks to Michael Hathorn, who encouraged me to publish, to my editor Jill Morris-Ehmke, and to Chris O'Byrne and the team at JetLaunch for their fast and efficient services.

Finally, and most of all, I'd like to thank my wife Katrin, without whose endless patience and loving support I never could have brought this to fruition.

PROLOGUE

The peasants smelled the crash site long before they stumbled upon it, the watery dawn light high on a saddle in the northern Sierra Madre Occidental.

A thin column of smoke and a hard morning's mule ride from their village over the ridge in a rocky valley to the north had brought them to the general area; the reek of charred manzanita, juniper and scrub oak guided them the rest of the way.

The scarred strip of terrain ran for one hundred meters or more up the slope between two peaks spotted with Yecora and Piñon pine, forming a swath of churned earth strewn with debris. The exposed stony soil had been burned black by the intense heat, and small fragments of aluminum and Plexiglas and other materials littered the area. Two larger dark lumps at the upper end of the dark scar seemed to be the remains of engines, the stubs of propellers bent backwards. Up close, the stench was penetrating and overwhelming, and kept changing with the wind: burned metal, gasoline, melted polyester fabric and, presumably, somewhere in the devastation, charred flesh.

The peasants gazed in bemused awe at the site. They were farmers, a father and son, from a nearby *ejido,* who eked out a living running a handful of wiry cattle and trying to coax corn out of the arid, marginal soil. The muffled thunderclap the previous evening on a cold clear night had been out of place, and had roused them early.

Explosions were a familiar phenomenon in the region, where dynamite assisted the illegal-timber operations with their product extraction and helped ranchers clear debris off narrow roads. Sometimes, warring gangs blew up farmers' trucks to make a point, or just for fun. But that usually happened during daylight hours when you could see what you were doing. Gunfire was even more common, popcorn staccatos occurring *veinticuatro horas del día.* The *policías* never showed up, unless they were already involved in assisting someone's turf war.

The elder was bandy-legged, with a spit-stained western shirt, a black claw of a mustache, and a creased visage the color of a weathered saddle tree. He was somewhere in his mid-fifties – he didn't know for sure – but to someone from the north he would have looked twenty years older. His son, in his early twenties, wore dusty jeans, a Kansas City Royals tee shirt, and a worn trucker cap with '701' emblazoned prominently across the front.

Opportunity had led them there, the chance to find something worth money before other scroungers arrived. That, and a concern for fire. Though it had rained the previous morning, there was still a fair amount of smoke still coming from the wreckage. The plane had crashed in an area characterized more by low shrubs and high grass than trees, and it looked to the older man like the heavy morning dew had suppressed the worst spots. He knew if it flared up, local timber interests would pressure the authorities in Chihuahua to send the fire-bombing planes. Up here, pine wood was the second biggest cash crop after drugs – too valuable to go up in smoke.

The boy kicked at some pieces of burnt aluminum, scavenging for anything of value, while the old man lit a cigarette and gazed south at one of the larger *narco* spreads. He adjusted his dirty straw cowboy hat, and spat, his mouth set in a grim line. To supplement his farming, he used to tend a small field of *yerba*, the 'good stuff', for the local boss. When traditional subsistence farming couldn't keep the family fed, 'the crop that pays' was always in demand, and often the only way a man could make a living in this place. But that was before the *hijos de putas* from the western coast had rolled into town. They had coolly presented the boss' widow with his head in a sack after he had refused to let them simply take over his operation. The still-living members of the entire family had fled by evening.

A few weeks later, another gang from the Chihuahua side had ascended to the valley to reclaim the territory for their cartel. The ensuing struggle had laid waste to farms and families for miles around. Farmers were dragged from their beds and shot in front of their children, just for harvesting a patch for their aggressors' rivals. When anyone could get killed for merely making a living, all sense was gone.

The old man watched his son sadly as he picked up a black piece of metal, then quickly dropped it, fanning his hand. He was a good kid, but the mayhem would get him one way or another. He'd be found on a blood-soaked dirt road after speaking to the wrong girl, or he'd be coopted by a cartel recruiter, handed a wad of cash and a bag full of *perico*, and told at gunpoint what his new job would entail. The old man had already been warned by his second cousin that the hat his son wore bore the number of a *narco* lord's wealth on some *norte* money magazine list.

Maybe it was time to run. Pack what little he had in the truck and go to one of those camps on the coast near the army. He would lose his land and everything his family had worked for, but that would happen anyway when he was dead.

He stubbed his cigarette out with the heel of his left boot, moistened his cracked lips, and whistled to the boy that they were leaving. *Federale*, *judiciale*, or mafioso, someone was going to eventually stop by to find out what happened to their load, and he didn't want to be around when they did.

* * *

A few hours later, a jacked-up Ford pickup with knobby off-road tires, shiny rims, and an oversized chrome grill, blaring *narcocorridos* at top volume, growled its way up the mountain from the south on a gut-numbing set of switchbacks that looked like they were made for mules more than trucks. When the road disappeared a few hundred meters below the saddle, two men wearing white straw hats, mirrored aviator shades, black leather jackets and ostrich-skin cowboy boots climbed out and started working their way up the stony slope.

The side brims of their hats were rolled up *cinco en troka*, so-called because it allowed five hatted men to ride abreast in the cab of a pickup. In the Sierra Madre, hats can talk. These two told anyone who cared to look…basically, look somewhere else.

Gold watches, gold necklaces and silk shirts proclaimed the men's stature in their field, which was further identified by the Kalashnikov-pattern assault rifles they wore slung over their shoulders. The ascent was arduously slow, and made all the more demanding by the relentless noon sun. But the appalling heat didn't deter the traffickers from reaching their goal, let alone removing their shiny goatskin jackets. Apparently, this task was too important to be left to run-of-the-mill hired hands.

Only thin wisps of grey smoke emanated from the blackened furrow by the time the *narcos* attained the saddle, and they only took a brief smoke break to catch their wind before casting an analytical eye on the junk-littered burnt turf. Though their employer hadn't lost any shipments, it could only enhance their cartel's competitive position if they could figure out who else had.

Twenty minutes later, they called it quits and started the steep hike back down to the pickup. Not only was there no evidence of a narcotics payload in the wreckage, but the plane was a light, piston twin, incapable of hauling a load worth the time of any respectable trafficker. Upon reaching the truck, they blasted off in a cloud of road dust and wailing *norteño* music, leaving the charred saddle to the merciless afternoon heat.

* * *

One week later, in response to an inquiry from the U.S. Consulate in Ciudad Juarez, a U.S.-registered commercial helicopter on an aerial-spraying contract to the Mexican drug authority landed at the site to examine the wreckage. Photos were taken, and the remains of the pilot, which had been enthusiastically gnawed-upon by scavengers, were bagged and strapped into the cargo area for further investigation. The wreckage of the fuselage was left where it had crashed.

* * *

CHAPTER ONE

S omething to the west, moving low and fast, flashed silver in the morning sun, then disappeared.

Traffic. Cook strained forward against his seat harness, rapidly scanning the dull haze between the arid scrub horizon and the dun-colored Tehachapi range for another look at whatever had caught his eye, before flicking his attention to the pale-breasted locust hawks effortlessly circling the thermals bordering the freeway. Many things were flying in the valley today, feathered and aluminum both. An impact with any of them could be fatal at his velocity.

He inched the throttle forward with his Nomex-sheathed hand, pouring more high-octane aviation fuel into the eighteen coffee can-sized cylinders of the aircraft's 55-litre Wright R-3350 radial engine, listening to the furiously churning steel symphony for any stray harmonics indicating a timing issue. At just under two hundred and ninety miles-per-hour, a thrown rod could turn the massive powerplant into a smoking mess in seconds. Cook had seen it happen many times during air races. And at a hundred thousand a pop for a custom-tuned model, which they all were, you couldn't do it very often and still stay in business. Heartbreaking was one word for it. Bankruptcy was another.

Cook checked his airspeed, and swept over the fuel, pressure and temperature gauges before shifting his glance to the windscreen and scanning the horizon again. Like all well-trained pilots, he did this religiously while flying. In his experience, radial engines liked to quit when you weren't looking. Maintaining a constant watch on an engine's temperature and pressure helped prevent unpleasant surprises. Diligence in flying was its own reward – complacency at the stick could turn you into a black, greasy stain across the sun-baked desert floor below.

He paused his scan and squinted forward through his helmet's darkened visor to see if he could make out what had caused the earlier flash, but whatever it was had faded into the pale, desert haze. No matter. At his aircraft's speed, the mountains were growing in the forward glass, and he would have to make a turn soon.

Cook was piloting an experimental-class aircraft, a highly modified fighter plane from World War II that had borrowed parts from several different aircraft in an attempt to optimize it for air racing. The fuselage and engine were from a Grumman F8F Bearcat that had flown in the Pacific Theater. The wing sections, thinner than the originals, were spirited from a North American P-51 Mustang that had fought with the US Army Air Force in North Africa. The 'tail feathers', the control surfaces in the rear, were largely custom work done by Cook himself. She was a mongrel and looked a bit strange to those in the know, but she was agile and fast – very fast.

A short burst of static barked in his helmet earphones, followed by a 'chunking' sound and a flicker in the display of the aviation-band radio in the instrument cluster.

That would be a gentle reminder from Gorman, in the chase plane. Cook was about to reach the limit of his aerobatic 'box', a special-use airspace on the aviation charts spelling out a giant, virtual polygon in the sky that permitted all kinds of fun activity in aircraft. Cook let back on the throttle significantly and dipped a wing to the left to clear any cross-traffic below; planes with wings mounted on the lower part of the fuselage created a large blind-spot. He then looked side-to-side and tried to locate Gorman's position, which should have been far aft given Cook's velocity.

Not seeing him, Cook squirmed his butt into a more comfortable position in his seat-pack, inhaled deeply, and took one last look around. Then he advanced the throttle, and pitched the plane into a steep left bank, his helmeted head pinned to the headrest – looking up, relatively speaking, into his turn.

Gravity descended on Cook like a blanket of lead, causing the calf, thigh, and stomach pads of his gravity suit to inflate pneumatically, preventing the blood supply in his upper torso from rushing down to his feet. These 'speed jeans', as they were affectionately called by military pilots, were worn on the outside of a pilot's fire-retardant flight suit and helped prevent him from blacking-out under the intense pressure of high-G maneuvers. They were supposed to support consciousness up to 9 times normal gravity, about double that of a Top Fuel dragster doing the quarter mile in 4.4 seconds.

In theory, anyway, Cook reminded himself as he clenched his abdomen and sucked in air – they didn't always work.

He continued banking, listening to complaints from the airframe as he pushed the hybrid racer through the punishing turn. Cook's plane, even in its base, unmodified configuration, was faster than some of the early jet-age aircraft, and the original design was never intended to handle the kind of stress that Cook was putting it through. Key sections of the wing spar, landing gear wells, and fuselage had been strengthened with spar doublers and shear panels, but everything was theoretical until you got her in the air.

Cook smirked, baring his teeth with the effort. Planes were women, in his world. Some beautiful, some not, some cranky, some bitchy. But each with her own personality, no two the same. Like all the women in Cook's life, they weren't around long, and they always seemed to have some sort of issue. Like the creaking that was emanating from beneath his seat.

Rivets letting go sounded like gunshots in the plane's interior. This was more like the sound of a wooden ship's timbers groaning as it plowed into oncoming swells. Probably just the reinforcement plates flexing a bit. Cook retarded the throttle a bit, letting the big propeller slow his velocity. He didn't want to break anything on the first real test flight. Gorman, his boss, wouldn't look kindly on Cook damaging something that was easily worth fifty times his annual salary. And a structural failure at any speed necessitated a bailout – it wasn't for nothing that a test pilot's seat-pack doubled as a parachute.

But Cook knew the plane could take it. He didn't own her, he couldn't even afford a day's fuel to keep her running – but she was his work from the ground up.

As the numbers on the directional gyro spun toward a true east heading, a nearby ridge looking somewhat like a sleeping dog slid into view through the arc of the giant propeller that had been cannibalized from a P-3 Orion antisubmarine patrol plane. Cook, who liked naming things from the air, called it 'Fido' and found it useful as a navigation marker. He began his roll out. His craft responded beautifully, the wing leading edges slicing through the turn like a hot scalpel through excess belly fat. Pleased at the response, he relaxed a notch to scan the terrain ahead.

Fanning out in a sideways V-shape to the east, the Antelope Valley was an immense, arid bowl that marked the beginning of the tortuously hot Mojave Desert, which extended as far as Las Vegas and the northern part of Arizona. To the south were the Sierra Pelona and San Gabriel ranges, which formed part of the mountain ring surrounding the Los Angeles basin, efficiently trapping pollution and ensuring the air was always thick and brown.

Empty, for the most part. For a flight test, you couldn't ask for more.

The California high desert was where the back of sound had been broken in the heyday of manned flight, where rocket planes like the North American X-15 had lit-off their liquid oxygen torches and pierced the blue-black veil of space. Just a bit east of Cook's position were the massive, restricted airspaces of the legendary flight test centers, Edwards and Armstrong, where virtually every aerospace technology commonly taken for granted in today's commercial aviation had been developed and refined. After Kitty Hawk, this boundless scorching basin was as close as you could get to the cradle of the pure essence of flight.

The private-sector successors of the early pioneers were still at it today, further north at Mojave, recently-renamed a 'spaceport'. Wild-eyed visionaries, backed by billionaire fellow travelers, launched spaceplanes powered by rockets burning tire rubber, driven by ego and commercial impulse to hurl tourists and thrill-seekers on six-figure jaunts into the black void.

Cook frowned under his visor. It was also where he'd worked up until three years ago. Before his life had gotten turned upside down.

Another hash of static broke squelch, interrupting his reverie, followed by a second's hum of carrier tone in Cook's headset. Gorman again, trying to focus his attention.

"Ennex fah-ve wun ho-tayle nanner, fee-ool stayte." Parsing Gorman's thick Arkansas twang, Cook checked his fuel gauge. Gorman wasn't really asking how much fuel he had left – he just wanted to know when Cook was planning on ending this particular daydream and coming back to earth.

"Chase One, NX51H9, fuel 'bingo' plus thirty, ETA Whisky Juliet Fox one zero minutes." Cook's formal reply was a jab at Gorman's homespun, Ozark drawl. The radio was tuned to a 'chat channel' on the edge of the air band, to a frequency that professional pilots often used when passing traffic that didn't concern air traffic control. No one else would be listening.

A static bark and 'chunk' were Gorman's equivalent of a grunted 'kiss my ass'.

Curious how the stiffened wing spar would handle the bounce of ground turbulence, Cook cleared his immediate area with a lazy, left-turning orbit, then chopped back aggressively on the throttle, dropping to within a hundred feet of the desert floor. Gorman's Skyraider floated into view above him. He then pushed the throttle forward to 75% of the engine's 'buster' rating, which meant 'best continuous power'. At this setting, over five gallons of high-octane fuel were pouring into the giant cylinders every minute. Cook held his foot down on the right rudder and leaned left against the stick, fighting the giant propeller's propensity to flip the entire aircraft upside down after an abrupt acceleration. The transition pressed Cook back against his seat as Gorman's chase plane flashed away aft, leaving him impossibly far behind.

Strictly speaking, this maneuver was something saved for a far later phase of the flight test procedure and simulated the conditions one would experience during an air race. It was also illegal, violating Federal Aviation Administration speed restrictions under ten thousand feet. But Cook was impatient to see what his plane could do, and he was pretty sure nobody from the FAA was watching. He knew he'd have about ten seconds before Gorman jumped down his throat.

A radial engine of the type Cook was testing normally ran at a comfortable 30 pounds per-square-inch of manifold pressure at normal cruising speeds, and was cautiously considered capable of increasing to about 50 'inches'. Extended use at high pressure would blow an unmodified engine intake manifold, throwing viscous black aircraft oil onto the cowling and the canopy, turning the aircraft into a smoky mess.

Cook was running his engine at 62 inches and turning his oversized prop for a groundspeed of just over four hundred miles per hour. This was the automobile equivalent of NASCAR racing loads on a typical Chrysler minivan. But since virtually nothing on this plane was stock anymore, Cook figured it could take the punishment.

Speed was everything. Agility around the race pylons looked pretty, and made the ladies ooh and aah, but brute-strength power matched with the right propeller and a low-drag profile brought the checkered flag every time. And in the end, that was what counted. Wringing every ounce of speed out of an airframe was what Cook did, and, for him, getting to the high end of the airspeed gauge was the only way to really feel alive.

Cook gripped the throttle quadrant, advancing it and the propeller RPM forward slightly, taking care not to 'over rev' the power or 'overspeed' the prop. The straining whine of the engine heightened its pitch infinitesimally, as internal engine nozzles sprayed a water-alcohol mixture into the cylinders to keep temperatures sustainable. The supercharger and a Nitrous-Oxide injection system brought the cylinders up to a cringe-worthy 410 degrees Fahrenheit.

Screaming through the roiling air at speeds that would actually heat the plane's aluminum skin, every pocket of air instability in the plane's path translated into a sharp blow, the fuselage shuddering as the specially thinned and clipped speed wings sent increasingly frequent kicks to Cook's gut through the heavily-stressed wing spar. Vibrations rattled his cheeks, and his left hand started to go numb with the effort. Air racing always looked smooth from the audience perspective, but it was a carnival ride in the cockpit.

Cook's ten seconds of latitude ended.

"Get that nose up and R.T.B. or you're history."

The corner of Cook's mouth twitched. 'R.T.B' meant 'return to base'. When Gorman was pissed, the Arkansas dropped right out of his voice. Cook keyed the mike, responding with effort.

"Roger. One Hotel Niner returning to base."

Cook knew he had tested his boss' patience enough. He held on for another few seconds as sand pans and twisted scrub flashed away below, his diaphragm tensed as he savored the sensations rolling through him. Then, with a sharp exhale, he relaxed his gut and shoulders, pulled the throttle back to a mid-range drone, and eased the stick back to gain some altitude.

The plane was liquid magic; mercury flowing across a hot skillet. He knew every inch of her lethally beautiful, shiny polished body, and it amazed him how the simple act of flying it transported him. It was like brushing the flank of the divine. Not many aircraft did that.

But just like good sex, the feeling was fleeting. The plane belonged to some asshole developer out of

Phoenix who wanted to race it once or twice a year so he could brag to his buddies about his super slick Topgun stick-jockey skills and sniff the crotches of real, working pilots at race briefings. It was a depressingly familiar story in the business. With the exception of very senior airline pilots, the guys who flew for a living rarely had the money for these toys. Only the super-wealthy could play in this arena.

Cook shook off his mood, further reduced his speed to a normal cruise, about 260 miles-per-hour, and pointed his nose toward the airfield. The fun was over – back to work. He redirected the tedium by scanning groundward.

Up close, at reduced speed, the desert floor flashing beneath the engine's shiny metal cowling looked different. Lumpy gray-green scrub tufted with pale yellow blooms carpeted an endless flat interspersed with brittle brown tumbleweeds. The drabness of the landscape was relieved by an occasional tar-paper shack, blasted black by the unrelenting desert sun. The soil under the scrub looked so white and flat that it seemed to have been underwater and only drained recently, rather than a geological age before.

It was a hard landscape to love, and it took a special need to make someone stay. For Cook, the association with the raw, primal edge of flight was all it took. He would have a tough time being happier anywhere else.

Reality intruded in the shape of the Skyraider in the canopy's rear-view mirror.

Gorman had finally caught up with him. He had been flying the chase plane inside Cook's racetrack course, and had closed immediately aft when Cook slowed, trailing in tight behind the racer's right wing now that he could keep up. The Skyraider was a Korean War-vintage Douglas A-1, dressed in Marine camouflage livery, with an unmodified version of the same engine running in Cook's aircraft. It belonged to an orthopedist in Santa Monica, and most of the year it schlepped from airshow to airshow as a static display. At full power it could do about two-thirds the velocity of the faster plane.

Cook knew Gorman had formed up closely to examine the fuselage for any fluid trails indicating leaks, or aluminum panels shaken loose during flight. Or anything else he could take out of Cook's paycheck in retribution. He probably also optimistically thought that sheer proximity would encourage Cook to bring the plane home. Gorman's nagging always made Cook restless, like an anxious mother coming into his room to check whether he was actually doing his homework.

Sighing mentally, Cook pulled back on the control column to get some altitude, punched the radio selector to the local traffic frequency and pickled the microphone on the grip. "Fox traffic, Bearcat One Hotel Niner is two west at one thousand, inbound for midfield break, left traffic runway two-four."

Gorman jumped on that. The transceiver lit up; his helmet earphones crackled.

"Negative on the break, Hotel Niner – standard entry into the pattern."

Cook waited. Instead of gradually descending for miles like an airliner or crawling slowly in a rectangle at a thousand feet around an airport's flight pattern, military pilots usually flew straight in over the runway threshold and pulled a hard bank called a 'break' to establish their landing pattern. Airfields like Fox with a lot of warbird traffic were used to it. For Cook, it was icing on the cake of an exhilarating flight test.

"Acknowledge my last." The threshold was moments away.

Cook ignored him, and hauled back on his stick, propelling his mount into a punishing climbing turn toward a low ridge to the north. As gravity tried to push him deep into his seat, Cook watched his boss fall behind like a shot buzzard plummeting earthward.

* * *

Gorman was leaning against a tow-cart in front of his hangar wearing a scowl as Cook rolled to a halt, braked, and advanced the throttle to 1,000 rpm for thirty seconds. He then throttled back to 800 rpm and pulled out the mixture handle to 'Idle Cut Off', starving his plane's engine. The blackened cylinder exhaust pipes on the sides of the cowling coughed in protest, then spat smoke, as if quitting wasn't something the engine wanted to do. The massive four-bladed propeller shuddered to a halt, shaking the entire airframe in the process. Cook waited until the vibration stopped and flicked the magneto switch to 'Off'.

Fighter aircraft like the Bearcat never had had any air conditioning installed; it was a luxury that just added weight. The instant you landed at a hot airport like Fox the cockpit would turn into a tropical greenhouse. Cook had already cracked the canopy open on the taxi to Gorman's hanger, but clammy rivulets of sweat were running down his neck.

He squinted through the heat distortion as he shoved the hot Plexiglas canopy back all the way and saw that Gorman's sweaty gray comb-over was askew, bobbing with agitation. The five-foot-seven bantam frame harbored a ferocious temper when provoked, and Cook expected the usual tongue-lashing for his stunt. He sighed and started unbuckling the four-point harness connecting him to his parachute seat-pack, wondering if it was time to start looking for another job.

Cook skinned his gloves and unplugged his radio cord as Gorman vaulted onto the wing with a spryness that belied his sixty-two years. The older man gripped the cockpit rail with both hands, the intensity of his grasp paling his thickly ribbed knuckles.

"You unhappy with your job, or something?"

Cook shrugged. "Wanted to stretch her out a bit, see how she handled."

Gorman's lips were compressed into a thin line. He was angry.

Cook closed his eyes for a two-count to stop himself from saying anything he'd regret, then looked back at the older man.

"Look, she handled it just fine. Temps were all green, and only a few groans – no squawks." A 'squawk' was a problem with a plane serious enough to merit a note in the logbook.

Cook gripped the cockpit rails to haul himself up out of the seat, but Gorman wasn't finished. His Ozark upbringing predisposed him to hang on to things like a razorback hog with a melon rind. A rough, work-calloused hand pushed down firmly on Cook's shoulder.

"That's a three-million-dollar bird you're sitting in...minimum. More, if it wins at Reno." Gorman peered under Cook's visor, looking him right in the eyes. "You hand me a check for that, you can rub up on her any way you like. Until then, you act like a fucking adult – understood?"

Cook pursed his lips, glancing sidelong at the hand on his shoulder.

Not expecting an answer, Gorman continued. "And, no, you ain't quitting either, shithead. There's still four hours left on the clock, and you're gonna rip that engine apart by sundown – see if you burned anything up playing Chuck Yeager."

Cook sighed – he was doing a lot of that lately – and ripped the Velcro band on the kneeboard strapped to his left leg. He knew his boss really wasn't angry at the impromptu speed trial, just pissed off at being ignored. Cook pulled off his helmet, exhaling with relief as it released his matted black hair, plastered under a sweat-soaked cotton skullcap. The baking mid-morning air started the evaporation process, instantly cooling his head. The skullcap kept the foam padding inside the helmet from becoming greasy and brought the temperature down fractionally.

Gorman put out his hand for the helmet.

"By the way, before you get dirty, Stubbsie told me there's some guy waiting for you in the diner." 'Stubbs' was Gorman's nickname for his apprentice mechanic, who was at this moment kneeling on the tacky asphalt under the Bearcat's nose, attaching a tow bar to the aircraft's spindly white gear legs. If Stubbs had a real name, Cook had never heard it.

Cook's face took on a perplexed look, as he distractedly wound the helmet's radio cord into a loop around his hand. "He got a name?"

"Fuck if I know." Gorman generally maintained a profanity-laced patter throughout the entire workday – off radio, anyway. "Lawyer. Said he wants to talk to you about your uncle or something."

"Huh." Cook handed over his helmet with his gloves and helmet cord tucked inside, grasped the hot canopy rails and lifted his torso up like he was performing on a set of parallel bars. He then pulled his long legs out of the cockpit footwells, an operation that took a bit of finesse considering its design for people from a shorter era. Sitting perched on the rail, he swiveled his feet onto the wing's tarry-looking patch of grip tape that covered the walkable area of the wing root; Gorman had already moved up the wing root towards the propeller to give him room.

Cook's lanky build stood a bit over six-two, tall for a pilot. His facial lines were usually worked into an easy grin, browned by too many hours in the cockpit sun, but he wasn't smiling. A pair of mirrored bronze Ray-Ban aviators, replacing his helmet visor against the blinding glare, covered any expression in the washed hazel eyes underneath. "Didn't say which uncle, did he?"

"Nope." Gorman studied Cook's face for a moment, noting his abnormally stiff posture and vacant aspect, then nodded. "Look...take an hour if you need it. Stubbsie and I'll get things started."

Cook stirred. "Yeah. Thanks."

* * *

Cook made a cautious exit out of the back of the cool hangar into a blazing parking area that seemed hotter than the tarmac, if such a thing were possible. In contrast to the somewhat more recently paved aircraft ramp, the parking lot behind the hangar was bleached white and crumbling. Asphalt didn't last long in the furnace sun. Nothing really did.

Off to his left was the airfield's imposing but faded military-style entryway, with its sweeping brown lawns and classic 1960's-style façade that hearkened back to the Strategic Air Command era. It was designed at a time when the B-52 jet bomber was the height of technology. For Cook it always evoked a sense of nostalgic loss, the decline of a black-and-white superpower in a multihued world. The antiquated and defunct terminal, now housing a worn-out diner called Foxy's Café and not much else, was straight ahead.

As he thoughtfully approached the tired-looking building, Cook ran through what he liked to call his situational state.

He had been working for Gorman for about two years, and he hadn't gone to any particular pains to disguise that fact. Anyone with an axe to grind or grievance to settle wouldn't have had a very difficult time finding him. As far as he could remember, he didn't owe anyone money, and he hadn't slept with anyone's wife recently.

But one thing he was very clear on. He didn't have an uncle – not one living, anyway.

His pulse quickened as he saw a white Ford Crown Victoria parked in front of the diner door. There were never many cars parked outside Foxy's, but he knew them all. Activating old instincts that usually lay dormant, he summoned the details with relative ease. The owner had an outdated Acura that he kept in immaculate condition, polishing it in the mornings to avoid the midday sun's blaze and parking it in a carport he had built to give it shade. The illegal Honduran cook drove a beat-up Corolla that had suspiciously new-looking plates. Lupe, the Mexican waitress from Nogales, slept with the diner's owner and rode with him.

In Cook's prior life, if you drove a Crown Victoria, or its close cousin the Grand Marquis, you were a cop or a government official. Usually, though not in this case, there would be an antenna or two poking out of the trunk lid, and another low-profile knob on the roof. Not a heavyweight, though. Higher ranking officials and VIPs rode around in Surburbans, Escalades, or other large sport utility vehicles with blacked out windows.

But no lawyer would be caught dead in one, not even the ambulance chasers. Anything that looked too much like a cop car could be bad for business.

Cook's senses keyed up to their highest awareness level as he squinted at the vehicle, the harsh sun alternately bouncing off its light body color and getting sucked in by its dark window tint. California plates, current tags, nothing out of the ordinary. The body was dusty, but so was everything else out here. He could see a window sticker inside at the bottom left front of the windshield, but he couldn't make out what was written on it. By that point, he didn't have to.

Cook turned and pulled open Foxy's glass door, tinted black against the searing sun, and waited for his eyes to adjust to the shaded interior. It only took him a moment to locate Porter sitting at a table against the wall in the far corner.

Cook's jaw clenched, and he felt his fists ball up reflexively. He inhaled deeply through his nose, holding it for a moment, then exhaled, his mouth forming into a cold grimace. He started forward stiffly. Might as well get this over with.

* * *

CHAPTER TWO

Porter's head was down, reading the local community rag.

The booth he sat in was positioned in the back corner of the diner, next to a dark tinted glass window that looked out on the runway. It had a clear view of the main entrance and a smaller door on the opposite side of the diner that gave access to the transient aircraft parking area. It also was close to the swinging service door that led out of the kitchen, offering an easy path out the back, should one be needed.

Cook usually sat there. He was always more comfortable with a wall at his back and unobstructed views of the exits. Porter had probably chosen it instinctively as well.

The man had aged in the past few years. A little less hair on top, the grey finally winning over the coarse black thatch, carrying a little more weight around the neck, an expanded paunch he had clearly grown comfortable with. But he still had the barrel-chest and massive chop-like forearms he'd had when Cook had met him thirty years earlier.

Since Porter had an unobstructed view of the flight line from his table, Cook assumed he had monitored the Bearcat's landing, and the taxi back to the hangar. A matte-black handheld radio on the vinyl banquette next to Porter confirmed it. He had probably timed Cook's entrance at the diner to the minute.

Cook slowly approached and stood a couple of steps back from the table, hands on his hips, waiting for acknowledgement. Porter continued to read, ignoring Cook's presence. Cook felt the blood pounding in his cheeks.

"Goddamned donkey-sucking left-wing hippies… those ass-clowns couldn't piss in the shower without help." Porter's deep bass was rife with exasperation. He still hadn't looked up.

Cook just stared at him. He briefly envisioned grabbing what was left of Porter's hair, yanking his head back, and punching down on the bridge of his nose. That might get his attention.

The older man stirred, folded the paper, and glanced up casually at Cook. "How are things, Guy?"

"What the fuck you doing here, Ted?"

A thin smile broke across Porter's face.

"You haven't aged a day, Cook. What's your secret?"

"Clean living," Cook snapped. He wondered why he even answered. Common courtesy? "You get lost or something?"

Porter ignored the question, kept smiling, and nodded at the other bench. "Take a load off."

"Thanks, I'll keep standing."

"Suit yourself." Porter reopened his paper, resuming his reading.

Cook hesitated, realizing that he'd lost any advantage the anger had given him. Goddamned Porter. That fat bastard could always play him.

He snorted and sat. Lupe, the café's waitress, who had waited patiently during the standoff, brought a cup of coffee over to join the one on the table in front Porter, then left without a word. She knew Cook's habits, that he drank coffee at all hours, and that he liked to be left alone. Perhaps she had recognized this trait in Porter as well. She obviously sensed the tension in the air and didn't want any part of it.

Porter had thrown his coat with his usual carelessness on the seat next to him, and still wore the short-sleeved shirt with a dark clip-on tie that he had favored, as a business attire, since the early seventies. If he was trying to look like a lawyer, Cook scoffed, he'd missed it by about fifty years. His hairy forearms, browned from a lifetime in hot climates, looked darker than Cook remembered. Must've been in the sun recently.

Porter took a sip of his coffee, his gray eyes studying Cook's face.

Cook took a sip and stared back levelly across the table as the black brew steamed lazily in the heavy, Navy-style mug. Foxy's coffee was so strong and bitter that creamer just made it muddy, barely blunting its caustic bite. Usually, it was just the thing for cutting through Cook's customary morning hangover, but at the moment all it served to do was make his scalp tingle.

"So, what's the deal, Porter?"

"Can't a guy drop in for a cup of coffee with an old friend?"

Old friend. Cook snorted again, shaking his head. The last time he had seen his former boss was a lunch three years ago at a timeworn airport diner called Flo's. Porter had looked apologetically across his biscuits and gravy as he delivered the unsettling news. Suspension from flight duty, an ongoing investigation, likely termination from the firm. Since the firm in question was a covert contractor for the US government, there hadn't been much of an appeal process. Management had acted swiftly, for a change. Cook had been let go the next day.

Not for the first time it occurred to Cook how odd it was that most of the important business in his former occupation was transacted in cheap eateries situated in low-rent, backwater airfields.

"Of all the places I thought I'd find you, twenty-five miles from the old ops hub wasn't it." Porter raised his scraggly eyebrows. "You get homesick?"

Cook's patience for Porter's labored bonhomie was disappearing fast. The waitress had some scratchy AM mariachi music competing with the fan in the exhaust hood above the grill, and it was beginning to work Cook's nerves. He decided to go on the offensive.

"So, you fronting as a lawyer, Ted? You take night classes, or was it online?"

Porter nodded; his expression clearly satisfied. "People drop everything for a lawyer. Adaptive coloration – you remember."

Cook smiled affably. "Sure. But that was before I got shit-canned and you didn't lift a finger to help me out."

The last comment came out louder than Cook expected.

"Still chewin' on that, huh?" Porter glanced cautiously around the room to see if anyone was listening, his aspect blank. Lupe was leaning on the counter, paging through People and bouncing minimally to whatever dance routine accompanies mariachi music. The grill exhaust fan and clatter from the kitchen served to mask their conversation from anyone outside the immediate area.

Cook's grinned thinly. He'd had enough. His gut thrilled to the icy numbness that precedes violence. Porter was baiting him, seeing if Cook would lose his cool, testing his control. He didn't care.

"Why wouldn't I, Ted?" Cook said loudly. "You covered your ass, I got the shaft. Seems fair enough. Pound salt, jerkoff."

He pushed himself up from the table.

"*Sit your ass down.*" Porter hissed sharply, glancing at the waitress again, who had looked up for a moment, then resumed her reading. "Why the hell do you think I'm here?"

Porter's demeanor had gone from cocky to alarmed. Cook hadn't seen that before. He felt a tinge of anxiety. Something was off. Nostrils flaring, he forced himself to relax. He levered himself back down slowly, carefully examining Porter.

"I give. Why you here?"

"Dick Massey." Porter's eyebrows lifted again. "Remember him?"

Cook froze, cold flame rekindling inside his gut.

How could he ever, ever forget? Massey was the reason Cook had lost his job and had been working a series of transient contract gigs at boondock airports like Fox. No, he didn't think of Massey much. Except maybe those nights he couldn't fall asleep and found himself chugging down shots of generic whiskey to forget about him. Which was a lot of them.

Cook blinked a few times to try to clear his thoughts. He was all over the place.

"Sure. How's he doing these days?"

Porter grunted approval at Cook's response. Cook briefly closed his eyes, rubbing the bridge of his nose wearily. He was getting tired of the back-and-forth volleying and hoping the old man would finally get down to business.

"Baked into a half-acre of Sonoran mountaintop." Porter studied Cook over the rim of his coffee cup. "Word has it they didn't find enough of him to fill a coffee can."

Cook nodded, sipping his coffee to hide an upsurge of conflicting emotions. Pilots never like to hear about other pilots crashing. It forced them to think about their own mortality. Unless that pilot was someone like Dick Massey.

Massey had pooch-screwed him good, no doubt. On a routine freight haul out of Chang Mai, Thailand, Massey had cached a twenty-pound load of methamphetamine under the forward cargo-deck floor plating of their aging McDonnell Douglas MD-80 freighter, apparently part of some brilliant unofficial retirement plan. Cook was the pilot-in-command, and Massey was a relatively new first officer, having moved to the international schedule from short-haul Central American runs.

Ordinarily, Massey would have gotten away with it.

Because of the company's special relationship with the U.S. intelligence community, their aircraft generally landed at fields where a hands-off arrangement meant Customs officials gave them only a cursory glance. But a novice company scheduler had routed them into Newark by mistake, a port-of-entry airfield with hyper-competitive Customs officers bucking for promotion. Much of the company's 'white' traffic went through that airfield, so the mix-up was later judged understandable, even forgivable, if not for the consequences.

During the long delay, while the management honchos burned up the phone lines trying to get the freighter cleared, a canine unit's drug dog caught scent of the package, and a combined Customs/DEA task force tore the plane apart. The next thing Cook knew, all four crew were handcuffed in a detention cell, and the company's general counsel was cheek-and-jowl with Homeland Security in Washington trying to quiet everything down.

The whole night in lockup, Massey swore up and down the cell that it wasn't him. Cook hadn't cared. The loadmaster and the cargo kicker had turned toward the wall in their bunks and gone to sleep.

The company's damage control machinery went into overdrive. Because they lived and died by U.S. government contracts, there was no question of a public scandal. The corporate brass got the intelligence community on board and called in a tall stack of official markers to make it all go away. Since the incident happened during the graveyard shift, the press never got wind of the flap. The investigation was kept off the books as a personal favor to the company's chairman.

Massey pointed the finger at the loadmaster and the kicker. The kicker might have been an accomplice, but the chief had been reassigned from another flight at the last minute, and therefore made an unlikely candidate. An unfortunately-timed urine test revealed that everybody on board had availed themselves of company-issued modafinil 'go pills' to cut the boredom of the twenty-five-hour flight, which didn't help matters. There were no fingerprints on the black duct-tape covering the Ziploc baggies, or anywhere on the nearby aircraft ribbing, leaving the investigators with no leads and an inquiry that quickly succumbed to frustration.

A deal was cut. Company higher-ups had been embarrassed and forced to expend precious political capital; they were hungry for scalps. The price was the heads of the entire crew. Business went back to usual, and Cook started his new career as a pilot-mechanic pariah in the civilian, general-aviation community.

Cook took another sip from his mug to bring himself back to the present. The rim had a hairline crack that captured his attention as he parsed his response.

"So, not so good, huh?"

Porter grinned broadly, nodded, and leaned back against the worn vinyl bench seat.

"I thought you might like to hear that. They found traces of about twenty kilos of burned up goofballs in the wreckage." Porter used archaic slang for barbiturates. Cook remembered that Porter never could quite keep up with current slang. He reminded himself that they were both getting older.

"Nothing ever changes," mused Cook.

He glanced out the window towards the tarmac. A Cessna pilot was walking around his plane, performing a preflight. Probably flew in for the proverbial 'hundred-dollar hamburger', or its breakfast equivalent, though in reality flying anywhere to get a meal cost well in excess of that.

Cook suppressed a deeply felt need to signal the waitress for a beer. He turned back to Porter and shrugged. "So, why're you here...other than to tell me about Massey buying some high-end Mexican real estate?"

Porter's grin widened.

"Well, it seems like Massey had some regrets about getting you all kicked to the roadside. Felt so bad about it, seems like he wrote a letter about it being his fault and all."

Cook went absolutely still, then slowly lowered the coffee cup he had brought up to his mouth. Massey was the most self-serving asshole Cook had ever known and had shown no shame in sending everyone up the river. And Massey had basically been illiterate – his flight plans were filled with misspellings. No way he had written any letter.

Cook marveled at what Porter was saying, and to what lengths he had clearly gone to get a forged letter into Massey's effects. Porter was watching him closely. His smile was straining the cracks in his weathered face.

Cook couldn't take it any longer.

"Cut to the chase. What's the skinny?"

Porter's grin mutated into a full-fledged leer.

"You're clear. The company wants you back. Full reinstatement." Porter paused, still grinning ear-to-ear. "Now what do you think of them apples, huh?"

Cook's jaw was clenched so tightly he thought he might split a molar. He looked sharply into Porter's focused gray eyes, searching intently for any signs of deceit.

"Back on the line?"

Porter nodded. "Probation for six months, regular rotation after that."

Porter was offering his old life back.

"Time?"

"Hours, seniority – everything."

Even in his most fevered dreams, Cook had never imagined this. Late nights staring at a plastic pint bottle of no-name whisky in his bare month-to-month apartment, trying to figure out his next play. Waking up on sweaty couches with dry mouth and hauling himself to jobs he could barely tolerate, he never saw this.

The drug bust had never made it into the press, but everybody in the business knew he had messed up somehow, and Cook was a leper. Thousands of flight hours were lost when he was fired, most of them acquired in places the company couldn't even acknowledge being present. As a rule, clandestine aviation work happened in the background, hidden in plain view. If done right, no one ever knew you were there.

It had made for awkward job interviews after his firing. The company kept two flight logs for their covert pilots, the real one and a sanitized 'white' version, bland but detailed enough to satisfy FAA scrutiny. More than one potential employer had wondered how Cook had gotten an airline transport pilot rating having barely the minimum fifteen-hundred hours logged to show for it. Usually at that point the prospective boss had shown him the door, figuring Cook was lying, omitting crucial negative information, or had somehow faked the certificate.

Cook blinked hard, banishing reminiscence from his thoughts, and looked intently at the man across from him. He needed more from Porter. He needed a reason. Something more credible than corporate regret.

"What's the deal? Why the second chance?"

Porter's grin softened. He pursed his mouth for a moment, and nodded speculatively, an affectation Cook remembered with a startling familiarity. Porter had always done that in the past to buy himself time to think. The older man spoke slowly, in a low tone, his eyes glassily downcast.

"Call it a retirement present. I'm going to be hanging it up soon, and I wanted to make things right with us."

Cook gawped internally. The revelation that Porter might voluntarily retire rather than be dragged out of the job by his boot heels would have stunned anyone who knew the man. It was like hearing a politician say he was leaving to spend more time with his family. You always wondered if there was a teenage boy, nanny, or hooker involved.

Cook had known Porter since he was eighteen, freshly arrived in the steamy Honduran rainforest from the foggy timber ranges of the northern Oregon coast, where he had been slinging bundles of pine trees off steep mountain slopes for about a year. Already a seasoned helicopter operator with a couple hundred hours of stick time, his prodigious abilities were obvious to all. Cook could knock over and pick up traffic cones with his helicopter's skid, then drop them into a truck bed, as easily as thinking about it.

Porter had taken that raw talent and nurtured it into a solid aviation skillset. He had thrown Cook into the tail-end of the company's involvement in the Contra-Sandinista conflict, flying resupply and 'dust-off' medical missions from Aguacate and other clandestine Honduran airfields deep into the Nicaraguan interior. He had taught Cook how to drink, swear and hold his own surrounded by cold-eyed intelligence officers and grim-faced mercenaries. He was as much a surrogate father as a mentor, in one of the most remote and harshest places for a young man to mature, an undeclared war as unforgiving as any conventional one. And Cook had thrived on it.

To Cook, especially in that place, and at that time of his life, Porter was the embodiment of all flying, a fixed point in the spectrum of the aviation world. The thought of his departure was like a classic rock song abruptly ending in the middle of a whining guitar solo. It just didn't happen that way.

The same kind of thing had happened with Cook's father. At some stage in his life, Cook had fixed his dad's age, never thinking of him as getting any older. That mental image had lasted for about thirty years. Then Cook noticed the gray hair, the wrinkles, the forgetfulness. Then his father was gone.

Cook shook off the spell. He sat up straighter in the booth and looked at Porter intently.

"What do I have to do?"

Porter looked pointedly at Cook's coffee mug. "First you got to convince me you can handle it."

Cook kept his face blank. "Why you asking?"

"The cashier at your local grog shop says you're a regular, but seems to think you have it together," Porter mentioned nonchalantly. "Looks like, in his world, if you don't drive three sheets to the wind or ask for credit, you're doing alright."

Cook turned to the window again, stung from the shock that he hoped wasn't showing in his face. That Porter had had him under surveillance bothered him less than the fact that he hadn't felt a thing. How long had he had people watching? Cook began to wonder if he was getting rusty.

"Don't take it personally," Porter chuckled, "You know me, just like to keep tabs on what my boys are up to."

Cook expressed what he hoped looked like earnestness. "Not a problem."

"Good. Make sure it isn't."

Porter reached into his shirt pocket and pulled out a business card and a pen. Cook glanced at the card across the table, seeing the logo and partner names of a fictitious law firm across the top. Porter flipped the card over and wrote a five-digit alphanumeric on the back, and pushed it over to Cook, who pocketed the card without looking at it. The number of the unmemorable law firm on the front would ring a professional-sounding receptionist at one of the company exchanges, who would respond with the appropriate cover story.

Porter paused and looked around Foxy's again before continuing.

"You've got a flight out of LAX at eight in the morning, terminal 2. There's a reservation in your name at the usual hotel. Pack for three days, hot climate. Bring your passport."

Porter finished his coffee and slid out of the booth. He stood and arched his back slightly to the sound of audible spinal cracking. He spoke in a lowered tone.

"I'm trustee for your dead uncle's Henry's estate, and you have to travel to Ohio for funeral arrangements, being the only surviving family. Tell your boss you need this week off to handle his affairs." Porter shrugged. "After we're done, you can tell him whatever you like. Any questions?"

A timetable, a cover story, a mission. Cook sat immobile, staring with a strange intensity at the empty seat opposite, then looked up at Porter's midsection.

"Nope."

Porter started to turn, then paused. "Need any money?"

He shook his head again. "I got this."

The older man held out his hand. "Stay off the jackass juice. And see you tomorrow."

* * *

It finally hit Cook on the highway south of Lancaster just how fast things had moved, were still moving, and just how much he needed to attain a sense of perspective.

Getting the time off was easy. Gorman was tiring of his workplace antics, and probably felt he could get more work done without Cook around. Packing went fast. As a pilot, Cook had learned early on to pack efficiently and compactly for a range of environments, and despite some areas of his life being in decline, he had always managed to maintain a professional-looking, and mostly clean, wardrobe. Suspending relationships was also a simple affair – he didn't have any. Occasional tumbles with local barmaids didn't exactly require advance notice of departure, exactly why he favored them.

No, things were moving, and Cook desperately needed a framework on which to hang the emotional and mental shards careening around his head. Porter had provided the catalyst, but Cook sensed he wasn't getting any more enlightenment from that direction. He needed perspective. And perspective meant Bellamy.

CHAPTER THREE

The unremarkable two-story office building just to the north of Santa Monica airport had the same conventional, businesslike exterior as every other building in the airport-vicinity office park, with its stucco façade, deep-set darkly tinted windows and forgettable corporate markings fixed to the upper corners. Cook pulled into a recently paved and painted parking lot, drove past the building's main entrance, and parked near an unmarked delivery bay at the rear of the building that was surprisingly well-covered by tinted camera domes.

A startlingly vivid orange and pink late-June sunset reflected in the blue glass wall of the Pacific Aviation Museum across the street.

The company, Transvector Aviation, maintained the museum in Santa Monica primarily as a tax write-off for its plane-loving CEO and owner, Hugh 'Hal' Hallett. The 'Old Man', as he was popularly known to the troops, loved flying his historical collection of WWII warplanes and showing them off to his business cronies, afterward wining and dining them at the overpriced and money-losing restaurant on the second floor. The company also hosted corporate team-building events and dinners there, in a half-hearted attempt to placate the accountants and justify the exorbitant cost of keeping the lights on.

Few, even inside the company, knew about the connection between the two buildings, or had ever had cause to be invited to the museum's plainer-looking cousin.

A cell phone call on the drive down Interstate 14 from Lancaster had secured Cook a numeric code. Inside the delivery bay, he punched a green backlit button in the bottom right corner of a blank, blacked-out number pad affixed to the concrete wall next to a reinforced steel door. There was a light chime, followed by a random distribution of nine green numbers on the keypad's buttons. An entry device of this sort indicated an unusually high desire for privacy – scrambler pads were used by the US Treasury, amongst others.

Cook keyed in the one-time code Bellamy had given him, and the heavy steel door's electric bolt released with a heavy chunking sound.

The door gave access to a hallway with numbered, but otherwise unmarked, doors stretching off directly ahead, with a carpeted stairway leading up to the left. An elevator with black chrome doors sat silently to the right. In all his years at TVA, Cook had never divined exactly what went behind the closed doors in the building, but there were obviously many more offices than needed to run a modest museum and hangar complex.

A 24-hour manned security post was stationed at the main entrance of the facility, but this entrance accommodated those who needed, or preferred, for whatever reason, a discreet method of access. A casual observer could be forgiven for thinking that Cook was entering a secure military facility or hardened government facility. In truth, the building embodied aspects of both.

Another tumbling keypad was attached to the wall next to the elevator. Cook entered the same sequence, and the door quietly swished open. He selected the lowest basement level as the door clicked shut. The elevator descended smoothly in absolute silence.

An hour and a half earlier, upon his arrival in Los Angeles, Cook had checked into the Grand Metropolitan near Los Angeles International Airport, the company's usual hotel. After he had gotten to his room, and dropped his unopened bag on the desk, he had reclined on the bed to gather his thoughts. It had been about three years since he had just dropped everything and deployed for a job; life was moving fast again after a long drought.

Cook had thrilled to the feeling, the myriad unknowns just adding to his anticipation. He was an explorer by nature and inclination, craving new experiences like normal people sought food. From his introduction to TVA to the recent past, it had never stopped.

The elevator door opened with another subdued swish, giving on to a cheerless, concrete-floored room with loudly buzzing fluorescent lights. An unattended security window flanked a set of open blast doors proffering a grim welcome directly ahead, while a shut steel portal wide enough to accommodate a vehicle brooded in darkness to the right. A feathery plume of dust swirled in his wake as Cook passed through a grilled security chicane and worked his way back.

The 'Vault' was designed as a bunker complex for Douglas Aircraft executives during the Second World War and was originally located under one of the company's factory production facilities. It was abandoned when Douglas left Santa Monica airport in the 1970s, and Hallett, baptized in the chill atmosphere of the Cold War, thought it might prove useful. In any case, trying to remove it would have been ridiculously expensive. TVA used it as the foundation of their office development on the site, and it now served as a corporate continuity redoubt in case of a mass disruption event. Its outer shell was thick, ferro-concrete bedded in a shock-absorbing cradle of gravel, and its ceiling was rumored to be eight feet thick. Cook supposed it wasn't state-of-the-art anymore as bomb shelter, but then again Santa Monica airport wasn't likely to be high on anyone's ICBM target list.

The security tunnel opened to a wide, but dimly lit room filled with dust-covered data and communications consoles, separated into sections by pillars clustered with overhead video monitors. Though dormant, the equipment looked to be of recent vintage, and likely retrofitted in the funding gush following 9/11. Despite the technical upgrades, the room's color and décor were reminiscent of the last great era of defense spending, the mid-1980s. Scattered monitor lights indicated that the capability marshaled here merely slept.

A figure moved in a brightly lit doorway at the back.

Bellamy was wearing a wry grin on his lined face as Cook approached. He held a tumbler of whiskey in each hand and proffered the left one to Cook. "Still drinking, I hope," he growled in his trademark rasp.

"Yep." Cook took a deep sip, savoring the blended Scotch for a moment before throwing the rest back.

Bellamy was pleased. "Good to see civvy life hasn't turned you into a pussy. Get your ass in here, kid."

He seemed shorter than Cook remembered. Bellamy, like most career pilots, didn't seem to age so much as shrink. Despite being a year shy of seventy, he still had a fit frame and piercing blue eyes under a shock of stiff, grizzled hair. His wrinkled skin was a deep brown color, seasoned in so many Third World hotspots that the shade was probably permanent.

Bellamy led Cook into a familiar looking conference room, which, for the younger man, was the real museum in the complex. The walls were lined with mementos of international clandestine conflict from the last half century. A Swedish K submachine gun shared space with Vietnam-era military rifles of all flavors, an antique Lewis Rifle, a Polish anti-aircraft cannon, and a pair of Czech machine pistols. No one seemed overly concerned that Bellamy kept ammunition for all the weapons and maintained them in perfect working order. Bellamy and Hallett went way back, and the Santa Monica facility was his own private fiefdom.

A small indoor firing range was located a few doors over, ostensibly for the qualification of the healthy security force that TVA maintained on site. In Cook's experience, it was a big-boy funhouse for Hallett's favored dinner guests to enjoy some postprandial fully-automatic gunfire, liberally fortified with hard liquor.

Because of his clean-looks and relative youth, Cook had been something of a black-ops mascot for TVA's older generation back in the day and had gotten a lot of invites to this place. Hallett had liked to show him off as the future of the clandestine side of the firm. Cook was pretty sure the Old Man didn't hold him in that kind of regard anymore.

Bellamy busied himself at the sideboard where, by the tinkle of ice and splash of liquid, Cook knew his drink was being freshened. He reminded himself as he sat to drink some water at some point to cut the booze. Bellamy was hard to stop when he had command of the wet bar, and with several similar drinking sessions under his belt, Cook figured he'd be lucky if he maintained only a slightly illicit blood alcohol content.

The whisky was already warming Cook's midsection, and he felt the tension he'd been carrying in his shoulders all afternoon drain away. He decided to get things rolling.

"I see the missus still picks your shirts."

"That mean bitch left me when I turned down retirement," Bellamy shot over his shoulder. "She's spending half my savings on some has-been golf pro in Palm Springs."

"Sorry to hear that."

"Don't be. Golf is for assholes," he responded, deliberately misunderstanding. Bellamy slid Cook's drink across the table and dropped himself in one of the plush, leather conference chairs opposite him. "Never getting hitched was one of your smarter moves."

There was a pregnant pause while they both sipped their Chivas. Bellamy never drank anything else, and always had a case with him on missions during his operational days.

Bellamy had been the prime deity of all covert operators for Cook when he started flying for the company in 1989, attached to a subcontracted helicopter outfit. The Boland Amendment in 1984 had halted direct U.S. military aid to the Nicaraguan Contras, resulting in a scramble by the intelligence community to line up private contractors to fill the gap. TVA's shell company was offering triple what he was making from his then-employer, and Cook was bored with slinging Christmas trees destined for southern California tree lots. It was an easy sell.

For the next year or so he shuttled advisors, black operators, civilian cowboys, and hard-faced Contras all over the Honduras-Nicaragua border, operating out of a variety of covert airstrips and occasionally forward operations bases in cleared patches of rainforest. Cook quickly became known as kind of heliborne *wunderkind*, someone who could get the job done, day or night, in any kind of weather. That dedication had engendered him somewhat of a reputation. More than one copilot had sworn on his mother's grave never, ever, to fly with Cook again.

The peace treaty between the Contras and the Sandinistas was officially signed in 1990, but TVA kept operating until it was clear that the remaining rebel groups had devolved into narcotics and weapons smuggling enterprises, making them politically unpalatable even to Republicans. Then Cook was shipped out to the Persian Gulf, where the Iraqis had occupied Kuwait.

Bellamy had recognized talent when he saw it and took the teenage Cook under his wing, prepping him for a career in the field. Porter had been ten years in with TVA already, skippering logistics for the aviation shell company, but Bellamy ran the show.

As he nursed his Chivas, Cook wondered how much he'd get from of his former boss. Bellamy was officially out of the spook side of the business, but old habits die hard. As it was, he needn't have worried. Bellamy was clearly starved for shop talk.

"So, Porter plucked you out back of the minors," the old man chuckled. He sucked an ice cube out of his tumbler and crunched it noisily. "'Bout time, too. Never figured you stupid enough for that speed thing."

"Porter called it a retirement present."

The old man snorted. "That's a load of shit. He's getting shoved out, just like I was. The company's bringing in Langley CPA-types who can handle all the lawyers and red tape." Bellamy smiled thinly. "Porter's too old school. They want assholes who write kindly emails and make pretty slideshows to impress the scuzzballs out in D.C."

Bellamy never let an opportunity to heap scorn on the political establishment to pass unscathed. TVA had so much contract work from the federal government – mail delivery, troop transport, munitions, materiel – that savvy observers often considered the company a virtual Pentagon subsidiary. Such a distinction, however, didn't endear Bellamy to his paymasters, nor stop him from frequently biting the hand that fed him.

To Cook, this was all ancient history. The old man had been serving up the same diatribes, with minor variations, for the past twenty years. He was more interested in current affairs.

"So why bring me back now?"

Bellamy's eyes narrowed. "You got something better to do?" He chuckled at his rejoinder. "Company's pretty stretched right now, working triple shifts flying all kinds of crap for the towelheads and sand chiggers out in the tar sands."

Cook winced, belatedly recalling his former boss' propensity for ethnic slurs increased proportionally with his drink intake. Bellamy was referring to the firm's work in the aftermath of the Iraq and Afghani conflicts. Coming from logging country Pacific Northwest, Cook had grown up surrounded by a fair amount of blue-collar antipathy toward people with a different skin color, but his father had instilled in his family a firm Protestant stance, judging his employees by their work ethic and little else. Cook had never grown comfortable the underlying racial biases that ran through vast swathes of the older pilot ranks. In Bellamy, he had never seen it as anything personal, just the unfortunate casual habits of an earlier generation.

Hoping to shift focus, Cook looked over to the large world map that dominated the far wall of the conference room. "Is that where Porter's been lately?"

Bellamy stared at the map, wistfully. "Not from what I hear. Word has it he's been working South China and the 'Nam for the last couple years. Pretty soon after you left, I think. Company's making some big changes out there."

"What sort of stuff?"

"Lots of deals with the Chinks. They've got the cash, and Hugh's been trying to wean us off the federal tit for the last few years." Only Bellamy called the company's owner Hugh – they went back that far. "They're even moving into surface shipping, I hear," Bellamy swiveled back towards Cook, his eyes suddenly rheumy and red in the fluorescent light. "Got some deal with the slant-eyes down at the Long Beach terminal breaking up ships. Probably some reciprocal thing to get more mainland business. Fuck if I know."

Cook suddenly felt lightheaded, his mouth too dry, the effect of too much liquor on an empty stomach. He shook his head, feeling a need to eat something. He didn't want to drive back to the hotel with this much booze in his system.

"What say you we get a bite to eat?"

Bellamy's reddened eyes narrowed.

"Not a day on the company dime and you already mooching for a free meal? Damn, boy, you haven't changed a bit." The old man drained his drink and stood steadily, the alcohol showing absolutely no effect. "Jesus, you always were a lightweight bucket of piss."

Cook grinned and followed the old man out of the conference room, back through the operations center, and past the security chicane.

To the left of the elevator, looming over the two men, was the large steel portal, painted battleship grey with cryptic numerals stenciled in black. Bellamy lifted a switch cover on the wall next to it, exposing large green, orange and red buttons. He punched the green with the butt of his fist, and the massive hatch ground slowly to the left, divulging a cavernous maw of pitch-black emptiness.

It was the entrance to a tunnel large enough to accommodate an armored personnel carrier or field ambulance, built when the prospect of the Japanese bombing Los Angeles was a real and present fear. It ran far beneath the road separating the Transvector corporate building from the museum and connected to a similarly-sized subterranean complex located under the main hangar. Cook supposed it had long ago disappeared off any public works department utility maps.

With an effect that he had always loved, a stuttering cascade of hundreds of feet of activating fluorescent tubes created a lightning-in-a-tube effect straight out of Disney's 1950s version of Tomorrowland. Bellamy shook his head at Cook's beaming grin and ambled off in a rolling stride that looked like something he had picked up on ship.

Cook ignored the other man's derision and kept smiling as he followed.

* * *

They dined on steak in the deserted museum restaurant, with whisky instead of wine. Bellamy thought wine drinkers were candy-asses, and had no problem saying so. Halfway through, Cook mouthed the phrase 'Ginger Ale' to the waiter in an attempt to sober up, hoping Bellamy wouldn't notice and unleash another wave of abuse.

Back in the day, when Cook occasionally found himself on the guest list for company dinners there, he and Bellamy would finish off the evenings in folding chairs on the roof deck, with the airport beacon and local traffic providing a nighttime backdrop to cigars and colorful flying stories culled from the old man's rich life.

Cook begged off more drink and the rooftop cigars by pleading an early morning flight. Bellamy taunted him for being a worthless cunt and bade Cook goodbye from the bar. Old fart probably sleeps in his office, Cook mused.

* * *

Cook drove back to his hotel on the freeway with the windows down to get some air on his face. Coffee after dinner had burned away some of the Scotch, but had also jacked up his nervous system, making his mind race.

Soft piano music emanated from the dimly lit entrance to the bar as Cook walked into his hotel, and all of a sudden he wanted another drink to put him to sleep. Flight regulations typically mandate twelve hours from bottle-to-throttle, and Cook was especially mindful of not doing anything to jeopardize his unexpected reprieve. But if company policy remained the same as three years ago, he wouldn't be flying the next day anyway.

He was also curious to see if any of his former colleagues were transiting LAX, possibly on the same job. If so, odds were they'd be in the bar.

Dim, glass-ball ceiling lamps spilled wan yellow pools of light on walnut-veneer cocktail tables grouped around couches on a herringbone parquet floor. Cook surveyed the room with a connoisseur's eye. Back in the day, it used to look like a feeble copy of a British public house, down to the Association football club signs and an annoying London Tube plaque. He guessed this was an improvement.

An engrossed pianist in a turtleneck and dark corduroy jacket played easy-listening favorites on an electronic keyboard to a bored Latino bartender and a stocky sales-type with white hair and a flushed wattle neck sitting on a barstool. There were some other patrons occupying a few tables, but no one he recognized. A fat, Midwestern-looking couple necked unattractively in a booth at the far end of the room.

Corporate airport hotels were the same the world over, Cook observed, the realization depressing him. The steady diet of harried business travelers and stranded tourists was locked in, so aesthetics and atmosphere take a rear seat to financial expediency. Throughput was the girding philosophy.

He stood at the bar, acknowledged the other patron with a nod, and ordered another Chivas on the philosophy of better-the-devil-you-know. At home, store-brand Canadian blended was the best he could afford, but being with Bellamy had given him a taste for more up-market refreshment. And even though he didn't have a dime of his new pay yet, he felt flush. The bartender shook himself awake at Cook's approach, straightened his posture, and took the drink order with an obsequious napkin flourish and an ingratiating smile.

Reflexively, Cook scanned the room again. Habits that had lain latent in the last few years were reawakening.

Being a pilot, Cook was not a field man by any stretch of the imagination, but a lifetime of getting things done in a covert manner had inculcated a healthy wariness. As in flying, the moment one lost focus and relaxed was the most likely time for an engine to quit running or a downdraft to drop your aircraft a thousand feet. The company had provided some remote operator training after Honduras, but Cook didn't bother to pretend he was secret agent material.

Even for a Tuesday night, the place was deserted. Airport environs usually had an ambient level of human density, regardless of the day of week. Besides the sales guy and the couple in the corner, who had by this point taken a pause from their amorous fumbling to drink more booze, the only other occupants were two mid-fortyish women chatting at a table by the window, and a younger couple talking in low tones on a couch.

Picking up his tumbler, Cook decided to take a booth near the back, with both a view of the room and the bar's entrance. He couldn't quantify the likelihood that Porter was still having him watched, but he wasn't going to take any chances. Slowly sipping the Chivas, he casually scrutinized the bar's patrons, this time with more concentration, his gaze lingering for a moment on the two women.

They were comfortable, self-assured, and both wore decent-sized stones on their left-hand ring fingers. Maybe a couple of flight attendants catching up off duty. Assertively not on the make, although far too attractive to be out unescorted. Transvector wasn't the only airline with contracts at this hotel, and if any front-seaters from the major air carriers turned up, their peaceful chat was likely to get interrupted.

In addition, or perhaps in preference, to his former colleagues, Cook had hoped he might find a woman when he wandered in. Airport hotels were notorious congregation spots for mid-range pros, but he wasn't looking for a hooker. He just needed to take the edge off the day's whiplash revelations, and Lancaster pickings were always pretty lean.

As he turned back towards the bar, a promising female voice ordered a Herradura stinger on the rocks, with salt. It was a good drink order.

Cook hadn't seen her enter. He shot a quick appraisal, and liked what he saw, especially from the back. She sat two stools down from the salesman, who, unlike Cook, was staring at her openly. She reciprocated by paying him no attention whatsoever.

Long, slim legs encased in tight, dark denim caught most of Cook's initial focus. Women who wore jeans well rated highest in Cook's book, and she filled out the rest of the bill quite well – clingy chemise, svelte torso, ballet dancer's carriage, long neck. When she turned slightly at the bar to glance around the room, her short brunette bob framed a tan face with intelligent brows, a sharp nose, and full, defiant lips. When her eyes briefly met Cooks', he saw a hint of street credibility in her manner: journalist, sales rep, something hands on. For a moment, he thought she might be a pro. If so, she was definitely out of his price range. Even if TVA had already paid him.

She returned her attention to the bartender, who had short-served her drink, probably hoping to make her lean forward so he could get a better look at her cleavage. From Cook's vantage, it seemed like the woman knew what he had done and why, and either didn't mind or accepted it as standard practice. She duly leaned forward and said something inaudible. If the barkeep's reaction was any indication, it had made his night. He smiled broadly under his extravagant black mustache, hooked another tumbler off the rack above the bar, and got busy making another cocktail.

The white-haired salesman two seats down had stopped overtly gawking but was now snatching furtive glances at her as he took long swallows off his highball. From the booth, it looked to Cook like he was fortifying his courage to make a play.

Cook felt his gut tighten with indecision.

He wanted to get her attention, but was too far away to do anything subtle. The drunk next to her was obviously running through his mental Rolodex of pickup lines between swallows – the pale line on his fourth finger indicated that he was well-practiced at ditching his wedding band. If Cook wanted to be a part of this, he would have to get up, walk over, and take command of the situation.

He wanted to. Personal pride prevented him from letting such a fine woman fall prey to the slob down the bar. But he had nothing. Totally out of practice. His increasingly damp shirt was pinned to the seatback by a case of opening night flop-sweat and a complete lack of anything to say.

The bartender slid her a glass of something amber on the rocks.

Another drink? This woman likes her sauce, Cook thought, reconsidering. Maybe he was better off taking a pass.

She leaned forward again, and made additional comment as she took the drink with a clinking sound. The bartender bestowed another mustachioed smile, this time accompanied by a deferential nod. The white-haired souse was looking directly at her again, and now grinning, apparently ready to deliver the goods.

She picked up the other cocktail in her left hand, pivoted gracefully from the bar, and walked straight towards Cook, smiling prettily.

His mouth agape, Cook was completely frozen in place. Before he could process anything, she was standing over him, holding a fresh whisky on the rocks. She arched an appealing eyebrow.

"Is this seat free?"

Cook couldn't do anything more than nod slightly. He couldn't really believe this was happening. Really good-looking women in bars just didn't walk up and ask if they could join him.

She slid with poise into the booth, her sinuous movement divulging well-toned abdominals through her tight-fitting top and straining the light fabric against firm and well-shaped breasts. Cook's mouth went dry. She pushed the now sweating tumbler towards him with another clink of ice.

"Sue Stokes. Chivas, right?"

"Guy Cook," he managed, forcing himself to come back to earth and be hospitable. He picked up the proffered drink. "Uh, yeah. Have we met?"

She smiled knowingly, clearly recognizing his discomfort.

"That lizard at the bar was about to start drooling on me, and you looked somewhat harmless. Can I stay?"

Cook assumed her query was rhetorical, but had to clarify something. His listless thought processes lurched into action.

"Harmless?" he repeated, working the self-deprecation angle purely on intuition. "Does that go in plus column?"

She narrowed her eyes, regarding him closely. "Let's just say you're not at zero – so far."

* * *

She was from Tucson and sold customer resource software.

Since neither item particularly interested Cook, he half-listened to her chat about her life while glancing sidelong at her legs next to him in the booth. They were long and toned, and snugly encased in what looked like really expensive denim.

She grew up in San Diego, and her mother made her learn French even though she wanted to learn Spanish.

Her arms were smooth, lithe and deeply tanned, and he wondered what they'd feel like wrapped around his back.

His reverie was interrupted by the awareness that she had asked a question.

"My job? I field test thong underwear." He arched his own brow in mimicry. "For a major designer."

Truth be told, Cook was getting a bit bored with the small talk at this point, and figured he'd cut right to the chase. After all, he had an early morning flight, and would just as soon hit the rack if things weren't going to pan out.

Her eyes narrowed as she considered this. "Are you wearing some now?"

"Well, I'm not, really," he admitted, feigning a world-weary attitude. "I conduct site inspections, checking for fit, thread count...the usual."

She nodded, understandingly.

"You're a pilot."

Cook aped a frown, secretly pleased at her speed of uptake. "Is it that obvious?"

"Pilots are lame-ass closers – they're always in a rush." She was counting on her fingers at this point. "You're drinking alone. And we're at an airport hotel. How am I doing?"

"Saw right through me, huh?" Cook smirked unashamedly.

"I've heard worse," she agreed, nodding slightly. "But that was pretty feeble. Especially," she added primly, "if you don't need it."

Cook's blood stirred as she stared innocently at her drink. She was good.

* * *

The rest of the evening was a blur.

The next thing Cook remembered, he had his hands on her hips and was nuzzling her neck as she fussed in her purse for the card key to her room. Her silky, dark-chocolate colored hair was an intoxicating floral scent, and he couldn't help pressing his hardening erection against the smooth denim stretched tightly across her firm ass.

He was aching to take her – her supple legs, tan arms, perfect champagne-glass breasts – all of her, and quickly. The pent-up frustration of years in exile had distorted into a remorseless lust that almost frightened him with its intensity. His already swollen cock became as stiff as concrete rebar when she pushed back against him.

She fumbled with the card and slammed it in the slot as he pressed against her more firmly, kissing her neck ardently. She arched her back as the lock indicator went green, the electronic chime rang, and the two of them tumbled through the doorway into the black room. As Cook pulled her back to him, she turned inside his embrace, her hands hot against his writhing stomach muscles.

"Easy," she exhaled, her cheek hot against his face, her breath like a feverish nighttime monsoon caressing his left ear.

Cook was drunk with his hunger for her warm, perfect body.

"I want you, Sue," he rasped, his voice hoarse with lust, "Right now."

A deep male voice responded in the dark, like a china plate dropped on a tiled floor.

"We want you too, Guy."

The lights in the room snapped on with blinding intensity.

CHAPTER FOUR

S tokes shoved Cook hard in the stomach, pushing him back towards the door, winding him and throwing him off balance.

Three men in dark clothes were standing inside the room. One was slightly behind Cook working the light switch, the other two in front of him. All had their hands loose at their sides, ready.

Cook, still out of breath from her shove, lowered his shoulder and charged the one on his left. The man parried Cook's outstretched right wrist, twisting it smoothly into a painful armbar, and took him to the floor. A knee across his head and neck had him expertly pinned, his arm immobilized in a vertical position.

The room was absolutely silent except for Cook's labored breathing and the quiet rustling sound made by his captor's gunmetal synthetic shell. His mouth was pressed firmly into the room's cloying, sticky carpet, causing him to drool on the prickly synthetic fibers. Cook's rapidly deflating erection throbbed painfully as it became increasingly pinched against his belt buckle. He struggled to roll over but found he could barely move.

A calm voice cut through his straining efforts.

"Mr. Cook, I'm Special Agent Romero of the DEA, and we need to talk." The voice paused, then resumed reasonably. "If you don't try to play tackling dummy again, we can have this talk sitting up. You good with that?"

Feds. At least he wasn't getting mugged, Cook thought.

"Sure," he croaked. His scotch-induced buzz was fading fast, rapidly being replaced by a pounding headache generated by all the unexpected calisthenics.

"Get him up."

The goon who had his arm took his weight off Cook and hoisted him to a standing position, skillfully transitioning Cook's wrist to a hammerlock behind his back. The fact that Cook experienced very little pain, but near total immobility, meant that he was dealing with a pro. A second large man, this one in a black fleece, slowly and methodically patted Cook down, paying special attention to his groin and armpits. He then turned and nodded to a third man wearing a suit, presumably Romero, who nodded back. Cook was escorted by both men to an armchair behind a coffee table in the room's corner and dumped into it.

Romero took a seat in another chair facing him.

He wore a dark grey single-breasted suit, without pinstripes, and sported a pale blue shirt with a conservatively patterned dark tie. His short-cropped black hair and tan skin favored his Hispanic surname. Thin, steel-rimmed glasses and a crisp white handkerchief in his coat's pocket completed the ensemble. Very much the professional law man.

He studied Cook for a moment, the silence in the room broken only by a faint chime of an elevator in the distance, and the rumble of an ice machine. His two hard guys silently flanked Cook in his chair.

Cook glanced over at Stokes, who was leaning against a credenza and regarding him impassively, over crossed arms. All warmth in her face was gone. He stared dully at her for a moment, his earlier passion utterly extinguished by her expression, then shifted his attention back to Romero.

"Let's talk about Massey."

Cook's mind churned with whisky-fueled inefficiency. What the fuck? How did this guy know his name, and how the hell did he know Cook knew Massey? It had only been a few hours since Porter had told him that Massey had gone to see Elvis, and before that Cook hadn't heard the name in years. Why was Massey so popular today, and what kind of shit had he been into?

"Who?"

Romero extracted a grainy, eight-by-ten, black-and-white surveillance photo from a manila folder on the glass tabletop between them and held it vertically in front of Cook for a moment before resting it on the table's shiny surface. It was unquestionably Massey.

Cook blinked hard at Romero, his mind still dulled by exertion, liquor and emotional whiplash. Blood pounded painfully in his temples as he tried to figure his next move. As far as he was concerned, he'd never heard of Massey.

"You flew with Massey in Central America, later in Thailand." It was not a question. Romero paused, cocked his head slightly. "Any of this sound familiar? Richard Massey?"

With a cold flash of clarity, Cook regrouped internally. Just a fishing expedition – nothing to get worked up about. Lots of people could have heard about Cook's previous association with Massey, if their clearance was high enough.

Cook's anxiety dropped a peg. He looked at the photo, then at the minder to his left, and shrugged slightly.

"You know what happened to him, right? Give me that at least." Romero grinned wryly. "Not feeling chatty, huh?"

To buy some time, Cook decided to deflect a bit. He nodded toward Stokes, who was still leaning against the furniture, but whose stony expression was directed now at the opposite side of the room.

"Don't much care for your approach."

Romero pursed his lips, nodded ruminatively. "Sue, why don't you go next door for a while?"

The woman, still favoring Cook with less-than-friendly regard, nodded, uncrossed her arms and walked through an open door that connected to an adjoining room. It closed with a soft click. Romero blessed Cook with what he probably thought looked like a sincere smile.

"Nothing personal, right? She's just doin' a job, OK?" Romero seemed to be taking pains to put Cook at ease, something Cook felt might give him some leverage.

Which reminded him.

"Let's see some ID…from all of you," Cook looked pointedly at each of the men flanking him.

Romero reached in his coat with his left hand and smoothly pulled out a black badge wallet. "Here's mine, Guy. These guys are with me – you don't need theirs."

The gold DEA badge sat flush against the shiny black leather, an official-looking ID card with Romero's image mounted behind a plastic window beside it. Mentally, Cook shrugged. It looked legitimate, but that didn't mean much. He'd seen DEA credentials previously in Honduras, but that was around twenty years ago.

Romero acted like a Fed, in any case. He opened his jacket with a practiced move and replaced the wallet. "So, you heard what happened to Massey, right?"

Cook relented somewhat. He figured he had to give a little to discover why he was here, and he felt a deep need to get this over with quickly. "Massey flew into some hard clouds west of Chihuahua. Just heard about it. Bad luck, I guess."

Romero stood and started pacing slowly. Cook, on no evidence whatsoever, decided this was a tic of Romero's when he needed time to think. He seemed like someone given over to amateur, shop-worn dramatics. The muscle on either side of Cook shifted slightly, reminding him of their presence.

"The story in the papers is that Massey went down in bad weather, cause of accident indeterminate by local authorities but presumed to be weather-related." Romero paused his pacing to inspect a generic hotel landscape on the wall, frowned, and then looked at Cook over his glasses. "We both know that's bullshit, right? A little cover story to protect the family and the company, make everybody feel better?"

Romero's insinuations were starting to hew awfully close to subjects Cook couldn't talk about, even to Feds. Romero continued pacing as he spoke, as if lecturing a class.

"The file jacket at EPIC has Massey moving loads of Mexican black tar heroin." Romero was referring to the El Paso Intelligence Center, a multi-agency border intelligence group. Cook knew of it from pilot friends who had spent some time flying for the DEA. "But since he wasn't flying a Transvector plane, the company gets a pass, and it's just another unfortunate flying accident. Am I boring you, Guy?"

This last comment was directed at Cook's gaze, which had wandered over to the room's window. The curtains were slightly open, and through them he could see the LA's lights spread out like a sea of dusty orange jewels, like a treasure city sunk beneath an ocean of dirty haze.

Cook jerked back, his anger rekindled.

"So, Massey was moving dope. What the hell does any of this have to do with me?"

Belatedly, he realized his outburst played straight into Romero's hand.

"Good question, Guy! Welcome to the discussion." Agent Romero smiled broadly, energized by Cook's flare-up. "We'll get to your part in a second, but first I want to know what Porter told you about your mission this morning."

Cook stared dumbly at Romero's shoes, his mind reeling. Romero's loafers looked Italian, rich black leather shined to a high luster. They seemed out of place on the garish carpet. Cook idly wondered what made that smelly carpet so sticky. Must never steam-clean it.

Romero snorted heartily, obviously enjoying Cook's shock. "Speechless, Guy? Just when we were starting to get along so well?"

Cook's mind roiled furiously. They must have been watching him all day, to catch his meeting with Porter. Hell, they could have been watching him all week, though intuition told him it was more recent. He mentally recast his day. Nothing and no one had been out of place at the airport, except Porter. Cook kept his face deadpan. He didn't want to give anything away yet. At least nothing he might be able to trade with later.

"You don't even know where you're going tomorrow, do you? You've got a confirmation number and a three-day bag of clothes."

A laser on the window. That was how they knew about the mission. A laser microphone could have been shot from anywhere on the airport and would have picked up the whole conversation. It could even have been planted in that little Cessna outside the diner window.

Romero slid another black and white photo out of the folder he was holding. "Recognize this location?"

Cook squinted. The grainy shot showed four C-130 fuselages at a distance, lined up on a ramp. The hull and tail feather markings looked like one of TVA's subsidiary lines, but it was hard to tell at that distance. There were what looked like low hills in the background, and the climate seemed hot and arid, with dry grass poking in places through the tarmac.

"Nope," he said carefully. In truth, it could have been one of a dozen southern fields Cook had flown into. It sort of resembled Gallup, New Mexico, only bigger.

"Don Miguel Hidalgo International, Guadalajara." Romero dropped the photo next to Massey's. "That's where you're headed tomorrow."

"You will be flying one of four Hercules transports carrying narcotics into the United States," Romero added in valedictory tone. "And we will be greeting you upon arrival."

* * *

The mood in the room settled, and Romero's men relaxed now that their boss had dropped his bombshell. Even Cook was subdued. How the hell did Romero know so much, and what made him think TVA was smuggling drugs? He had to hear this out.

"You feel like jumping in here? Don't hesitate to contribute." Romero sat on the bed now, confident Cook wasn't going anywhere. He was grinning again, almost mischievously, as if he had just pulled off a complex magic act, calling out numbers and suits as he pulled cards from the deck.

Cook, for his part, was calculating the odds that this was a sting of some kind, run by a government faction hostile to Transvector's interests. Romero could easily be a shill, limelighting for another federal agency. Absent knowledge on where the information was originating, the percentages were no better than those of

Romero being straight. And besides, Cook was pretty sure any handicapping was going to be dicey in his current state.

Romero seemed content to let Cook run through whatever thought processes he had to. He gave off the air of a man with time on his side. He waited for Cook to look up, then pointed at the photo.

"Those are spray planes, C-130s contracted by the USDA for firefighting and aerial forestry work in Jalisco state. TVA has them scheduled to come north for routine maintenance in the next few days. Massey was working directly for Porter over the last year, running support for the spray operation."

"On U.S.-bound flights, he loaded crates labeled," Romero paused, consulting a sheet of scratch paper covered with notes, "'AN Fittings/Adapters' and 'Control Systems'." Romero replaced the sheet on the bed next to him and focused intently on Cook. "Dick made a fatal mistake. He got entrepreneurial, tried to move some black tar up on his own. We caught him, and he turned snitch."

That explained Romero's source. Cook wondered if any of it was true, or if Massey had tried to buy some immunity by throwing the company under the bus. Anyone flying clandestinely for TVA for a substantial amount of time had more than enough horsepower to give the firm serious problems.

And Dick always thought he was a lot smarter than he really was. In all the years Cook had known him, Massey was constantly moving from one goat-rope to another. His fondness for company 'stay-awakes' probably only exacerbated the problem. Cook was a little surprised Porter kept someone so accident-prone around, though this lent only a bare shred of credibility to Romero's story.

Romero pulled a final photo from the folder and held it in front of Cook.

"Look carefully at this one," Romero's voice became quiet, "because this is what happens to Porter's guys when he thinks they're going to drop a dime on him."

The third grainy photo showed the wreckage of a light twin on a scorched and blackened mountainside. Nothing except the twisted cores of the reciprocating engines was larger than a toaster.

"It was a clear night, with a quarter-moon. Plenty of light. And Massey was bringing the load to us, the last one he was going to carry."

Romero set the photo down, and the room became hushed again.

Cook examined the photo while he internally ran through his options. If Romero actually had anything on him, he would be under arrest, so the Feds needed to buy his cooperation. TVA had a lot of political protection, so Romero probably wouldn't have much luck going that route: details of the investigation would leak, and the company would simply shut down operations until it had blown over.

And there was no earthly reason to believe what Romero was saying was true.

Individual pilots or crew occasionally got caught engaging in illicit activities, mainly because it was easy, and the upside was huge. Only idiots like Massey got busted, and the collateral was generally limited to the

individual. Cook's case had been a painful exception.
But Porter?

TVA had made itself indispensable to the government, a Faustian bargain where federal contracts
kept the company afloat in lean times, and the firm
did the dirty work no one wanted publicized. Like
transporting Stinger missiles and ComBloc ammo to
the Mujahideen in Afghanistan. Or ferrying formerly
useful war criminals out of their home countries to
discreet, politically tolerant locations. Cook had done
these, and many other morally questionable activities.
But the company hierarchy itself was oddly prudish
when it came to illegal activities unsanctioned by the
Pentagon or the intelligence community.

As long as Cook had known Porter, he'd never seen
anything to indicate a desire for self-aggrandizement
or profit-taking. Porter, like Bellamy and Cook, was in
it because, ultimately, they were doing *right*. The best
anyone expected after their twenty years of service was
a defined-benefit pension and satisfaction for having
fought the good fight. Some, like Bellamy, were too
restless to retire and stuck around filling postholes and
making themselves generally useful, but most went on
to other lives. The smart ones scammed consulting
contracts with Uncle Sam, but most ended up in the
commercial aviation trades, flying corporate, or failing
in real estate. It was the rare pilot who hit the jackpot.
That just wasn't the business they were in.

That Hallett had gotten as far as he had was a
matter of luck and timing. The government dumped
tons of equipment after Vietnam at fire-sale prices.
Transvector was the descendant of an Air America

subsidiary, sold off in its entirety for cents on the dollar. Following the fall of Saigon, the CIA had grown uncomfortable about the massive size of its aviation shell company, and they were in a hurry to unload it.

If Romero was trying to bring down TVA on the basis of this evidence, he had a lot of work on his plate. Cook decided to get some breathing room, create some space within which to haggle.

"So, what part of this story is supposed to make me want to work for you? I'm not seeing the incentive here."

Romero smiled widely again, which made Cook uncomfortable.

"You lost a lot of hours when you left Transvector." Romero held up his hand. "We can't get those back, but I can promise you steady government work with guaranteed hours."

Cook looked back to the window for a moment. Wow, everything a guy could hope for. Guaranteed government flying hours. Sounded like a special hell on earth. The fact that he was already getting all that stuff back rendered Romero's point moot, but he didn't want to give that away. And didn't Romero know this if he was listening in at the café? Cook felt a weariness assail him. Why all this now? He really wanted to get some sleep.

"What if I just go to Porter and tell him you're leaning on me?"

Romero nodded slowly, as if he were a teacher, and a dull but attentive student had just made a particularly astute comment. He stood and resumed his slow pacing.

"Good point," he acquiesced, ruminatively stroking his chin. "Porter shuts his deal down, and we get *bupkis*. End of story." He stopped, and turned to Cook, and raised his finger. "Problem with that scenario is you never fly again. In fact," regarding Cook with what looked like a sympathetic look, "you'll probably spend the rest of your life in prison."

Cook frowned, genuinely puzzled at where Romero was heading.

"I've got your file jacket, Guy, the real one." He looked at Cook pointedly. "It wasn't easy to get. I had to twist some arms, call in a few favors. You were real lucky Porter was there to fix things after that speed bust, otherwise you might still be in the can."

Cook exhaled, feeling inwardly relieved. Whatever Romero had would never see the light of day. The company would make sure of that.

"Not impressed, huh?" Romero studied Cook's face carefully. "Well, here's something that wasn't mentioned in your file, but I think you know what it is." He reached into his folder and pulled out a color-copy of an old photo, the edges of the image seamy and dog-eared, its dull tint indicating it was taken decades ago. He held it in front of Cook's face for a moment before tossing on the table in front of him. "Got your attention now?"

Cook stared at the photo in stunned disbelief.

It was an old aerial shot, apparently taken at a low altitude and high velocity. Part of an aircraft's engine nacelle and wing could be seen at the leftmost margin of the image. The main part of the image consisted of a large, blackened area in a deep, green jungle from which several thick columns of smoke were emanating.

It was impossible. He barely heard Romero continue.

"Even Transvector will run for cover if this gets out. Assuming they ever knew you were involved." Romero's voice seemed muffled, as if it came from a great distance. "They'll throw you to the wolves in a heartbeat, say it was an off-the-books action or something. Some might even call it," he paused for emphasis, "a *war crime*."

Cook couldn't take his eyes off the old photo. A dull roar across time rang in his ears.

Romero regarded Cook with what might have been pity. "You decide not to play, or tell Porter, whatever – that photo goes into your file, along with the accompanying story. The only thing you'll be flying after that is a prison mop."

Romero pursed his lips, looking almost regretful.

"Did you really think I was going to give you a choice?"

He then nodded to one of his henchmen, who tapped Cook lightly on the shoulder, indicating he should stand up. As Cook was escorted to the door, he heard the clink of ice as Romero, or someone, fixed himself what sounded like a celebratory drink.

"We'll be in touch."

* * *

Cook blearily opened his room door, tossed his card key on the nightstand table, and fell full length on the quilted polyester spread, staring up at a white textured ceiling painted orange by the streetlights below. His mind spun like a helicopter rotor floundering in a steep downdraft. And about as productively.

How the hell had Romero gotten that photo, or uncovered what it signified? Only a handful people had known of it, even fewer had been involved, and Cook was one of them. Some might have heard about it anecdotally, but all of them would have had a vested interest in making sure the information never saw the light of day. And nobody, absolutely nobody, had any actual proof – those in authority had made sure it was deeply buried. Until now, it seemed.

Too many hits in too short a time, he mused. Could've handled this twenty years ago, he thought, deeming the theory ludicrous as soon as it surfaced. He tried to remember if he had arranged for a wake-up call, and decided he had. What the hell did it matter now if he missed his plane? He was finished.

He knew he wouldn't sleep tonight.

* * *

CHAPTER FIVE

Ajolt from a pocket of turbulent air forced Cook awake, his face sweaty from being pressed against the hot airliner window. His shirt was soaked with perspiration, and his mouth felt as pasty as crumbled drywall. An askance look from the passenger in the neighboring seat told him that the reek of alcoholic sweat coming off his skin was as strong as it smelled.

Cook had finally fallen asleep about three in the morning, having polished off a good part of the hotel minibar. It took both an alarm and wake-up call from the front desk to rouse him from his stupor, and even with that stimulus it had taken several minutes for him to regain consciousness. As it was, he barely made his flight.

The blinding sun coming through the window was well past its apex as the airliner touched down in the dusty, brown air filling the elongated bowl of the Atemajac valley surrounding Guadalajara. Cook searched for the C-130s out his cabin window as the plane taxied toward the terminal and caught a glimpse of them at the cargo terminal at the north side of the field. The company appeared to be occupying an entire large hangar complex for its operation.

The airliner porpoised to a halt on the tarmac, victim of an over-enthusiastic stomp on the brakes by an Aeroméxico pilot, and a sun-bleached jet bridge pressed against the fuselage. The crew cracked the cabin door, allowing searing summer air smelling of sulfur and burned jet fuel to pervade the cabin. A collective groan went up from the mostly North American tourists unaccustomed to the 85-plus degree temperature and cloying humidity, while homecoming locals smiled at the familiar warmth.

Mexican customs was a perfunctory process that clearly inconvenienced everyone involved, especially the officials. Cook had flown dozens of times into smaller Mexican airfields where a discreetly tendered twenty-dollar bill assured a very cursory and inattentive inspection. Gratuities in Mexico, and throughout Latin America, brightened the mood of civil servants and engendered cooperative attitudes in the absence of adequate pay. Mexican officialdom at its most efficient was an entrepreneurial occupation.

With Romero's ambush the previous evening taking up an unreasonable amount of rent in his head, Cook went through the *Aduana Mexicana* with a detached disinterest.

He hadn't seen anyone on the flight paying him undue interest, but he accepted that such scrutiny was present. Significant time on the job in foreign countries, hostile or ostensibly friendly, had taught Cook to function unconsciously as if under virtually constant surveillance. He needed time to think, to work out whatever advantage he could retrieve from this mess. In all probability, Cook doubted that luxury would be available.

Cook hadn't seen anyone on the plane he recognized as TVA either, and he guessed pilots would be coming in all day or were already there. Outside of the immigration area, Cook hunted for the customary van driver. A short, heavy Mexican with slicked hair and a well-groomed mustache, sporting a tan guayabera and rolling a toothpick with his teeth, held a handwritten sign misspelt 'Amrstrong' in black felt pen. *Armstrong* was the name of the phony law firm on the card Porter had given him.

Cook stepped over to the man, handed him his carry-on, and without a word spoken was riding in an air-conditioned van toward downtown. On the way to the hotel, Cook got the driver to turn on the radio. He leaned back in his seat and let the jaunty beat of *narcocorridas*, extolling the exploits of local heroic and usually deceased drug traffickers, distract his restive mind.

Cook noticed some subtle differences since his last trip down. Back in the heyday, the sharper drivers always had a cooler of frosty *cervesas* available for thirsty aircrew – it assured good tips from weary pilots. They also seemed a little cheerier and more talkative than this one. Perhaps the driver sensed Cook's unbalanced mental state and decided to leave him alone.

The route from the airport to downtown ran by constantly growing housing ghettos of shacks made from salvaged building materials with foundations cobbled from pieces of broken concrete. Wires ran riot across corrugated roofs of scavenged metal, providing electricity in the absence of any central planning. But at least the residents of this shanty town had their priorities straight: satellite dishes peppered the rooftops like a crop of desiccated grey mushrooms. They might have a dirt floor and no running water, but dammit if they're going to miss their *telenovelas*. The sickly-sweet odor of chemically treated raw sewage leaked past the van's air conditioning. Cook belatedly remembered you could almost describe your location blindfolded in Guadalajara by the smell.

After a forty-minute fight through Guadalajara traffic, the driver deposited Cook at the Hotel Encantador and sped off without another word. Cook did not tip him. In the absence of an extra incentive like a cold beer, no *propina* was required. The company took care of all such logistics.

In general, the airline crew experience in foreign countries is completely spoon-fed, something at which Cook, as a recently self-employed pilot, never ceased to marvel. All procedures and protocols were detailed on tear sheets given to the plane crew the moment they disembarked, and their employers conspired to insulate them against unscheduled contact with the disorderliness of the real world. Reception staffs never had to check identification because they knew the van driver who brought the crews in. Lobby drop-off and pick-up times were established – the driver showed up with a flight number, and even the tip amount, paid by the firm, was listed on the sheet. Drivers never needed to see credentials because the flight uniform was identification enough. In Latin countries, an international flight uniform conveyed more status than most of the indigenous people would ever possess. They were a pass in themselves.

Over the years, a few con men had taken advantage of the situation, enjoying gratis shuttle van transport and hotel accommodation. Some were even former company pilots who saw no reason to give up the life just because they'd been let go. Anybody making the right noises and wearing something resembling the correct outfit would blend right in.

Like all major transport lines, TVA treated its pilots pretty well, primarily because they had a good contract. Compared to the past, when cargo pilots were the red-headed stepchildren of the industry, Transvector pilots rated as good accommodations as the commercial passenger carriers. In Mexico, the hotels were four-star or better, usually clean, with decent restaurants and pleasantly efficient service.

Registration at the reception desk was an expedited process. An impeccably groomed receptionist, her black hair pulled severely into a tight bun, smiled professionally as she took Cook's name and ticked a mark against a list of rooms reserved for 'Asterra', presumably one of the shell companies TVA operated under in Mexico. Cook's brief glance at the sheet showed a listing for eight pilots, with space for a dozen aircrew listed separately. The 'aircrew' designation covered all the non-pilot types staying at the hotel. Then she offered him a margarita.

The Encantador was an old standby, a rustic Mexican colonial-style *albergue* with a fountain pool in the middle of the open-air courtyard that was popular with company pilots. Airline management was always trying to divert their staff to more staid corporate chain hotel accommodations downtown, but the pilot's union wouldn't budge. More than one tequila-fueled evening had ended up with entire aircrews cavorting fully clothed in the central fountain to high-energy mariachi music.

The formalities concluded, key card in hand, Cook scanned the lobby for familiar faces. Besides seeing a couple of pilot uniforms in the bar, he didn't recognize anyone. Delta, as well as the Detroit/Ypsilanti cargo lines servicing U.S. auto plants in the area made regular stops down here, which could sometimes make the lobby resemble Homecoming week.

He found himself relieved. After the previous night's grind session with Romero, some time alone wouldn't be such a bad thing. Cook headed for his room.

He exited the elevator on the eleventh floor and walked down a hallway reeking of bleach and that special Mexican carpet cleaner that somehow manages to make everything smell worse. He inhaled a lot of it, as his room was at the far end of the hotel's east wing. A cleaning cart blocked his door partially; the room next to his was being cleaned. He slid the card into the slot on the door to his room and got no reaction. It took three tries, and a rub of the card on his trousers, for the lock to blink green. The latch uncoupled with a tired whine and a click.

Cook pushed open the door and walked into the dark room, made darker by the thick curtains which were drawn tightly. As he fumbled for the light switch on the wall to his right, he heard the door slam behind him. A voice with a Latin accent barked, "*¡Policia! ¡Manos Altos!*"

Shit, Cook thought, his heart beating wildly. Not again.

*   *   *

"I almost pissed myself when I saw your face, Guy. *Jesus* that was funny."

Kane sat across from Cook, laughing so hard tears were forming at the corners of his closed eyes and flowing into the dark creases at their corners.

Kane's skin was so black it almost looked blue in the bar's dim yellow light. Shorter than Cook by half a foot, he more than made up the physical disparity with his wrestler's shoulders, bull neck, and clean-shaven bullet of a head that looked like it had been spit-shined. The hands that gripped his beer bottle looked like they could easily crush the brown glass and not even notice it.

Cook had known Ron Kane since soon after he started with Transvector in Honduras. Back then, Kane was a field engine specialist who would show up at remote sites when local personnel couldn't solve the problem. He was also a multi-rated ferry pilot and could fly the serious maintenance cases back to the States for heavy work, assuming, of course, the planes weren't so shot-up that they could still fly.

Ron was also one of his closer friends from the past, a frequent flying partner, and hence a source of recurring wistful nostalgia after he'd been tossed out.

"You'd have almost thought you were getting jacked, the way you jumped," Kane snorted, provoking both a sidelong scowl and simultaneously heightening Cook's anxiety surrounding the Romero situation. Kane was no idiot and had known Cook longer than most. If he wanted to keep everything he'd heard from Romero quiet, Cook had his work cut out for him with Kane.

"You ready for another one, Wonderbread?" Kane chortled, knocking back a shot of tequila and chasing it with a long pull on a bottle of *Tecate*. Even though Cook's complexion was fairly tanned and weathered, Kane seemed to like emphasizing that Guy was fish-belly white next to him. Usually, in Mexico, Kane blended far better with the darker skin tones of nearby patrons than did Cook, although no one seemed to pay them much mind at all.

It was late afternoon, and word had filtered through the pilot ranks earlier that the schedule for the day was scrubbed. Pilots being natural loafers, many had chosen to head to the hotel pool to catch some sun and get some drinks. Cook and Kane had headed out of the hotel to drink in peace.

The cantina was dark and smoky, with a rudimentary bar and battered tables and chairs scattered about. The booming-voiced proprietor took care of customers on the bar stools, while an elderly waiter in a ribbon tie and black vest slowly hovered around the room, emptying ashtrays and serving tortilla chips and dried chilis along with an endless stream of *cerveza*. This was a locals' place, Cook's favorite kind. He sought them out wherever he traveled.

Sometimes, that penchant for cultural realism could prove dangerous. Years earlier, Cook had taken some fellow pilots to the outskirts of Culiacan searching for an authentic Sinaloan dining experience. They had been seated at the bar about ten minutes when two hard-looking men walked in the door carrying Uzis and riddled a booth of men from a competing drug cartel. With brass cartridge casings still rolling around the floor, cordite smoke wafting toward the rafters, the shooters had departed without bothering to glance at any other patrons. Cook's arm, holding a beer, had been frozen halfway to his mouth for a good minute before he had finally lowered it to the bar.

Kane was shaking his head as he signaled the waiter for another round.

"This guy moves like he's being paid by the minute, or something." Kane gave up for the moment, and cocked his head, scrutinizing Cook. "So...you been behavin' yourself?"

Cook knew better than to try to gull him. A black man making a career in an overwhelmingly white field had to have good antennas to survive, and Cook rated his buddy as sound a judge of character as could be found anywhere. Which made his response all the more uneasy.

"You know me, Ron." Cook offered a nonchalant grin and sipped at his beer in an attempt to hide any obvious facial cues.

Kane's smile narrowed, and he nodded slowly. "Yeah, if anybody does." He again tried to attract the old server's attention by waving his empty bottle, finally getting an exasperated nod in response. "Who's into you, and for how much?"

It wasn't an unreasonable question.

Lots of pilots had gambling or serious debt problems. It was sort of built-in to the high adrenaline lifestyle. Many lived paycheck-to-paycheck, paying more attention to flying than what toys they were spending their money on. And there were always lots of toys to buy – tablets with moving maps and weather, slick flight bags, really cool sunglasses – all of them marked up with a pilot's premium.

Pilots were also notoriously poor businessmen. It came from a lack of patience, from being accustomed to receiving instant output for every input on the controls. Somehow, they expected life outside the cockpit to work that way as well.

Cook sensed a real danger in leveling with Kane – not to himself, but to his buddy. There were a lot of good reasons to keep him far out of the DEA's orbit, friendship aside. And Cook didn't have history with too many people like he did with Ron.

"It's not like that," Cook backpedaled, buying some space. "Just waiting for some pieces to fall in line, get my game back."

In the back of his mind, he wasn't yet sure that Porter hadn't sent Kane to give him a once-over. Or even possibly someone from Romero's side. For all Cook knew, Romero could have leaned on the whole flight.

"As if you ever had any." Kane's expression conveyed grudging acceptance of the response, if not actually buying into it. "What kind of crap you been up to out there?"

"Racing iron, mainly," Cook offered, relieved by the change in topic. "Owners bring them in stock, and we trim the body fat, put in some extra muscle, hook them up with nitrous and spray bars." Cook found himself surprised by the enjoyment he felt discussing a job that had so completely exasperated him only a day earlier. Yesterday, life had been a lot simpler. "Been a couple different places, the usual drill. How about you?"

It looked to Cook like it was Kane's turn to weigh his responses. The expression was very familiar. Though Cook was back on the line, he wasn't quite family yet. More like a semi-distant cousin.

"Been out in the sand box for last couple years, lots of green lift." Kane's dark brow furrowed. "Not too much fun stuff."

The 'sand box' was the Middle East and Egypt, while the rest of Africa was the 'dark side'. 'Green lift' was military cargo, and 'fun stuff' was covert spook work. Kane spoke in the terse, clipped lexicon of the military or clandestine operator, intended to be opaque to the casual listener. "Company's grown some since you left."

"How so?" Cook needed as much information as he could get if he was going to parley something tactically useful out of his current predicament with Romero, and pilots always have the best raw intelligence – they tend to be right where the action is. He hadn't yet identified an angle he could play, but if he could get Romero to orchestrate an early move on TVA – before the mission began, that was – he might be able to cut fence and slip out anonymously.

"Mainly logistics for the major players in Bahrain and Qatar." Kane frowned at his empty beer glass.

"They also opened some marine division down at the LA harbor. Beats the shit out of me what they do there."

Cook emptied his beer and felt some warmth return to his emotional state. He missed the companionship lost when he was drummed out. The gossip, the shop talk, the sense of being one of the gang. The rhythms of the past were reinserting themselves into his consciousness.

The senescent waiter finally ambled by with the next round. Having learnt the drill, Kane immediately ordered another one. Cook felt like he needed to eat something if they were going to keep drinking at that pace.

"What say we get some chow after the next one?"

Kane grinned widely around the bottle mouth as he downed half his *Tecate* in one gulp.

"You fadin' on me, Cream Cheese?"

* * *

Dinner was a boozy affair, punctuated by a meal heavy on refried beans, rice, and Guadalajara's special take on carnitas, the *Torta Ahogada*, which was heaven to Cook's Lancaster-bland palate. As the evening progressed, Cook became more and more relaxed, dropping his earlier concerns about Romero, Porter, drugs, complications. Kane whipped up some *mariachis* who had wandered in and led them in a fair rendition of "*Rancho Grande*." The local senoritas began to look prettier, and he found himself wanting a woman again.

Instead, he got Porter. When the taxi finally disgorged the drunken pair on the Encantador's doorstep, they made for the rooftop deck to get a nightcap. Cook found his former-and-current boss sitting alone at a table, smoking a cigar. He pointed the cigar at Cook and shrugged his head at an empty seat, indicating Cook should join him.

Kane rolled his eyes, gave Cook a hearty slap on the back and lurched toward the elevator. Cook tightened his gut, obliterating the carefree afterglow of the last several hours. Time to face the music.

* * *

Cook had been wondering all evening how he'd act around Porter when he saw him. Guilty? Evasive? His brain roiling, Cook fought through the alcoholic fog as he negotiated through the tabletops on the gracefully trellised terrace, with its candle lanterns and slowly revolving overhead fans. Cook had always gotten along well with Porter in the past, so he decided to try that and see how it went.

"Lookee what the cat dragged in."

Porter smiled broadly as he wiped sweat off his forehead with a hairy forearm. Despite working in hot climates for most of his adult life, Porter never had seemed to acclimate to tropical weather. His madras print shirt was dark with sweat over his prominent belly, and the armpits were soaked through. And at nearly a mile above sea level, Guadalajara wasn't even that warm compared with Honduras or many of the company's previous job sites.

An attentive staff member appeared next to them.

"*Café por mi amigo*," Porter ordered, raising a knowing brow. Cook nodded with a faint grimace. "*...y una otra Damiana por mi*." The waiter vanished.

Cook waited silently while Porter puffed his cigar to life, the orange tip rasping faintly with the effort. Out of country, Porter always maintained a healthy stock of Cuban cigars close at hand. When it came to tobacco, his deeply heartfelt American patriotism ended at the U.S. border. It was like Bellamy and his never-ending supply of Chivas.

"So, Kane worked you over pretty good tonight?" It wasn't really a question.

"You put him up to it?" Cook smirked, hoping his tension didn't show. He equivocated. "Out of practice. I'm fine for tomorrow."

"Well, keep your powder dry. We're in a holding pattern right now, waiting for some pieces to fall in place." Porter's voice seemed to betray some impatience, and his body language conveyed restlessness as he shifted in his rattan chair, the material creaking audibly under his mass.

"Problems?" Cook accepted a thick brown mug of coffee from the waiter, who had quietly reappeared at his elbow.

Porter waited until the server had finished his efficient ministrations before continuing.

"Nothing crucial. Still waiting for a couple guys to make it down here – I had to pull them off other jobs." He took another generous draw off his cigar, then tapped it against the heavy crystal ashtray. "This one's a little delicate, and we're saddled with some bureaucracy for the duration."

Cook ran through his limited data set, weighing options. The coffee helped him think but elevated the chilly anxiety that had returned in full force. He might not get another chance alone with the old man, but Porter wasn't giving him anything like a natural opening for confession. He decided to stand pat.

Porter interrupted his mental calculus. "Something on your mind?"

Cook's initial and abiding instinct was to come clean to Porter as soon as he saw him. Romero's story seemed flimsy, and Cook would rather throw his lot in with the devil he knew than some slick-suited DEA hack who liked to throw his muscle around. He hadn't let Romero in on that decision, but then again Romero hadn't looked like he was going to let him go until he heard that Cook would play ball. Better to bare it all and get on with it.

But Romero's final revelation with the photo tempered the urge somewhat. If he knew about the Nicaraguan village, what else did he know? And regardless of Porter's helpful intentions, he couldn't help Cook from the inside of a prison cell, which is where they'd both be headed if Romero dropped that ace-in-the-hole.

Christ, he had been a teenager. Porter should have known better than to get him involved.

The fatigue of constant deception was starting to weigh down on Cook. Three years in the wilderness had dulled his edges, and evasiveness wasn't his normal mode of operation. He couldn't think clearly and wasn't up to parrying the older man's penetrating gaze. He decided to finesse it, to say something honest in lieu of the truth.

"Women. Even the locals were starting to look good an hour ago."

Porter smiled appreciatively, looking past Cook's shoulder. "Well, I can't help you with that, but a couple aircrews came in earlier, so maybe you'll catch some luck," he remarked with the detachment of a balding senior beyond all such concerns. He braced heavily on the chair arms, eliciting a loud screech from the rattan, and stood, looking down at his former protégé. Muttering around his cigar, "I'll leave you to it. Good hunting," he sauntered off with his drink, smoke trailing in his wake.

Cook sipped at his coffee and stared off into the dim yellow haze that softened the lights of the city spread out below. Muted sounds of *narcocorrida* hip hop rose and receded from a passing car with a giant subwoofer, and a few faint pops indicated the late-night gangster crowd was just getting warmed up. The swirling fans overhead stirred the warm odor of bougainvillea across the terrace, causing the candle lanterns to gently bob and flicker.

Porter and Romero. Cook found himself having a difficult time squaring his loyalties with the need for self-preservation.

What did he owe Porter, or the company for that matter? They had provided him a lifetime's worth of exciting and challenging employment he would've been hard pressed to find anywhere. Despite the unjust termination and his transient existence of the last few years, Transvector had been a foster home, and Porter an adopted father, for someone who had abandoned his own origins decades ago. And frankly, without too much self-consciousness about patriotism or the emotions it evoked, the company had fulfilled Cook's heartfelt need to be fighting a good fight, whether for country or just the men he worked with.

Did the sum total of all this oblige a confession?

Romero's case had been persuasive. No matter how much Transvector had nurtured and supported Cook in the past, revelation of that one Nicaraguan night flight would force the company to weigh anchor and sail for the horizon. They would disavow any relationship as a matter of course, and probably throw Porter overboard for good measure. They would try to ferociously avoid the fate of other government contractors caught in similar circumstances: congressional testimony, boycotts, civil suits, the lot.

Cook's coffee had gotten cold during his ruminations, and he wanted something stronger anyway. Maybe even a cigar. The ashes from Porter's Cohiba were still warm, their scent tantalizing. A woman would be too much to hope for, but he was probably better off. The memory of Stokes persisted in his mind despite his abject loathing of that nasty, hard-faced, cock-teasing bitch.

As he signaled the attentive waiter hovering discreetly by the lounge entrance, he heard the click of a woman's heels, then the sound of a rattan chair being pulled out from a table behind him. Another click followed by a rustle might have been a cigarette being lit. The overhead fan wafted an ephemeral odor of a faint, floral perfume lightly tinged with a spicy tobacco hint.

When the whiskey Cook ordered arrived, he savored it for a moment while contemplating the prospect of an unattached female advertising her availability by coming out solo for a smoke on a sparsely occupied patio, and in close proximity no less. Maybe he would catch some luck, to use Porter's cumbersome phrase. As the waiter occupied her attention with his drink service, Cook shifted his seat slightly to hazard a quick glance at the new arrival.

And froze. It was Stokes.

* * *

She was ignoring the waiter completely, smiling through her cigarette at Cook's blanched countenance and clearly enjoying the effect. After her drink was served and the waiter departed, she indicated by slight nod of her head that Cook should come over.

Cook panicked, looking uneasily around the terrace. After verifying that it was nearly empty, and there was no one he recognized, he picked up his tumbler and threaded his way between the cane chairs to her table. He quickly sat down, pulse pounding in his temples, as he tried to formulate a method of telling her to get the hell out of there without attracting an undue amount of attention.

Stokes cut off his frantic mental gymnastics.

"Relax," she said evenly, in a quiet but firm tone. "We've got eyes all over this place. Porter's on the way to his room for the night, and anyone coming out here will think that you're chatting me up." She tapped her ear. "My people will let me know if we're going to be disturbed."

Cook's breathlessness and inebriation made speech a labor. "What in the name of Christ are you doing *here?*"

Stokes took a long drag on her cigarette, smiling through her exhale.

"Romero said he'd be in touch." She transferred the cigarette to her left hand and extended her right, which Cook took unthinkingly in his dazed state. "I'm Sue Stokes, freelance photojournalist. Nice to meet you."

Cook snatched back his hand as if burned, causing Stokes' smile to stiffen slightly.

"Stay calm or you'll only look guilty," she warned. "I've been out all night drinking, we're meeting for the first time, and you're trying to pick me up to get me to your room," she glanced at her watch, "which is where you're taking me in fifteen minutes or so."

Cook's gut chilled. "Think again, honey."

Stokes' smile became tight and thin-lipped. Her voice dropped to just above terse whisper.

"Listen, asshole. You're about as appealing to me as a goddamned root canal. If you want to act cute, I'll burn you so completely they won't find any ashes." Her smile returned to its former pleasantness. "Play ball, and I'll get out of your hair."

Cook stared daggers at her, riding a rollercoaster of fatigue and resentment. His father had taught him growing up that real men never hit women, and he never had. But right now, he wanted nothing more than to break that streak, along with several important bone structures in Stokes' face. And then throw a few in for Romero and his crew.

A hot deluge of shame flowed over him for even thinking that. Not his best night. By a long shot. He leaned back in the rattan chair.

"Ok, so what do we do until then?"

Stokes' posture relaxed as she sunk back into her chair, her penetrating gaze softening as she took another drag on her cigarette. A cerulean blue silk top flowed sinuously over her torso, evoking a reaction in Cook's midriff despite his resentment. She crossed her denim-sheathed legs comfortably, dangling a manicured foot clad in a fashionable three-inch stiletto pump. Her eyes and smile widened as she assumed the role of a potential quarry, simultaneously skeptical of and enthralled at the prospect of hooking up with a pilot. Cook shuddered internally at the accuracy of the deceptive mimicry.

"You tell a gullible and intoxicated photojournalist about C-130s," she responded smoothly.

* * *

The sensation of claustrophobia and dismay Cook had felt in Romero's hotel room had returned. As he stood by passively, Stokes had taken total ownership of the scene the moment they entered Cook's room, drawing the curtains, switching on the television to a music video channel, and turning up the volume to an almost uncomfortable level to defeat possible listening devices. An uneasy sweat broke out on Cook's forehead as the hideous rust-colored wallpaper seemed to close in on him.

Without a word, Stokes removed a large-scale aviation chart depicting Mexico and the southern United States from her handbag, unfolded it, and spread it on the garish orange bedspread. Guadalajara was prominently circled in black felt marker, as was Transvector's aviation operations hub at Mojave. The U.S.-Mexico border between the two airports was segmented into four sections by short vertical lines, with each section labeled from A to D in green, blue, orange, and brown. Stokes pulled a red-capped Sharpie marker out of her bag and held it out to Cook.

"Put a circle around the most likely U.S. landing location for each section in the event that you had to make an emergency landing about 20 minutes after crossing the border."

An annoying series of music videos on the television behind Cook flashed striking hues across the chart as he studied it in the otherwise dimly lit room. Solid blue circles scored with clear lines depicting runway headings marked the major airfields, while smaller uncontrolled airports were colored magenta. Airspaces and VFR routes were demarcated in similar, but faded colors. He sensed Stokes watching him over his shoulder.

The tangy floral scent she wore made his mind wander as he absently stared at the aviation chart. Though he resented her presence, along with its implicit coerciveness, he still felt his earlier drive to touch a woman, to feel her warm skin and press against it. For a fleeting moment, he wanted this all to be a big misunderstanding, to have her really be there for him, so he could throw her on the bedspread, chart and all.

"You still with me?"

Stokes didn't bother disguising the impatience in her tone. Cook snapped back to the present, an onset hangover pulsing at the back of his neck. He really needed to stop drinking so much before getting bushwhacked. It really messed with his buzz. Her foul attitude made him want to smack her again – this time without the accompanying shame.

"Hold your piss – I'm thinking." He resumed his inspection of the chart, mentally calculating a twenty-minute distance based on airspeed and started marking airfields in each section. A minute later, he had circled two or more locations in each of the four areas. The red marks looked like a rash of chicken pox across southern California and Arizona.

He handed the marker back to Stokes, who examined the chart carefully.

"Our problem is to get the information from you after your briefing, without Porter or your left-seater catching on. Could you wear a wire into the mission brief?"

Cook shook his head.

"Unless they've changed the procedures, pilots are issued clean flight suits on site and change under observation to deter smuggling. Personal bags are searched too. Company learned its lesson after Massey."

Stokes frowned, furrowing her brow and tapping her lips with her index finger. "That rules out radio. And a light would be too obvious."

She straightened up, stretching her arms over her head, an action that strained her silk top against her breasts. She really has to stop moving like that, Cook concluded. It wasn't doing his blood pressure any favors.

"Describe your pre-flight to me."

Cook shrugged, looked at the ceiling, and ran through a mental checklist.

"We board, check with the loadmaster, then get in the cockpit and grab our paperwork. We pull charts and flight plans, and stow the flight bags. Then we do a walk-around."

"What does that involve?"

Cook ran through the various stages of pre-flighting a C-130, which he had mentally rehearsed earlier that morning on the flight down.

Stokes listened carefully, waiting until he finished. "We can do finger talk. Flash two numbers to give sector and airfield." She paused for a moment. "Do you adjust the sun visor as part of preflight?"

Cook shrugged minutely, tired and not really interested in helping anymore. "There aren't any."

Stokes' eyes flashed, then narrowed. She regarded him for a moment, her expression unreadable. Then she sighed, closed her eyes, and lifted her shoulders as if to relieve some muscle strain. She sighed again, and walked slowly over to Cook, her hips loose as she moved.

He stiffened uncomfortably. She lowered her head as she came close, gazing searchingly from under her perfect dark eyebrows. Cook's gut tightened, his skin crawled, and he readied himself for a punch to the gut or a knee to the groin. She put her hands on lightly his hips and her lips close to his ear. Lavender and citrus flooded his nostrils.

"Listen, Guy. I work for a living – just like you. Under different circumstances, you seem like a nice guy, and maybe we would be hitting it off. But right now, I need your help, and then we can get this over with, OK?"

Cook closed his eyes, momentarily intoxicated by her scent, then expelled a breath as he nodded slightly.

Her unexpected soft approach had totally thrown him off, and all the fight left him. He nodded again, and she drew away, looking at him tiredly.

He saw the fatigue in her eyes and inexplicably found himself feeling protective of her. She was just a professional doing a job, Cook told himself. Like him. Maybe he could be a little more helpful.

"There's a grip bar on each side of the cockpit. I usually hang my flight gloves on it. There's also a clip on the side stanchion for holding IFR printouts. I could do it either way. But how are you going to see it at night?"

Stokes nodded. "I'll use a long lens. What's the illumination like in the cockpit on the ground?"

"Dark. We keep the lights down to preserve night vision." Cook stroked his chin. "I just don't know how you're going to see anything."

Stokes' face hardened. "What you need to figure out is how to bring the plane to us. Can you briefly turn on a light?"

It was Cook's turn to nod ruminatively. "I'll figure something out. I take it this has to happen without the pilot getting wise."

Stokes cocked her head. "That would be ideal, but in any case, you need to get the message out. After that, you're clear."

"Right – steady government flying job," Cook scowled. "Every pilot's dream."

Stokes nodded cheerfully. "Better than prison."

Then, as if remembering something, she abruptly turned and walked over to the room's minibar. She opened it, removed three mini-bottles of scotch, and cracked them open. She poured a sip of one of the bottles into a tumbler located on top of the bar. Cook stared at her uncertainly.

"I'm…uh…done for the night," he said, perplexed.

Stokes ignored him and walked into the bathroom. Cook heard her pour liquid into the sink, and then run the tap. She walked back in and placed the empties along with two glasses on one of the nightstands next to the bed. She turned to Cook.

"We had a couple more drinks tonight. Throw the bedspread and a pillow on the floor, and mess up the sheets in the morning. If Porter has the cleaning staff in his pocket, it will look like we spent some time in bed."

Cook closed his eyes and shook his head slowly in disbelief. "Want me to rub one out on the pillow too?"

Stokes arched a brow, causing another tinge in Cook's groin. "Do what you need to do."

She walked towards the door, and paused before it, lightly touching the ear with the communicator in it. Apparently receiving a favorable response, she cracked the door open and peered out, before turning her face over her shoulder to Cook.

"Get some rest. You look like you need it."

And then she departed.

* * *

For the second time in two days, Cook found himself alone on a hotel bed, sweaty and staring at the ceiling, pining for a woman who alternatingly tormented and exasperated him. He closed his eyes, willing himself back to her LAX hotel room door, his hands on her fluid hips, hungry to taste the saltiness of her warm, tan skin. He pictured her long legs wrapped around him, her hands locked behind his neck.

Laughter came from a comedian on the television, followed by loud applause from the Mexican audience. The booze made him feel sleepy, but the caffeine and the conversation with Stokes caused his mind to wander restlessly. Yet again, Cook's mind was completely blurred on where his obligations lie.

He also wondered just when he was expected to get a night of untroubled sleep.

* * *

This mission started a little differently than usual.

For most tasking, pilots would get verbal notice to standby, or a BPT – 'be prepared to' – to do something that was needed to be done. Following that would be a briefing from the intelligence crew with charts, payload weight data, expected weather enroute, objectives, approach/departure vectors, alternate fields in case of an emergency, extraction information, and the like. Finally, the pilot would suit up, preflight his aircraft, sign off with the operations supervisor, and standby in the ready room, or in a rack, on a ten-minute alert status until given a green light or a 'mission abort' command.

On this one, Cook was shaken out of a deep, sweaty sleep in the sweltering night air by one of Porter's flunkies, who told him to be ready to jump in five minutes. No charts, no route info, no preflight. Not even a shower. Cook shrugged on faded blue jeans, a pair of hand-tooled cowboy boots, a tropical-weight pilot shirt with pen slots on the left sleeve, and grabbed his canvas flight bag on the way out the door.

The plane's engines were already running when Cook arrived at the field, and he could see Porter's silhouette outlined against the window by the cockpit's red night-light. A kicker wearing tan mechanic's coveralls crouched in the cargo hold, tying down a load that Cook couldn't make out despite a dim red work light illuminating the hold's interior. Upon entering the cockpit, Porter handed Cook a cold-frosted can of Coke and proffered two 15 milligram Dexedrine time-release capsules to cut the fog from sleep deprivation and last night's cocktails. Cook chugged down the "go pills," shrugged himself into his seat harness, and struggled to catch up with Porter on the preflight checklist.

Cook sped over gauges indicating manifold pressure, fuel state, mixture, and propeller speed, and wondered where this plane came from. It was an older model Grumman C-1 Trader, a battered high-wing twin powered by aging Pratt & Whitney radial engines which had lived a previous life on an aircraft carrier as a delivery bird. Cook hadn't flown one in years – thirty to be exact. The passenger cabin had been stripped clean of seating to make way for cargo, two 55-gallon drums of which he could now make out over his shoulder, lashed onto the floor tie-down rings.

As Porter counted off the final item on the checklist, and Cook advanced the overhead throttles forward to start the taxi rollout, he tried to focus and shake off the numbing confusion that fogged his awareness. Everything seemed standard procedure, but wasn't he supposed to be flying a C-130, and why was Porter with him?

With a sustained throaty roar, the shuddering Trader leapt into the dark night.

Porter navigated from a sectional aviation chart on his knee marked up in red felt pen, occasionally punching coordinates into a LORAN navigation unit on the panel. Why was he using LORAN – Cook thought they'd shut down that system years ago. Porter called out heading changes with increasing frequency. Cook's grip tightened on the yoke as the plane's velocity increased seemingly beyond the ability of the engines to sustain it. Wispy clouds flashed by in the faint moonlight. Cook's calf muscles strained as he fought increasing pressure from the foot pedals controlling the aircraft's rudder. He gritted his teeth with effort as his left leg started to ball into a cramp.

It was a revenge mission, and he knew it wouldn't end well.

A Nicaraguan guide leading a reconnaissance team of American contractors about twenty-five miles northwest of Bonanza had been turned by the communists, and led the unit into an ambush by a platoon of Sandinista infantry reinforced by Soviet advisors. The simple probing mission had turned into a running gun battle, then a rout, with three Americans dead and a messy night extraction. A local intelligence asset that was still considered reliable had pinpointed the traitor's village and confirmed that the Sandinistas were bivouacking there for the night.

The dry taste in Cook's mouth accompanied palms so sweaty they could barely keep grip on the yoke. The plane roared and strained through the damp cloud cover as if tearing through endless sheets of damp black felt. Porter's finger on the map moved inexorably toward the red felt-pen circle.

A faint cluster of lights appeared suddenly beneath the transport's nose, and the kicker let out a war cry as he shoved the barrels of 'hot soup' – Jet-A fuel mixed with detergent soap, basically homemade napalm – out of the Trader's side hatch. Static cables attached to a roof rail went taut, yanking pins out of thermite charges attached to each barrel as they fell toward the cluster of village lights. Tiny sparks trailed in their wake like expended fireworks falling earthward.

The brilliant orange fireball illuminated the entire valley as liquid fire splashed indiscriminately, burning everything it touched.

Sharp, staccato cracks raked the cockpit, unleashing faint wisps of smoke and the odor of burning insulation. Giant hands reached up and shook the plane by its tail section. Most of the warning lights on the annunciator panel flashed red, and it seemed like every alarm horn was going off simultaneously.

Cook heard Porter calling out map coordinates in his headset as he dove the now fiery plane toward the burning valley, toward a thin river lit by the twisting and curling orange pillars, now towering over the village as they consumed the forest canopy. More lurches indicated that the anti-aircraft fire battery still had them in their solution.

A tremendous thud whacked Cook in the back of his head, setting off a ringing in his ears and causing his vision to go red. He quickly recovered his sight, but his head felt heavy and his brain was having trouble understanding the instrument panel. When Porter shouted a question at him regarding their location, Cook's tongue felt swollen and unable to form words. Things started moving slower and didn't seem so important anymore.

A hurricane of branches whacking the cockpit glass woke Cook from his sleepy state. The glow from the fire was much dimmer now, though its much closer reflection in the river made up for the loss of illumination. A second later, Cook felt an incredible and instantaneous weight on his chest, a giant dark hand crushing all the air out of his lungs, as the cockpit windscreen went dark with an onrush of dirty river mud. With a giant bang, everything stopped moving. He flopped his head to the right with effort and saw Porter slammed up against the yoke, blood streaming from his forehead, unleashing a storm of profanity against the flashing red light of the instrument panel.

Flashing, roaring, burning.

He shook his head back and felt pressure under his arms and against his heels. Why is it so quiet, Cook wondered, and dark? He smelled something that resembled heavy armpit sweat, and realized Porter was dragging him through mud and underbrush, somewhere. He managed a squawk. "What happened?"

"Still with us, huh?" Porter's voice. "Hang in there, killer, we'll get you back in the game."

But Cook didn't want to go back. No more games.

Cook arched his back against his harness restraint and screamed as the fiery liquid death exploded again over the tiny farming village, burning every soul into charcoal mannequins – again and again, endlessly through the night – like it had myriad times before.

* * *

CHAPTER SIX

Fierce pounding on the room's door caused Cook to bolt upright, his sweat-soaked sheets adhering to his body like an unwanted skin.

"Wake up, shithead! Bus rolls in 15 minutes," Kane shouted through the door, and pounded it a couple more times for emphasis.

"I'm on it!" Cook rubbed his face and jogged to the bathroom to get ready. It was two in the afternoon. He had clearly made up for his earlier lack of sleep by missing the first half of the day. Red-rimmed, bruised eyes stared back at him from the mirror. His quick shave and shower did nothing to remove the soiled feel of the previous night's torment.

Scowls from the other pilots greeted Cook as he slung his gear bags through the van's cargo door and took the place Kane had saved him on the passenger side of the bench seat at the rear. The van driver slammed the door with a glower and hustled around to get his shuttle back on schedule. Fuck 'em, Cook concluded as he rested his pounding head against the already warm tinted window glass. They probably all whooped it up last night over hangar flying and daiquiris and then passed out face down in bed, instead of shaking awake every hour with angry burning ghosts screaming their names out of charred lungs at them.

Cook raised his hand to rub his forehead, as well as shield his eyes from the blaring morning sun and the bald-faced glares of the other pilots. He felt Kane staring at him, glanced over, and infinitesimally shook his head. Kane nodded, and leaned back against the seat – they'd talk about it later.

Sure, they'd have a long talk about it.

About Cook getting shanghaied by the DEA into selling out Porter and TVA and bringing whatever chump he got stuck with in the cockpit along. Yeah, that'd be a fun conversation. Cook peeked around the van from beneath the hand still shielding his eyes. Kane, finding something more productive than mothering Cook, had donned a set of noise-canceling headphones, and was communing hypnotically with downloads on his mobile. Cook examined the others. One of them was going to get co-opted into his caper – if he decided to go through with it – and he didn't feel any the better for it.

For what it was worth, he hadn't decided, yet. There might still be a chance to confide in Porter – he would know better than anyone how to handle this kind of thing. Hell, he was Romero's main target anyway. And maybe this time the company might show some gratitude for his effort.

Of course they would…just like last time. They did gratitude like nobody's business. Transvector might be so grateful they'd kill him for his own good.

A thought had reoccurred to him as he lay awake the night before, struggling to get to sleep. He might not have been the only one in this group that Romero had tried to bend over. The DEA agent had good information on the company and its personnel, and pilots were always stepping in it. It shouldn't have been too hard to find another stooge to blackmail. For the moment, he decided to give up – without better insight, he was just churning.

They entered the cargo end of the airfield and sped toward the hangar TVA had leased.

Bone-white tails of four C-130 transports reared above them, together resembling the bleached shoulder blades and vertebrae of some humongous quadruped in an open-air dinosaur museum. The white fuselages were adorned with the word 'InterSur' in twenty-inch red letters, but the airline name and the red symbol painted on the vertical stabilizers were meaningless. The putative owner or lessee would be a lawyer administering 'Asterra' or whatever cover name they were using, a Cayman or Panamanian shell that could cease to exist in a week, if needed, and reappear just as quickly under a new moniker at a pen stroke.

The van pulled around the tail of the last plane and drove straight into the dark maw of a cavernous, unmarked hangar.

Inside, the massive, shaded space was relatively cool and a veritable hive of activity, with uniformed mechanics laboring over large assemblies of tanks and piping mounted on pallets that sat on flatbed semi-trailers. To Cook, the palletized assemblages looked like nothing more than a series of micro-brewery fermentation tanks tipped over on their sides. He assumed it was high-end aerial spray equipment, but far more complicated than anything he'd ever used. A couple of tanker trucks with Mexican logos on the side were parked along the hangar wall, with hoses rolled in neat piles nearby. Large reels of thin steel cable were stacked towards the back, the purpose of which Cook couldn't guess.

Four construction-type trailers were huddled up together in the hangar's rear left corner surrounded by a chain link fence, like suspects crouching together in the holding area of a county lockup. Cook supposed the fence was a vain attempt to prevent theft of the trailer contents rather than any real security measure – in Latin America generally, unmonitored equipment tended to disappear quickly. Power, water and waste lines snaked between and around the trailer support jacks.

For Cook, camp jobs always had the same transitory feeling about them. Temporary buildings, jury-rigged utilities, portable toilets – nothing about them suggested any kind of loyalty to place. There was an atmosphere of transportability: the whole place could be packed up and vacated in a half a day.

The van stopped outside the fence around the trailers and disgorged its passengers.

Cook waited his turn and stepped out into fetid hangar, which felt like a sauna after the arctic chill of the van's air conditioning. The heat and humidity, combined with his hangover and lack of sleep, conspired to reinvigorate the previous night's migraine, which was crawling slowly from the back of his skull forward. This was going to be a fucking great day.

His fellow pilots formed a line at a gate in the fence surrounding the trailers, where a corporate flunky sporting aviator shades and a company flight shirt was scanning IDs and checking names off a clipboard. Since Cook hadn't had time to get company identification before arriving in Mexico, he pulled out his pilot's and driver's licenses, as well as his passport.

Kane glanced at the pilot's license in Cook's lightly quivering hand.

"Still got that, huh? You bribe the flight surgeon to pass the medical?" Muffled chuckles could be heard up the line. Cook sensed he wasn't very popular this morning.

"Eat me, Oreo." He felt Kane stiffen behind him as more startled snorts erupted. Cook knew Kane was largely immune to racial slurs, but he usually bandied them in private with his former colleague.

"You're just lucky I'm not a racist…Cool Whip." That got more smiles.

Cook stepped up to the company screener and handed over his identification. The functionary carefully checked each piece of identification against Cook's face, twice, then slotted them into a small manila envelope, which he duly labeled and tucked inside his clipboard box. He then ticked off a box on his list and extracted a laminated swipe badge with a large blue 'Flight Crew' and Cook's old TVA photo from a nearby table. "You'll get your ID back at destination."

Standard procedure for jobs on foreign soil was to surrender your personal identification and carry company credentials in their place. This was done for a couple of reasons: it was easier for the company to bail drunk pilots out of jail if the authorities called them directly, and it usually took an extra-large bribe to get U.S. government-issued papers back from local law enforcement.

"Thanks, buddy – keep up the good work." He shot the screener a facetious grin. The office flacks who pushed the paperwork and pulled security on jobs like these were always annoying junior G-Man types, off on a glamorous adventure with the flyboys. They usually dressed like they were in a combat zone, or on some dangerous secret government mission, and they all came off as mouth-breathing idiots. The pilots uniformly despised them, not the least because they routinely searched through everyone's luggage as part of their job.

Cook clipped his badge to his left shirt pocket and proceeded through the reek of hydraulic fluid and jet fuel that permeated the squalid hangar air toward the steady droning of industrial air-conditioning units mounted on each of the trailers. In the hallowed tradition of American overseas corporate enterprises, the coolies got to sweat in the noisy, sweltering heat while the Anglo brass labored in quiet, machine-cooled comfort. Cook's shirt was already wet under the arms as he mounted the steps to the first trailer. Inside it was cool and dim, and Cook shared in the audible groans of relief.

The room contained a couple of couches, several recliners, and a few camp beds at one end – obviously the ready room, where the flight crew would change and rest before the mission. Clothing lockers lined part of the walls, and assorted flying gear was piled next to them. As other pilots entered behind Cook, he noticed a large LCD television and satellite box on the opposite end of the trailer from the cots – the life of company pilots had definitely improved in his absence.

The screener, having locked the gate behind him with an officious clank, walked through the gaggle in the middle of the room and opened a door on the far side. He waved his clipboard, gesturing that they should follow him through. A short, steel-grate gangway led to the next trailer, which they entered in turn accompanied by the clanging of heavy feet.

Cook took a seat in a folding chair at a long conference table with a humming LCD projector commanding its center. A blank screen covered the short wall toward the hangar's center. This was clearly a briefing room – a connecting door in the center of the back wall presumably led to the operations center in one of the other two compartments.

The remaining pilots filed in and took their seats. Cook wondered, as he looked around, who he would be paired with on this junket. Word on Cook's background had apparently already filtered out on the pilot grapevine, but there were only a few familiar faces in the group. He recognized Sobek from some work in the Congo over a decade ago, and Margolin, who had once dropped a wing into a field during a low turn in Argentina. We're always remembered for our failures, Cook mused. He was relieved to see that he wasn't the only one with a reputation in the bunch. Kane sat two seats away, gazing up at the trailer's ceiling.

The pilot sitting next to him looked vaguely familiar and was typical of the breed: hairline beginning to recede, face that had seen a lot of sun and foreign soil, wiry build that spoke of high resting metabolic rate and an active life, but probably little actual exercise. Khakis and a short-sleeved button-down, both wrinkle-resistant so they could be washed in a hotel room sink and hung dry in the field if needed. And always the regulation undershirt. Seemed like every flight school drummed that one into its graduates – some holdover from military training. Cook always wore one himself.

Cook thought the guy's name might be Evans. He leaned toward him slightly, keeping his voice at a murmur. "You got any idea what the job is?"

The man just stared at Cook for a moment, as if irritated that he'd broken some unspoken silence protocol. Then he shrugged.

"Been down here four days – haven't heard squat," he responded in a low tone. "Waiting on you and Marszalek, I guess."

Cook nodded, leaning back. He had no idea who Marszalek was. As if a spell had broken, other low conversations broke out as the men waited in the dim florescent light and hypnotic droning of the air conditioning.

* * *

Mission briefings in Cook's former world were pretty consistent and predictable affairs, always following a prescribed format. A bunch of pilots sat in a room, received the who-what-why-when-where and how, wrote it all down, were given the current weather, and then sat around waiting until it was time to light up the engines.

Things had obviously changed while he'd been gone.

Muffled footsteps announced activity in the adjacent trailer, and the adjoining door swung inward to admit the operations staff, making the already cramped conference area seem even more crowded. Porter, wearing the trademark Hawaiian shirt he always wore in tropical climates, its armpits darkened with sweat, led the group into the trailer, but he broke off to the rear of the space as the others took the head of the room by the whiteboard covered by a projection screen.

Cook wondered what was going on. Porter had conducted every clandestine briefing since Cook had started with the company, even when Bellamy was ostensibly in charge. Must be the changing of the guard Bell had been referring to. He switched his attention to the front of the trailer.

A clean-cut, preppy-looking corporate operative was giving the introductions. His short brown hair was creased by a sharp part, and his pale chin was shaven so closely it looked like he had never grown facial hair in the first place. He sported khakis and a navy polo shirt, and introduced himself as Blair.

Cook detested him on sight, and if his glances around the table were any indicator, so did everyone else present.

This was normal. Transvector periodically rotated talented up-and-comers into the field on the covert side to give them some seasoning before slotting them behind a desk somewhere in the operations hierarchy. Occasionally, mid-grade CIA clandestine branch officers did tours through TVA to give them a taste of the contracting side of their business. All were universally loathed by the line personnel who pretended to listen attentively to their naïve and dangerous ideas, and largely tuned them out.

Blair started without introducing anyone else in the room.

"This mission has been designated 'Sideshow'. Aircraft callsigns are 'Strongman' One through Four, Guadalajara is 'Carousel', and mission control at headquarters is 'Boardwalk'."

He consulted his notes.

"Though the current Mexican administration has diminished its participation in the war on drugs, there is still substantial cooperation in politically non-contentious activities such as aerial drug crop eradication...."

While Cook waited for the meat of the matter – the headings, airspeeds, fuel figures, cargo details, weight and balance, conditions, etc. – he focused on the most interesting person in the room, slightly apart from the others, leaning against the left wall.

Like the Ivy League-type at the head of the room, his dark hair was well-groomed, but his expensively tailored light gray suit and tie made him stand out. He was young and good-looking, with intelligent dark eyes that quietly roamed the room while Blair droned on up front about the benefits of close cooperation with the Mexican government. His darker skin made him a local, and Cook figured he was with the Mexican attorney general's office or another internal security group. His perceptive gaze carefully examined each person in the room while feigning interest in what Blair was saying. When their eyes met, Cook quickly refocused his attention back to the front.

Blair was starting to get into stride, as evidenced by his higher voice pitch and choppy, excited hand gestures. He flicked a remote at the LCD projector sitting on the conference table, and an image of a C-130 sprang to life on the screen. Blair glanced back at the screen with satisfaction. Clearly, digital slideshows were this idiot-child's bread and butter.

Cook closed his eyes momentarily and groaned internally, his migraine slowly increasing its pulsing tempo.

"As some of you have guessed by the equipment in the hangar, this is an aerial spray mission, utilizing the Modular Aerial Spray System, or MASS, units that are mounted on…"

Blair seemed determined to bore everyone to death even before the mission started. Novice operations types always found comfort in the technical aspects of the missions, while the line personnel just wanted to know the practical aspects that affected their flying. Kane was staring at his hands on the table in front of him. Cook hazarded a glance back at Porter, who favored him back with a vacant smile and a rolled-eye look.

Like most pilots, Cook had a good memory for important details, such as altitudes and assigned frequencies, and could play back information as needed while he divided his attention elsewhere.

Basically, the MASS system had a capacity of 2,000 gallons in four large tanks connected together by tubing and pumps and controlled by a fairly sophisticated computer console that was hooked into the aircraft's navigation system. You could control the volume of spray exiting the C-130 on two booms which protruded from the aft end of the aircraft's fuselage, and two other spray arms mounted under the wings. The whole thing rested on military-standard 463L aircraft cargo pallets and was designed as a 'Roll On/Roll Off' system that locked into the C-130's dual rail system.

Blair lovingly flicked through image after image showing glossy pipes and shiny tanks, as if he was a sales representative for the firm that manufactured them. Cook didn't bother concealing his yawn. This information was better suited to the loadmaster, who was in charge of the cargo area of the aircraft, than the flight crew in the 'office' up front.

His mind wandered to more pressing concerns.

If Romero wasn't talking out of his ass, and Porter was smuggling drugs aboard the planes back into the U.S., there was virtually no way he would be able to find out. Images of the cargo bay interior beyond the spray system only reinforced for him just how cavernous the C-130 Hercules aircraft was. His initial thought that he might be able to search for the contraband during the flight now seemed quaint. It could be cached anywhere in that massive airframe, and it might not even be on his plane. And the technical personnel in the back might even rouse themselves to wonder what the hell he was doing.

An image of a large-scale aeronautical chart of Mexico and the U.S. flashed on the screen, and Cook switched his attention back to Blair's brief.

"The cover for this mission is that the current operation assisting the GOM" – he nodded at the Mexican official when saying this, 'GOM' being officialese for 'Government of Mexico' – "with aerial forest spraying for the Javanese Bark Beetle has concluded for the season, and the aircraft are being repatriated back to the U.S. for a heavy maintenance class-D inspection and retrofitting of aerial firefighting systems."

A 'D' check was a major maintenance event that commercial aircraft underwent periodically. It was a mission rational that TVA often used when they needed to move large amounts of equipment quietly on short notice. And it was getting toward the time of year when forest fires would break out in the southern US states. Cook noticed other pilots nodding their approval – as cover stories went, this was probably as good as it gets.

Cook also knew that even though Mexico and the U.S. didn't get along on most issues, they were in lockstep agreement on protecting timber interests. Mexico gladly received the bug eradication and airborne firefighting help as foreign aid, and American timberland owners were thrilled to be better protected from foreign pests working their way north and killing trees. It was win-win for everyone but the taxpayer, who, as usual, got wildly overcharged by inflated contracting fees.

Blair turned and aimed the remote control's laser pointer at the position of Guadalajara on the screen, to the sound of stifled snorts. The fact that he was standing right next to the projected image and could have used his finger made the situation even funnier. Blair squinted out at the darkened room, not comprehending the titter, obviously thinking there might be a question.

On the spur of the moment, Cook decided to nickname him the Sock Puppet – his naiveté and imperceptive nature reminded Cook of a character from a children's TV show.

Colored lines sprang up on the aeronautical chart leading from Mexico into the U.S.

"The most direct route from Guadalajara International Airport, or GDL, to Transvector's Mojave facility lies over the western portion of the Sierra Madre Occidental, which certain federal agencies in both the U.S. and Mexico have recognized to offer targets of a fruitful nature." Blair nodded again at the Mexican government representative and paused as if waiting for him to respond. The liaison, who was looking at his phone, didn't react.

Porter sallied forth from the back to fill the awkward silence. "Basically, someone noticed you'll be flying over some of the best poppy-growing fields this side of Chang Mai and the Helmand Valley."

Blair paused his presentation, staring at the back of the room. A full three seconds passed in silence.

"Thank you for your input, Mr. Porter," he enunciated carefully. "There will be a comments section at the end of the presentation."

Dead silence reigned for a moment, followed by subdued sounds of awe among the assembled pilots. Cook was dumbstruck. In all his years of working for TVA, no one had ever heard of Porter getting slapped down in public before. He glanced back at the older man and saw his face redden and jaw muscle tighten, apparently stifling a strong reaction. Cook turned back to the front and saw that even the Mexican official looked surprised at such an obvious put-down by the younger man.

The Sock Puppet continued, oblivious to his snub's effect.

"In conjunction with the GOM and the U.S. war on drugs, Transvector has been tasked with testing a new delivery system that will revolutionize aerial drug interdiction efforts...."

Blah, blah, blah. Cook wondered why Blair bothered with the finer political ramifications in front of a room filled with pilots, who could obviously care less. Maybe he was practicing for briefing upper management. If so, his behavior toward Porter made some sense. If Porter was getting pushed out, as Bellamy had suggested, this man-child might already be his designated replacement. Cook decided to cut down on his obvious displays of boredom and yawning and clock back in. After all, this guy could be his new boss. Besides, the brief was getting juicy again – the Sock Puppet was consulting notes.

"Aircraft dispersing the chemical will be flying at night over variable terrain at between 100 and 150 feet, at a velocity of approximately 200 knots."

Jesus H. Christ, it was a suicide mission.

Loud enough murmurs erupted around the table that Blair hesitated in his heretofore mechanical delivery and looked up from his notes.

"Does someone have a question?" he asked, in a tone indicating that there shouldn't be. A pilot across the table raised his hand.

"Just how variable is this terrain we'll be flying 100 feet over?"

Blair smirked with satisfaction, as if he'd anticipated the question and was tickled at his own clairvoyance. "Mission terrain elevations range from approximately 600 to 3100 feet above mean sea level."

Everyone had a comment on that one. Evans was loudest. "Just how do you expect us to navigate at night at those altitudes and airspeed? With a fucking Ouija Board?"

Porter barked from the back. "Settle down, guys. We've got a solution."

Blair fixed Porter with another glare, apparently peeved that he'd had his punchline stolen. He then looked down at his sheet and advanced the slides. The image showed a glass screen in the instrument panel with a sophisticated-looking, multi-color GPS-like readout, including flight path vectors marked with purple arrows.

"TVA has been selected by DARPA and the Defense Spraying Agency to field test a new gene-based herbicide tailored to opium poppy eradication...."

More propeller-head mumbo jumbo. Something about surfactants, and droplet size. Basically, the stuff would kill the shit out of an opium poppy and leave everything else around it standing, which in the Sierra Madre was some evergreens and pitifully small Indian corn plots.

So why didn't Blair just say that? Cook was already pining with nostalgia for Porter's breezy briefing style. In his book, only pilots should be allowed to brief pilots. If this new guy was going to be replacing Porter,

Cook was going to have to reconsider how much fun this reinsertion into clandestine life would be.

What the Sock Puppet didn't get is that pilots saw themselves as essentially over-educated, overpaid truck drivers, hauling stuff from point A to point B. Cargo was cargo, regardless if it spoke, moved, dropped, or exploded after falling out of the plane. What Cook and the rest of the men around the table specifically wanted to know was how in the hell they were going to fly over that topography, at those altitudes and airspeeds, *at night*, and make it out alive. Flying low over mountains was always dangerous. Flying low over mountains in the dark was asking for an early exit from life.

With *sotto voce* comments continuing around the room, Blair belatedly seemed to realize that he was losing his audience. Cook thought Porter might have thrown him a signal to speed things up, but when he glanced back again, Porter seemed absorbed in slowly typing an email on a smartphone with his large clumsy thumbs.

"Can I get your eyes back up front, folks? This is crucial information." The neophyte clearly had imagined an enthralling briefing before the fact, unmarred by a boisterous, uncooperative, attention-deficient pilots. Now he was presiding over a full-scale pilot revolt.

With the briefing devolving into chaos, Cook once again craved for Porter to reassert control. But Porter, still hunched over his mobile phone, had no such intention, and his slight smirk might have even indicated that he was enjoying the show.

Blair was rapidly advancing slides to try to find something to regain his momentum. The other Transvector personnel in the front of the room awkwardly stared at the conference table, quietly talked amongst themselves, or consulted the tablets everyone seemed to be carrying. The Mexican government liaison indulgently glanced at his expensive wristwatch and examined his manicured nails.

Not looking nearly as smooth as when he started, Blair finally found what he was searching for, a time-lapse video with a multicolor terrain map depicting the geography between Guadalajara and TVA's Mojave base. Miniature C-130s were staged on a runway schematic and started to taxi slowly to the runway as the digital video advanced. There were some snorts at the ridiculous level of detail, and suddenly Blair was tripping over his notes in a rush.

"Departure is scheduled for 2030 hours local, contingent upon favorable meteorological conditions. At approximately 2055 hours, mission flight will reach cruising altitude, and the uprated TERMIT system will automatically actuate and synchronize between aircraft. Upon initialization, aircraft are hands-off until you're past the ADIZ, barring an emergency abort."

The pilots let out a collectively held breath.

The TERMIT, or TERrain Mapping Integrated Technologies, was a highly sophisticated terrain-following autopilot that combined ground-proximity radar, GPS input, inertial guidance, and laser-based terrain interrogation. Each individual system in itself had its shortcomings, but together their redundancies overlapped to make the business of flying nap-of-the-earth that much safer. It was head-and-shoulders above what the average cruise missile had on board. The military had used it extensively in Afghanistan and Syria, and it had a good record from everything Cook had heard. It was usually seen in fighter jets and drones, but there was no reason it couldn't be used on a C-130.

Basically, the 'Termite', as it was affectionately known, was going to act as a black box that ran the whole show, right up until the Air Defense Identification Zone, or ADIZ, that wrapped around the U.S. and warned NORAD of any approaching threats. Had Blair mentioned it earlier, he could have saved himself, and his audience, a whole lot of anxiety.

Blue colored lines trailed the aircraft icons on the map video, inching their way north to the US border.

"Strongman aircraft will fly mile-in-trail. At approximately 2105 hours, the formation will enter the area of operation, and Strongmen One and Three will depressurize their fuselages, lower their ramps, and deploy modified KT-04 towed aerial targets with electronic decoy packages on board."

An insert appeared on the mission map video showing a light-gray aerial vehicle that looked like a miniature version of a jet from the 1950s. Cook saw others nod in recognition. TVA personnel had towed them for UNITA rebel anti-aircraft training in Angola back in 1990. So that's what all the cable in the hangar was for.

"The aerial targets will spool out to approximately nine-tenths of a mile, at which point their transponder packages will activate simultaneously with Strongmen Two and Four's transponder deactivation. Strongmen

Two and Four will then extinguish navigation lights and descend and fly the spray mission profile."

Red lines snaked and twisted away from the straight blue flight path of the main flight, with little purple squares lighting up along the way to indicate areas that were being sprayed.

It was a nice touch. Even though Mexican radar coverage was pretty thin outside the major traffic centers, if anyone caught the flight on their scope it would look like all four planes were still in formation. Since TVA apparently never got rid of anything, and Angola had been almost thirty years earlier, Cook guessed someone other than Blair had generated this aspect of the plan. It was a classic subterfuge, and it had Porter written all over it.

Cook snuck a look back at Porter for the umpteenth time and saw that the older man was staring at him. He started inwardly, but casually shot a questioning eyebrow and received a minute head-nod in response. To Cook, it looked like Porter wanted to huddle with him after the briefing, and he forced himself to nod nonchalantly in return.

His insides started to twist with an increase in stomach acid. This was it – Porter knew about Romero, and Cook was going to have to come clean. No worries. Cook had already come to the conclusion that his loyalties lay with TVA and Porter, damn the consequences. He'd let Porter ask, then give him the goods.

Cook looked back to the front.

Blair was pathetic. Even now, as he dribbled gratuitous details on a laser detection-and-ranging system called LIDAR that was going to measure herbicide dispersal over the opium fields, the other pilots were shaking their heads and exchanging glances. His inexperienced and disjointed delivery clearly telegraphed that he was both an amateur and a fool, and reduced his already scant credibility to nothing.

The moving graphic ended, with the tiny aircraft taxiing to the TVA facility at Mojave. Oblivious to the absurdity, Blair waited until the planes had actually stopped before he resumed his brief. Cook overheard one of the other pilots ask his neighbor in a whisper if they would "actually park in those spots," and got a snicker in response.

The briefing ended pretty much as it had started, awkwardly.

"Ok, guys, that's the profile," Blair concluded. "I want you all to remember how important this effort is to the company, and the war on drugs...."

The Sock Puppet clearly had taken some sort of motivational speaking course, and was trying for a big finish, but his audience of hardened aviators had already tuned out and were mentally going over the mission details or quietly conferring amongst themselves. One of Blair's flunkies passed around navigation charts that indicated emergency landing areas along the route should there be a problem. These were 'clean' charts that would have been issued if this were a normal maintenance flight. They were necessary because, although they contained no indication of what the actual operation would be, things occasionally did go wrong, and you had to land the plane somewhere. Cook noticed with a jolt that at least four of the airports so marked in the U.S. were airfields he had circled for Stokes.

Blair finished with a lame attempt at a joke that nobody but Porter chuckled at. Flushing at what he obviously, and correctly, read as a failed performance, he waved at his assistant in the background to approach the head of the table with his clipboard. Chatter halted as the other pilots refocused their attention.

The assistant read off the crew assignments from the list of names. Each flight had a pilot, copilot, a loadmaster, and a utility crewman as technician to monitor the spray rig. Cook listened attentively, his apprehension burgeoning as he waited to hear which unlucky schlub would be paired with him, and possibly have to undergo some sort of post-mission scrutiny, regardless if Cook played ball with Romero or not.

"…and Strongman Four. Kane PIC, Cook FO."

Kane was his pilot, and he was first officer. Things were looking up.

* * *

"Sideshow is right," Porter grunted, wiping a copious amount of sweat from his forehead with a shaggy forearm, despite the room's frigid temperature. "Jesus, what a circus."

The briefing had broken up, and the pilots had shuffled next door to the ready room to change into their flight suits and relax on cots and recliners in the brutally efficient air conditioning until 'go time'. The Sock Puppet, the Mexican government liaison, and the rest of the TVA operations staff had exited the opposite door to the inner trailer. Porter had not followed, and Cook had dawdled at the back of his scrum until the two were alone in the room with the doors closed. With the previous occupants gone, the thrumming drone of the industrial cooling unit only seemed to increase, conveniently screening any conversation from outside ears.

"And that little ass-sucking Langley cheesedick. Who the hell does he think he is?" Porter continued from the corner of the room, scowling myopically into a cube fridge on top of the TV credenza. He pulled out two chilled cans of Coke, threw one to Cook, then flopped his bulk into one of the conference room folding chairs, which squealed in protest. Cracking open his can with a satisfying hiss, Cook wondered if he should spill to his boss immediately, or let Porter vent.

And Cook could understand why he'd want to. The whole feel of that briefing was different from any he'd seen in the past – more like a corporate board meeting with all the suits and polo shirts than the cowboy-rodeo atmosphere of previous decades. Porter's pit-stained Hawaiian garb was itself a relic of the late-Seventies.

As it was looking, Cook thought he might have trouble getting a word in edgewise anyway.

"After all the shit I've done for this company… Hallett? You think he'd take that crap? He'd kick that fuckface punk straight in the balls for that prima donna shit he pulled!"

Cook decided to chime in, just to prime the pump a bit. The desire to confess Romero's extortion had been increasing in proportion to his re-immersion into the company milieu, and, at this point, he felt like a Catholic schoolboy holding onto a fistful of sins in a confession booth. He assumed an air of detached speculation that he wasn't really feeling.

"Maybe he's back against the wall on this one? Bellamy was telling me the Feds are tightening up on all the contractors since the Iraq cluster." Cook's oblique reference to the scandals surrounding Halliburton and Blackwater during the second Gulf War needed no further elaboration. Every private military contractor had felt the increased government scrutiny in their top-line accounting.

Porter roused himself from his musings, which was the intended effect.

"You been talking to Bell? How is that old rat-turd?"

"Still kicking…still drinking." Cook thought the latter detail might please him for some reason.

"Good for him," Porter mumbled. He seemed to brighten a bit at the mention of the other man's name, but was showing his age more than Cook remembered.

Cook wondered if the older man had been drinking himself. Porter took a dim view on alcoholic beverages during flight operations, but these were different times. In Honduras, late night decompression sessions had often resulted in semi-licit blood-alcohol levels the following day, and a discreetly poured Irish coffee hadn't been unknown. But Cook had never seen Porter or any other pilot actually flying impaired. Not one that wanted to live long, anyway.

As if sensing Cook's train of thought, Porter suddenly fixed him with a rheumy eye.

"There anything you need to get off your chest? You seem more wound up than usual."

It was now or never. Cook stared at the tabletop, trying to form his thoughts.

"Listen, Ted …there is something I wanted to talk to you about…you see, uh…."

The connecting door to the operations area crashed open, and Blair stuck his head into the room, his face expressing sheer exasperation.

"Porter – we need you in here now."

Porter's eyes, which had been focused on Cook's face, narrowed with what looked like barely suppressed rage.

"Gimme a minute," he snapped.

Blair switched his attention from the back of Porter's head to Cook, and raised his eyebrows, as if he was waiting for Cook to stand up and walk out. Porter, sensing insubordination, slowly turned halfway around in his seat. The back of his neck was flushed red.

"I said give me a goddamned minute – I'm finishing something up here."

Blair's impatient eyes showed a flicker of aggravation.

"One minute." The door slammed as he departed.

Porter continued seething at the closed door, breathing heavily. Cook decided to just blurt it out while he had the opportunity.

"There's something you need to know, Ted, about tonight's gig…."

Porter turned back abruptly and held up his hand, cutting Cook off. The blood vessels on his temples stood out prominently, and his eyes were aflame with repressed fury. His chair scraped the floor as he stood and fixed Cook with a steely glare.

His supervisor's tone brooked no dissent.

"Save it for later, kid – I'm done taking this meat sack's shit. You can tell me whatever it is when we get back to Mojave. I'm riding with you guys."

The door slammed as he left the room.

Cook heard heavy clanking on the walkway grate, and a muffled crack as another door was wrenched open. Porter's voice boomed Blair's name, then something forceful and drawn out, but indistinguishable as the door slammed again, shaking the thin trailer wall.

Cook sat still in the room for moment, staring as tears of condensation ran down the side of the Coke can and letting the inexorable throb of the environmental system wash over his taut nerves with something akin to, but not quite like, relief. He'd made his choice. He'd tried, and failed, to warn Porter and come clean. The decision had been made for him, and the rest was easy.

His increasingly calm resolve diminished the specter of Romero's photos and Stokes' galling manipulations. He would play their game up until mission time, but run things according to the company playbook thereafter. Misgivings about trusting the organization that had previously betrayed him were steadily fading away. Deep down, he knew it wasn't their fault, that this situation was completely different, and they wouldn't do it a second time. They'd have to side with him. The bad press alone would topple them. If he started talking to investigators and the media, it would be Iran-Contra all over again.

He was in this with Porter and TVA to the end.

Whatever that end would be. Bellamy, Porter and Kane, and the others were the only family he'd really ever known. The DEA and their threats were nothing compared to that. If he had to go down for it, lose his ability to fly, or even his freedom, well…so be it. He would do it for family. At least now he knew what he was fighting for.

Cook stood, opened the trailer door, and walked out to the ready room.

* * *

Time often seems to stand still while you're waiting for an operation to begin. All the military-standard gripe phrases clambered through his consciousness. Hurry up and wait. Standby to standby. No wonder they existed – they were all true.

Cook lounged alone on one of the trailer's brown Naugahyde sofas with his arms crossed on his chest, and his legs stretched out in front of him. A company issued InterSur ballcap sat low on his forehead covering his eyes, both to block the room's light and deter any potential conversationalists. The olive-drab flight suit he had changed into was brand new, its perfect fit a testament to the efficiency of the company handlers. The glossy Nomex chafed a bit; he was more accustomed to second-hand gear that was well worn in. He'd traded his street shoes for a pair of black leather Lucchese roper boots – for his money, the best flying boot made. They were comfortable as hell, they looked good with jeans or slacks, and had good pedal feel.

A couple of pilots, who had likely stayed out too late the previous evening, had immediately commandeered the cots at the end of the trailer nearest the hangar wall. Kane and a few others had repositioned the

Barca loungers around the television and were watching ESPN Sports Center. The rest, joined by flight crew that had finished working on the spray systems, sat opposite Cook on another couch surrounded by folding chairs, and conversed in low tones.

That Cook had the couch to himself spoke volumes. With the exception of Kane, Sobek, Margolin and Evans, he didn't recognize any of the other pilots or crew. He assumed most of them had been hired since he left the company. But if the area of quarantine around him said anything, it was that they didn't want Cook's jinx rubbing off on them. The private chat with Porter had sealed it – he was officially a leper, and probably bad luck as well. That was fine with him. He needed time alone to think.

Cook had hoped to catch some sleep himself before takeoff, but his mind kept chewing over the Romero situation. He had to give Stokes a signal as he left, or they'd be waiting for him in Mojave. Playing along would buy him some time. He could always say he tried to initiate a system malfunction and failed – or maybe Kane managed to stop him. He'd think of something in the air.

The route they were taking was fairly straightforward, and he had imprinted the general details from Sock Puppet's slideshow into his memory: from Guadalajara, northwest up the Sierra Madre to Fort Huachuca; then west-northwest through southern Arizona to Yuma, and from there into California. Once the flight entered the United States, they would be traveling primarily through military and restricted airspace, thus remaining innocuous to most air traffic control centers. At Brawley, California, they'd pop back into the commercial aviation system, fly over the Salton Sea, and northwest up the Coachella Valley to the home field.

He decided he would give Stokes the hand signal for Palm Springs International, one of the emergency landing fields enroute. It was about twenty-five minutes flight time from Mojave, but if Romero was driving from Los Angeles, it could take him two-and-a-half hours to get there. And by that point, Cook would have told Porter everything. With any luck, Porter would put him in a jumpseat on a cargo flight to Africa or the Middle East until the whole mess had been cleaned up. Romero could hardly arrest Cook if he couldn't find him.

Cook inhaled deeply, then exhaled slowly, feeling tension seep from his frame.

He felt more relaxed than at any time since he'd arrived. He snuck a look at his watch from under his hat brim – still about four hours to go. Maybe he would be able to catch a few winks before departure. He glanced enviously at the pilots on the cots to his left. Both were out cold, one snoring lightly with his mouth wide open. Maybe he would head over and try it himself.

He felt a light kick on his foot, and his seat cushion was abruptly lifted as someone sat down heavily next to him.

"Peso for your thoughts. I saw you check the time, so I know you're not sacked out."

Cook sighed with resignation, pushed up his cap's brim and looked over to see Kane grinning at him. The man had a cheery quality that just never quit. Cook grunted, and, scowling, pulled his cap down again.

"Seriously, Guy, everything with you and Porter alright?" Kane asked in a quieter tone.

Cook pushed the cap brim back up and saw that his friend's gaze was punctuated with concern. There was nothing that needed telling at the moment. He decided to assuage Kane's apprehension by playing it light.

"Copacetic." Cook shrugged himself upright on the couch, adopting a thoughtful posture. "Porter just wanted to make sure I was okay flying second seat to such a second-rater." He paused, as if considering the matter. "I told him I'd probably sleep most of the time anyway."

Kane pursed his lips and nodded, stifling a grin. "Not the way we're going to be flying, you won't. Nap of the earth, baby. Going to be the next-level Vomit Comet."

"Yeah, no doubt. You ever used the TERMIT?"

"No, but I heard from the guys at Bragg that it's bombproof."

Cook shrugged. "So, I guess our chances go from zero to better than average?"

"If you can keep your hands off your stick." Kane grinned, then, as if recalling something, he peered at Cook intently.

"You get that other thing sorted out with Porter?"

"No problemo – just had to straighten out how I get my ratings back." Cook turned to face Kane, his face portraying disbelief. "Hell, twice your damn hours and I'm still your copilot."

Kane leered, showing some teeth. He glanced around furtively, making sure no one was eavesdropping, then leaned in, speaking in an undertone.

"It's 'cause I'm sneakier. When I bring in my *mota*...I do it real quiet-like."

Cook groaned, sliding back down on the sofa and replacing his cap brim over his eyes.

"Great...just what I need. Another dickhead-in-charge."

* * *

CHAPTER SEVEN

The fading light on Guadalajara's high plateau turned the matte white skin of Cook's C-130 a golden-sand color as he paced around its periphery, performing the pre-flight inspection while Kane shuffled flight paperwork in the cockpit.

Great, thought Cook, first officer – again. Back to being a goddamned gear puller. He patted the aluminum skin of the fuselage and tried to muster some excitement about it.

A crucial procedure on smaller planes, like Cessna 172s and single-pilot racing aircraft, the mandatory walk-around on a crew-maintained aircraft like the Hercules was a largely a redundant exercise. If there was a bad system somewhere in the enormous fuselage looming over him like a dry-docked submarine hull, a hasty examination like the one Cook was performing as first officer wasn't going to reveal it. He felt like one of those uniformed airline pilots people saw from the concourse looking up into gear wells and peering into the engines – largely cosmetic, a bit of showmanship to placate the nervous traveler.

As Cook slowly trudged the perimeter, he was mainly concerned with making sure all the dust covers and control locks were off the four gaping turboprop engine intakes and the control surfaces on the wings and the tail. After all, mechanics were human, and forgot things like everyone else. More than one aircraft had been brought down by a missed 'Remove Before Flight' tag that rendered the plane completely unflyable.

In this instance, however, Cook found nothing to complain about. The proficiency of Transvector's mechanics and crews was well-known in the industry and had been since Cook's Honduras days. But procedure was procedure, and on this flight, he was particularly concerned with adhering to the checklist.

He had always marveled at the size of these aircraft, especially since most of his time had been in smaller bush planes, like de Havilland Caribous, Twin Otters, and a variety of single-engine cargo hoppers. Each of the C-130's four curved propeller blades was almost the width and height of a man, and the bulbous auxiliary fuel tanks mounted under the wings between the engines were longer than his car. The upper-mounted wing was half again as long as a tennis court, and created a vast shady space underneath that was a particularly nice place to work in hot climates.

The basic airframe had been around since the mid-Fifties, being heavily upgraded over the intervening decades. This particular C-130 was a newer 'J' model, a so-called Super Hercules, which had a reinforced center wing section retrofitted to prevent the explosive fuselage separations that had infamously occurred over the years on ex-CIA planes used in firefighting. The avionics in the cockpit had also been completely swapped out, resulting in a mostly glass-cockpit that bore a partial resemblance to a modern airliner.

For Transvector, it was a departure from past practice. Usually TVA bought used equipment, and kept aircraft flying long after they should have been retired. But these things were pristine, looking fresh off the assembly line. Cook suspected that the US Air Force's generosity in loaning TVA the planes wasn't out of the kindness of its heart, and that they were getting something juicy in return. Like free testing of a new avionics package without putting any of their own pilots in harm's way.

Still, he couldn't shake the feeling that there was more going on here than he'd been told. He also wondered if Stokes already had eyes on him. It made the whole exercise seem creepier, somehow.

As he walked toward the aft cargo ramp, Cook gave a wide berth around one of the pair of many-nozzled spray booms that protruded six feet out from the side of the cargo bay. A green-gloved technician in a Tyvek bunny-suit and respirator was making final adjustments on one of the spray spigots. Cook didn't know how toxic the experimental herbicide was to humans, but he didn't care to get close enough to find out. Looking something like the spiny arm of a metallic Saguaro cactus stuck on the fuselage, these booms, along with spray bars on the outboard section of the wings, would discharge the contents of the chemical tanks in a thick, foggy plume over the target poppy fields. Cook had seen them used before for mosquito spraying after hurricane Katrina and oil-spill mitigation in the Gulf of Mexico.

His circuit around the Hercules complete, Cook ducked his head and swung around one of the hydraulic arms on the rear cargo ramp to look inside. As large in diameter as a small subway tunnel, the cavernous hold of the C-130 was filled to the bulkheads with the shiny steel tanks and pipes of the MASS spray system components. Each tank unit had been filled by hazmat-suited crew inside the hangars, with roaring exhaust ventilation fans running nearby. Because they were supposed to be returning to the U.S. with empty tanks, this was done in the interests of operational security, to shield their purpose from drug cartel observers who were almost certainly watching the festivities.

As was presumably Stokes. Cook turned and gazed at the landscape outside the airport's barrier fence through the faint evening haze. She would be using a long-focus or telephoto lens, with a vantage of the taxiway leading to the active runway. Probably in one of the commercial buildings to the south, or with her cover as a journalist, possibly in the terminal itself. Anyway, it wasn't his problem. He gave up trying to guess and turned back to the cargo hold.

Having given the spray technicians a thumbs up, and received one in return, Cook jumped down and proceeded up the far side of the fuselage. About twenty feet forward of the props, he mounted the side stairway-hatch in the front of the cargo area, then clambered up the ladder to the cockpit area.

Kane looked up from checking the pre-programmed flight information on the TERMIT unit's display.

"How's the gear in the rear?"

Cook smiled thinly.

"Why don't you go back and look yourself, Mr. Pilot-in-Command?"

"No thanks. I've got flunkies to do that for me."

Cook closed his eyes and shook his head side to side. "This isn't gonna get old for you anytime soon, huh?"

Kane showed a wide grin, his teeth flashing a brilliant white. "Not a chance."

Cook slid sideways through the narrow space next to the cockpit floor instrument cluster and stepped into his seat, which was set in an aft position during the pre-flight period. He reached behind his back into his flight bag and grabbed a Velcro-strapped thigh clipboard which had navigation charts already attached to it. He glanced at his watch – still an hour before takeoff. "You think we're going to get shot at?"

Kane paused from twisting one of the input dials to glance up at Cook. "Probably. You worried?"

Getting shot at from the ground was never fun, but the likelihood of the narcos having any kind of serious anti-aircraft capability was low. Aircraft Cook had flown in Honduras had been peppered from time to time with fire up to a 14.5mm Soviet ZPU cannon, but he'd only been shot down the one time, and he didn't care to think about that particular incident at the moment. They might have some .50 caliber heavy machine guns, but it was awfully tough to hit a flying object without practice, especially one running low to the ground without lights. And a C-130 was a whale – it could take some damage.

"Nah. I'm more worried about pancaking into one of those barrancas than getting picked off."

Kane leaned back and put his arms behind his head, audibly cracking his spine.

"I wouldn't stress too much." He pointed at the glass screen. "This avionics package is something else. It's got the whole route plotted out, with a 'tunnel in the sky' and synthetic vision on the heads-up display, and it'll pipe straight into the infrared headset. Nails your position to within a meter or two – plenty of room for us." He glanced out the side window. "What the hell is Porter doing…a preflight?"

Cook looked over through the window. Porter, carrying a flight bag, was talking to the crew chief at the next plane over, and looking up at the wings.

"Yeah, forgot to mention that. He's sick as hell of that new turd-stain Blair, and he's coming with us."

Kane turned his head back to Cook, impressed. "No foolin'? Bet he hasn't flown a job in ten years – being management and all."

Cook grinned. "Don't load your shorts. He's just along for the ride."

Kane nodded. "I just hope he ain't ridin' with us."

* * *

At twenty to eight, Porter called all the pilots to a pow-wow in the entrance to the hangar.

The C-130s had been preflighted and were buttoned up and ready to go. They all looked identical, despite their differing payloads and functions. The planes that would be towing drogues still had their spray bars attached, for all intents and purposes indistinguishable from the others. The two unused MASS systems removed from Strongmen 1 and 3 would go north in container trucks.

As the group gathered round, Cook observed a subtle but ambient change in the demeanor of the aviators, one that was visibly lacking at the earlier brief. This was an interesting mission, with a little danger mixed in – basically the sort of thing that caused them to sign up with Transvector in the first place. Any residual trace of hangovers from the previous evening had been replaced with a calm alertness. They waited with anticipation as Porter made his way from the trailer cluster up to the front of the hangar.

In his customarily breezy manner, he jumped right in.

"Let's cut to the chase. Boy Wonder's briefing sucked. Here's what you need to know."

"This is a standard plain-wrapper gig on semi-friendly soil, so let's keep things smooth and steady. We're running this one hands-free. Trust your gizmos, and don't feel the need to engage in self-help unless you've got a full-blown Mayday. Keep an eye on the map and your emergency alternates if you have to take her down. One and Three, try not to fall asleep, okay?"

Scattered sniggers broke out. Porter turned towards Cook and Kane.

"Strongmen Two and Four, it's basically an uprated crop-dusting job. You're going to be low, and when you're dropping the load, it'll be noisy. Some of the targets may have advanced warning and there might be some ground awareness, so be prepared to take some flack – not that you can do anything about it. Stay calm, trust your armor, trust your aircraft. Remember, speed and darkness are your friends."

Cook nodded, feeling the adrenalin pump into his system. This was the feeling he missed, the mission-time high. He looked at Kane, whose face was showing the same reaction. Let's get this thing on.

Porter turned back to address the entire group.

"On the plus side, we don't have to worry too much about exposure. No one affected is going to run to the cops or the media. The people we're hitting are dirtbags, so the public won't give a damn."

"If we do this right, we'll all make it home by zero dark thirty. You never know," he winked, "we might even make the early breakfast special at Denny's."

He scanned the pilot's faces and paused, his eyes flicking mischievously.

"Some of you have heard a rumor that I'm flying with you tonight. Well, my new boss," he raised his hand slightly at the low chuckles this prompted, "tells me that although I'm absolutely crucial to the success of this mission, they can spare my presence in operations for the next couple of days."

Porter paused and glanced over his shoulder before resuming in a low tone.

"Basically, I'm gonna strangle that drippy shit-stain if I have to spend another minute with him."

All the pilots nodded their agreement. Cook exchanged an "I told you so" look with Kane.

"So, you're probably wondering who's the lucky crew." Porter paused again for effect, and looked around the circle at each man before landing on a pair to his right.

"Stongman One, you drew the short straw."

Low groans erupted from two of the pilots, while the others smiled or sniggered at their obvious discomfort. Cook felt a tide of relief sweep through him. Even though he had yet to come clean on the Romero situation, having Porter ride the whole way with him would have worked his nerves into a knot. Much easier to put something together over the radio.

Porter grinned. To Cook, he seemed to be in a much lighter mood than earlier.

"What, you guys thought I was going to sign on to one of the rollercoaster rides? Relax you two. I'll be in back with the chief, manning the daiquiri blender. We'll send a couple forward after we cross the border."

There was outright laughter. This was vintage Porter. Cook felt a tinge of sadness creep up on him, and for some reason Bellamy's seamy face came to mind. It must have been like this when he was replaced.

Porter got back to business. His eyes found Kane.

"A couple of you in the spray planes have asked about the fuel load, and whether we have the range for the mission with the payload you're carrying."

Kane nodded agreement and looked over at the other spray pilot.

"You can relax. Since this is a test run on these systems, they're only carrying half the normal payload – we chucked the flush tank, and the other pallet is extra gas. So, you'll make it to Mojave with room to stretch." He paused, looking around the circle again. "Any last questions before we launch?"

* * *

At exactly ten to eight, the radio hashed to life with a "start engines" command from the operations trailer. A ground marshaller in a neon lime-green vest and headset stood in front of the C-130 with a pair of illuminated signaling batons. He pointed one baton at the first engine and began twirling the other baton over his head. With Kane reading from a checklist, Cook flicked the start switch on engine number one, and watched the massive propeller slowly turn clockwise as the turbine blades spooled up with a rapidly ascending whine. When the turbine compression had reached the correct RPM level, he flicked the igniter switch, lighting off the compressed fuel-air mixture in an inferno of combustion. The noise increased, driving the engine up to its full 4,600 shaft horsepower. Cook carefully watched as the temperature gauge rose up into the red zone, then settled back down to green. After the first prop spun up to full velocity, he repeated the process with each of the other three engines.

The marshaller made the 'ground power disconnect' and 'chocks out' signals with his batons, and Kane rotated the yoke and pushed the rudder pedals to check control surface movement, receiving a confirmatory thumbs-up. When all the craft were warmed up and running, the marshaller in front of Strongman One gave the 'start taxi' signal with his batons, and then pointed the direction to proceed.

As the last plane in the flight, Kane waited for the other three C-130s to lumber down the taxiway before receiving his signal and advanced the four power levers forward. As the massive aircraft started to roll, Kane used a small steering wheel to turn the Hercules' nose to follow the rest of the flight. While Cook monitored the engine gauges for any over-temps and ran through the takeoff checklist, Kane kept his right hand firmly fixed to the throttle quadrant.

As the Hercules taxied in the direction of the active runway, Cook took a deep breath. He had no idea where Stokes was located, or if she was even watching. But he had to go through with it, if only to give himself more options down the road. Now or never.

He fumbled at his flight suit's chest pocket and casually dropped his reading glasses.

"Crap." He looked over at Kane. "Dropped my specs. Can I turn the Grimes light on?"

Kane smirked, without looking away from the windscreen. "Already got the shakes? Sure, go ahead, washout."

After Cook toggled the red Grimes night-light, he reached down and fished for his glasses on the deck, bracing his right hand against the side window. He held his first three fingers together with the fourth finger down, then two, giving the code for Palm Springs. A thin sweat broke up on his forehead. He glanced over at Kane, who was completely absorbed with maintaining his spacing on the C-130 preceding them. Cook swept his hand back and forth, knocking his glasses against the console and exclaiming "goddamn it" to sell it a bit. He repeated the finger code for about fifteen seconds to make sure Stokes could see it, then discreetly transformed it into a raised middle finger. Suck on this, Romero.

He'd done his part. If Stokes hadn't seen it – well, that was tough. He straightened up and inhaled deeply to relax his taut abdominal muscles.

Kane flicked the intercom button on his yoke. "Everything OK over there?"

Cook glanced left and pushed his button in reply. "Affirm. Just trying to remember how to make it go up."

Kane telegraphed an expression of mock disgust, then pushed on the pedals to brake their forward movement as the flight stacked up in front of the runway to await clearance. They sat, engines running, while two commercial airliners on approach landed and cleared the active runway. The short wait had created enough space in the approach pattern for the TVA flight to depart in succession.

Spanish-accented English came over the radio.

"InterSur flight, Guadalajara tower – you are cleared for departure, runway two-eight."

Although English was the international language of aviation, and one all pilots and air traffic controllers were required to learn, competency and proficiency were variable. Some calls, usually by Japanese trainee-pilots, never failed to evoke laughter from the regulars. In this case, however, it seemed like Guadalajara ran a pretty tight ship.

The lead C-130 replied.

"Guadalajara, InterSur flight – departing two-eight."

One by one, the C-130s lumbered onto the threshold, braked, ran up the engines to full takeoff power, and lurched down the runway. When it was their turn, Kane slowly advanced their Hercules into position on the active, and firmly mashed the brake pedals to the floorboard. He then advanced the four power levers to the forward limit, Cook supporting his hand from behind. With the engines straining at full power, Kane released the brakes, and with a jerk, the plane rocked forward down the runway, slowly building speed.

The higher the airfield and the hotter the day, the longer the runout would be. Especially with the heavy load they were carrying. Fortunately, the main runway at Guadalajara was over 13,000 feet long, so they had plenty of room to build up to the 'Vr' rotation speed, roughly the velocity at which the lift from the wings exceeds the mass of the aircraft, thus allowing flight. The gross lift-off weight, or GLOW, of the J-model Hercules was over 75 tons, and since they were under that by a good margin, they wouldn't be using all the asphalt available.

At rotation, Kane gently eased back on the yoke, bringing the nose up and letting the plane fly into the air by itself. Once airborne, Cook continued reading items off the checklist as Kane cleaned up the C-130's configuration: gear up with three red lights, flaps to climb, etc. As they rose above the dry scrub field northwest of the airfield, Kane put the aircraft into a shallow bank north, giving them a vector to form up in a long trail with the rest of the flight.

Takeoffs in any aircraft can be a risky business. An engine can suddenly quit, hydraulic pressure can fail, the entire instrument panel can go dark, or a dozen other gut-wrenching mishaps. All necessitating an immediate turn back to the runway you just left for an emergency landing. Cook had previously experienced many of these exciting events and was quite content that none of them had occurred on this departure. Things were looking up.

As Kane piloted the Hercules towards the others, Cook scanned the twilit sky for any traffic, glancing occasionally outside at the terrain below as he did so. The departure path took them just north of the pine-covered cone of the Tequila Volcano, a landmark that never failed to spur wry comments from thirsty southbound pilots.

Cook loved the rugged, almost primeval landscape below. The Sierra Madre Occidental was a high volcanic plateau, cut by river erosion into steep stony barrancas and breathtakingly deep gorges. There were more ancient volcano cones along the route – Ceboruco, Tepetiltic, Sanganguey – all dressed in dark pine and fir, all crumbling with the forces of wind and rain. They were part of the Trans-Mexican belt of volcanoes running west to east across central-southern Mexico, caused by Pacific Ocean tectonic plates diving under North America.

Years earlier, on a U.S. government contract for Transvector, Cook had ferried heavily armed 'agricultural inspection' teams made up of Mexican drug agents and DEA 'advisors' to remote strips in the mountains for marijuana scouting and eradication. While the Mexican peasant growers had despised them for destroying their livelihoods, Cook had had friendly interactions with the indigenous Huichol and Tepecanos. He had sat out hot afternoons near the dirt strips under scraggly pine trees, sharing warm Tecate and hand-rolled cigarettes, struggling to communicate with his rudimentary Spanish, while the Mexican agents had wearily piled and burned every cannabis plant in sight.

Even then, when to Cook the job was just a job, he had found it ironic that the government enforcers were constantly hitting the poor farmers, just trying to make a living growing weed, while further east there were massive plantations of *sinsemilla* growing in plain sight. It was basically a given that the Mexican agents were working for a local cartel, going after low-hanging fruit and eliminating small competitors. He remembered reading later that the entire agency had been disbanded on charges of corruption and drug running.

A loud crackle on the radio disrupted his reverie. Cook glanced away from the darkened sky as he turned down the volume on his headset.

"InterSur Flight, InterSur One, radio check."

This was the prearranged signal to switch to the satellite communications system. While Kane keyed up the VHF aviation radio and answered *en clair* in turn, Cook punched a button on the encrypted satellite radio, and received a squelch chirp in return. From then on, all mission-related information would be unintelligible to any listeners without the transmission code key. The lead C-130 would handle all regular navigation calls to the various air traffic control centers *en route*.

"Strongman flight, this is Boardwalk. Commence radio check."

'Boardwalk' was this mission's name for TVA's control center in the U.S. The operations trailer in Guadalajara was 'Carousel'. The personnel there were already packing up to leave in case of blowback from angry cartel interests.

Transvector's mission code words were always kind of bland these days, Cook mused. It all went back to Churchill during World War II. He never wanted to have to tell a soldier's parents that the combatant had died in 'Operation Bunnyhop' or some other absurdly named venture. Things had been lot looser back in Honduras – contractors got latitude the military could only dream about.

Cook pipped the intercom unit and keyed up. "We ready back there, chief?"

The loadmaster on their plane was a guy he'd never seen before named Hendricks, who, as far as Cook could tell, was competent. A voice came back over the headset.

"The gizmo is five by nine, boss."

Cook decided Hendricks was okay. He gave Kane a thumbs up signal, even though Kane had clearly heard it himself.

The C-130 flight sounded off once again in order, reporting their readiness.

"Strongman flight, approaching cruise altitude. Standby TERMIT system initiation."

Cook looked over at Kane and shrugged. There wasn't much to do for this. The system would engage automatically at a signal over the satellite data link, and after that the crews would be passengers. Cook had brought a couple of magazines in his flight bag to read while the plane flew itself.

When the 22,000 foot altitude Kane had programmed into the regular autopilot was achieved, he eased back the throttles to the mission cruise speed of 150 knots. The sluggish pace, about half of what the Super Hercules would normally cruise at, would allow the ramps to be lowered on the drogue planes, and let the spraying planes catch up to the formation when they finished their work.

Cook scanned the instrument panel again for any warning lights. Altitude good, velocity good, rate-of-climb zero – all green. The TERMIT screen was displaying a moving color map of the terrain below, with four green squares on it representing the flight. Outside it was approaching pitch black, except for the faint reflection on the wings of their aircraft's blinking navigation lights, and those of 'Strongman Three' approximately fifteen hundred yards ahead.

Kane keyed up. "You ready to have some fun?"

Cook smirked. "Let's light this candle already."

"Amen, brother."

Both of them hovered with anticipation, the delay seeming to stretch endlessly.

Thirty seconds later, an electronic chirp emanated from the moving-map screen, and the green squares were filled by four small green triangles. Kane took his left hand off the yoke, and it remained rock solid. Since all the autopilots were linked, the transition was unnoticeable. Kane nodded at Cook, who also removed his hands from the yoke and slouched back in his seat.

The scrambler crackled to life.

"Strongmen One and Three, prepare to stream drogues."

Cook looked ahead through the windscreen at the lights of the Hercules ahead of them. He saw a faint glow up ahead, and although he couldn't make out any detail in the soot-black darkness he knew that the loadmaster and his crewman would be lowering the cargo ramp at the rear of the aircraft. Since pressurization was required for the crew to breath over 12,000 feet of altitude, and it was already negative fifteen degrees Fahrenheit outside, they would be wearing insulated coveralls and oxygen masks. The pilots would also be on oxygen because there wasn't any door between the flight deck and cargo hold. Cook charted their next movements from the briefing. Wearing safety lines so they wouldn't get blown out the back by the turbulent, roaring air, they would attach the winged drogue unit to the looped end of a cable that ran through a sealed aperture in the aft fuselage above the ramp door. They would pay out a few dozen yards of cable, letting the drogue unit drag freely in the dark behind the plane. Then they would reseal the cargo ramp door, restoring pressurization to the cargo area so that they could remove their oxygen masks and breathe freely again.

"Strongmen One and Three, stream drogues."

At this command, the crews would activate the winches, which would pay out approximately thirteen hundred yards of cable. Again, Cook could not see anything, nor did he expect to. But he knew the drogue would be drafting in the night somewhere in the neighborhood of three football fields in front of him.

This was the dangerous part. Although the spacing of the aircraft would be fixed to within a meter by the TERMIT, Cook's still had a numb feeling in his stomach that there was something large hanging just in front of him in the dark. And, if the loop on the cable slipped, or the friction mechanism on the winch somehow failed, it would impact their cockpit glass at about 170 mph. Of course, it would happen so fast he wouldn't even have time to cry out.

There was a pause, then two confirmation calls on the satellite radio.

"Strongmen One and Three, activate drogues."

Cook imagined the buffeting drogue suddenly snapping level and releasing three sub-drogue elements on thin woven-nylon tethers, each a self-stabilizing mini-drogue in its own right. There was another, lengthier, pause, and two more confirmations.

"Ready five second countdown for mission execution."

The voice on the radio sounded primed for action. Cook snugged the straps a bit tighter on his shoulder harness.

"On five, four, three, two, one – mark."

On the command, the autonomous system extinguished all their aircraft's external lights and turned off the location-giving transponder. Simultaneously, the drogue flashed to life in front of him like bolt of lightning. He heard Kane gasp.

"Strongmen Two and Four – good hunting."

On the moving map screen, the display now showed six dots, but the icons representing Strongman Two and Cook's C-130 were now colored red.

Their craft abruptly dove.

Not expecting such an aggressive maneuver, Cook threw his hand out to the window stanchion to avoid falling forward on the control yoke. Kane swore. Cook jerked his head left against the negative gravity that was threatening to launch him up out of his seat, and saw that Kane was holding on as tight as he was.

"Could you have given us a goddamned heads-up?" An irritated voice yelped over the intercom from the back.

Through momentary rising bile, Cook guessed this might have been a little joke on the part of Porter and the boys to keep them on their toes. But there was a practical aspect to it as well. Even though the transponder on their plane had been silenced, a C-130 still had a large radar cross-section that any air traffic control radar could easily see. When the drogues activated, the second and fourth aircraft had to get to a lower altitude quickly in order to avoid being 'painted' by the next radar sweep. Any duplicate images while this was occurring would likely be chalked up to phantom radar 'echoes' at Mazatlan Center, or whoever was looking at them.

Still, it would have been nice to have a warning.

Porter's plan was inspired. The three mini drogues would glide behind and to either side of the main unit about the distance of a Hercules' wingspan, and aft the distance of the plane's tail. Each of the elements contained lights, which mimicked the strobes and colored navigation lights on the wingtips. The main drogue body, which was highly radar-reflective, held an active transponder unit, which would give the air traffic control centers they encountered a bright return signal. From twenty-two thousand feet below, on a moonless night like this one, a ground observer would see something that looked very much like the aircraft that was towing it.

As the lights of the drogue constellation and its tow-plane diminished above them, and their C-130 gradually leveled off, Kane removed his arm from the side window and keyed up the intercom on a yoke that had assumed a life of its own.

"Sorry guys – surprise to us too. Stay strapped in."

Their ride had begun.

* * *

On the roof of the three-story warehouse in the industrial zone southwest of the airport, Stokes carefully packed her camera lens in a foam-lined case, the faint sound of departing turbine engines long erased from the soft and sweaty evening breeze.

It was almost dark, and the surrounding commercial area was quiet with the exception of a few barking dogs. A faint tinkle of *narcocorrido* music could be heard from a truck in the parking lot below. That would be Gustavo, my attentive and friendly security drone, Stokes mused, snickering internally at the thought.

She had looked for various places to stage her camera for a shot at Cook's cockpit window, but there were no easy perches in the immediate vicinity of the airport taxiways that wouldn't attract a lot of unwanted attention. Especially for the long, thermal-imaging telephoto lens she was using. Local law enforcement would have had a few questions to ask if they had seen her photographing aircraft at night.

In the end, she was forced to take direct action. Earlier in the day she had scouted the warehouse and ascertained that there was only one elderly security man on duty. At six o'clock, the older man's predictably younger replacement had arrived for the nightshift. He was sitting in his pickup truck, smoking cigarettes and listening to the radio, when Stokes decided to make her approach.

Gustavo had listened to her story about being a photojournalist doing an undercover article on InterSur Airways with polite interest, nodding when she showed him her camera with the mortar-tube-like super tele-photo lens. He was a good-spirited sort, who smiled a lot and stared openly at her breasts to show her he wasn't gay. Stokes had sensed that he really didn't care if her story was true, but that his job wasn't very interesting, and talking to an attractive female photographer was a pleasant way to pass the time.

His smile had widened broadly when she offered him a hundred US dollars. That was more than he'd make pulling a double shift. He had suggested the roof as a good place from which to get her shots, and he'd be happy to help her up the ladder. And he had, getting a nice view of her jean-clad ass in the bargain.

From her rooftop position, with the camera resting on a façade ledge, Stokes' 800mm telephoto lens with 2x magnification adapter brought her right up to the portside cockpit window of the Super Hercules almost a half a mile away. Normally, in such low-light conditions, she wouldn't have been able to make out much detail. But the crimson glow from the cockpit's Grimes light illuminated Cook's hand from behind. She clearly made out the finger code he held up to the window, as well as the subsequent middle finger he flipped.

She grinned behind her view finder. I get it, jerkoff – more than you could possibly know. Back at you, flyboy.

She broke down the heavy telephoto into its constituent parts, and carefully set them in their individually padded compartments. Stokes took her time. The lens cost about eight thousand dollars, and she didn't want to be the one explaining why it was broken. The SLR camera body went in last.

Shouldering the camera backpack, Stokes walked along the grating over the corrugated roof to the back wall where the ladder was located. She looked down. Gustavo was nowhere in sight. Good a time as any.

She pulled out her phone and dialed a number. When it connected, she said, "Palm Springs," and hung up. Then she started her climb down. She had to get to her ride pronto.

* * *

CHAPTER EIGHT

Nap-of-the-earth flying is something every pilot tries at least once in their flying career, or wants to, because it tests their capacity for risk and requires both nerves and skill. It is also exceptionally dangerous. Experienced pilots, often those who've done it many times before, frequently become complacent, with predictably bad results. Novice pilots – well, sometimes their first experience is their last.

Cook both loved and respected ground-hugging flight. The roller-coaster thrill and the inherent danger were the ultimate adrenaline kick. The military used it for 'terrain masking' – i.e. to evade enemy radar and avoid 'skylining'. But, actually watching yourself do it, at night, in a hands-off situation, was a new encounter.

Even though the TERMIT was considered reliable, and Cook, like most pilots, truly believed that your number was up when it was time, he still found the aircraft's descent into pitch blackness unnerving. And now they were banking slightly, still in a descent. To help quash his anxiety, which by long experience never even made an appearance on his face, he reached up behind his head and unclipped a pair of infrared goggles from the rear cockpit bulkhead. They were standard issue on clandestine TVA flights that might need to go totally blacked out, and because of the company's relationship with the military, these were the new panoramic variety that the military used. They had four tubes instead of the usual two, and doubled the green-tinted, night-vision field of view to about 95 degrees. Though Cook thought they made the wearer look like a creature from the cantina in the first Star Wars movie, he couldn't deny their improved effectiveness. As he wrestled the module's strap to a comfortable position around his forehead, the C-130 made a sudden pitch-up, then another rapid banking descent.

Cook fingered the power toggle, and almost wished he hadn't.

The sensation was like flying low and fast over giant green ocean swells. Except that these waves were made of eroded volcanic rock, didn't move, and any contact with them would be immediately and explosively fatal. The TERMIT was maintaining an even hundred feet of altitude over the tops of peaks and ridges and exploiting the barrancas by dipping down into them. The terrain-following system used phased array radar coupled with GPS input, laser interrogation, and satellite mapping data to make the exercise completely hands-free, which may have been normal for B-1 bomber jocks, but wasn't Cook's preferred mode of travel.

He pivoted the visor up while leaving the strap on his head, and looked over at Kane, who seemed engrossed in a Mexican graphic novel he had picked up somewhere on the street in Guadalajara. In the dim red cockpit glow, Cook could just make out some gratuitously explicit porn. Kane licked his left thumb and turned the page, glancing over as he did so.

"How was it?"

Cook gave a ruefully thin smile. "Weird. Not my kind of thing."

Kane nodded, and pointed at the map display. "Gizmo says we're coming up to a target."

A bright red box had appeared ahead of their flight path on the map. Cook keyed up the intercom.

"Target approaching. What's the payload status?"

"Nominal." The guys in back were always passengers – one trip to them was very much like another.

"Roger. Keep us posted." Cook looked over at Kane. "How much, and what kind?"

Kane pursed his mouth. "Twenty bucks, two-to-one on .50 cal."

"I'll take that action. I'm going with light rifle."

"AK or AR?" Kane was referring to the difference in caliber between Kalashnikov-pattern and U.S. military Armalite-style rifles, like the M-16 or M-4.

"Really? Ok, AK then, and if we get nothing it goes in the pot."

"Deal."

*   *   *

Leaning against a railing of a patio that jutted out over a sharply descending slope of a forested ridge, two sentries talked quietly in the cooling night air, pausing every so often to take drags on cigarettes cached in their palms. They did so not only because their employer, a stickler for security, punished blackout violations quite harshly, but also not to tempt snipers with an easy target. Not that it was likely there were any shooters near the remote ridge top compound this cool summer evening. There was another ring of security personnel further down the mountain from the hacienda, not to mention redundant lines of electronic sensors and infrared cameras.

Both men were locals, reared in the giant *barrios* east of Mazatlan, destined by birth to be part of the vast service underclass that preyed on the fat, pasty *gringos* who frolicked year-round on the sugar-white beaches of the coastal resorts. But these two had escaped, and gotten better jobs than they could have imagined, considering their limited marketable skills, which included torture, serious bodily harm, and murder. They worked for one of the biggest *narco* bosses in the region, and enjoyed fearsome respect, endless pliant women, and the best booze and drugs, when off-duty of course.

Which was not tonight. This night they were part of an eight-man team guarding their boss' hacienda and adjoining ranch land. There were some thin cattle roaming the dry fields, as well as a respectable horse stable, but the real objects of value were the extensive greenhouses near the main barn. These housed the experimental marijuana and opium plants, over which a couple of Colombian botanists labored diligently to enhance their potency and output. Such was the importance of this facility to the boss' operation that it had its own separate four-man security detail around the perimeter.

The older of the two sentries, a thirty-year-old everyone called *Flacco* because of his skinny frame, took a final discreet drag on his unfiltered Camel and ground it out in a small metal mint box that he had repurposed as an ashtray. *El Jefe* himself smoked like a factory, but his bitchy new young wife hated to see cigarette butts littering the ground – she thought it made the place look trashy. Flacco never dared voice his true feelings on this to anyone. He liked his job too much.

The other guard finished his own smoke and faded off toward the other end of the rambling hacienda with a wave. Flacco straightened his shoulders and shifted his slung Kalashnikov into a more comfortable position on his back. The Russian assault rifle was his most prized possession, a visible symbol of his status as a heavy player. Everyone called them *cuerno de chivo*, or 'goat's horn', because of the long, curved thirty round magazine that stuck out of the bottom. It identified him as a bad ass, and he was proud of that, but the *pinche cabron* magazine always dug into his ribcage when he walked post.

* * *

Cook tightened his safety harness again, settled himself more comfortably in his seat, and rocked the night vision goggles back down over his eyes. The moving-map display had shown them situated one valley over from the first target, and he wanted to see firsthand what they were hitting. Kane had also unclipped his eye-set and was adjusting it around his smooth pate.

The C-130 was just bottoming-out from a long descent in a broad, steep-sided barranca. Cook had earlier confirmed the terrain-following system was set on 'soft', which meant the smoothest ride over geographical features. While fighter-bombers and other jets often used the 'hardest' setting possible, they were much better suited to the G-forces generated by the abrupt pitch-ups and dives than this lumbering, prop-driven whale.

The Hercules climbed toward the intervening ridge top, which served to mask the aircraft's noise from the upcoming target. At its current velocity, they'd never know what hit them.

Hell, Cook thought, it was probably deserted anyway. More money for the pot.

* * *

Flacco had just finished walking his quadrant of the big house and was thinking of hitting the cooler in the guardroom for an energy drink. Unlike many of his co-workers, who snorted *chivo* to make it through a night shift, he liked to keep his head straight and took his duties seriously. Though nothing had ever happened in the five years that he'd worked for the boss – the action with the rival gangs usually went down in the Mazatlan cantinas and discos – he was angling for a promotion. After all, turnover in his field could be high, what with all the competition, and the shift chief's position came with its own tricked-out 4x4 pickup truck and a separate *hacienda*.

He decided to postpone the beverage and walked over to the south side of his sector by the pools and *cabanas.* A former security boss, who had recently died in a hail of gunfire at his mistress' love pad in town, had warned him that their enemies looked for patterns when probing for weaknesses in their defensive lines, and that he should avoid habitual movements. Too bad he hadn't followed his own advice, Flacco ruminated. He'd always liked that guy.

The cherry-red glow of a cigarette up ahead told him that someone was both flaunting their blackout protocol and probably reclining on the chaise lounges near the tanning pool. Flacco quickened his step. He was getting ready to deliver a sharp rebuke in the man's direction when heard a low, deep-bass thrumming sound that seemed to be building steadily. Sensing a threat, Flacco unslung his rifle and cradled it in the ready position while he pushed his radio's transmit key with his free hand.

"*Hombres, miren bien. Suena como un avión o un helicóptero.*"

He then raised his Kalashnikov, panning the moonless, ink-black sky, struggling to make out the source of the now louder noise. Around him, he could hear muffled shouts and the clacking sound of rifle bolts being racked, and the heavier thuds of someone charging the dual actions of a pair of Browning M2 heavy machineguns.

* * *

The green-colored ridge loomed massively as the Hercules climbed toward it at what seemed like breathtaking speed. Buildings appeared to jump into existence in front of them: barns, stables, greenhouses. Kane barked "Holy shit!" as dozens of small, white flashes sparkled from amongst the buildings. A light on the panel illuminated, indicating the spray system had activated.

*   *   *

Flacco loosed a long string of bullets randomly across the sky as something huge roared deafeningly overhead. Cries of ¡*fuego*! were interspersed between concussive blasts of the twin Brownings in a sandbagged emplacement on the roof of the *hacienda's* extensive carport. Yellow tongues of .50 caliber tracer licked across the jet-black night. Light spilled out of the house as the boss' personal security detail came piling outside.

It was over as quickly as it had begun. The night went abruptly silent as the shooting stopped, the faint buzz of the plane disappearing off to the north. Crickets, which had gone silent with all the racket, slowly resumed their nighttime calls.

*   *   *

"Jesus!"

Kane snapped his visor up with such force it almost peeled the retention strap off his dark crown, now beaded and shiny with sweat. "You see that shit! Tracer…that was like downtown fucking Kandahar!"

Cook, breathing rapidly, nodded his agreement. "Looks like you scored – I think they threw the whole goddamned hillside at us."

*   *   *

Flacco, fully alert, with his assault rifle still pointed skyward, glanced over at a gaggle of house guards, who had their weapons similarly raised in the now brightly lit compound. One of them met his look and shrugged. Everyone listened intently, trying to ascertain whether more *cagada* was coming down, or that it was over. Faint, rapid radio calls punctuated the tension as units from elsewhere called in to find out what had happened.

A cool, clammy mist slowly descended from the sky, blanketing the entire compound in a thick veil of fog. Flacco heard a sentry on the carport roof cough lightly. What the *mierda* was this? To him, it seemed to be over.

* * *

Kane was still fidgeting two minutes later.

"Maybe it was those greenhouses. You see them?"

Cook hadn't seen Kane so agitated since Honduras. Age, and long-term stress from the job, was clearly taking its toll.

"Yeah, that must've been the target," Cook agreed, trying to calm his partner. "Didn't know they grew poppies in greenhouses, though."

Kane adjusted his seat harness, checked the engine gauges, and minutely tweaked one of the power levers. "Porter sure as hell owes us some beers after that."

Cook was glad his partner seemed to be regaining some composure. He remembered Kane as being a cool head under pressure, especially when getting shot at, and had no desire to see him flip out. Kane could be obsessive and detail-fixated under normal circumstances and flying with an uptight basket case would make for a long trip.

The intercom light illuminated.

"I think we took a couple of taps back here, but everything's still green."

Kane keyed up. "Keep us updated and stayed glued to your seats. There's more where that came from coming up."

"Roger. I'll find some epoxy."

Cook chuckled at the laconic response. Backseaters.

* * *

The next two targets followed the same procedure: dip down, sharp climb and spray. But they were a lot quieter; only a couple muzzle flashes could be seen through the goggles. Cook figured they were actual fields rather than large, fixed grow operations. After the third target had receded, Cook punched up a wider view on the TERMIT. Five more target squares to go. Total flying time to this point had been 1.6 hours, with 5.2 left in the countdown box on the display. Culiacan International's Class B airspace was off to the west, but at the altitudes they were flying at, no controller would come close to catching them on radar.

The fourth target on the readout was in the bottom of a broad valley that ran north-to-south. The C-130 dipped down in the bowl-shaped depression and stayed low, skimming about sixty feet over the tops of scattered farming shacks that appeared in the infrared headset. At that height, Cook mused, they'd probably shake loose a few tin roofs in their wake.

Distant, but rapidly approaching, lights told him this one would be hot. Several of the light clusters were concentrated in one area, a settlement density indicating a major installation. And because they weren't hiding behind any terrain features on their approach, whoever was located there would have a lot more time to hear them coming – bowl-shaped valleys tended to magnify sound. Cook could almost hear the rifle bolts being racked in anticipation.

Kane leaned in a bit.

"Want to bump up the action? A crisp fifty on this one?"

"What stakes?"

"We get painted." Kane pointed at the radar warning detector.

"You think? Done." Cook glanced over, impressed at Kane's regained swagger, but less so by his wager. 'Painted' meant being brushed by ground controlled anti-aircraft radar, which in turn meant a ground-based gun or missile-flavored anti-aircraft battery. Their plane had a radar detector as part of its avionics package, which was straight out of military stocks.

Though Cook had been stunned by the amount of ordnance on their first dust-up, he rated the likelihood of radar here as low. Because of their rural locations, most narcotics grow-sites in the Sierra Madre foothills operated more or less like farms in the open, relying on corruptible local officials for their protection, and obviating the need for air defense. If anything was likely to come from the sky, it was going to be a bent military general or narcotics cop in a helicopter, his hand held out for a generous bribe.

The real danger came from a portable infrared homing surface-to-air missile, or SAM, like the U.S. Stinger, which various cartel groups were rumored to possess. The Hercules came complete with anti-heat-seeking missile flare ejectors and some laser-based sensors and countermeasures that ran automatically in the background, but they were occasionally buggy and, depending on the weather, didn't always work.

The light cluster grew larger.

Idly wondering if he and Kane should petition Porter for a combat bonus due to all the shooting *en route*, Cook almost missed a yellow line that appeared on their moving-map screen to the left, which was steadily merging with their flightpath.

"What do think that is, Ron?"

"Pretty sure that's Strongman Two's flight path. Looks like we're going to run in parallel for this target."

"Must be some mother-huge grow fields then." The maximum spread of aerosolized herbicide from their aircraft was about 300 feet using a low-power vacuum system, plus usually a bit more as it settled to the ground, depending on the wind direction. With two planes in parallel formation, that width would double. It would be the equivalent of spraying something the size of the Los Angeles Coliseum in one pass.

Jesus. They were bringing down some holy wrath on this one.

* * *

In 2003, Cook had flown a series of resupply missions into Anbar province in Iraq, a few weeks after the 3rd Infantry and Marines had taken Baghdad. He had originally been scheduled to be in Colombia, but the company had him filling some holes in their schedule. His de Havilland Caribou was loaded to its full weight capacity with MREs (Meals-Ready-to-Eat) and ammunition, and presented a fat, slow target from the ground, especially when landing. Insurgents trying to slow the U.S. advance had greeted it each evening with a mix of light arms and heavy machinegun fire. Looking like a non-stop stream of Roman Candles in the cloudless nighttime skies, it was as hot as he'd ever seen up until that point.

This was worse.

The heavy bass drone of two C-130s barreling down the stadium-like valley at near-maximum cruise velocity must have sounded like the inside of a sub-woofer playing WWII bomber approach sounds at high volume. Fully alerted by the noise, the ground contingent at the massive compound opened up early, judging that the unseen sky-borne threat was a lot closer than it actually was. Anti-aircraft fire ascended like a glass-beaded curtain strung with Christmas lights.

Only the heavier guns would have the brightly-glowing tracer rounds – anything under .50 caliber would be invisible, unless it was coming from a belt-fed machine gun. Nonetheless, it seemed to Cook that there was plenty to go around. He could even make out some of the smaller rounds whizzing past the cockpit, the heat of their passage visible in infrared.

Gaps appeared as what looked like 20mm tracer waved blindly back and forth amongst lighter ordnance, but with no control over the direction of flight, he and Kane couldn't exploit those opportunities. They were just going to have to hunker down and take it. Cook felt his buttocks tightening involuntarily in anticipation.

Then they were in the middle of it.

A couple of light taps had the sound of a car hood being swiped by a passing hailstorm. In something the size of a C-130, the smaller projectiles did relatively little damage: the fuel tanks in the wings were self-sealing, and the cockpit area had some lightweight armor built into the flight deck. The biggest threat was usually a severed fuel or hydraulic line. But the .50 caliber or 20mm rounds were a different story. Cook had seen holes the size of a golf ball running straight through a pilot's seat and out the roof in a similar aircraft. In that case the entire cockpit was painted wall-to-wall with blood – the impact had been immediate and fatal.

The spray light activated once again.

The TERMIT had programmed an ascent from their earlier low altitude to about 150 feet over the target area, but even so it was likely the aircraft hulls could be seen in the reflection of the compound's illumination. Cook glanced over at Kane, and was shocked to find himself looking at the fuzzy glow of Strongman Two's fuselage. In the dim red light coming off the other plane's instrument panel, he could just make out the contorted grimace on the copilot's goggled face.

The stress made the image hilarious. Cook found himself cackling crazily at the man's expression. Kane's goggled face swung toward him, his mouth agog.

Abruptly, the spray light switched off, the rattling ceased, and they once again plunged into total darkness.

Cook flipped the visor up on his sweat-matted hair and quickly scanned the panel for any warning indicators. There were none. His undershirt was wet under his arms and pasted to his seat in the back, but otherwise he was strangely calm. A glance over a Kane received a steady thumbs-up.

"Looks like we slipped through."

Kane grunted his agreement, jerkily performing his own survey of the cockpit. "Check with the back office."

Cook nodded. "Everything shiny back there?"

"Ruined my nap, but otherwise solid," came the unruffled reply.

Cook stifled a snort.

"Roger."

The pitch of the engines had increased as the C-130 began climbing again. Cook's abdomen felt strangely tight. He looked down to see if there was any blood. He'd known a couple pilots who had taken a round while flying and not noticed due to shock, but the legs and torso of his flight suit were clean, if a little damp. Then he realized he'd been holding his gut in since the beginning of their approach. Cook took a couple of deep breaths to relieve his tension, hoping Kane wouldn't notice.

The satellite radio chirped a squelch tone, providing a convenient distraction.

"Strongman flight, this is Boardwalk. Be advised of a mission change. Strongman Two is not responding to radio calls, and onboard telemetry is reporting a MASS system malfunction, but no mechanical damage. We are declaring a mission abort. Standby for nav-system update."

Cook's eye went to the moving-map screen. Strongman Two's red display pip was tracking away from them, presumably toward their next target, but otherwise acting normally. "You think they took one in the satcom system?"

"Probably. Beats the hell out of me." Kane had his visor back down and was scanning outside. "What's the display doing?"

"Nothing yet."

The map display went black. "Hold on – it just went dark."

Kane snapped up his visor and joined Cook in staring intensely at the screen. The readout flickered, and the words 'Update in Progress' started blinking. A hollow loading bar appeared beneath the script, slowly filling up from the left.

"Jesus. I hope that thing's not using Windows."

"Amen to that."

Cook shared his concern. New technology on aircraft always had bugs, and they were barreling along at high velocity and low altitude in pitch black conditions. He hoped the programmers were smart enough to have the system retain the old course until the update had fully downloaded. It wasn't like they were sitting still on the tarmac under optimal conditions.

Both men watched intently as the loading bar continued its leisurely plod across the display, willing it to hurry up and finish. When it finally reached its terminus, the screen went dark again. To Cook, this was a serious user-interface failure. Pilots really like to know what's going on with their aircraft, and screens going black didn't help.

The display flickered again, and the map snapped back. New yellow lines now had them vectored to rejoin the drogue aircraft who were plodding along at the reduced cruise speed overhead. Simultaneously, the engine tempo rose again, and the nose pitched up into a steeper climb.

"OK, that was fun." Kane's expression mirrored Cook's sense of relief.

"Definitely exciting." Cook loosened his shoulder harness, and stretched his arms over his head, twisting his torso from one side to the other. His spine cracked audibly, and he felt a deep sense of relaxation course through his frame. The mission was over – nobody would be shooting at them for the rest of the trip. All that was left was a long, hands-off ride back to Mojave, with a brief approach sequence at the end.

Kane cracked open a Coke he had stowed next to his armrest. "I'll let the guys in back know they can shut down the gizmo and break out the sports pages."

Cook nodded, and gazed wearily around the cockpit, idly wondering where they'd get breakfast in Mojave when they got in. Recalling Porter's crack about Denny's for breakfast, Cook began to salivate. He was already getting hungry, and the thought of some chicken-fried steak with a crispy side of hash browns was making him a bit light-headed. His eye caught the map display – 3.8 hours to go. Nearby on the panel rested the radar detector, an occasional light flicker reflecting extremely distant radar interrogation signals. It had remained quiet the entire flight.

Cook snapped his fingers at Kane, and pointed at the instrument.

"Guess who's buying breakfast."

* * *

The remainder of the mission over Mexico was uneventful, if not interesting to watch as a passive viewer. During the rendezvous with Strongmen One and Three, they reversed the procedure they had performed earlier in the flight. The TERMIT was almost uncanny in its precision as they slid up to a cruise profile directly behind the brightly lit drogues trailing from their tow aircraft. Cook watched Strongman Two's symbol rejoin with them and concluded their damage must be minor.

Boardwalk gave another countdown, and on the 'mark' command, the system reactivated the navigation lights and aircraft transponder. The drone in front of them simultaneously went dark. Strongman Four's square icon on the map display changed from red back to green, and they were all once again in trail formation as the drogues were reeled in.

Now all they had to do was count down the time.

Cook was happy for the lull in activity, as it gave him time to think about his next moves. Romero, and presumably Stokes, would be waiting for him at Palm Springs as he cruised overhead, and they could already have someone waiting at Mojave as well. He would have to act quickly upon landing, executing a seamless disappearing act. A ground-based solution was out of the question – it would have to be by air.

The Transvector hangars in Mojave had small corporate jets and other transport available on standby for rapid deployment, in case the company needed to send repair teams to fix one of their cargo craft. Porter could get one of those spooled up and waiting on the tarmac for their arrival, and later manufacture some sort of mission for the accountants.

As he absentmindedly paged through the latest Sports Illustrated Swimsuit Edition, Cook ran through the likeliest scenarios. Mojave was about two and a half hours by car from Palm Springs, so Cook would have a two-hour head start. Even if Romero had a helicopter, and took off immediately after the TVA planes passed overhead, he would still be about seventy knots slower than the C-130s, and therefore would arrive at least twenty minutes later. Tight, but doable, if all the preparations were in place.

If there were feds waiting for him at Mojave, a contingency Romero had surely put into place, it was probable that they would wait until the aircraft had landed before making their presence known; otherwise, TVA could simply divert the flight to an alternate airport, claiming some sort of exigent necessity in order to stall any investigation long enough to get their legal team in action. So, it would most likely be a DEA ambush. They would be delayed by TVA gate security for at least ten minutes while any warrants got sorted out, giving Cook a small window. But long enough for Porter to get him on another aircraft if it was fueled and ready to depart.

But would he do it? Cook hadn't managed to tell his boss about the DEA agents before they left, and

Porter might think he had been holding back. Cook needed to get in front of that issue. He had to talk to Porter.

And there was also his file to consider. If Romero broadcast it, as promised in the event of non-cooperation, Cook would be instantly toxic, dumped by TVA like a batch of bad jet fuel. But the contents of his file would take some time to disseminate, possibly more than twenty-four hours. And by that point, he'd already be in the wind.

Cook stared blankly at a perfectly tanned seventeen-year-old body wearing a wispy bikini on a sugar-white sand beach, he realized that all the planning in the world wasn't going to be of any use. He'd have to improvise quickly depending on how things fell. He tossed the magazine in his flight bag and grabbed his Coke from the armrest. Too many unknowns, too many options. He was barreling along toward his fate, one nautical mile at a time.

He looked over at Kane, who had put his head back and closed his eyes. Screw all of them. He would stick with his own.

* * *

Borders can be dangerous places.

Outside of Europe and a few other places where sovereign nations have shared customs agreements, most countries carefully monitor their frontiers for groups attempting to enter without permission. And not only do they generally have corps of military or paramilitary sentinels stacked on either side, but also layered defenses in depth, including walls, fences, electronic sensors, and cameras. They are usually intentionally difficult to traverse, often following rivers or mountain ranges that aren't easy to cross.

The obstacles notwithstanding, myriads still try.

The advantages in circumventing frontiers can be enormous. Governments hungrily tax imports, so their evasion can add percentage multiples to an importer's bottom line. Alcohol, tobacco, and luxury goods are particularly popular.

But the imports you can't get legally at any price, on either side, really drive the traffic. Evaders spend millions, while countervailing efforts by governmental authorities tally in the billions. The result of these opposing forces can be measured in the body counts that litter either side.

The U.S.-Mexico border illustrates this concept perfectly.

Over nineteen thousand U.S. Border Patrol agents guard a nearly two-thousand-mile-long line stretching from Brownsville, Texas in the east to Imperial Beach, California in the west. While over 350 million people cross it each year at one of 46 legal border-crossing checkpoints, in 2019 around a million illegals tried their luck either by swimming across the Rio Grande or trudging overland through the pitiless Sonora and Chihuahua deserts. Often these hopefuls are forced by their 'coyote' guides to carry drugs as part of the price of admission.

The river is easier, both for the immigrant and the border authorities. The constant pressure of would-be crossers meeting an undermanned human wall of olive-green uniforms, horses, helicopters, and patrol boats virtually guarantees hordes slipping through. The deserts are deadly year-round. Clothed skeletons, still strapped into homemade marijuana-bale backpacks, offer mute testimony to the hazards of the route.

The lucky who survive the scorching wastes sometimes make it. The rest are picked up either at the border, or at one of the numerous interior checkpoints scattered about seventy miles inside the US line. If they don't request political asylum, which their apologists instruct them to do, then they are sent back, usually only to try again as soon as they can raise the cash.

Official interest in US-bound aircraft theoretically begins even before the engines are spun up. The Transportation Security Administration, and other parts of the US Department of Homeland Security, want to know who and what is coming into the country well before it arrives. Prior to entering US airspace, inbound traffic encounters the Air Defense Identification Zone, or ADIZ, where they have to announce their impending arrival to whatever air traffic control center handles that region. Failure to do so captures official interest, usually in the form of a fighter jet intercept. U.S. Air Force F-15 Eagles and F-16 Falcons, and even some of the newer F-22 Raptors, are deployed on a five-minute alert status just for that purpose.

For the flights that don't care to broadcast their presence, the U.S. Department of Defense (DoD) has tethered several blimps in vulnerable areas at fifteen thousand feet with look-down radar capability. Anything generating a large enough blip on a military radar scope is checked against civilian control center listings. If they don't have it, uniformed personnel start to pay a lot more attention.

* * *

On the moving-map display, the Arizona border approached at a relatively gradual pace, so much so that Cook only glanced away from his National Geographic article every few minutes to confirm their position. Kane was snoring quietly in his marginally reclined seat, having drifted off almost immediately following the resumption of formation flight. TVA flight protocols had two pilots awake for the entire time a C-130 was in the air, especially when they weren't flying with a relief crew. But as with most commercial aircraft on autopilot, there just wasn't that much to do, and after all the fireworks down south, the two of them had decided to spell each other at the yoke. And with the advanced systems these planes were running, Cook knew that both pilots could have slept throughout the entire mission, with the approach alarms waking them for landing. He was pretty sure the techs in back were sacked out as well.

A slight change in engine pitch told Cook that they were beginning their descent toward the ADIZ.

In addition to the aerial drug spraying, one of the secondary goals of the Sideshow mission was to minimize, or entirely avoid, detection by US military radar. Blair had suggested as much when he profiled the flight's entry into US airspace. It sounded like they'd be skimming scrub brush when they crossed the line.

As the rugged spine of the Sierra Madre Occidental moves north, it loses both altitude and coherence, as if the effort to reach America exhausted its ability to maintain its majestic stature. With Arizona creeping closer, the TERMIT increased the rate of descent, the engines cutting back further to bring them closer to the dwindling northwestern foothills. Kane's snoring paused briefly, then resumed without him waking. Cook stowed his magazine and punched the zoom button on the map display.

Most drug flights came in low and fast, to get as far inside the border as possible before air-dropping their loads to transport crews on the ground. The pilots would then kick the plane into a steep one-eighty and beat a hasty retreat to the safety of Mexican airspace without getting shot down. It was a simple and effective technique, if not pricey in the occasional lost airframe or pilot.

Strongman flight's entry into the U.S. was designed to test the DoD's border detection capabilities and verify that military controllers were awake in their seats. While the blimp radars scored an impressive hit rate, there were gaps in the coverage, usually near civilian point-of-entry airfields such as El Paso and Nogales. The C-130 formation's route was vectored through one of those holes to see if they could slip by unnoticed. Needless to say, getting caught was going to be considered a failure for that part of the mission.

Cook watched as the altimeter steadily declined and lightly punched Kane's shoulder.

"Ronnie...wakey, wakey time."

Kane stirred without opening his eyes. "Blow me, Cook. I was just dreaming about your future ex-wife."

Cook smiled. "Were you in divorce court watching her get half my stuff? That's my favorite."

"Half of nothing? Sounds like a pretty shitty deal for her." Kane blinked. "Where are we?"

"Coming up on the line."

"'Bout time." Kane readjusted his seat to its upright and forward position, and rapidly scanned the panel. Pilots wake up faster than most, especially to the sound of voices. You only had to hear one repeated call from a major ATC center to know that someone had gotten a little comfortable on autopilot and had dozed off. Professionally embarrassing, but pretty much everyone had experienced it at least once. "Fresh Meat tell us how low we'd be?"

Cook shook his head. "Nope. Probably didn't want to scare us off."

"Right." Kane reached down to the map display and widened the view. The altitude indicator continued its steady drop in the corner. Watching Kane, Cook noted that the newer multifunction glass instruments – newer to him, anyway – had replaced the need to scan the entire instrument panel, a standard pilot task that kept one situationally aware. Basically, it was a video game – you could fly the entire plane off its two glass screens, or even a headset. Like a lot of things Cook had encountered since his return, he wasn't sure how he felt about that.

Cook gazed out into the inky darkness as the altimeter ticked off their descent, reflecting that even though he couldn't see anything, and wasn't actually piloting the aircraft, this might be the most dangerous part of the whole mission. The deck here was somewhere in the

4,000-foot range, and notwithstanding the less densely clustered nature of the Sierras at this stage, there were still jutting peaks here and there that could terminally ruin your day. He was used to flying in zero-visibility conditions, even on autopilot, but never so low and fast. It reminded Cook of pylon racing up at Reno, fifty feet off the scrub, except doing it on a moonless night at max velocity wearing a blindfold.

Their route on the map showed a fast-approaching defile, a low spot between ridges in an otherwise continuous furrowed wall.

Kane broke into Cook's tension.

"Twenty says they tag us."

"Don't you get tired of losing? No bet."

Cook actually thought the odds of them popping up on a military scope somewhere were pretty low, but he was starting to feel the encroaching frontier as a palpable thing, a curtain of decision that, once crossed, wouldn't permit backpedaling or second-guessing. Cortes burning his ships on the beach, or Caesar crossing the Rubicon. He would have to run, and keep running to stay ahead of his file jacket. No stateside work until everything had run its course. Thailand, Philippines maybe – assuming Porter and Transvector backed him this time.

Really, they'd have to. The revelations in his leaked file guaranteed years of Congressional investigations, special prosecutors, the works. The firm would be gaffed, strung up and gutted like a billfish on a Loreto dockside. No company, no matter how well connected, could survive that kind of onslaught. Hallet's close buddies in intelligence and elsewhere would fade into their paneled woodwork, never to be seen again. With those prospects, Cook's inaccessibility would be highly sought after. No witness, no testimony.

If Kane had noticed Cook's introspective odyssey, he chose not to comment on it.

"What's it look like groundside?"

Cook found himself strangely irritated that Kane was obviously preoccupied with the mundane things that could kill them, such as their altitude. The TERMIT had turned off the ground-proximity radar – it would have blossomed on the blimps detection systems like a line of fireworks cutting across the landscape. And the altimeter readout in the corner was flashing a bright red terrain warning with no numerical figures.

"Why don't you take a look yourself?"

"'Cause I'm left seat, and you're the hired help."

"Yeah, that's some tough flying you're doing." Cook yanked the goggle headset off its cradle and re-snugged the band to his brow. When it fired up, he realized he'd left the magnification cranked up from earlier. He felt for the dial near his temple, then started. It was set to the neutral detent. Everything looked large because it was close…really close. They were skimming low ridgelines about thirty feet below the fuselage. Peering aft, Cook could see the occasional puffs of a dust trail billowing in their wake. Only the utter lack of moonlight, the absence of any kind of habitation, and the dim glare of the panel kept Kane from seeing the terrain clearly in ground reflection from the bright haze of the Milky Way. Cook considered him lucky.

"We're close."

"Do I even want to know?"

Cook grinned under his headset. "Nope."

* * *

Romero sat quietly in his apartment, the lights off, a faint glow from street lampposts outside peeking through a slit in the beige curtains. He looked at the luminous dial of his watch again. 12:15 am. Cook and the C-130 should be in Palm Springs in the next couple of hours.

Of course, it had been Palm Springs. It was the only logical approach from the south. The Tijuana-San Diego corridor was just too noticeable, too upfront for Transvector. And with their operations hub in Mojave, it made no sense navigationally. So, Palm Springs. Romero had been so sure about it, he'd already booked the motel rooms.

He always had two rooms. A private one in which to think, plan, and rest; and another for dealing with the outside world, including setting up stings on suspected narco-traffickers and paying off informants. It was a compartmentalization he needed in order to function. Romero had thrived on counternarcotic work in the Los Angeles division. He was easily able to mingle in a crowd, chat comfortably with suspects, and improvise flexibly according to changing circumstances. But he was also a planner, a strategic, methodical thinker who patiently gathered information and recorded details for the big busts. And that required quiet solitude, a safe space.

Prior to his transfer to the DEA's LA division, Romero had been in Denver, where he had run down heroin distribution networks run out of Juarez. Before that, he had operated in Miami as part of an organized crime drug task force intercepting shipments from South America. A posting in Panama during Operation Crankbait and stint in Chang Mai, Thailand rounded out the international experience on his resume.

But he found work in the US most rewarding. International investigations were filled with bureaucratic diplomacy and endless paperwork, in addition to the necessity of interfacing with foreign law enforcement. Corruption and leaks were rampant. More than once he had led raid forces into warehouse complexes that had been stripped to the walls days beforehand. Stateside investigations were more predictable, less chancy. When you made your move, you usually got the goods.

Not so with Transvector. Romero had been stalking the company for years, biding his time for the inevitable slipup that would provide the opening wedge. It had never happened. Their government protection was just too strong; magic curtains of influence screening off the unwashed. Close ties with the intelligence community hedged them with cast-iron immunity and forestalled any DEA incursions. By the time he could obtain permission to enter the secure airport cargo areas, the flights had always moved on.

In past undercover operations, he'd had guns pointed at his head, and had calmly talked his would-be assassins down. He'd had knives held to his throat and been shot at multiple times, and still succeeded in maintaining his composure. But Transvector was a faceless enemy, one which threatened him not with bullets and blades but with stalled promotions and career-ending sanctions. He could deal with scumbags and sleazy traffickers, but the quiet lawyers and gimlet-eyed departmental bureaucrats were worse by far. They had made the company untouchable.

Until now. He'd managed to bust Massey, who, in his desperation to avoid jail time, had given up a confidential informant in the TVA hierarchy. The snitch was a mid-level manager in the covert operations wing with some drug issues that would've gotten him fired had they come to light. Massey had some leverage on him, having sold him some product from time to time, and offered to act as the go-between. But Romero hadn't bitten, insisting on speaking to the informant directly. A series of discreet and hard-to-hear conversations conducted from truck stop phone booths near Mojave had given Romero information about the Guadalajara mission. Ratcheting the pressure up a bit had gotten him the company file on Cook. By some stupendous stroke of corporate carelessness, the photo of the unidentified napalmed village had been tossed in the back of the file.

Romero had never been able to find out what the photo actually signified, but its implication was clear: a jungle village had been scorched, and a lot of people had died. Somebody had screwed up, and someone else had made sure they kept a photograph as proof. The guilty nature of the image was unmistakable. And Cook's reaction back at the Grand Metropolitan had given him all the leverage he needed.

Now, all the pieces were in place, except for Stokes. Romero had scraped the barrel on his contingency funds to get her out of Mexico on a jet charter flight into Riverside, where he would pick her up. Her call, and the emailed photos from Guadalajara, were confirmation that all the groundwork had paid off. He was going to nail Transvector's hide to his wall, and damn the consequences.

An alarm quietly rang on his phone. 1 am. Time to go.

*   *   *

CHAPTER NINE

The first *en clair* radio call since Guadalajara came as they intersected a visual-flight-rules, or VFR, airway about forty miles east of El Centro, California. It was Porter's voice on the call, activating a preexisting VFR flight plan with a local flight service station. Cook was reassured to hear that years of flying a desk hadn't dulled Porter's command of the aviator cant.

"Prescott radio, Transvex 65, with you at 10,500, flight of four C-130s mile-in-trail, 55 nautical on 247 radial from Gila Bend, *en route* Mojave, activate VFR flight plan with Whiskey."

'Transvex' was the company's callsign when conducting civilian operations worldwide, because anything with 'vector' in it was confusing to controllers. Porter's call told the civilian FAA specialist who and where they were, and their destination. 'Whiskey' tagged on to the end meant they had the current weather forecast for the area.

"Transvex Six Five, squawk 2455, reduce speed to 220 knots, maintain spacing at 10,500, contact San Diego Center 124.35, good day."

After the radio call was acknowledged, the satellite radio chirped with Porter giving them the real skinny. "OK guys, we're on positive control up to Mojave approach, ETA seventy-five minutes. Strongman One makes all civilian traffic calls unless it's an emergency. Otherwise, use the sat link. Out."

Kane stretched upward and yawned. "Where do you want to get breakfast? Denny's, or Tomasino's?"

Cook bunted. "Not sure what I'm hungry for yet. Too early."

"Lose the yoga-chick pose, Angel Cake. You eat when Papa Ron tells you to eat."

Actually, Cook was too preoccupied to even think about eating. He'd been tossing over what to grab from his apartment, or even if he had time, ever since they crossed the border. There really wasn't much, but what he had, he liked. Some cool flight gizmos, a few favorite t-shirts and ballcaps, the Oakley shades he traded off with his Ray-Ban aviators, depending on the job and his mood.

Their on-the-down-low entry across the border had put them in the Fuzzy Military Operating Area (MOA), a deserted section of Arizona airspace restricted to military training flights. The closest habitation was a defunct mining hamlet called Ruby, five miles to the east. The US military had been informed of their activity, and once they got over the fact that the Transvector flight had skunked them at the border, they grudgingly provided assistance. That had been followed by a discreet series of doglegs along low-level military training routes through the border region, until they turned on their navigation lights, intercepted a civilian airway, and climbed to a normal altitude as if they were any other commercial aviation traffic.

Porter had said it was about an hour and fifteen from their location to Mojave at the current rate of travel. If Romero and his crew were driving, Cook would have plenty room to maneuver. But if the DEA agents got into the air as soon as Cook sailed overhead, they would be running only twenty to forty minutes behind. Not enough time, and he couldn't take the risk. Cook ruefully accepted the worst-case scenario – he'd be buying new stuff on the road.

His phone.

He had left his phone in Guadalajara during the gear and uniform swap, and presumably it was on its way up to Mojave on a TVA King Air carrying the support crew. It was turned off, but the battery and SIM card were still in it, and he didn't know if someone with the right equipment might still be able to track it.

It was possible the phone would make it back to Mojave before he did. But then again, he had told Stokes that he would have to turn in his mobile. Romero wouldn't be following that lead, not yet anyway.

He paused his reverie to find Kane staring at him.

"Guy, nothing personal, but what the hell is eating you?"

Cook glanced down at the map. Thirty-five minutes to Palm Springs. He looked back at his friend, and saw the worry written across his forehead, the real uneasiness it was causing. It felt like a kick in the midriff.

"You don't want to know, Ron – I mean, you really don't. It's something I've got to hash out with Porter."

He closed his eyes and exhaled. "Can you give me a couple minutes on the radio?"

Kane's face registered the hurt expression of a concerned friend who's been told his help wasn't wanted. "Yeah, I'll be in the head, then check on the guys in back." He unbuckled and started to push himself up when he paused.

"Nothing to do with me, right? We're good?"

"We're solid. Always have been, by the way." Cook tilted his head slightly. "Sorry if I made it seem otherwise. Just may have to take a rain check on that breakfast."

Kane nodded gravely, apparently satisfied, and slipped out of the cockpit. Cook adjusted his headset's boom mike and pondered how to convey his message. Avoiding specifics was going to be crucial. He chirped the satellite link.

Strongman One, Strongman Four for the top kick. He available?"

"Standby."

Thirty seconds passed. Porter came on.

"What can I do you for, Four?"

"Can we go to a side channel?"

"Copy. Go to Orange." Cook knew from the briefing that 'Orange' meant an alternate, inter-aircraft channel. While anyone on the mission could theoretically listen in, professional courtesy dictated that the other pilots would give them privacy.

"One for Four on Orange, go."

"I'm going to need to bolter on arrival – that appointment I tried to tell you about earlier. I can't wait for the crew van to take me back to L.A."

There was a pause. Cook knew Porter was sharp enough to appreciate both the extraordinary nature of the call and the unspoken nuances. Still, he was suffused with uncertainty as he awaited a response.

"You need a lift somewhere?"

Cook pushed out a held breath.

"That'd be great. You got something available?"

"Roger that. We'll get you set up. Anything else?"

"It's got to be a fast turnaround."

"Understood. That it?"

"Buy a round for me at breakfast."

"Copy. We'll sort out what you owe me later. One out."

It went better than Cook expected. Relieved, he discovered he had been sitting erectly on his seat cushion, as if he just concluded an interview. He sprawled against his seatback as the tension dissipated. Porter was keeping the faith. Cook wished he had been able to tell him earlier.

There was a light knock on the cockpit hatch. Kane poked his head in. "Everything simpatico?"

"Yeah, thanks." Cook waited until Kane had worked his way back into the left seat. "And thanks for the space. I'll fill you in on the whole thing after."

Kane's dark features still bore concern, but his look was less hurt than earlier.

"Sounds riveting. Can't wait." His voice barely betrayed any irony.

* * *

Yuma to El Centro, then northwest. San Diego was following them on radar and gave frequent heading changes as the flight worked its way through the congested border airspace of southeastern California. It helped that most of the airspace in the area was considered military or restricted, and that TVA planes were often tagged by the FAA as a special government cargo flight. The early hour didn't hurt either – their vector changes came like clockwork.

Night navigation is far easier in populated areas than it is during the day. In daylight, haze and glare conspire to make ground features blur together, and locating airport beacons could be a bitch. But at night, streetlamps and road lighting make populated areas stand out just like their shapes on the map. Cook could recognize a half dozen cities from a nighttime sky by their illuminated outline alone.

Night flying had also always given him a feeling of being above it all, the world's problems passing dreamily below. Like coasting smoothly over a glowing carpet of habitation, embroidered with bright red-and-white freeway arteries. It was almost two in the morning.

Kane South, Kane East MOAs. They caught a VORTAC radial out of Thermal which would lead them past Bermuda Dunes up to Palm Springs.

Cook tried to imagine what Romero and Stokes and the nameless minions were doing right then, where they were waiting. And, most importantly, how they would react when they would realize that no one was landing. He shifted in his seat. He'd know soon enough. They were now only about ten minutes out of the Palm Springs airspace.

The dark tranquility of the skies above the Salton Sea up ahead provided a respite from the tangled light tapestry below. The other aircraft of Strongman flight were strung out like brightly glowing gems on an invisible chain, winking intermittently against a black sky.

Entranced by the view, Cook pondered how he would have forced a landing in the first place, had he decided to go through with Romero's plan. There were too many crewmembers present to get away with anything subtle, so it would have had to have been a blunt-force event, with explanations given after the fact: a screwdriver lobotomy on the TERMIT, shorting the electrical, starting a fire in the lavatory. He hadn't really thought it out that much, and was grateful that it wasn't going to be necessary.

Forty minutes to go. Kane rustled in his seat, adjusted his harness, and resettled his radio headset. He then sifted through his approach plates, found Mojave, and clipped it to his kneeboard. Finally, he took a stick of gum from his shirt's left breast pocket, peeled the metallic wrapper, and popped it in his mouth.

It was a ritual Cook had witnessed as long as he'd flown with Kane, and it made him a good partner to fly with. Some pilots waited until the last ten minutes of a flight to scramble to get their gear wired tight, but Kane was a conscientious, detail-obsessed aviator, a creature of habit who followed the same procedures with Swiss-timepiece regularity, every time. And it was always Wrigley's – never anything decent – and always the old Doublemint sticks. God only knew how Kane was going to fly if the Mars company ever discontinued that product.

Kane glanced over, aware he was being observed, and offered Cook the mint-green packet. "Want one for the road?"

Cook's refusal was ritual as well. "Can't stand that grey crud – tastes like mint-flavored cardboard. Why don't you ever buy the good stuff?"

His standard rebuke delivered, which always seemed to elicit a quiet grin from the other man, Cook gazed back out the windscreen towards the lights of the Coachella Valley, at the black emptiness of the Salton Sea, slowly receding off to the right.

To the right.

Cook felt his gut tighten and his skin go cool, goosebumps breaking out on his arms. He pointed at the urban cluster ahead. "Those lights should be dead center."

Kane's voice was tense. "Yep. You want to call that in?"

The satellite radio chirped. It was Porter. Being the lead plane, he'd obviously beat them to it.

"We're...uh...having some problems with the TERMIT...it seems, uh...standby...."

Cook's tension increased. When Porter dropped comms procedure, things were bad indeed. Then another chirp.

"Strongman flight, Strongman One...," there were unintelligible voices raised in the background, their pitch suggesting something approaching panic. "Uh, at this point we're going to recommend...."

The satellite radio went dead. Not just the audio, Cook noted with alarm, but the entire radio module – it wasn't getting any power. Cook punched the satcom's power button, then all the others, in an attempt to get it running, when Kane suddenly erupted, pointing at the map screen.

"What the hell!" The display had gone dark and was updating. Cook went cold. "Kill the autopilot."

Kane fingered the micro-switch toggle on the yoke a few times, then quickly reached over to the main console for the primary switch. "Negative response. Pull the Termite."

Cook mashed his index finger on the TERMIT power stud, then a few more times. "Nothing. Still updating."

"Yank the fuse."

Cook ran his hand on the ceiling mounted breakers. "Looking for it."

They were both working with choreographed, mechanical efficiency to isolate and resolve the problem. With their combined experience, checklists were largely unnecessary. Regardless of the aircraft type, most of the systems were fundamentally the same.

Cook ran his finger over, across and down the myriad numbered fuse caps until he found the one for the TERMIT and popped it out. The update on the map screen was unaffected. Cook grimaced. "Negative. What next?"

Kane activated the intercom. "Chief, get in here ASAP."

Since TVA cargo aircraft usually ran minimum spec crews, the loadmaster was cross-trained as a flight systems engineer. In most circumstances, this aspect of his knowledge was rarely needed. Not this morning. They heard him barrel up the ladder.

"What's up, Boss?"

Kane's voice was taut as he strained against the control column. "I'll stay on the yoke. Guy, you and Hendricks get this goddamned thing unlocked."

Cook looked at the chief and pointed at the TERMIT. "We're off course, this piece of shit is frozen, and we can't shut it down. Main and essential buses?"

Hendricks shook his head. "It'll still have power. Battery disconnects and generators should work – power down and reset?"

"Yeah, both."

Kane cut in. "We'll lose comms. Call it in before we go dark."

Cook reached for the hand mike, but was beaten to it by a crash of static on the VHF radio and Porter's panicked shout.

"Mayday, mayday! Strongman – abort, abort, abort!"

* * *

Romero blew into his cupped hands, in an effort to ward away the dry desert chill. The cold air was spiced with the sweet tang of sage and yucca absorbing night dew on their leaves. A light breeze occasionally buffeted the collar of his tightly-buttoned raid jacket, emblazoned with 'DEA' on the front and back in gold block letters.

Next to him, a similarly attired Stokes stood impassively, her dark hair pulled tightly into a ponytail under a navy ballcap and her distant expression inviting no conversation. A few paces behind, Romero's two helpers wore tactical DEA vests and lounged against the quarter panel of a plain-black SUV, conversing in low murmurs.

Twenty feet away, as if observing a separation more visceral than jurisdictional, was another cluster consisting of a lieutenant and two deputies from the Riverside County Sheriff's Department. The lieutenant was leaning against his department-issued Dodge Charger, chatting with his shift sergeant, while a third deputy napped in another marked cruiser.

A faint drone resolved itself to the south, bouncing off the granite mountainsides on either side of the valley. The lieutenant turned from his conversation. "That your package?"

Romero checked his watch, and looked over at Stokes, who gave a curt nod. "A bit early, but should be."

The lieutenant walked over to the second department vehicle and lightly kicked the door. "Showtime, Rodriguez."

Romero turned to Stokes.

"You know what to do." It wasn't a question.

Stokes didn't respond for a moment, her face tilted up to the still dark sky. "Why aren't they overhead?"

Romero followed her gaze up to the west, his eyes narrowing, searching for whatever was making her uneasy. The San Jacinto Mountains were a curtain of jagged blackness against the stars on the moonless morning, revealing nothing. The drone of multiple aircraft was growing louder, but still more distant than they should be.

The flash, though small as seen from the airport, must have been huge to appear at that distance at all. It was followed a few seconds later by a rolling boom that all of them could feel.

* * *

"Strongman One just went in!"

Cooked jerked his head up from the panel. The fireball three miles directly ahead of them was bright orange, internally illuminating a growing mantle of thick black smoke. The extra fuel, Cook thought dully. Porter had told them about it after the brief. It would have made the impact explosion that much greater. Porter.

The VHF radio erupted with the loud, dissonant screech of multiple, simultaneous stepped-on transmissions.

"Eeeee....screeeee...we can't...eeeee...frozen!"

Kane's wide-eyed face turned on Cook, who along with the chief, was still staring forward.

"Get this fucking thing unstuck!"

*   *   *

Stokes swore inaudibly.

Romero stared openmouthed at the fire, which had diminished greatly since the initial impact, but was slowly starting to increase in size. He looked wildly at Stokes, who was staring back at him intensely.

"What the hell just happened, Vic?"

Behind them, the lieutenant was barking into his handheld radio while gesticulating wildly at his deputies. "Copy! Looks like just south of the tram station...we're going to need wildland crews and CDF bombers...yeah, helos too...this thing's going to go big time...right, standing by!"

He let the radio drop to his side, still chiming fire call-out tones and crew assignments, while his deputies busied themselves hauling kit bags out of the Riverside cruiser's trunk. "Was that your guy, Romero? Just what the hell is going on here?"

Romero jerked around. "Not part of the plan! I have no idea what that is."

"I do. It's the start of a motherfuckin' massive wildfire."

* * *

"Yoke is still locked! Bus shutoff has no effect! We're going to…." Strongman Two's transmission cut off as another fireball blossomed somewhat closer in the windscreen. Cook stared dumbly at the windscreen and calculated feverishly.

Two miles. Just over thirty seconds at this velocity.

Kane slapped Cook's arm. "Wake up! Generators and batteries now!"

Cook violently twisted the generator switches in rapid succession. The panel lighting dipped for a moment as the onboard battery banks took up the slack. The TERMIT screen continued its update. "Still locked!" Kane shouted. "Batteries!"

Hendricks fumbled at the battery toggles and slapped them to the off position. Every instrument and light in the cockpit went dark. "Batteries off!"

The view outside was eerily clear without the cockpit lighting glare. Cook could easily see Strongman Three's navigation lights ahead, the shape of the plane outlined by the spreading flames on the mountainside. The thrum of the four turbine engines continued unabated, the fuel running on mechanical pumps tied to the turbine engines. As long as there was fuel, they would keep running, and powering the hydraulic systems.

Suddenly, the yoke in front of Cook started to gyrate.

"I've got it!" Kane shouted. He immediately initiated a climbing bank to the right. "Chief, strap in! Cook, get me a flashlight!"

Cook reached behind his seat into his flight bag and waved his hand around until he felt a couple aluminum shafts. He yanked both lights out, punched the butt switch on one, and held it out to Kane, who grabbed it and put it between his teeth. He aimed it at the mechanical compass, the altimeter and the airspeed indicator, three non-electrical instruments on the panel that were still functioning.

Because of their climbing turn, Cook couldn't see the plane in front of them, but from the bright flash that lit up the windscreen, he guessed they had just exploded on the mountain below. His jaw clenched as he held tight to a grab rail – nothing he could afford to think about right now.

Kane leveled off and peered ahead at the lights of the valley now filling their cockpit glass.

"What's the nearest field?"

"Palm Springs!"

"Give me a vector!" Kane struggled to fly the plane with a dark panel while Cook frantically scanned ahead for the airport beacon. He found Interstate 10 from the red taillights of vehicles heading northwest, and then looked below to the left and right. "Got it! Two o'clock!

Kane searched intently.

"I've got it! Give me fifty degrees of flaps!"

Cook turned on his flashlight and found the flaps lever. He lowered it to the fifth detent. "Fifty degrees flaps!"

Kane reduced the throttles to increase their descent rate. "Can you find a handheld to call this in?"

Cook reached back into his bag and grabbed his air-band transceiver. He turned it on and waved his light's beam over his kneeboard with its attached charts. He flipped through until he found the Palm Springs sheet's tower frequency.

"Got it! Tower is 119.7 – standby!"

* * *

The vehicle and handheld radios of the sheriff deputies were spitting out a nonstop barrage of traffic on multiple command and tactical channels as an airport fire department Surburban sped out to the gathering on the tarmac, all its lights flashing. It screeched to a halt with its external speakers blaring, and a stocky battalion chief in full turnouts jumped out. He ran over to the group.

"Who's Romero?"

Romero looked up from the aviation chart spread on the hood of his SUV that he was consulting with Stokes. "Right here."

"The chief wants to know what type of aircraft hit the ridge and how much fuel it's carrying."

Romero's expression telegraphed his frustration. "Tell him it was probably a C-130, and a lot."

The battalion chief's look was frosty. "Thanks, you're a big help." He abruptly turned to the sheriff's lieutenant. "We're setting up a joint command here. You want to come over to the tower, find some space?"

The lieutenant regarded Romero with disdain. "Let's do it. You two," he added, turning to his subordinates, "keep an eye on our guests."

They began to jog toward the airport control tower when its external radio speaker, the volume dialed to maximum, was activated by the controllers inside. Scratchy sound exploded over the parking area.

"…Mayday, Mayday, Transvex 68 inbound for emergency landing, electric power failure, Mayday!"

* * *

Emergency landings can span the spectrum of everything from a relatively normal approach with a troubling engine light to a controlled crash. Cook knew this one was going to be more like the latter. He had wrestled his way back into his seat, cinched down the harness straps until he could barely breath, and shouted at Hendricks to do the same.

When Cook had located the beacon, Kane basically steered straight toward it and aimed for the numbers on the nearest available runway. Emergency checklists tend to be concise and Cook focused only on the highlights in the frantic atmosphere: flaps, negative on lights, throttles. As first officer, Cook's role was to cover Kane on the controls and do anything else needed so his left seater could land the plane. At about two thousand feet above the airport, Cook lowered the landing gear. Kane kept the speed up so there was no chance of a wing stall.

When they were twenty feet above the threshold, Kane flared, Cook following him on his yoke. It was eerie experience landing with a black panel, Kane using runway lights and landmarks to gauge their position. The plane's control surfaces, powered by hydraulics, were unaffected by the power outage and operated normally. They wallowed on the air cushion of ground effect for a few seconds until the aircraft slammed into a jarring contact with the runway asphalt.

On the rollout, Kane feathered the propellers and steered the nosewheel as Cook shut down the fuel pumps in case of fire. Then they coasted for a moment until Kane floored the foot pedal brakes brought them to a shuddering halt towards the end of the runway. With the engines starved of fuel and the loss of any air velocity, the plane lost all power, and the cockpit became utterly silent. The only illumination other than the flashlight in Kane's mouth came from the high-intensity edge lights along the runway and the approaching strobes of emergency vehicles.

Cook sagged in his seat while Kane pried his damp hands loose from the death grip he had been holding on the control yoke. He spat the flashlight into his lap and turned his shiny, sweat-beaded face to Cook, his breath rapid. "You ok?"

Cook wiped his forehead with his sleeve and examined it. It was dark with moisture.

"Pretty sweet piece of work, Ron."

"Check on the guys in the rear."

"You got it."

Cook snapped the taut buckle of his harness and hauled himself up. His undershirt was soaked through with sweat, and his legs trembled from strain as he hobbled across to the cockpit ladder. He descended cautiously, not trusting his footing. When he tried to swallow, he found that his mouth was bone-dry, and his lips were cracked. Cook coughed to get some moisture back in his mouth as he looked for his flashlight, then remembered he had left back in his seat. It was too dark to see clearly. He flailed for an emergency flashlight tacked onto the bulkhead and activated it.

The LED light shocked him with its intensity. Cook waved it around for a moment, looking for any smoke or damage, then stiffly shuffled through the hatchway to the cargo area.

Hendricks and the kicker were both still strapped into their seats in front of the control console.

"You two alright?"

The loadmaster grimaced. "Can we get our money back? I think I left my spine back at the threshold."

"Complain to management." Cook withdrew and pivoted to the main hatch. Through the Perspex viewport he saw Romero and Stokes standing at the head of a growing group of public safety personnel. He paused for a moment, his head down, his hand resting on the main door latch, calculating.

With his original plan in tatters, he was going to have to do a deal with Romero. Porter was gone, and so was any prospect of protective treatment from the company higher-ups. They would probably treat him the same way as last time. Files would get dusted off that demonstrated a propensity for criminal behavior, and he'd be brusquely discharged. Again.

It also occurred to him that he was now the only one left alive who had participated in the misguided Nicaragua debacle.

A chill ran down the drying sweat on the back of his neck. Why had the navigation system gone haywire, starting an update precisely when they had the least possible chance of survival? What if this wasn't just run-of-the-mill corporate IT incompetence. What if it had been the corporate plan all along, Transvector's version of cleaning up embarrassing messes?

A pounding on the plane's hatch broke his train of thought. He closed his eyes. He couldn't think clearly, the extreme physical exertion of the last five minutes catching up with him. Probably shock, he thought dully – after-action strain. Maybe, at this stage, going with Romero was the safe play. There were no good options. He heard Kane shuffling out of his seat on the flight deck above and made the call. Cook cycled the door's handle, and let the hatch slowly sink down on its hydraulics.

Romero was ready for him, his badge in hand.

"Mr. Cook, Special Agent Romero, DEA. I am authorized to take you into protective custody for your own safety. Will you come with me now?"

The Sheriff's lieutenant pushed forward from behind. "Hold on a second, Romero, this isn't a federal airfield. We've got some questions…."

"*Lieutenant*," Romero hissed, cutting him short, "This individual is a material witness in an ongoing federal investigation. My authority here supersedes your jurisdiction." Romero paused, still looking directly at Cook. "The rest of the crew is all yours for questioning. Stokes, take him to the car."

Cook nodded, and walked down the hatch stairs to Stokes, who turned and led him to the SUV without a word. Behind him, he could hear Romero still issuing directives.

"Lieutenant, I want you to get a CSI team out here and tear this plane apart and look over every inch of it. Do you have a K9 drug unit available?"

"I can call one out. What're you looking for…?" The conversation trailed off as Cook and Stokes approached the blacked-out Chevy. One of Romero's helpers held the rear door open for Cook as he climbed in. When the door shut, it was utterly silent, and Cook was again left alone with his thoughts.

Porter. What in Christ's name was he going to do without him? Cook was pretty sure Romero's dope idea was crazy, but he had nothing other than his intuition on that one. Porter had been his fallback plan – actually, his only plan. The crash didn't leave a lot of room for maneuver.

He looked out the tinted window toward the plane and felt like he'd been gut-punched. Kane was standing on the hatch steps blinking at all the emergency lights and the rapid-fire questioning that Cook couldn't hear but knew was being directed at his friend. He felt his cheeks flush and grow hot from a mounting sense of betrayal. He hadn't taken the opportunity, when he had it, to explain to one of his most steadfast and worthwhile friends the mire he had stumbled into. And now the chance was gone. Kane's record was unblemished, but he could still get tarred by association. And Cook was leaving Kane to fend for himself.

Maybe the fact that he hadn't told his friend anything would help. Kane could plead ignorance honestly; he was just doing a job. Cook dropped it. Stokes and Romero were back, and Romero stood outside talking to his muscle while Stokes got in front and turned the ignition. Doors clunked shut one after another, and Cook found himself being chauffeured off the airfield toward the exit, the backseat to himself.

No one spoke, the only sound being an occasional call on whatever channel the DEA radio was monitoring. Cook was grateful. The county's public safety communications systems must've been going berserk with the fires and dealing with the aircraft search.

It was still a couple hours before dawn. The SUV rushed smoothly past hazy orange halogen streetlamps on nearly empty streets. The only traffic was early commuters and trash trucks. Cook dully wondered if trash trucks were starting or finishing their shifts. He decided he didn't really care and realized how exhausted he was to even pursue the thought. He yawned deeply and reclined back on his seat. He was feeling dopey, and he'd been up way too long. He hoped wherever Stokes was driving him had a couch he could crash on for a few hours.

Cook had his answer shortly. After about ten minutes, Stokes turned into the parking lot of a Great Western motel and parked in an empty space in front of a row of ground floor rooms. They exited the SUV and Stokes brusquely escorted Cook by the arm through one of the orange pastel doors. The room was modernly furnished in subtle browns and tans, and had an open adjoining door leading to the adjacent room.

Stokes indicated with her head that Cook should go into the next room. Her reddened eyes had black bruises under them, and her face seemed paler than he remembered. She looked tired. Probably had been up all night too. "Get some rest. We'll let you know when we find something."

Yeah, back at you, Cook thought, his mind foggy. He splayed himself out on top of the covered bed. Sleep found him as he stared at the fan on the ceiling.

* * *

The dream had changed. Porter no longer flew in Cook's plane, but in one flying in tight formation, with too many engines on the wings, all of them trailing greasy plumes of bright orange flame. They weren't over rainforest, but dry graben-and-pan terrain like in the desert West. And instead of dropping home-made napalm on a village of unsuspecting innocents, Porter, with a wide, bloody grin on his face, piloted his strangely smoking air contraption straight into a sheer cliffside. The resulting explosion kept growing in illumination, like a nuclear warhead, until his vision was saturated with brilliant white light...

Cook's eyes blinked open. A ray of hot, high desert sun had found its way through a chink in the curtains and was beaming on his face. With grouchy anger, he vaulted from the bed and yanked the curtains together until they overlapped. He then fell back onto the cover of the still-made bed, staring at the tan textured ceiling above.

A brass and wood fan rotated slowly above him, its four stubby blades reminding him of a propeller. Not something he wanted to think about. The sounds of muffled voices from next door, intermittently upraised, were punctuated by the occasional slammed door and car horn outside.

He looked down at his chest. Damp spots on his undershirt remained from his sweat-soaked dream, and he tried to remember the last time he'd been in such a constant state of perspiration. Malaysia, maybe Diego Garcia. Your clothes always stuck to you for days on end, nothing ever dried. Cook took in a deep breath. Sweat from exercise and stress smelled differently. Anxiety carried an acidic tang that most animals recognized as fear. Got to get this showered off at some point, he thought.

He looked at his watch – almost nine in the morning. Wondering if they'd found anything yet, and craving information, Cook hobbled up to the adjoining door and knocked. The muted voices immediately ceased, and after a moment, Stokes opened the door.

"What do you want?" Her voice and demeanor weren't particularly friendly, and if anything, she looked even more tired. Cook didn't really want to antagonize her or Romero until he had a better appreciation of his situation.

"Just looking for an update."

"We'll let you know when we find something." She shoved the door closed before Cook could squeeze another word in edgewise.

Cook heaved a frustrated sigh, and stumble back to collapse on the bed. In a few seconds, he was back asleep.

* * *

The scene around the C-130 kept growing, with each new arrival proceeded by flashing strobes of blue, red and white.

A Fire Department lieutenant showed up, followed by an official from the Riverside emergency management department and a sheriff's crime scene investigation unit. Kane watched from a window on the ground floor of the control tower building with a bemused look on his face. Behind him, public safety minions were setting up an incident command post on a large, U-shaped conference room table with a projector and wall screen. Current emergency management protocols dictated a large space – interagency cooperation was the word of the day.

He was happy to be alive. He kept telling himself that as he wondered what kind of massive organizational incompetence could have led to this cocked-up catastrophe. And Cook. Why had they rushed him off like that? What had he done? Kane knew he was perfectly capable of getting himself into all kinds of sketchy jams, but this was so far beyond his usual scrapes that Kane couldn't believe he was even remotely involved.

Kane saw some CSI types talking to the loadmaster and kicker about forty feet to the rear of the plane. The loadmaster was gesticulating rapidly, pointing back at the fuselage. Sensing a mounting problem, Kane tapped the arm of the deputy assigned to watch him, but who was currently staring at his smartphone. The deputy flinched at the contact and regarded Kane suspiciously. "Something I can help you with?"

Kane pointed at the Super Hercules. "You might want to tell your techs that the rear of that aircraft is coated with an experimental herbicide, and they should probably get some protective gear on...and maybe stand a little further away."

The deputy nodded, and stepped away to radio the information in. Kane watched as the Sheriff's lieutenant peeled off from the group he was standing in and marched quickly toward the tower. A few seconds later he was in the room, steaming.

"You mean we've been standing near this crap for hours and nobody thought it might be important to tell us?" he asked pointedly, squinting.

"I would have told anybody who asked, but I've been cooling my ass in this room," Kane retorted. "Anyway, I'd tape the back end of the plane off out to about thirty feet, just to be safe."

"Thanks for your advice. Any other pieces of information I should know?"

"Only thing I can think of right now."

The lieutenant frowned, then found a new target for his ire.

"Hey," he barked, calling to Romero's men sitting across the room, "you guys know when your boss is showing up? I've got some more questions for him."

"No idea."

"Jesus! Everybody's so goddamned helpful today...." The lieutenant stomped out of the room, muttering.

Kane looked back out the window at his plane, and at the smoky haze that was slowly filling the valley.

* * *

CHAPTER TEN

Cook started awake, suffocating in the close air of the room, which was punctuated by a faint smell of burnt pine. He sensed by the weightier darkness that considerable time had passed, and it was probably evening. A thin line of light leaked from under the door to the adjoining room.

Rest had given Cook's brain time to resume something resembling normal function, and now he wanted answers from Romero. Like, did he know anything about what had gone wrong with their mission, and what exactly had they found on the C-130? His earlier shock and exhaustion had transformed into a bloody-minded pugnacity, and if Stokes tried to kiss him off with another bout of attitude and a slammed door, he was going to raise some holy hell.

He could again hear muffled, raised voices in Romero's room, which may have been what woke him. From the differences in high-and-low pitch, it sounded like Stokes was carrying most of the conversation, with Romero occasionally responding. Cook pounded the heavy door with his fist, and the talking again ceased. This time, when the door opened, it was Romero.

"Listen, Romero, I need some...."

"Guy," Romero cut in quickly, "I don't have anything for you yet. They're still searching, and it could go on for another few hours. I don't have to tell you that it's a big plane. And that they've got a lot of other things to deal with right now."

"No, you don't, but you can't keep me cooped up in here forever. I want to talk to someone from Transvector, like now."

Romero sucked in his lower lip, as if considering Cook's proposal.

"Guy, we're doing this for your protection, and because you're my best witness for this whole catastrophe." Romero nodded, possibly to himself, continuing. "You, better than anyone, should know that those planes didn't crash into the mountain by accident. Your company may actually have been involved somehow. They may not be the best folks to touch base with at the current time."

Cook smiled thinly.

"Don't pretend my welfare is your biggest concern, Vic." Cook saw Stokes stiffen. He hadn't used the DEA agent's first name before, and it looked like she was sensing a precursor to violence. "You just don't want to lose control of your primetime case before you make the big score, maybe cost you a fat promotion."

Stokes strained forward against Romero's shoulder, her face snarling. "You don't know shit about...."

Romero hastily raised his arm, cutting her off.

"Look, Guy. I tell you what. Give me a few more hours, and you can call whoever you want. Fair?"

Cook inhaled, then blew it out slowly through puffed cheeks. "Ok, I can work with that. But I want to know as soon as you do. And I want some food – the last thing I ate was some coffee in Guadalajara."

Romero nodded, smiling. "I've already got something coming. Should be here shortly. Chicken salad or a burger work for you?"

"Yeah. I can do that."

"Good." Romero regarded Cook. "You may want to get out of that flight suit. There's some jeans and a sweatshirt in the dresser under the TV. Should fit."

There was a loud knock at the door. Romero looked at Stokes, then back at Cook. He lowered his voice.

"Speak of the Devil." Romero glanced to the door, then at his colleague. "Sue, stay with Cook in there, just to keep things discreet. Keep the light off, ok?"

Stokes nodded, and shrugged her way past Cook, carrying a black tactical duffel in her hand. She closed the door quietly, standing next to it with her ear cocked. Cook walked to the dresser and shrugged out of his flightsuit, not caring if Stokes was watching. The jeans were pretty much his size. It was a thoughtful gesture – the flightsuit had gotten clammy from all the time he'd spent in it. As he shrugged on the sweatshirt, he heard Romero say, "Be there in a minute."

As Cook slipped his boots on, he heard Romero's footsteps squeak across the thick brown carpet toward the door. Must've been covering stuff up he didn't want room service to see. While waiting in the dark, Cook realized that Stokes didn't smell much better than he did, an acidic tang emanating from her hair and clothes. Stress, and probably no recent shower for her either.

They heard Romero's attenuated voice through the wall telling the person at the door to wait a second, then the clacking sound of the chain being withdrawn.

The loud 'phutting' and cracking sound of suppressed automatic weapons fire penetrating wood rattled their adjoining door.

Stokes gasped, and threw an outstretched arm signaling quiet. Romero's door was kicked open with a bang. The line of light under the door dimmed as someone moved past it. There was silence for a moment, then the crunch of something glass or ceramic broken on the carpet. A thin wisp of white smoke wafted under the door from the next room, smelling of cordite.

Her lips trembling, Stokes knelt and quietly parted the zipper of the Cordura kit bag down with her finger, exposing what looked like a short-barreled assault rifle with a folding stock. She slowly tugged at the Velcro ties holding the weapon, but the noise was sphincter-clenchingly loud, with each tearing pop of the Velcro fasteners seeming deafening in the dark silence. Halting, she changed direction, fishing out a fist-sized black tubular container instead. She tip-toed next to the door handle, her eyes wide, and listened.

At first it was silent. Then there came the sound of muffled whisper as someone gave a command.

Stokes firmly pulled a pin from the top of the grenade, yanked the door open a hand's breadth, and tossed it in the next room. She then slammed the door and dove for her black bag on the ground.

A cry went up, but was quickly cut off by a tremendous, whamming explosion which rattled Cook's back teeth and outlined the door in a brilliant white glare. Clearly, some kind of stun grenade. While Cook was trying to figure out how he ended up sitting on the floor, Stokes had torn her weapon from the bag and had cycled the charging handle on a full, thirty-round magazine. She dropped into a crouch, jerked the door open fully, and went into the room low. Cook followed, crawling on all fours into the smoke-shrouded gloom until he could get his feet under him.

The first thing he noticed, after Stokes loosed at deafening string of automatic fire at a figure struggling to rise by the front door, was the strong smell of sulfur. Then he saw prone figures on the carpeted floor, reaching feebly for dropped submachine guns and wheezing for breath. Romero was splayed at full length over the bed nearest the door, head hanging over the side, his face an unrecognizable mess of red pulp.

Stokes marched methodically to each prone figure and fired a round point-blank into the eye socket. She then pulled another stun grenade from her belt, yanked the pin, and lightly tossed it out the room's open door.

She shouted to Cook, "Get down!"

Cook dived behind the bed not supporting Romero's corpse, covering his ears and opening his mouth to relieve pressure. The blast was louder this time, and he felt like he'd been kicked in the stomach as he tried to breathe. Through his forearms that were bracketing his head, he saw Stokes advance toward the doorway, scanning over the barrel of her rifle.

The man outside the door was apparently the last of them, because Cook heard only a single shot and Stokes reentered the room at a trot. She scurried into the adjoining room, where she and Cook had been less than thirty seconds before, and reemerged with her ballistic nylon duffel in her left hand. While covering the door one-handed with her assault rifle, she rapidly knelt near each body and patted it down for weapons and magazines.

Cook watched in a daze, his arms still up by his head, as Stokes doggedly stacked pistols, spare magazines and suppressed submachine guns into her sack. When finished, she slung the bag across her shoulders, and, with her rifle raised, slowly stalked out of the room, her knees bent in a tactical crouch.

His arms still covering his head, Cook rose to his knees and scanned the room, trying to assess what had just happened. The gaping cavity in Romero's ruined face, dripping gore down the side of the bed, mocked him like a macabre smile. Cook lowered his forearms and examined one of the corpses next to him. Beneath the powder burns covering his face, his skin looked light brown, the eyes Latino or Asian. The .30 caliber entry hole in his eye cavity was still smoking, and the back of his skull was a mushy pillow of bone, brain and tissue. Cook blinked for a moment, then vomited straight onto the dead man's surprised expression. He then wiped his mouth, looked at what he'd done, and puked again. Then he fell back against the side of the bed, coughing and hacking to unclog his mouth and nostrils.

Outside the room, he could hear a vehicle ignition turning over, then dying. Cook levered himself up, spat again to clear his mouth, and scampered outside. Stokes was bent over the steering wheel of a black four-door Jeep Wrangler parked in the middle of the lot, fiddling with the ignition harness. She was obviously trying to hotwire it.

Cook dove for the passenger-side door and yanked it open, staring at her. Stokes jerked up, looking over the front post site of a Glock pistol, her eyes darting wildly. "I couldn't find any keys!"

Not comprehending her, Cook responded. "Why aren't we taking the Tahoe?"

"Check Romero for the keys!"

Cook scuttled back into the room, keeping low for no reason he could fathom. Everyone was still dead. Thin ribbons of smoke curled near the only table lamp still emitting light. Romero was in the same place, his corpse in full extension over the bed as if he had leapt backward in the act of dying. Cook fished around in the left front pocket of the agent's gabardines next to a dark, damp urine stain where his bladder had let go. Nothing. A quick rummage through the other side produced a key ring.

He hustled back to the parking lot, hissing, "Got it!" and punched the unlock button on the key fob. Amber running LEDs flashed brightly in the darkening lot. Cook could see a few nearby window curtains twitch as the occupants peeked out to see what was going on.

Stokes abandoned the Jeep, her bag clanking as she spun, covering her departure with the Glock. When she was next to Cook, she put out her left hand. "I'm driving. Get in."

* * *

As Stokes roared down the boulevard, she punched up the sheriff department's main frequency on the dash-mounted radio. Pandemonium blared from the speakers. The dispatcher on the channel they were monitoring seemed to be having a busy evening: she was calling out incidents and assigning units virtually nonstop, pausing only to acknowledge responses. One call caught Cook's attention.

"...All units, shots fired, Great Western motel, 1509 S Palm Canyon Drive...."

If Stokes heard the call, she didn't acknowledge it, visibly to Cook anyway. She kept driving, making seemingly random turns and continuing to drive at high speed away from the motel vicinity. Wondering why she hadn't called the incident in yet, Cook thought she might be suffering from some kind of post-traumatic combat shock. He'd seen it often enough with other pilots and experienced it himself once or twice. Tunnel vision, coupled with simplistic, rote behavior after a hairy, adrenalin-inducing event. It faded with time, or a gentle tap-out from an external source.

After another high g-force turn, Cook leaned in. "You gonna call for backup?"

"Good idea," she responded, still scanning and maintaining her headlong velocity. She dug a smartphone out of her jacket pocket, thumbed her contacts while occasionally glancing up to steer, and selected an entry. When the call connected, she shouted "Prairie

Fire" into the handset, rolled down the window, and threw the phone out of the speeding SUV.

Cook sat silent for a moment, his body still except for the occasional brace against another lurching turn. Then he stared at Stokes. "What the fuck was that?"

Stokes stared straight ahead, accelerating.

Cook stabbed his finger repeatedly at the radio. "Call the feds – get us some help!"

They were careening down a commercial side street when Stokes stomped on the brakes, skidding the Tahoe over to the side of the nearly empty road. Ignoring the rifle on her lap, she drew her sidearm from its holster and pointed it at Cook.

"Get out."

He gaped at her, uncomprehendingly. Stokes, a federal officer, in whose protective custody he currently was being held, was drawing a bead on him. He tried to say something, but his mouth wouldn't form words. He managed a croak.

"What?"

"Get out. Now."

Over the years, Cook had heard anecdotally about how easy it was to get a pistol away from someone in a cramped space such as a car. If you moved fast enough, the other person wouldn't have time to react. But at that moment, looking at the vacant expression on Stoke's face, he had no inclination to even think about trying it out.

Cook raised his hands slowly, trying to buy time.

"What's the deal, Stokes? Why aren't you calling in the cavalry?"

Staring down the barrel at Cook, she chuckled eerily, a sickening grin contorting her face.

"You don't get it, do you?" she screeched.

Her mouth was twisting, her eyes surrounded by white. Cook, suddenly and increasingly scared, shook his head.

"Help me out here."

"There is no cavalry, no fed backup, no police." Stokes' eyes darted wildly. "I don't work for the DEA – I worked for Romero, same as you – with pretty much the same deal as you. So, get your ass out."

Cook leaned back against his door, his hands still up, stunned. The barrel of the Glock didn't waver.

It made sense. The summary executions and weapons collecting back at the motel. He tried to form his next question, but Stokes beat him to it.

"The operation is unsanctioned. Somehow Romero got your file and figured he could leverage it into a sting on Transvector. He's been obsessed with your company ever since I've known him."

She paused, still aiming at his face.

"Hayden and Keefer have the same deal I do – we all snitch for Romero. They probably aren't their real names."

"Was that who you called?"

"Yeah."

"What are they going to do?"

Her eyes flitted, the gun wavering slightly. "Probably head for the hills like me. Which means you've got to go. I'm running solo."

Cook thought furiously. He needed room to maneuver. Getting cut loose on a dark street, with no fallback, wasn't a good outcome.

"Who hit Romero?"

"I have no idea, and that's why you're getting out."

Cook's imagination had run dry. He couldn't think of anything to keep the conversation moving. The radio saved him.

"All units, be on the lookout for a male and female driving a black SUV with Federal plates, seen leaving the Great Western on south Palm, considered armed and dangerous – standby for further."

Stokes' pistol barrel wavered again as she heard the broadcast. It was all the opening Cook needed.

"Look, you've got to dump this ride anyway. At least put me near a pay phone so I can make a call."

Stokes showed her teeth, but seemed to be listening. Cook pressed on.

"There's got to be a mall around here, or something. Dump me there."

Stokes shook her head slowly.

"I'd be real careful calling your company. There's some shady shit going on there."

Cook nodded. "I can't argue with that. But I've got to try." He paused, lowering his hands. "If it goes sideways, I've got a fallback."

Stokes was silent for a moment.

Then she holstered her firearm and hit the accelerator, pressing Cook back into his seat.

* * *

Kane snapped awake in his chair by the window as the command post door slammed open, the sheriff's lieutenant leading two men in dark suits. The beleaguered lieutenant seemed to be fighting a rearguard action against them as he entered, and failing badly. From what Kane could infer, the two suits, who looked like Feds, wanted Kane to come with them, and the lieutenant was trying not to lose his last eyewitness on scene.

"...and the other pilot went with Romero. The two guys in back didn't see anything, so I need him here to answer technical questions for the fire guys."

The taller of the two suited men nodded sympathetically while the lieutenant spoke, but even Kane could tell that the transfer of custody was a foregone conclusion.

"We appreciate that you're busy right now, but things have developed on our end, and we need him for questioning."

The taller agent, obviously the senior of the duo, kept nodding while he spoke, treating the lieutenant like a slow learner requiring remedial instruction. The lieutenant seemed to pick up on this, and Kane could see the man's neck redden. He responded angrily.

"That's the same shit Romero spewed! I've got a fucking toxic plane to search for drugs, and the DEA guys have vanished. Is Homeland Security now in charge, because I could sure use some of your goddamn help! What do you think they were going to do – use those fucking planes to blow up the damned convention center?"

To Kane, the last retort seemed to be emitted with an equal quantity of sarcasm and spittle. But he knew a lost cause when he saw one. The two federal agents were smooth, assured and confident in their abilities to surmount bureaucratic and jurisdictional barriers, and the tide had turned. The lieutenant bore the look of an overwhelmed middle manager struggling to assemble resources for a job that had outgrown him.

Kane quietly gathered his flight bag and jacket and stood. At least he was getting out of this miserable conference room.

* * *

A tan steel latticed screen offered a partially concealed vantage from which Cook could observe the entrance to the Haydon's supermarket without being easily seen. He was sitting at a table on the terrace of a Pedro's coffee shop, nursing a steaming large coffee while he waited. The caffeine was helping keep him alert. He had paid for it with the thin roll of bills Stokes had left as a parting gift.

Cook had pleaded for more time, and would have begged on his knees in the plaza parking lot if it wouldn't have attracted too much attention. But she was adamant, stiff with resolve. Better off alone, she kept saying.

There was some truth to that. The cops were looking for a man and a woman traveling together. And from what she had said earlier, she didn't even have the possibility of backup – there was nobody coming for her.

Unlike for Cook, who had made his call.

She wouldn't tell him what she had planned or where she was going. She merely focused on getting the old wagon she had chosen started, while Cook kept a casual-looking vigil from a nearby bus bench. The lot of the Avalon Theatre on East Baristo was packed with the vehicles of patrons enjoying a movie in the artsy theater adjacent to a nearby mall that was largely untenanted. Most would be in there for a couple of hours, depending on what showing they had caught. If there was security for the complex, it was busy chasing off the hooded teenage skateboarders who kept trying to grind every concrete corner in the area with their axles.

Cook sipped pensively at his paper cup, his eyes locked on the supermarket entrance.

The crowd at the independent theater tended toward older model vehicles, which they kept in pristine condition. That meant both elderly owners, and a less difficult electronic ignition to circumvent. It had taken Stokes less than thirty seconds to get the chosen station wagon running.

She had quickly maneuvered to the bus stand to allow Cook to jump into the back seat. As they left the parking lot, Cook slipped down to the floor. Since the theater was only a few blocks away from the airport, Stokes wanted to keep their profile low. Police are always less likely to stop a woman than a man.

While she was driving him to a good location to make his phone call to TVA, Cook had tried to persuade her to wait. But he could tell that her mind was already on the road, planning strategy, mentally canvassing and evaluating her contacts. He might as well have been talking to the seat back.

An argument broke out terrace behind him. He glanced back to see a young and very pregnant Latina with heavy mascara crying at an indifferent black man in an Oakland Raiders jersey across the table. The man stared back at him. Cook quickly resumed his vigil.

He had made the call from the customer service center of the supermarket across the parking lot, telling the attendant that his car had broken down and his cell phone battery was dead. The man had been sympathetic, happy to help. Cook had dialed zero and given the operator the ten-digit mission emergency number and the name Ridgecrest. When the collect call was answered and accepted, he was given the standard interrogatory. "Which extension are you trying to reach?"

"Market research." There was a pause, and then dead silence. Then a voice came on.

"Hoover, Research. Who's calling?"

"Sandy Ridgecrest." Where did they come up with these things? More silence while someone checked a code word list on a screen in the TVA covert operations center.

"What firm?"

"Trent Valley Aggregates." Another pause.

"What can we do for you, Mr. Ridgecrest?"

"I need a pickup in Palm Springs, California, 415 South Sunrise Way, Haydon's Supermarket."

"How many product samples do you have?" He was asking the priority level, on a scale of one to five.

"Five cases. Can you give me an ETA?"

"Hold on." There was another, longer pause while the voice on the other end digested the information. "We can arrange a taxi pickup in about twenty minutes. Will that work?"

"That's fine."

"The cab will take you to one of our facilities, and we'll make further arrangements then. See you soon, Mr. Ridgecrest." The line went dead.

The taxi would take him to a hotel where the operations personnel were already arranging a room. There he would wait until the company could send a couple of representatives in a helicopter for a direct extraction. He'd be back in Mojave before morning.

He tilted the coffee cup back, sucking the warm dregs of coffee and milk from the bottom of the cup. After his rollercoaster evening, it tasted fantastic. Cook looked at his watch. Only fifteen minutes had gone by. He had time to order another. He was turning to get out of his chair when some movement in the half-full parking lot caught his eye.

A silver minivan with heavily tinted windows had slipped into the parking lot and cruised slowly towards the entrance of the supermarket, stopping on the curb by the main entrance. The side door slid open and two short men with spiked black hair and dark jackets stepped out. They looked around the parking lot for a moment, then one turned and spoke something into the van before sliding the door closed. The pair walked inside. The minivan then started to slowly circumnavigate the parking lot.

Cook squinted at the two men as they disappeared into the Haydon's entrance. From this distance, in the weak light from the parking lot lamps, their complexions looked dark – Vietnamese, Filipino – it was hard to tell. But they stood out against the largely white and Latino crowd doing their marketing that evening.

And to Cook, they looked a lot like the hit team that had taken Romero out.

Fury surged through him. Apparently, the company was trying to liquidate him, and this time they were being methodical. Stokes had dusted their tracks too well to be caught through aerial surveillance, and Cook didn't believe in coincidence. This crew was here as a direct result of his contact with Transvector. And that meant the C-130s, the hit team, and this group were all laid on by TVA to cross him out.

He didn't stand a chance. Transvector had more logistical reach than most of the world's nations, their oversized clandestine branch larger than many countries' militaries. The hundred-plus aircraft fleet gave company paramilitary and intelligence operatives the capability to influence policy in some places, and even help change the outcome of brush-fire conflicts in underdeveloped regions. Theoretically, this was all done according to the Pentagon's or CIA's marching orders, but Cook had been awestruck by the level of corporate autonomy in Honduras and other tense hotspots.

He stared at the empty coffee cup in front of him, wanting to crush it and hurl it at the window. Though he wasn't the type to whine or complain, the wrongness of it all stung. He had given the majority of his life to the company, and now they were trying to take the rest of it. He was really alone.

He needed to move.

"Phone call wasn't everything you hoped for, huh?" Cook spun around. Stokes had managed to get right behind him without him hearing.

"Why are you here?"

"Heard on the Motorola that they set up traffic checkpoints on all the good routes out of town. Thought I'd come back and check out your fallback idea."

"What makes you think it's still available?"

"Them." She jabbed in the direction of the minivan with her head. "Saw them just after I showed. They don't look like a standard company extraction team, do they?"

"Not really."

"Let's chat about it in the car. I'm parked next door."

* * *

When Stokes heard his idea for getting out, she almost dropped him off again.

But, laying again on the rear floor mats, he managed to convince her that they were out of options, and running out of time. Law enforcement would eventually have the area sewn up so tight that their apprehension would be a fait accompli.

Stokes stuck to major boulevards and surface streets and made careful turns if she thought a call from the handheld radio resting on the front seat made it sound like patrol vehicles were nearby. Cook thought the police might have already had a report on the stolen station wagon they were using, but nothing had come over the airwaves. Must've been a long film at the Avalon, he guessed. Law enforcement had also seemingly failed to find Romero's Tahoe, but Stokes had cached it pretty well in a dark corner of the mall by the theater.

Cook's mind wandered as the wagon chugged cautiously along, his calves warmed by the chassis' driveshaft hump. Though not generally prone to intro- spection, the down-time situation practically lent itself to self-inventory. How the hell had he gotten here? He was just a pilot, doing his job – nothing special. Why was everyone gunning for him now? It couldn't be the Nicaragua thing. The company either didn't know about it or didn't care, despite the photo in his file. They could have easily taken him out anytime during the past three years. Porter had found him pretty easily. And if the plane crashes were laid out to get rid of him, it sure seemed like the firm was going to a lot of very messy public effort to finish the job.

Cook shifted his back into a more comfortable position against the rear passenger door and rumi- nated over the past few days. What drove him? He understood planes and liked turning wrenches. He got satisfaction from jetting ports and fining valves, making things run better. And flying faster. That was pretty much it. There weren't a lot of people in his life; those that had stuck around through the decades were his true friends, even if he hadn't seen them in years. The others were like rest stops on a deserted highway; convenient places to park for a break, but ultimately, you'd be moving on.

Why had he come back? Comradery, excitement. Civilian life hadn't provided much of that; he had been going through the motions, filling time. Porter had offered him a path forward, restitution for past transgressions, real or imagined, the corporate equivalent of a religious indulgence. But the anticipated thrill of being back in the covert world had been short-lived. Subsequent events had completely overwhelmed that.

Cook knew TVA wasn't really in the business of world betterment, but he had seen the other side too, the arbitrary beatings and murders, disappearances, totalitarian systems that ran on the whims of megalomaniac autocrats and dour-eyed cadres. He always felt in the balance that he was doing some good. Nicaragua – well, that one had been an impulsive act of revenge on Porter's part, but even that mess had its nuances. Innocents had died, but so had a brigade of hardcore communists who were executing villagers, at least those who didn't subscribe to their idiotic dogmas. Still, it didn't justify scraping an entire village off the landscape.

And so it went – assembling and reassembling the pieces of his jumbled life. After about fifty minutes Stokes needed Cook to rise upright for directions. They were on a deserted road with tall grass fields on one side and what seemed to be a large horse-riding complex on the other. Cook nodded – he recognized the area. He laid back down.

"Good. Next road on the right. Head down to just before the airport fire station, then turn right on the street just after the fence. Drive about two hundred yards down, flip a one-eighty, and park."

"You resting comfortably back there?" Stokes seemed irritated by the long, tense drive.

"Just do it."

Cook's instructions put them just inside the airport perimeter fence, close to a gate that led to several rows of general aviation hangars. He quickly sat up and scanned the area. It was quiet, and except for the lighting by the terminal parking lot, dark as well.

"Perfect," he muttered.

Stokes didn't seem quite as happy. "How exactly are we supposed to get a plane out of there?"

"Guy I know, he never locks his hangar door – figures that way he'll never lock himself out."

"What if his plane isn't here?"

"Then you can break the lock of the hangar next door, and we'll take that one."

"That easy, huh?"

"Well, we do have to get over that fence." Cook pointed at the chain-link gate about twenty yards in front of them at the end of the road. Stokes snorted. It was all of about five feet tall.

* * *

CHAPTER ELEVEN

As the cellphone buzzed on his bedside table like an angry wasp, Craig wondered why calls always seemed to come just when he had comfortably gotten to sleep.

He looked at the screen. It was Simms. Which meant it was important. He swung his legs out from under the hotel bed's comforter and sat up. "Craig."

"Get dressed. There's a car outside, and a chopper waiting for you at Wilshire."

"What's going on?" he asked, with little hope. After all, it was Simms, and an open line.

"I'll brief you there."

Big, then, if Simms was awake at one o'clock in the morning to see him off personally. In a helicopter, no less. Simms was the ASAC, or Assistant Special Agent in Charge, of the counterintelligence section of the Los Angeles FBI field office. Craig had been at his unit for the past two weeks conducting crisis management refresher training classes.

As a senior special agent in the FBI's Critical Incident Response Group, or CIRG, Craig was accustomed to both late-night wakeup calls and being flown to unknown places with minimal notice. The unpredictability was the reason he took the job, the aspect of it that appealed to him the most. Sitting still was death to him. He always operated at his best during crises, a leftover from his days as a Force Recon marine, where to not move is to die. The downside to that particular personality quirk was that, without constant catastrophes occurring, he often felt rudderless and grew complacent.

Craig shook himself, banishing the unsolicited tangent as a hangover from the abrupt wake-up call and the metabolic aftereffects of the previous night's chicanery. He had destroyed a steak and a bottle of Jamison's with a few of his former colleagues from the LA office at Di Ciccio's, which had never worked out too well in the past. No rest for the wicked, especially when the wicks were burning at both ends.

He decided he had time for a quick shave and a rinse. Past experience with CIRG assignments had taught him that the next one might be a long time in coming. It always put him in a better frame of mind to feel clean and sharply dressed when launching into a typical turd-hitting-the-fan situation. His garment bag and toilet kit were streamlined for maximal efficiency, and he was ready to go in less than fifteen minutes.

Comb in hand, he gave himself one last look in the mirror before departing.

His hotel was close to the FBI office in the Wilshire Federal Building for convenience, and he arrived at the field office in his agency-issued vehicle within twenty minutes of the initial call. He drove up to the barrier gate and touched his parking card to the sensor. The gate swung up like a semaphore, and he drove to the unmarked Bell 412 helicopter waiting in the middle of the empty parking lot.

Craig smirked at the incongruity. The Wilshire building didn't have a helipad. If Bureau personnel needed to get picked up by helicopter, they had to go to the Veteran's Administration hospital complex across the freeway. Except at this hour, when the parking lot was basically wide open.

Simms was waiting for him near the unmarked helicopter, a thick plastic document folder plastered with confidentiality labels tucked under his arm. He had obviously not cleaned up before driving out from his place in Flintridge. At least there wasn't much traffic at this ungodly hour, Craig thought.

"Feeling clean and refreshed, Denny? You sure smell pretty."

Craig grinned. Before his posting to CIRG, he had been one of Simms's counter-intel minions in LA, and being back there was like a homecoming weekend. Giving Craig a hard time about his spit-and-polish demeanor was Simms's equivalent of 'good morning'.

Craig responded in kind. "You look like day-old puke, boss...where's the fire?"

"Palm Springs – literally. The SSRA in Palm Springs took one look at this cluster, and immediately called for some subject-expert backup. I wanted to get some eyes on this before the whole LA office relocates there."

An SSRA was a Senior Special Resident Agent in one of the LA FBI's resident agency offices. He or she would be supervising the special agent to whom the case was assigned. Usually, cases stayed at the local office, and resources were attached as necessary. The fact that the Palm Springs office had called for help without hesitation meant it was the kind of case Craig was really going to like. Simms was still talking.

"A DEA agent named Romero was gunned down two hours ago at a Palm Springs motel. Local police took the case, then called us in when they found Romero's credentials. They are thinking it's a dope gang revenge hit, but it actually gets more complicated – Transvector Aviation is involved. A bunch of their planes crashed, and one of the surviving pilots seems to have been Romero's informant."

Craig nodded thoughtfully. Transvector had a thinly veiled intelligence community link, and anything they were involved in would be extremely sensitive media-wise. His quick summons was starting to make sense.

"Palm Springs PD's still technically in the lead, but it's already outgrown them, and they asked DEA and us to join their task force after about five minutes. Special Agent Brent has the case. He's a solid agent, but still a little wet behind the ears, and doesn't have your background with contractors and spooks."

Craig had done a few months in Iraq checking up on some of the private military companies that had flooded in after the second Gulf War, making sure they were operating in compliance with US law. As unofficial adjuncts to Pentagon and CIA efforts in the Middle East, dealing with them had required a deft touch. Most of the stuff he uncovered never saw the light of day.

"What do you want me to do?"

"While they sit on their thumbs working everything out, I'm attaching you to the investigation to monitor any Transvector connection. Prop up Brent and keep him from stepping in it. You're reporting directly to me on this one. I want to know everything as soon as you know it. Are we on the same page?"

"Affirmative."

Simms tapped the folder before passing it to Craig.

"This has got everything relevant we could put together on Transvector since we got the call. The file's pretty thin. Also, some local PD reports on the crashes and the Romero scene. The encrypted jump drive inside has some extra eyes-only stuff, as well as aircraft specs for background. No idea how long it'll take, so you're taking your luggage with you in the chopper."

Craig tossed the folder into the helicopter's open rear hatch and walked to the rear of his vehicle to get his bags. Simms followed, still giving instructions.

"I've alerted the operations center staff, and we'll be fully manned within the hour." Simms nodded at Craig's surprised look. "I'd rather get everyone on deck and find out it's nothing than be scrambling for asses to fill seats if it's the Superbowl. Call me as soon as you get there. The ADIC," Simms was referring to the Assistant Director in Charge, the head of the LA office, "is going to want a detailed play-by-play later this morning, so pump the local guys for everything they've got at the command post. You'll get whatever resources you need. Toss me the keys – we'll get you another Bureau car when you get back."

Simms pocketed the thrown keys, and helped Craig get settled in the Bell 412's rear seat. He banged on the front hatch to signal the helicopter pilot to spool up.

"Now I'm going to get a nice, hot shower and some java." His thin smile betrayed his fatigue. "Have fun."

* * *

Craig was already into the folder before the helicopter lifted off the ground. It looked like a hastily assembled sheaf of executive summaries on Transvector Aviation, as well as the parent company, Transvector Worldwide. Simms had probably gotten some probationer on the 24-hour command center staff to put together anything he could find quickly. Also included was an initial Riverside sheriff's report on the aircraft crashes, as well as a draft copy of the Romero crime scene report from the responding police officers.

Craig knew from experience how tenuous early incident information could be, and how important it was to actually speak with someone on the ground. The police officer leading the crime scene investigation would have been rushed to get his draft report out as quickly as he had. He'd have been typing it on his vehicle's computer while taking calls from the watch commander and anybody higher up the food chain who'd been woken up for this, including the chief.

Looking out the window at the shiny sea of Los Angeles passing below, Craig reflected that everything seemed to be joint teams these days, and overall, it was a good thing. From years in the field, he had learned that federal agencies could be insular and clannish, leading to parochial modes of thinking. Working with personnel from outside the Bureau brought in fresh perspectives and opened up better lines of communication. Hell, he wouldn't be surprised if Homeland Security and ATF were in on this by lunchtime.

Simms had included a resume on Brent, the FBI agent leading the case. He must have been posted to LA after Craig had left. Brent had been selected for the Palm Springs residency because of his experience in high-end fraud and embezzlement in Chicago. Apparently, Palm Springs had enough white-collar federal criminal activity to support his assignment. Craig stared at the man's photo for a moment, trying to see if he could gain any insight into the agent's character or judgment. The fact that Brent had known to call for support rather than trying to glory-hog it was a good sign. Self-aware agents knew what they didn't know, and knowing enough to reach out for help was never a sign of weakness in Craig's book.

A slim folder marked 'Top Secret' contained a couple of recent, and heavily redacted, National Security Council reports on the company that presumably emanated from the FBI's NSC branch. Craig didn't have any real in-depth knowledge on the firm, but he was well aware of their reputation. And, unlike most of his agency, he knew that TVA had done some quiet rendition work for the Bureau, not long after 9/11, transporting hooded suspects in chartered aircraft to locations where the CIA thought interrogations would be most fruitful. Craig had been involved in developing the crisis management strategy in case the news leaked.

He skimmed the local law enforcement reports, paused, and stared out the window.

The sheriff's report gave Craig a skeletal narrative. Four Transvector C-130s had taken off from Guadalajara airport the day before yesterday, had done some anti-drug spraying *en route*, and three of them had crashed into the shoulder of Mount San Jacinto west of Palm Springs, starting a massive wildland fire. One plane had managed to make an emergency landing at the airport, was partially covered with a potentially toxic herbicide, and was going to be searched by drug canines after the plane had been cleaned off.

Craig mentally flagged the information on the drug dogs. It seemed unusual that they'd be searching TVA aircraft for drugs. Had DEA agent Romero been on to something? Did TVA have any history of smuggling narcotics? He'd have to look into that later.

The draft police report on the murder was written about eighteen hours after the aircraft incidents. Romero, who was leading the investigation into TVA, had been killed by what looked like an Asian gang, particulars currently unknown, in what might have been a revenge hit. The DEA agent's informant, one of the surviving pilots, was missing, along with three other DEA agents, two male and one female, names unknown, who were working with Romero.

Craig considered the reports. The information on the TVA planes seemed solid. The addendum on Romero was filled with a lot of conditionals. Other than the fact that Romero was dead, there wasn't a lot of hard information.

Judging that he was basically in the loop, Craig stuffed the papers back into the folder, and considered whether he should call Brent and get things going. He pipped the intercom. "What's our ETA?"

"Twenty-three minutes," the pilot responded without hesitation.

"Thanks." Craig decided he'd wait until landing to make contact. After all, the man knew he was coming, and was probably as busy as all hell anyway.

* * *

The airport was eerily quiet as Cook and Stokes pushed the light single-engine Cessna into the alley between the hangars, and turned it facing south. Cook double-timed it back into the cavernous hangar and hit the 'down' switch on the corrugated, bifold door that loomed above him. As the twin electric motors ground the chains to bring the door back down, Cook winced for the second time that night at the noise. Then he ran back to the plane.

As Cook remembered, his buddy's hangar had been unlocked, and the key to the plane wasn't only handy, it was actually in the ignition. His friend's rationale was that if someone wanted the little 172 badly enough, they would find a way to take it. Flawless, if not extremely useful, reasoning. Especially tonight, Cook thought.

Thermal airport, renamed 'Jaqueline Cochran' after a famous female aviator almost no one could remember, didn't have a control tower and was attended only during daylight hours, which was a big part of the reason Cook had chosen it – that, and the fact that it was the only airport nearby where he could conceivably steal a plane. The downside was that small airports often had aircraft hobbyists and tinkerers who hung around at odd hours. This morning, they seemed to be lucky. The place was deserted.

Cook jumped into the left seat and told Stokes to buckle in. He hit the Cessna's master power switch and lit up the panel. He consulted the start-up checklist, set the throttle to 'start' and the mixture to 'rich', and rejected anything that would attract undue attention, which meant leaving all external lights off. Against long habit, he resisted the urge to shout 'clear' out the window before he turned the key. The engine cranked a few times and caught immediately. Foregoing the usual oil pressure and magneto check, he raised the engine RPMs after a few seconds, and began taxiing.

Nights in the Coachella Valley were often cold and heavy with dew, which rapidly accumulated on the small plane's windshield, and, with the condensation coming from the two of them inside, made it difficult to see. Cook reached behind the seat and felt around for a rag. He felt a surge of confidence as he pulled one out of the mesh pocket. Pilots like predictability, and so far, this little Cessna was meeting expectations beautifully. Cook cracked the pilot's side window and reached forward to wipe down his section of the windscreen as they passed the fueling station and turned right down the taxiway.

Riverside county maintained a sheriff's sub-station with a helicopter near the airport, and Cook knew they'd have to move fast. During the high-speed taxi out to the flight line, while he scanned intently for any activity, he had Stokes read from the checklist so he wouldn't forget anything crucial. It had been a while since Cook had flown anything quite this simple, with a fixed prop and *fixed gear* even, and he was mildly concerned he might overlook something important.

"Radio master on."

"Check." After the initial squawk, the radio, tuned to the local Unicom, was quiet.

"Navaids – set." Cook dialed in the frequency of a VOR he knew in LA, but didn't plan on using.

"Transponder – 1200/STBY."

"Forget it. We're good."

Cook made sure the fuel selector was on the 'BOTH' tanks setting and pushed the left pedal to align the nose with the taxiway running parallel to Runway 12. There, the asphalt widened to accommodate the run-up area, for final engine and instrument checks before flight. Ignoring established procedure, and not wanting to waste the time making the dogleg turn to the runway, Cook mashed the throttle against the panel, and started accelerating down the taxiway.

Stokes said nothing, but Cook could see through his peripheral vision that she was bracing an arm against the rim of the passenger side door. He grinned. He had always wanted to just blaze off down a taxiway, giving a stiff middle finger to the FAA. The opportunity was made for it.

At rotation, Cook pulled back on the yoke, but then abruptly cut their ascent and leveled out less than fifty feet above the ground – which ironically was still about seventy feet below sea level due to Thermal's depressed location. He then pitched the plane into a steep turn to the left and started climbing again.

Stokes keyed her microphone.

"What's the deal with east? I thought you wanted to go to LA."

Cook grinned again. "Just don't want to make it too easy for them."

* * *

Craig felt like he was landing in the middle of a war zone, or a major terrorist bombing incident.

The dull brown pall of smoke from the uncontained San Jacinto fire parted to reveal a landscape of flashing red, white and blue strobes, and pairs of yellow headlight beams scuttling back and forth on the ground. The red-and-white fuselages of a pair of fire bombers, both repurposed Navy P-3 Orions, were surrounded by support vehicles and tanker trucks pumping fire retardant ammonium phosphate and sulfate compounds.

Craig's pulse increased as the pilot called in a vertical approach to the apron in front of the control tower and began a rapid descent to the tarmac.

A Riverside fire attack marshaller wearing a respirator waved them down to a hover with glowing batons and directed them to a parking area on the apron in front of the terminal. The FBI resident agent handling the case was waiting for Craig with his hand out.

"Brent. We're set up inside."

Quick, no nonsense, efficient. Craig liked him already.

The incident command post inside the terminal's conference room was raucous with activity, with county fire and police dominating one side and the federal response on the other. Brent had carved out some space for the team at a table in the back. Short introductions were made, and then the briefing commenced. Brent had given it to an intense, red-haired young agent called Cecil, who seemed to stare at everyone for a full second through steel-rimmed glasses before answering questions. Amazing what you find in the sticks, Craig mused.

"At approximately 2030 hours on 26 June 2019, four Lockheed C-130J Super Hercules cargo aircraft, owned by Transvector Aviation and equipped for aerial spraying, took off from Don Miguel Hidalgo y Costilla International Airport in Guadalajara, Mexico. They flew a covert opium poppy eradication mission for the US government under the cover of...."

Craig put his attention on autopilot as Cecil continued his brief. He thought the younger man might have been getting too granular, but he always applauded an agent's attention to detail. In any case, Craig already had the general outline from his hastily assembled folder. He was essentially auditing the information while he pondered strategy, always keeping an ear cocked for something new.

It came sooner than he thought.

"We've identified the prints of one of the deceased suspects from the Great Western scene. He looks like a member of the Trask Lo Boyz Vietnamese gang out of Westminster, Orange County."

Craig's eyes narrowed. That sounded like Little Saigon. Brent jumped on it. "Any idea why he was out here?"

"We don't have motive at this point. The gang's got numerous suspected homicides in their file, but nothing's stuck. And they were all inter-gang activity – nothing like this."

"Drug related?"

"Strong possible. They move opioids, methamphetamine, and heroin. DEA has signatured some of their product as southeast Asian, but most of it comes from Mexico. They traffic for Chinese organized crime out of LA."

"The DEA give up any of Romero's case file?" Craig fished.

Cecil stared back longer than normally, then shook his head.

"They were unusually forthcoming on this one. They have no idea. Said whatever Romero was working on, he hadn't logged it in."

It was Craig's turn to stare.

He'd seen it before. Agents working on private cases, hobby projects. It was usually background on something tentative that could develop into a full-blown investigation later on. Generally, it caused no harm, as long as the effort was out of work hours and didn't involve agency resources.

But Transvector? Craig almost whistled at the audacity.

Where it could, and often did, go wrong was when a so-called pet project became an obsession, the kind you'd spend every waking minute on. Then the lines became blurred, and perspective went out the door. In cases like that, sometimes management would find out months later that their agency had committed significant men and materiel, often under the rubric of other investigations. Craig had been personally involved in cleaning a few of those up before they went public or attracted the attention of Justice Department's Inspector General. It wasn't completely kosher according to ethical guidelines, but then again no one wanted Congress to get involved, especially around budget time.

But the misuse of resources was hardly the key issue here. Maverick agents left little or no breadcrumbs to follow, let alone a paper trail, so there were no leads for anyone else to pick up. And they rarely called for backup, fearing discovery.

Brent looked at Craig and shook his head. "Ok, what else?"

"Romero doesn't have a partner assigned, according to their staffing, and they don't have a file on anyone named Stokes."

"Think it's a cover ID for a CI?"

"They can't say. The check on Romero's files didn't turn up any confidential informants matching the description either. We're going to download the motel and dash-cam footage from the sheriff's office, see if we can get anything. But," Cecil's mouth puckered, "that's going to take some time."

Brent expelled a frustrated breath. "Well, that's why they pay us next to nothing. What about Romero's pilot informant...uh," he looked at his notes, "...Cook?"

"Unknown."

"Looks like he took off at the same time as Stokes."

"What happened there?"

"After the hit team took down Romero, somebody popped a couple flash-bangs into the space from the adjoining room, and then finished the crew off with

300 Blackout ammunition, according to shell casings collected on site. The crime techs are still working on the scene, but they think it was probably Cook or Stokes."

Craig mulled on that for a moment. 300 Blackout. Now that was something you didn't see every day. It was a specialized cartridge that could be loaded for super- or sub-sonic applications. Supersonic, it hit with the force of an AK round, and had better terminal ballistics than the standard 5.56mm rounds that AR-15s used. The subsonic ammunition that was usually used with a suppressor. Craig frowned in thought. Definitely not standard DEA issue. Typically, only special operations personnel or extreme enthusiasts used that caliber, and it was expensive.

"What are we doing on them?" Brent asked.

"Federal BOLOs with full descriptors – images in Cook's case." Cecil used the common law enforcement acronym for 'Be-On-the-Look-Out'.

"Good. I want to question the other crew members as soon as possible." Brent looked down at a sheaf of papers while Craig caught something in Cecil's face.

"What don't we know, Cecil?"

Cecil looked at Craig and the others and shrugged sheepishly. "The rest of the crew is…uh…missing."

Brent jerked up, straightening in his seat, and surveyed his team.

"How's that?"

Cecil reddened, and looked around for support. None of the others seemed inclined to jump in.

"It appears that a couple of Homeland Security agents picked them up about an hour ago for questioning." He nodded convincingly. "We're trying to run that down right now."

Craig leaned back, pursing his lips. In his experience, whenever three or more startlingly coincidental events occurred in succession, somebody was running something in the background. The Transvector-CIA link was never far from the front of his mind. Three company planes crash, a federal agent is murdered, and the surviving crew disappears off the map – from this very airport.

Brent turned to Craig.

"I've got to stay here and get the command post set up – we've got about fifty agents heading out this way right now. We'll work from here and back at the residency. Since you're the expert on contractors, I want you to get back on the chopper for a bright and early sit down with Transvector's CEO – wait, scratch that. I want the company's chairman...whatever his name is…Haskett."

Cecil interjected. "Hallett."

"Right. TVA will give you the runaround, so go through the NSA branch Executive Assistant Director's staff and ask them to notify the CIA liaison." He stood and looked down at the team. "And I don't want you sitting across the table from some ass-licking TVA lawyer. If Hallett's not available, I want someone from the C-level or the board who we can handcuff and frog march to the lockup if I find out they're lying. Understood?"

Craig stood, gathering his belongings. "Got it."

"You're back with ASAC Simms, unless he attaches you here again. Keep your phone handy – I may have some follow ups on these squirrels."

Craig grinned. "Break a leg, guys. I think we're all in for a long one."

* * *

Stokes' face was pale as she maintained a white-knuckled grip on the glare shield of the instrument panel and braced firmly with her right hand against the padded ceiling on the passenger side of the cockpit.

The Cessna 172 was buffeting hard in the ground turbulence coming off the rooftops of buildings only a hundred feet or so below. Cook was flying just high enough to avoid getting snagged on power lines, occasionally climbing to ensure clearance. An abundance of light from the street grid below provided ample warning of upcoming obstructions.

Cook knew from previous airshow flights with Bellamy's museum collection that the aerial radar in the Los Angeles basin couldn't reliably acquire returns under about 150 feet. Everything below that got lost in the ground noise. Individual airports could see targets below that altitude on approach, but he had deliberately chosen a circuitous route into the area that avoided those zones. Skimming the northern edge of the mountains surrounding the basin had brought them to within about ten miles of downtown.

Upon departure from Thermal, Cook had headed south and then east, looping counterclockwise through the Joshua Tree National Park and staying as low as practicable to avoid detection by the Marine air-ground combat center at Twentynine Palms. The area was almost as dark as Mexico had been, but this time he flew without the benefit of night vision equipment or ground interrogating radar. The little Cessna had a moving map tablet that made the flight survivable, if not easy. Some of the peaks had antenna towers with flashing red beacons, which helped him avoid piling into the dirt, but it was still a nerve-wracking flight in the pitch blackness. He skirted around the northeast slopes of the San Bernardino mountains, using Big Bear and Arrowhead as navigation points, and ducked back into the Los Angeles airspace by following vehicle lights on Interstate 15 south through the Cajon pass.

If anyone had seen them leave Thermal, they might've thought he was heading toward Arizona. Cook didn't expect the ruse to fool their pursuers for any great length of time – hopefully just long enough to clear the area where he was planning on ditching the plane.

Another severe lurch elicited a yelp from Stokes. "What the hell, Guy? How much longer are we doing this?"

Cook pointed straight ahead through the windshield. "There. We're down in thirty seconds."

Stokes followed his finger to a patch of darkness in the lit cityscape with a languidly rotating green-and-white beacon. "I thought we were staying away from airports."

Cook snorted tightly as he fought the yoke. "Who said we're landing at an airport?"

They were flying down the darkened median strip of a wide, divided boulevard, just above streetlamp and powerline level, when he threw the Cessna into a crushing right bank that brought them roughly in line with the dimly lit threshold of a runway with a large '19' painted on it. Stokes, who had been peering below, screeched as she smacked her head against the Plexiglas window.

"Asshole! How about a goddamned warning…?"

She trailed off as they coasted over the short, latticed-fenced railing on the edge of a bridge overpass and plunged into a dark crevasse.

Los Angeles is a perennially arid coastal city, possessing few natural waterways of any size. Those that do exist tend to be highly seasonal, ranging in volume from turgid flows in April to stagnant trickles in late August. During the fierce, brief downpours that periodically pummel the California southland, flashfloods that can toss cars and disintegrate housing occasionally manifest. As a consequence, the majority of the basin watershed has been corralled into broad, concrete flood-control channels that safely, if wastefully, convey the raging brown flood waters to the Pacific Ocean.

Conveniently for Cook, the Rio Hondo River channel in El Monte ran exactly parallel to the El Monte airport and was in fact a good stretch longer than the active runway itself. Past conversations with warbird pilots at the local coffee shop after airshows had speculated on whether it could function adequately as an emergency landing strip. He had never seriously considered that he would have the chance to find out.

As Cook snapped on the landing lights, Stokes gasped with alarm at the rusty brown glimmer reflecting off the thin sheet of water on the channel floor. Cook flared hard and cut the engine and lights. They wallowed above the murk for a few moments, the channel shimmering a faint silver-gray strip in the ambience of streetlights. The wind whispering around the wing struts was the only sound.

Contact with the channel bottom jarred the cockpit, tossing the charts and checklists into the air. Cook gritted his teeth as a spray of brown muck piled up on the windscreen, and he fought to keep the aircraft straight against the tug of water against the wheels. Clumps of wet grass, sand and wood debris rattled them violently on rollout.

Cook held the yoke back to keep the front wheel light so they wouldn't do a nose-stand in the channel, and rode out the landing without using the brakes. After about fifteen seconds, the plane began to slow noticeably. Cook continued letting the plane roll until they approached a railroad trestle crossing the canal. He then alternated on the pedals to steer the Cessna toward the gap between two concrete bridge supports before mashing them to the floor, bringing the plane to an abrupt halt.

The air in the cockpit was tropical with sweat and smelled faintly of sewage. Cook unbuckled his harness and cracked the cabin door. He stepped down onto the gear leg footrest, then turned and indicated to Stokes for her to do the same quietly.

Off in the distance a dog barked repeatedly, but otherwise there was nothing unusual about the sounds of the city traveling down into the channel. Cook remained still and listened for a full thirty seconds. He then leaned against the warm engine cowl and whispered across the nose to Stokes.

"Help me push it under the trestle." She nodded, her eyes still wide.

For all its size, the 172 Skyhawk is a fairly light plane for a four-seater, and the struts angling down from the high wing offered a convenient place to push. The slight downward inclination in the concrete channel bottom made it easier as well. Within a minute, the two of them were shaded from the streetlamps by the trestle bridge.

Stokes looked tense. "They're going to find this as soon as it gets light. Where are we?"

"El Monte. East of downtown."

"Good. There's a Metro station here somewhere – be a good place to look for a car."

"Where you planning on going?"

"Better you don't know. What about you?"

Cook stared down the channel toward the ocean for a moment, marshalling his thoughts. He had had a vague idea of going to Hallett's compound and beating the truth out of the old man. But other than envisioning punching his tanned face several times in quick succession and kicking him in the junk for good measure, Cook realized he'd overlooked some of the practical details, like how to get there, how to break in, and how to find out whether Hallett was in town at all. He realized he was tired, too tired to think clearly. He needed someplace to rest and think. He looked back at Stokes.

She seemed to be studying him, her eyes narrowed and her mouth thin. He could still see the tension around her eyes and in her clenched jaw, but her expression appeared to have softened somewhat, eroding her formerly inscrutable streamlined façade. She shifted the strap of the gear bag to a more comfortable position on her shoulder.

"Why don't you come with me for a while? I've got a place you can crash, then I can drop you somewhere later."

He searched her eyes, not sure to trust what he'd just heard.

"Don't you need to run?"

She nodded, her mouth pursed as if she was assessing something.

"Yeah, but you got me to LA. Gotta be worth something, huh?"

* * *

The floor-to-ceiling wainscoting in the hushed boardroom was polished, quarter-sawn oak, flaunting a ribbony ray fleck across the finely striated grain.

Very classy. Craig had once been given a tutorial by a Hungarian forger who fronted as an antiques dealer during a lull in a hostile interview. Still somewhat bewildered that he had been caught by people he thought little better than uncultured savages, the refined felon had sought to preserve what was left of his dignity by showing off his deep knowledge of quality woodwork. He said quarter-sawn was the best cut to prevent warping and shrinkage, and thus ideal for fine furniture, musical instruments and decorative wood paneling.

It was also extremely expensive, just like the rest of the room's appointments. Craig could see the reflection of his hands resting on the highly polished mahogany conference table. It had a rich, red-brown translucence that was almost hypnotic in depth. Covering the floor was a thick, luxuriant burgundy pile that left visible footprints when trod upon and absorbed any stray sounds.

Craig had been waiting for twenty-five minutes in this sanctum of gentility and was starting to get impatient. A finely monogrammed porcelain cup on matching saucer sat empty next to his right elbow, its aromatic Arabic brew long-ago consumed. A blank scratchpad topped by a heavy Transvector pen sat next to his tablet and smartphone to the left.

Craig gazed around the walls, trying to submerge his bone-deep fatigue in the detail-absorption process. In his experience, you never knew what evidence might break a case. The framed pictures on the windowless walls were a black-and-white timeline of the previous century's military aviation milestones: a formation of Mustangs over Europe, a F-4 Phantom in Thailand, a Lockheed U2 on the ramp at Lancaster.

After finalizing his investigative strategy with Brent in Palm Springs, Craig had boarded the helicopter for west Los Angeles where Transvector Worldwide's corporate headquarters was located. During the short flight back to what was essentially the same place he had departed earlier that morning, Craig brushed away his torpor and tried to digest an agency précis on Hallett he had downloaded to his tablet.

The file described the career of a consummate and agile Cold War corporate player, a hard charger with the perspicacity to foresee the possibilities afforded to the risk-savvy in the aftermath of Vietnam by the growing conflict between the COMBLOC countries and the West.

Hallett had started as an Air America pilot, and then transferred to become a covert logistics manager in Thailand and Laos, running weapons, cash and supplies from Udorn and Nakhon Phanom to the Hmong hill tribes fighting the Pathet Lao and Viet Minh. Though not explicitly mentioned in the record, it was also likely that he transported the guerillas' opium base from the mountain poppy fields to the heroin refinement labs in northern Thailand. All above board at the time, when anything was game in the clandestine skirmishes with the communists.

When the US covert effort folded in 1975 and the CIA divested itself of an airline that had brought it an embarrassing amount of profit as a legitimate carrier, Hallett and an unnamed group of investors picked up the fixed-wing assets at cents on the dollar, essentially continuing the same operations under different management. The file intimated that the CIA provided the seed funding that put Hallett in business.

A lengthy list of operations in which the company was involved followed, putting Transvector alongside every major theatre of the US-Soviet conflict: Korea, Angola, Guatemala, Nicaragua, Honduras, Afghanistan – the list went on and on. Craig was hard-pressed to recall one Third World hotspot where TVA didn't have some form of participation. The cozy government-corporate alliance served both parties, keeping Transvector solvent with sweetheart contracts and providing the clandestine operators with built-in, hands off deniability.

Very tidy, Craig thought, as his annoyance grew unharmoniously in the stately chamber. And I could use some more coffee. If someone doesn't show up to talk in about two minutes, he promised, extending the interior monologue, I'm going to start handing out subpoenas just for effect.

ASAC Simms had greenlighted Craig's return with hasty assent, having other things on his plate. Usually, FBI agents didn't conduct interviews solo, but almost all of Simms's available able-bodied personnel were headed out to the desert. Craig was fine with that. Any Bureau newbie unfamiliar with the wily ways of Agency contractors would be easily rolled by TVA, and Craig, though a trainer by profession, currently didn't have the patience to shepherd some neophyte on his maiden foray.

No sound penetrated the room beyond the soothing purr of the air-conditioning, which was threatening to put him to sleep. The board room was located in the center of a six-storey rectangular block-shaped building, one of four in the broad, well-manicured grounds of an older corporate cluster near the San Diego freeway. By the look of it, Craig could tell it had been developed in the late Sixties – lots of solid concrete and plate-glass windows fronting the exterior. He had gotten a good look at it earlier that morning as his helicopter spiraled down to a landing on one of the rooftop helipads.

The style might have been dated, but the security measures had obviously kept up with the times. Thermal imaging equipment was evident in abundance, and the landscaped frontages had been updated with tasteful concrete bollards to foil vehicular incursion. The cluster was a non-descript fortress in the midst of gaudier corporate neighbors.

The boardroom itself was a throwback to the days when interior chambers with acoustic ceiling paneling and padded doors were state of the art protection against eavesdropping. However, Craig could also sense active quieting systems by the flattened sound of the ventilation fans. He surmised it would be a good place to hold a private conversation.

Without warning, a door opened opposite his seat, and Hallett entered with a man Craig recognized from his background reading as Transvector's CIA liaison. Clarence Veidt was a Yale lawyer and éminence grise who had worked on the fringes of the national security community for better than forty years, serving a few presidents along the way. He'd be sharp, Craig opined blearily as he rose to meet them, and I'm running short on caffeine. He could already tell by Veidt's pursed expression that the conversation wasn't going to be light and sunny.

Hallett looked all of his seventy-three years in the early morning, his ashy skin almost matching his light grey hair. Age had somewhat reduced what had obviously been a bear-like frame, but he still made an imposing presence. He leaned across the conference table, extending a large, veiny hand.

"I'm sorry to have kept you waiting, Mr. Craig. Clarence was just briefing me on the latest developments. Would you like some more coffee?"

"As long as it comes quickly. I'd prefer to get started." Craig's kept his expression non-committal as he shook. Veidt had probably been outlining to Hallett the phrases he should avoid uttering, so he couldn't be accused of perjury. Veidt confirmed Craig's intuition by jumping in first.

"Very well, Agent Craig, but I'd first like to point out that...."

"Mr. Veidt," Craig interrupted smoothly, "I'd prefer to direct my questions and receive answers directly from Mr. Hallett." He smiled aggressively. "You of course may advise your client before he responds."

Veidt was clearly not used to being cut off.

"*Special Agent Craig.* Let me explain to you how this is going to work. You do not have the clearance or authority to...."

Craig patiently let Veidt run on, at length, about the clandestine nature of the company's relationship with the intelligence community that precluded them sharing anything in detail with the FBI. He nodded agreeably as the lawyer went on to explain how all communication would, regrettably, have to first pass through CIA counsel. Veidt concluded with a "...and furthermore, nothing in this informal interview will be placed on record."

What a douchebag.

"Mr. Veidt," he said with a tranquility he wasn't currently feeling, "a federal agent investigating your firm has been murdered, one of your employees is wanted for a federal investigation, and three of your company aircraft are burning on a mountainside and sopping up the resources of at least two county fire departments, not to mention the California Department of Forestry. If we find *any* corporate culpability on your part on *any* of these issues, your charmed CIA connections are going to forget your phone numbers. I think it would be in your best interest to give me as much cooperation as possible at this stage."

Hallett, who had been watching the back-and-forth interchange between the two men with a weary impatience, interjected.

"Clarence, give it a rest." His rheumy eyes fixed on Craig.

"We've got as little or less than you do on this." He looked as tired as Craig was. "I was in the middle of a pleasant sleep in Telluride when the call came, and just got in about two hours ago. *En route*, I spoke to our operations section – every hand on deck is working this situation, and so far, they've got nothing."

In previous dealings with covert operators, Craig was accustomed to hearing half-truths, runarounds, outright lies, and other assorted deceits. He also had a good ear for salient omissions, relevant exclusions, and the studied pauses that were practically confessions in themselves. But he sensed none of that here, just Hallett's obvious fatigue and Veidt's tooth-grating manner. He shook off some of his own lethargy by sipping at his quietly refilled coffee and jumped ahead a few squares. If Transvector hadn't helmed this shipwreck, who in the hell had?

"Tell me what you know."

Hallett nodded at Veidt, whose expression took on a somber cast.

"The aircraft were tasked for a covert CIA/DEA spray operation at Guadalajara. They had been down there for a couple months doing bug control on Sierra

Madre timber for the USDA. Langley came to us with the concept, and brought along Blair as part of the package."

"Sorry – who?"

"Preston Blair. Young prick the Agency dropped on us to liaise for contract work. Annoying as hell. And," Veidt added, casually, "incidentally, he's dropped off the map."

"Come again?" Craig asked in astonishment. The main players were dropping like flies. In another couple of days, there'd be no one left. He banished the groggy thought.

Veidt nodded resignedly. "Exactly. Can't find him – read that as you like."

He continued.

"Blair was in charge of the teams getting the herbicide down there and upgrading the navigation system to the latest Milspec." Veidt glanced again at Hallett, as if concerned about his next statement. "Word from Porter…was that he was difficult to work with."

"Porter?"

"Ted Porter. Special operations director. He was on one of the aircraft."

Craig's fleeting look up from the notes he was taking caught Hallett staring sadly at his hands, which were clasped together on the darkly varnished tabletop. "Go on."

Veidt raised his eyebrows and spread his palms like a Vegas casino dealer changing shifts. "That's all we're working with. The sat-linked telemetry on the flight was normal, including the mission abort update after one of the birds caught hostile fire and took some damage."

He paused, looking towards Hallett yet again. "There was one last satellite update before the aircraft impacted the mountain, and it didn't come from us."

Craig frowned, studying both men. "Where did it come from?"

"We won't know until we get the black boxes," Veidt shrugged, "and we won't see those until the fires are out."

"We'll need to be included on that."

"Of course."

Craig sat back, expressionless, but was gratifyingly shocked and even a bit alarmed at the level of cooperation he was receiving. In his experience, intelligence contractors were notoriously reluctant to share anything with the FBI, invariably claiming some sort of national security exemption and deferring questions to their parent sponsoring organization. He was starting to warm to the idea that TVA might actually be an unwitting actor in this cascading farce. But empathy could be dangerous; he had to remain objective.

"Ok. What about Victor Romero?"

Veidt shrugged. "We have never heard of him. No paper whatsoever."

Craig squinted, not ready to give up on that one so easily. He slid his tablet displaying sheriff dash-cam photos of Romero and Stokes across to Hallett. They had been transmitted to him in the helicopter. "You heard he was looking at your firm, right, for narcotics? And got taken out by professionals?"

"Literally nothing," Veidt stated, shaking his head. He slid the tablet back.

There was a pause while Craig checked his notes. He directed his attention to Hallett.

"You do work in Asia?

"Lots of work. Why?"

"Any reason someone over there would be interested in doing you a favor, or making you look bad?"

Hallett shrugged. "We lose money every year just trying to maintain market share. Everyone's palm needs greasing, and ground crews steal fuel straight out of our wing tanks and sell it back to us at a profit."

"Thank you," Craig proffered, to fill the silence, underlining something on his pad. He looked up and paused, as if unsure exactly how to proceed. "How would you describe Porter's role in all of this?"

Hallett started from his reverie, as if he'd been awoken from a nap.

"Porter?" he stopped, his face wan, then resumed. "Porter was pissed about working with Blair, but he follows orders – always did...."

"He was your operations manager? Did he usually take part in air operations?"

"No. He was scheduled to fly back with Blair on one of the company jets after the mission flight departed." Hallett's grin was wistful. "I assume he didn't want to have to listen to that insufferable ass-hat all the way back to Mojave."

Craig frowned ruefully at the irony. "I take it the company jet did make it back?"

Veidt nodded. "Blair changed the flight plan mid-way and had himself dropped at Phoenix Sky

Harbor at 1 am. No one's seen or heard from him since."

"What did the CIA tell you?"

"Nothing so far."

Interesting, thought Craig. Next stop, Langley. Was the CIA stowing gangways and buttoning up the ship? His rapidly scribbled notes were bordering on the illegible as he flipped the page and started on a new one. His discreetly recording tablet would provide fill-ins, as necessary.

"What can you tell me about the crew that did make it – uh…Kane, Cook, and the rest?"

Here Veidt seemed to find surer ground, dispensing with his customary glance at Hallett before responding.

"Ron Kane has been flying with the company for over twenty-five years and is solid as a rock. Hendricks and Barowicz are also long-termers, proficient in cargo logistics and systems – Hendricks has an A&P rating with an inspection authorization."

Craig looked up from his writing. "And Guy Cook?"

Veidt paused for a moment, as if carefully choosing his words. "Mr. Cook was a former employee who was recently rehired."

Craig's antennae twitched. He regarded Hallett. "Former employee? Why'd you let him go?"

Hallett looked at Veidt, who nodded.

"There was an incident with a cargo flight, involving drug smuggling." Hallett pursed his lips. "There were four crew on board, and it wasn't clear who was responsible." He paused again. "We had to let all of them go."

Craig kept scribbling. "What kind of drugs?"

Hallett looked at Veidt, who assisted. "Methamphetamine. You won't have it in your files. We took care of it internally."

Craig scrutinized the two men, then focused on Hallett.

"Does this sort of thing happen often with you?"

Veidt interjected. "That's uncalled for, Agent Craig."

Craig acknowledged the rebuke. "Fair enough. Is there anyone else in your company I can talk to, maybe someone who worked with Cook?"

Rather than responding, Hallett looked at Veidt. "Did you call him?"

"He's awake…barely. Not real happy about it, though."

Hallett looked back to Craig. "There's a car outside for you. We're sending you over to Bellamy. He can tell you anything you need to know about Cook."

Craig frowned. "I'd prefer to talk with him here."

Hallett's expression was regretful. "So would we, but you'll get more out of him on his own turf."

* * *

Cook stared at a chipped, painted concrete floor that had originally might have been colored burgundy, but had been pummeled by grease, dirt and countless shoe soles into a textured patina resembling the bottom of a dirty garbage can. He scraped one of his boot heels to the side and left a stripe. Disgusted, Cook stared at his hands in his lap while Stokes talked down the hallway.

It turned out they didn't have to go as far as the El Monte Metro station to find a car. There was heavily Bondo-ed black Acura almost waiting for them in the parking lot of a window factory a hundred yards south of the railroad trestle. The windows had a bad purplish tint job with lots of bubbles, and there was no lock on the driver-side door. It was the perfect ride to blend in with the locals.

Stokes' contact was a fence called Holman, and he ran his business out of the back of a *carniceria* off West Adams, southwest of downtown.

Cook tried to overhear their hissed conversation while he focused his attention to the '*Hecho en Mexico*' canned goods on the shelf in front of him. It didn't seem to be going well. Holman, apparently, didn't have a lot of friends…and really didn't like *friends* of friends. He heard some emphatic negatives expressed as he surveyed the label of a can of '*La Morena*' pinto beans, not daring to look over for fear of spoiling the deal.

In the past, when in a particularly Latino part of LA, Cook had occasionally marveled how much it felt like being in Mexico. Trash pressed along the street fences, the reek of strange cleaning products, Aztec eagle symbols, the cloying stench of pineapple, cinnamon and hibiscus. If it wasn't for the reasonably maintained asphalt road surfaces and the street signs in English, he would sometimes forget he was in the States.

The conversation in the hallway had broken a bit, and out of the corner of his eye Cook could see Holman on a cell phone, a finger pressed tightly to his ear as if there were a lot of ambient noise, or the person on the other end was speaking softly. After a jerky nod or two, Holman signed off and faced Stokes. "*Bueno.*"

They conspired again for a moment while Cook moved his attention to a small glass bottle labeled '*El Yucateco*', which looked to contain an extremely hot green chile sauce. His eyes went vacant for a moment, thinking about a really good burrito he had eaten with Kane at a dingy hole-in-the-wall in Los Mochis – the scorching sauce had left him without the ability to taste for a good five minutes.

Kane. Cook sighed, wondering what was happening to his friend. Probably nothing good. The only thing working in Kane's favor was that he knew nothing, about Romero, Stokes, or anyone else. Cook hoped they weren't making it too hard on him.

Thinking of the burrito made him hungry. Cook glanced to the rear of the shop where a couple of butchers were dismantling a side of beef. Might make good hamburger, he thought. God he was hungry. A machete like cleaver struck downward a joint, neatly parting it. Cook looked around, as if in a daze. What in the hell were they doing here? It looked like a perfect place to get chopped up and put in a garbage sack.

Stokes jogged his shoulder. "We're moving."

* * *

They parked behind Holman in an alley about ten minutes' drive from the butchery, near a sign restricting parking to an '*Iglesia de la Santa Cruz*'. Cook's mood improved for a moment; after all, how bad could it be if they were meeting in a church? Neutral, even sacred, ground. Then the back door opened, spilling a dim red light onto the grease-stained asphalt and framing a muscular, shaven-headed giant wearing a dark wife-beater undershirt, who displayed extensive tattooing on all his visible skin surfaces. Cook's earlier relief evaporated into an ever-refilling reservoir of over-used adrenalin.

Stokes had some really terrifying friends, he decided, as he slowly got out of the Acura, his every move vigilantly observed by the hulking door minder. What the hell had she been into before she hooked up with Romero? The tattoos on the giant's arms were all prison-style, either indicating a lengthy period of incarceration, or just a high tolerance to pain during a short bid.

As he and Stokes were escorted down the ruddy hallway, the drug-blown eyes of overly made-up and underage Latina hookers peered out of dark doorways to either side, and then quickly retreated. So, not really a church, Cook reflected, but probably a lot of prayers and genuflecting going on, though not necessarily at the same time. An outpost on the prostitution-slavery trail from the southern border. Stokes' face was impassive as she strode ahead of him. Had she been in the trade at some point too?

Another enormous, tatted thug with a dark Mohawk patch crowning his shaved dome blocked a door at the far end, and Holman surged forward to whisper rapidly in his ear.

Cook slowed his pace, hanging behind Stokes until he felt something heavy and metallic prod him in the ribs from behind. Not looking good at all. This had all the hallmarks of a hastily-arranged execution – Holman had probably just been stalling to find a suitable, and suitably quiet, location.

As the group crowded up in front of the still closed door, Cook perceived a momentary tactical advantage. At this proximity, no one could move easily, and any shots fired would likely hit everyone in the scrum. He discreetly drew a deep breath to saturate his muscles for action. This opportunity might not come again. A sidelong glance at the stubbled neck of the thug next to him gave him his opening – he'd strike with a left backhand chop to the throat, then pivot right and trap the gun to his midsection. But what, then? His brawling skills rusty, Cook decided he probably wouldn't live through it, but felt like he had to do something.

He felt an extremely firm grip on his left forearm. It was Stokes signaling him to remain still. She must have sensed his heightened tension, or heard something change in his breathing.

A muffled voice, sounding confident and authoritative, issued an unintelligible command from the next room. Holman briefly glanced at his two captives, his expression taut with anxiety and something Cook couldn't decipher, and then nodded at the heavy with the Mohawk, who quickly pulled a slide bolt and pushed the door open. Bright yellow light flooded the hallway.

Over the threshold, Cook could see the outline of a figure with his back turned. The man wore dark slacks and an expensive-looking walnut suede jacket, which seemed out of place with the gang-style attire all around him. He seemed to be more concerned with talking to the people in the room than his visitors in the hallway.

Then he turned, and Cook's heart skipped a beat in shock. It was the sharp-looking Mexican official from Guadalajara.

* * *

CHAPTER TWELVE

Bellamy sucked down the dregs of his third cup of coffee and slapped it down on the Formica tabletop with a clatter. "Ok, I'm awake. What do you want?"

Craig had met the groggy and unshaven older man in the back of a coffee shop off West Pico in Santa Monica, the apparently safe ground described by Hallett and Veidt. The décor was dated and worn, given a washed-out and pallid cast by banks of fluorescent panels in the dropped acoustic ceiling. While the front rooms of the restaurant had been updated to resemble an idealized image of a 1950s American Graffiti diner, the rear stayed faithful to the original look of that era. Chipped tables worn shiny by the elbows of countless Elks lodge patrons were surrounded by battered chrome-legged diner chairs and cracked burgundy vinyl banquettes.

An insulated black urn of coffee rested between the two men, which Bellamy was steadily emptying, apparently on the theory that sufficiently large amounts of caffeine rapidly warded off morning inebriety. Without betraying any indication in his expression on what he thought about that particular belief, Craig had waited patiently until the older man had swilled enough brew to assure what he must have considered adequate functionality. After Bellamy's comment, Craig grinned accommodatingly and poised his pen over a fresh sheet of notepad.

"What can you tell me about Ted Porter?"

"He's dead," Bellamy frowned, gazing around the room as if he had just discovered where he was. One of Hallett's clean-cut young men in a dark polo shirt had deposited the older man into the room about five minutes earlier, then gone to the front to join Craig's driver at the front counter. "Gave him a hell of a sendoff last night."

"How was he as a co-worker?"

"What are you writing, his obituary? Good operator, dedicated to *the work*." Bellamy put emphasis on the latter statement as if he were describing a religious calling.

Craig nodded as if he understood. "Did you get any indication how he felt about the upcoming job transition with, uh…," he glanced at his notes, "Blair?"

Bellamy's frown deepened into a scowl.

"Thought he was a limp-wristed ass-suck like everyone else." He started on his fourth cup of coffee. "I never met him, but no one made much secret of that."

"Do you think Porter is likely to have been involved in any criminal activity?"

Bellamy's eyes narrowed and his face flushed as he half-rose from his seat, glaring at Craig, his frame trembling.

"You *trying* to piss me off, gumshoe?"

Craig raised a hand in supplication, backpedaling. "I had to ask, Mr. Bellamy. Please. No disrespect was intended." He motioned toward the banquette, "Please."

Bellamy sat heavily, his face still suffused with blood, the effort apparently exhausting to him. He shook his head wearily. "Porter didn't like it any more than I did when they shoved me out." He reached out a gnarled finger across the table and tapped Craig's notepad. "But Ted was a *real American*." The last was uttered with the same reverence Bellamy had used to describe *the work*. "You take it as it comes — like a man — and cry into your drink later." Bellamy leaned back again, much to Craig's appreciation. "*That* answer your question?"

Satisfied he'd gotten all he was going to get on the matter, Craig nodded. "What about Guy Cook?"

Another squint from the watery red eyes. "What's he done now?"

It was Craig's turn to shrug.

"We don't really know at this point, and we want to talk to him." Craig paused, calculating that some give-and-take might elicit better results from Bellamy. "We actually can't find him — he's totally in the wind."

The old man snorted. "Kid's done a runner on you, huh?"

Craig feigned a sheepishness that wasn't entirely contrived. "Yup."

"Hah. Boy's got good instincts, that's for sure."

Craig jumped on the comment. "How so?"

Bellamy tilted his head back, his expression reminiscent. "One of the most talented sticks I've ever

271

seen. Fly anything in any conditions, anywhere. But rash, and pigheaded when he wanted to be." Bellamy smirked at some private memory. "He'd just as soon get himself in a fix as out of one."

Craig made an encouraging grunt. It seemed to work with Bellamy, who grunted a lot himself.

"He's a survivor. Had to put down a couple of times in some hot spots, and made it out...more or less in one piece."

"Was that Nicaragua?"

Bellamy paused, snapping back to the present and eyeing Craig carefully. "What're you cleared for?"

"Pretty much everything, at this point."

Bellamy nodded, apparently satisfied.

"We used to put guys that showed talent through the same forward operator's course that the customers use – escape and evasion, forward air control, counter-surveillance, weapons, communications, the usual. We set it up under the cover of smokejumper training in remote areas. Cook was a natural. Got to use it a few times." Bellamy became wistful again. "He did some real hairball shit down there in Honduras, saved a lot of guys' asses."

"What do you know about his work after he left Transvector?"

"This and that." Fatigue had crept back into Bellamy's gaze. "Heard he was working the racing circuit. Speed merchant."

Craig snorted, smirking as he wrote. "That's appropriate."

He instantly regretted it.

Bellamy's eyes sharpened, and his visage reddened again. "Don't make my already low opinion of you any worse, *Agent*," he snapped. "That was just bad luck. He was flying with some known shitheads."

Craig made another placatory gesture.

"Sorry. Haven't had a lot of sleep lately." He took a deep sip of his own coffee, savoring the acidic bite and feeling a complete lack of effect. "What's a 'speed merchant'?"

"A train out of Boston…what do you think, flat-foot?" Bellamy chuckled at his own humor. "Airplane tuner. Makes birds go faster, for racing. Takes a stock warbird frame, cuts down the weight, adds horse-power." The old man smiled slightly. "Cook was a good wrench, and a talented fabricator, when he wanted to be."

Craig suddenly needed to get out of the dingy dining room, feel sunlight on his face.

"How can we find him?"

"Why'd he run?"

Craig found himself adopting Bellamy's terse, clipped speech.

"It's a bit foggy, but it looks like he was on the sidelines of a professional hit. On a federal agent."

Bellamy pursed his lips, nodding. "He'll go to ground, wait 'til the dust clears." He paused. "If he's got some help, he may try to backtrack, you know… hunt the hunters. I don't know…."

Bellamy trailed off, staring at the wall.

"Think he'd contact you?"

"Maybe." Bellamy's expression was once again vacant.

"Think you could call me if he did?"

Bellamy rolled his head around his shoulders a couple of times. Then he belched, releasing a whiskey smell. Craig wasn't sure he had heard the question.

"You got a card?"

* * *

The room was as swelteringly hot as the hallway had been, and suffused with the stench of adrenalin, testosterone, and too many male bodies on high-protein diets. But the sweat Cook felt on his scalp and palms was chilly. The fact that he was restrained, and his arms were duct-taped behind his back, didn't help.

Cook was taped to a scratched metal folding chair, in an otherwise unfurnished room. Quick glances as he was walked in showed him some tables and more folding chairs stacked in the corners. The floor was covered with cheap white vinyl tiles stained a dull gray from long use. He guessed from the room's small size that if this place actually fronted as some kind of barrio church, they were in an anteroom or meeting room behind the main gathering hall.

Stokes had been led away as soon as they entered the room. She hadn't looked happy, and seemed uncharacteristically passive in her demeanor towards the current company.

The Mexican government official no longer wore a suit, but he still managed to look dapper despite the surroundings. The tobacco suede jacket he wore over a French blue button-down shirt was well-cut, thin, and obviously expensive. His dark straight hair was still immaculately coiffed and conveyed the impression that the man was at home in any circumstances. His expression, however, was grim, and a slight red tinge in the corner of each eye betrayed that, like many others, he hadn't gotten a lot of sleep lately.

The fact that nobody had bothered to hide their faces ratcheted up Cook's anxiety level further. It indicated that his host didn't care what Cook saw. He shuddered, his thoughts running back to Holman's butcher shop. Was that where he was headed after they beat whatever they could out of him?

The crew that had escorted them down the hallway stood in a loose semi-circle behind the government official, if that's what he even was. Their expressions were tense, ranging from a confusing, wary tension to outright hostility. A couple of better-dressed minions, openly armed and covering the official, hovered at the back wall. Holman, standing toward the rear, looked almost sick with anxiety. What the hell's eating him, Cook wondered. At least he was standing.

To Cook, the gathering uncomfortably reminded him of the few CIA interrogations of Sandinistas he had witnessed in Honduras. He had been brought in a couple of times after the hard stuff to evaluate any aviation-related intelligence. They had always asked him to step out of the room before continuing. Cook had never forgotten the pleading expressions, the hopeless eyes, and wondered if he would look like that.

The Mexican official broke the silence. His tone was gently modulated, almost friendly, but his eyes were expressionless.

"Mr. Cook, I'm going to ask you some questions, and it is very important you tell me everything you know. Your future treatment depends on how you respond." He paused, glancing at what looked like a gold Rolex on his left wrist. "We have very little time."

Cook knew from his basic interrogation-resistance course, and a limited amount of real-world experience with this sort of thing, that emotional pleading was of little use, unless you needed to buy a few extra minutes of time. Usually, the interrogators would politely listen for half a minute, then proceed to do what they were going to do anyway. But he had no backup coming, so no point in that. Maintaining the respect of the questioner was key, and maybe even to appear interesting.

Cook also sensed that he might have something to trade. The fact that he was alive was one clue. And while he could think of a number of questions he'd like to ask concerning his personal wellbeing, he decided to focus on the Mexican's latter statement.

"What's the rush?"

"There are a number of groups actively looking for you right now, and I have made temporary arrangements with one of them to speak with you before you are turned over. Many of them would have already poured gasoline over your naked beaten body as an incentive to talk." He gave a gallows smile. "I prefer to give you the chance while your mind is still unclouded by the prospect of excruciating pain."

That explained Holman's unease.

"Who are you?"

The official seemed to consider the question for a moment before ignoring it.

"Did Porter explain to you why he hired you for this mission?"

Cook frowned, puzzled at the line of enquiry. "He told me he was short on pilots."

"Nothing about your termination from the company?"

Cook's apprehension increased. How much did this guy know about his record? "You know Porter's dead, right?"

"Yes." He nodded, then leaned forward, his expression intent. "You were fired for smuggling methamphetamine on a Transvector cargo contract flight. What reason did Porter give for rehiring you?"

Cook was impressed by the official's depth of information, but had no idea where the man was heading. He wracked his brain trying to remember the highlights from his counter-interrogation course, but he was just too tired. Give them something, he thought. Throw some spaghetti on the wall, see if it sticks.

"He told me that the guy who actually smuggled the speed confessed to it before he died."

"Did you believe that?"

Cook flexed his arms, trying to find a more comfortable position in vain. The gang members in the overheated room were starting to get bored, shifting from one foot to the other. Nobody sat. Cook assumed these things usually didn't take this long for them, or involved a lot more blood.

"Not really. I had the feeling the letter was faked."

The official nodded, as if confirming something to himself. "Did you get the impression that someone had told Porter to hire you back? Someone higher up in management. Hallett, for instance?"

The thought had honestly never occurred to him. He'd seen Porter throwing him a lifeline, and he'd grabbed it. "No."

The official tilted his head back for a moment, before resuming his examination.

"You spoke with Porter the night before the mission."

Since that wasn't phrased as a question, Cook simply nodded.

"Did he mention anything about the mission, or the type of chemical you'd be delivering?"

Cook surmised he'd been under near constant visual surveillance in Guadalajara, but that they hadn't been using parabolic microphones or lasers to pick up the conversation. He also concluded from the tangential nature of the questioning that they were expecting him to know more than he did. He would have to parcel out his answers carefully, to attempt to remain useful to his interrogator. He decided to equivocate.

"You were at the briefing. You heard the same thing I did."

The official looked at the men standing next to him, inhaled deeply, and held it a moment before blowing it out. Cook's response seemed to frustrate him, and his reaction telegraphed the sense that the interrogation might not be bearing fruit. Cook realized he needed to try and buy some more time, be more helpful. Give and take.

"He called it a milk run, made it sound like it'd be the first of many."

The official looked back at Cook.

"But no mention of any details, until the briefing?"

"Right."

Something bigger was going on here, thought Cook. Nobody gets this upset over a dead crop or two – you just raise the street price and move on. Assuming this guy was on the take from a cartel, he seemed to be spending an awful lot of time on non-drug-related matters. Cook canvassed his exhausted memory to find something that would make him valuable, would buy him a ticket out of this sweaty church-brothel. But the official wasn't interested in giving him leisure time to think.

"After Romero was hit, did Riggs make any comments on the crew that did the job?"

"Sorry…who?"

For the first time the Mexican seemed unsure, then quickly regained his composure.

"You know her as Stokes. Did she make any remarks on the hitters?"

"Who is she?"

The Mexican's face turned dark.

"No one you need to worry about."

Cook was tired of the man's circumventions. He gambled. "Yeah, well – if you want anything more out of me, bring her back here."

The Mexican official's momentarily surprised expression quickly turned to one of regret. "Mr. Cook, I'm not actually certain at this point that you know anything we need."

The chill that settled in Cook's abdomen jump-started his survival instinct and threw his cranium into overdrive. To not be useful was to be dead. He needed to smoke out the motive behind all of these theatrics. Something a lot heavier than a simple spray job had gotten everybody's attention – there had to be corpses stacked somewhere, or boxcars of money gone. He had a crappy hand, but he could bluff.

"Porter said Hallett called this one a game changer, that there was a lot of money behind it."

"I'm listening."

What the hell, it was worth a try, Cook thought.

"He also said something about building up the numbers, keeping the feds happy."

It was a long shot. But the Mexican official, who had been listening to someone whispering in his ear, raised his hand to indicate a pause.

"Was Porter saying this, or was he repeating a conversation with Hallett?"

Hallett was still alive and could potentially talk. "Hallett."

"To what did you think he was referring, Mr. Cook?"

"The girl?"

The official raised his eyebrows, his mouth not quite forming a smile.

"I have no problem keeping her around as an incentive, but," he shrugged, "I'm going to need more."

Cook played his last face-card.

"You want to talk to Hallett, right? So do I. He's got to answer for Porter and the rest of them." He leaned forward. "Of the two of us, who do you think can get closer to him?"

The official stared at Cook, as if trying to calculate how much he would lose by just shooting him right there. The eyes were no longer expressionless. In fact, they looked angry. Cook's anxiety level increased, and he hoped it didn't show on his face. There was just too much emotion in the room for what had been a standard antagonistic sally between narco and fed. What was this guy so upset about?

The Mexican turned to a surly-looking man at his side and whispered something. The grim face was still for a moment, then nodded. The official returned his gaze to Cook, his eyes reappraising.

There was dead silence, for far too long.

"Have you ever been to his house?"

* * *

After finishing his interview with Bellamy and leaving the old man in the diner to sober up enough to eat solid food, if he ever did, Craig was rerouted by a phone call from Simms back to the Los Angeles FBI complex on Wilshire.

He had Hallett's driver take him directly there, while making a mental note to get a driver or another Bureau car on standby. Then he decided to put it on his phone calendar, with an alert in two hours. If he didn't write it down at this point, it wasn't going to happen. He was starting to experience a serious sleep deficit from the last ten or so hours of continual wakefulness and geographical hopscotching, and he needed at a minimum a couple hours of downtime.

In a conference room on the tower's 17th floor, Simms waited with one of his section's Senior

Supervisory Agents, a weathered SSA called McCray who people referred to as 'grandpa', but only behind his back. Though nearing the mandatory retirement age of 63, McCray was still a formidable presence in the Bureau's western region. Legends of six-gun shoot outs and beatdown confessions awed raw recruits more familiar with plastic-handled pistols, touchscreen tablets, and politically motivated agent prosecutions.

Simms waved Craig into an opposite chair with an uncommon brevity, and, skipping any pleasantries, got right down to business.

"There are two more casualties out at Palm Springs." His frown deepened into a grimace. "Problem is, they're our guys."

Brushing his fatigue aside, Craig leaned in.

"What happened?"

Simms nodded at McCray, who addressed Craig with his customary scowl.

"They were Emergency Response Team techs looking over the TVA aircraft. They both got some exposure to the spray residue off the back of the plane – and they were wearing Level C Hazmat suits with respirators. They were down in about a minute. Everyone backed off pronto, and the whole area was quarantined." McCray paused, glowered at his notes, and then looked up. "Two hours later, the HazMat response guys put in a robot with an arm-mounted sensor. It tested like a G-series nerve agent, similar to sarin or soman."

Craig's jaw dropped. The ERTs were the Bureau's CSI people, and the HMRT, or Hazardous Materials Response Team, personnel were the all-stars of the dangerous crime scene cleanup world.

"Nerve gas?" He stared at the table for a moment. "TVA sprayed nerve gas on Mexico?"

McCray thrust his lined jaw forward as he nodded. "Yeah, looks like it. HMRT and medics are tenting off the whole airport, checking everyone who was there. Did you go near the plane?"

"No. Brent or one of our residents might have, but they hadn't gone out there before I left." Craig was dazed. "Any reports from Mexico?"

Simms took it from there.

"We've heard nothing at this point, and they may not have put it together yet, but it's going to blow up into a major international cluster. The National Security Council is setting up a meeting as we speak, and the president has been informed. They're keeping as tight a seal on this thing as they can, but it's going to leak at some point."

Craig felt more unraveled than exhaustion alone could account for. The spray capacity of two C-130s over large swaths of Mexican countryside meant there could be thousands dead. The implications were staggering. It was essentially a criminal act of war against a neighboring friendly state and trade partner. Why? And where in the hell did TVA get nerve gas?

"Who's taking over?"

"Brent's still on point, and you're still attached if you can stay awake." McCray smirked, showing some teeth. "The ADIC wants hourly updates, but we're getting calls every fifteen minutes, and that's not going to change." At this, McCray rolled his eyes. The Assistant Director in Charge was a petty Beltway-poohbah tyrant named Beauchamp, who ran the LA office like a sovereign kingdom, and wasn't well regarded by the foot soldiers. "Homeland and ONI are setting up next to the incident command center. CIA is keeping their distance, but said they'd give us a shout if Blair turns up." He tilted his head to the side as he regarded Craig. "That's bullshit, naturally. If they find him, he'll disappear down some memory hole."

"Does TVA know about this yet?"

Simms chimed in. "Unknown. We just got it ourselves."

"Good. We should probably keep that one here for now." Craig cast about the room, hoping the movement might dislodge more coherent thinking. "Who's on Mexico?"

Simms again.

"State and Justice will run cover as long as they can, but they're looking to us for quick answers." He looked intensely at Craig. "The president is going to have to make some kind of statement before the media starts up the three-ring circus. We can probably count our time in hours – maybe a day."

Great, thought Craig.

"Anything on Cook or Stokes?"

"Still quiet, but the BOLOs have been updated for a broader area."

"What about the rest of the aircrew? Did Homeland find them?"

"DHS says they didn't send anyone." Simms looked at McCray, who shrugged. "We're running blind there. It might be Langley, but it's pretty raw, and even they're not stupid enough to be behind the nerve agent."

Craig shut his eyes and inhaled deeply, then focused on McCray.

"Nate, can you give me a no-holds blueprint of what the hell's going on here?"

McCray's weathered visage went still as he pondered for a moment. He was renowned for catching the footprints of domestic intelligence agencies on US soil. Nothing ever made the papers, but heads had always rolled, quietly.

"Denny, the spooks will bend you over the table every chance they get, but I'm with Gil here. This is up-the-fucking-wall crazy. There's no plausible deniability, no cover story I can think of that would explain this cockup." His mouth bore an expression of extreme distaste. "This kind of shit-storm brings down presidencies. CIA DDO would never green-light this – nobody would. And Transvector sucks every dime they make from Langley's tit."

The DDO was the Deputy Director of Operations at CIA headquarters in McLean, Virginia, which everyone called 'Langley' because that was the name of a former colonial-era plantation their headquarters occupied. The DDO was the guy who actually ran all covert operations, including, ultimately, whatever Transvector did for them. Craig strained against an escalating impression that he was hugely out of his depth. They needed to take this from him, send him home, let him sleep.

He shook it off. No time for self-pity. When in doubt, go back to the basics.

"Who benefits from this?"

"We do. DEA, Border Patrol, everyone," said McCray, without hesitation. "So does Mexican law enforcement, *if* the planes only hit *narcos*. Competing Mexican drug cartels in the Gulf area. Some others."

"Who are the losers?"

"The US government politically, TVA and Hallett, bent police officers, the west coast cartels. Republicans."

Craig raised a finger. "What about other DTOs?"

The acronym stood for 'drug trafficking organizations', but nobody ever bothered to spell out the complete phrase, except in presentations. McCray's lips pursed, he shook his head, and looked over at Simms, who frowned. But Craig wouldn't let it go.

"How about Chinese, or the Russians? They were Vietnamese at the Romero scene – lot of historical interaction there."

"Nobody has that kind of reach, not even LA Triads." Simms was a subject expert on Asian criminal syndicates. Los Angeles offered a lot of scope for his experience. "And that's not their style. Too flashy, too public. They stay out of the limelight and let everybody else catch the heat. Russians," he paused, on less firm ground, "they stay close to their traditional territories, franchise out their stuff elsewhere. They have some presence in the Bay Area, but not as much down here. And the stateside Vietnamese hate their guts."

Nothing. Craig decided to approach from another angle.

"If Blair was behind this, he couldn't do it himself. Where'd he get a binary nerve agent – are we assuming it was binary?"

Binary nerve agents were chemical weapons, like sarin or soman, that were stored in separate tanks as precursors and mixed together to form a lethal gas. For the G-series nerve agent sarin, all it took was a restricted compound called DF and isopropyl alcohol. Alone, DF was dangerous, but not usually lethal. When combined, the resulting sarin was twenty-eight times more deadly than mustard gas. Very, very nasty stuff.

McCray sucked air through his teeth. "Binary's probably what it was – too toxic to handle otherwise. CIA shouldn't have access to that domestically, or if they do, they aren't saying. And Defense keeps that shit locked up tighter than a virgin's snatch. Syria maybe? Ex-Soviet stocks?"

Too many unknowns at this point, too many options, and creative thinking was getting increasingly difficult. Craig knew he'd had it. Time to check out.

"Nate, can you spare me while I catch a couple hours shuteye?"

"Sure thing, Denise." The older man smirked, and rose. "Just don't leave us hanging. We need some coherent answers on this, and I'm too old to go back to knuckle-dragging fieldwork."

McCray walked out.

Simms stood. "Two hours, Denny, then I need you back. I'm glued to the threat center. Washington's going to start calling every five minutes for updates, and we'll probably be briefing the Assistant Deputy Director soon."

Simms left, turning out the room's lights as he departed. Craig beelined for the boardroom's couch, stretched himself out full-length on the black leather cushions, and was instantly asleep.

* * *

The room was still stiflingly hot, but the body-odor stench had lessened somewhat with the departure of everyone but a lone sentinel, a brawny, t-shirted teenager who preoccupied himself with text messaging while seated with his back against the wall near the rear door.

Cook remained drooped but upright in the metal folding chair, his arms still bound by duct tape, but his captors had brought Stokes back into the room for company. She was similarly immobilized, with the addition of tape around her ankles binding her legs. Cook didn't want to think much about what they had been preparing for her.

"So, Riggs, huh? What's your real name?"

Stokes glanced at their warden, who was studiously ignoring the pair, then shot Cook a dubious look. "Better you don't know."

"Better for who?" Cook perceptibly surveyed the shiny gray tape that pasted her jeans flush to her ankles. "Looks like they had something special in mind for you."

"Don't lose sleep over it." Her expression held a combination of disdain and fatigue. "I've still got plenty to trade." Her lips straightened into a flat smile. "Holman just sold us to the wrong crew, that's all. Strictly a temporary thing."

"Yeah, like the man said," Cook mused. "You know who this guy is?"

"I can make some guesses."

"He's got heavy connections. He had enough juice to sit in on our preflight briefing."

Stokes, or Riggs, was silent for a moment, digesting the information. She started to speak, then paused, then changed her mind again. "He's probably with Mexican security, then…or CNI."

The teenager at the door glanced up at mention of the term, then went back to his typing. Cook frowned. He had never heard of it.

"Who are they?"

"National Center for Intelligence. Mexican CIA – new civilian group that handles national security. Took over from an outfit called CISEN after the lefties came in."

"Why would they be involved? They know the score…he was there." Cook assumed the room wired, and that every word uttered would be picked apart and analyzed, but he just couldn't, at this point, bring himself to care.

Stokes – Riggs, Cook corrected – was staring at the warden by the door as she spoke.

"While we were separated, I overheard some guys talking about piles of dead bodies."

Cook nodded. "Yeah, I threw out some smoke about the Romero hits and body counts, buying some time. They were probably just repeating it."

"Well, good guess." Stokes paused. "Whatever happened during that mission, there are stacks of corpses lying around somewhere.

She stopped talking, lapsing back into thought. Cook stared at her. Her neck muscles were taught, and veins stood out on her forehead. She was anxious, even if she wouldn't admit it.

"So, how long you been working for the cartels?"

Stokes glanced over, then looked at her feet. Cook tried again.

"I mean, you seem to blend in pretty smoothly here. Got your markers and connections, everything. If it wasn't for the duct-tape, I'm thinking you'd be on the other side of that table."

Stokes' head swung back. "Why don't you shut your yip, Cook. You don't know shit about anything."

She went back to brooding. Cook shrugged, as much as tape would let him. She didn't seem inclined to give him any more. On the plus side, though, at least she said his name. That was an improvement. Their relationship had progressed to a point where he was an actual human being.

He tried again.

"So, hook me up." Cook peered around, wobbling slightly in his chair. "Not like we got anywhere to be."

Stokes glared at him for what seemed like a full minute, then looked at her feet again. For some reason Cook felt compelled to understand her better. Or maybe he just wanted to fill the ominous silence with something more pleasant than thoughts of their captors returning with grim-eyed expressionless faces.

"I don't think they'd be hearing anything they don't already know."

Stokes closed her eyes and sighed, minutely shaking her head. "Have you always been this much of an asshole?"

Cook simpered mindlessly. "One of my best features."

"I was a cop, in Arizona." She blurted suddenly, clearly unaccustomed to personal disclosures. Warily glancing back at their monitor, who ignored them, she carried on. "Loved it. Was on the promotion track – made corporal after eighteen months. Chief was looking to put me in for detective. Things were looking up."

Stokes paused, pressing her lips wistfully. Then she looked directly at Cook.

"One of the dick sergeants had it in for me. Thought me being in his unit meant I was his personal piece of tail on the side. Basically, tried to rape me on a stakeout. I told him if he didn't cut the shit out, I'd write him up. Didn't go down real well."

Cook searched her face. He was finally getting some honesty.

"Next day, internal affairs gets a tip there's twenty grams of blow in my locker. Asshole planted it. Said he'd seen me dealing off-duty. My word against his. You can guess how that went."

Cook nodded, swallowed drily.

"After that, I tried some other things, but the bastard fried me good. Couldn't even get security guard work after that. Cartels sent a talent-scout with a fistful of cash – I was running out of options, so I bit. Romero popped me in Nogales, and the rest is history."

Cook stared forward. "How long?"

"Nine, ten years ago." She smiled forlornly and looked around the dingy room. "They had someone scrub the databases, change my pictures. The Feds aren't going to put it together anytime soon."

Stokes had put some extra emphasis on the last statement, as if for their monitors. Cook looked back.

"Did you set up Romero for them?"

Stokes scowled. "Jesus, Guy, what kind of dumbass are you? That wasn't us. I kept them updated on what Romero was doing, but they didn't seem to care much. Figured it was an internal *yanqui* thing."

Cook nodded again, reddening slightly. There was a companionable silence for a moment.

The mood didn't last.

The commotion of shuffling feet could be heard beyond the door, and the texting sentry scrambled to his feet, standing at what apparently passed for parade-rest in a Mexican street gang. The door slammed open, followed by the Mexican official speaking rapid-fire Spanish at Holman, and a smaller entourage of gang members than earlier. The two sharp-looking operatives, who had earlier accompanied the Mexican official, stood by nonchalantly in black jackets, their hands loose. Holman, appearing agitated, seemed to be arguing some heavily slang-laden position, with sharp gesticulations. Cook understood none of it, but it looked like the fence was losing badly. As the group approached the bound pair, the official terminated the discussion with an abrupt slice of his hand through the air.

"¡*Alor*! Mr. Cook, it seems that despite your almost total ignorance of what's transpired in the last few days, you can be useful to us. Furthermore, your new friend Holman," he indicated with a tip of the head, "heartily agrees, and has decided to extend our arrangement to include certain activities."

Holman's expression looked anything but hearty, but Cook was happy to hear he wasn't getting fed to the dogs just yet. "What sort of activities?"

"You're going to help us get to Hallett, who apparently is back in town. And he's going to tell us everything he knows."

* * *

CHAPTER THIRTEEN

C raig woke to a light tap on his shoulder. It was Simms, holding a thick mug of coffee.

"You got three hours – most we could give you. There's an all-star lineup including Beauchamp waiting for us in the SCIF."

His brain still screaming for sleep, Craig downed the cup, then went to an adjacent bathroom to throw some cold water from the room's small sink on his face and run fingers through his thick, greasy hair. He was really starting to want a shower at this point. Doing without one and wearing the same clothes for days-on-end was part of the job, just not his favorite part.

When he got to the SCIF, or Sensitive Compartmented Information Facility, it was packed. Designed to be a secure location for the discussion of top-secret information with special access controls, it was half the size of the conference room he had just woken up in. SCI facilities were not known for their comfort; all the counter-detection hardware cost money, so space was always at a premium.

Responding to Simms' wave, Craig shuffled sideways down the row and wedged himself into a free seat.

Presiding at the head of the conference table was the LA office ADIC Jim Beauchamp, surrounded by a phalanx of Special Agents in Charge, or SACs, ASACs, and lower-ranking functionaries, many of them staring at laptops while quietly murmuring into headsets. McCray stood scowling in the corner with Cassell from Homeland Security and someone Craig didn't recognize from DEA. It was a tight bunch, but the atmosphere was anything but congenial.

Beauchamp, who had everyone pronounce his name 'beech-um', got the meeting rolling.

"Please take your seats. The Deputy Director, the Assistant Attorney General and several security council members are conferencing-in." Beauchamp waved vaguely at the large screen dominating the opposite end of the crisis suite, where the heads and shoulders of few government officials could be seen, and others began blinking into existence. "Special Agent Craig of CIRG has been attached to the field investigation by ASAC Simms and has a solid overall picture. Agent Craig."

"Good morning." Craig could feel the second mug of FBI-sanctioned coffee he had gulped down cutting through the heavy fog of sleep-deprivation as he spoke. He knew he would pay a price for the deferred rest later, but at this precise moment he needed all the clarity and focus he could muster. This was not a crowd you wanted to look drowsy in front of.

He gave as terse and spare an outline of their current knowledge as possible, without offering either supposition or supporting commentary. He did this for two reasons. Craig knew his audience would engage in a spirited question-and-answer session, each participant thereby demonstrating his own insight and analysis, and he didn't want to deprive them of their enthusiastic, if amateur, sleuthing opportunities. And secondly, with his own plethora of questions and paucity of answers, he had ceased caring hours ago what anyone thought or who got credit for what, and just wanted to make some progress.

Kenton, a presidential advisor on the NSC, piped in with the first follow-up after Beauchamp solicited questions.

"We're huddled up with the GOM to keep this out of the daylight, but we need something hard to give them, and soon." A couple of field-types looked around the room, smirking at the affected operational lingo. Beauchamp quickly frowned down the dissension, before Kenton could comprehend the disparagement his tough-guy jargon engendered. Even Craig had to restrain his own smirk. "Do we have anything on who's behind this? Dysart? What's the agency's story?"

Dysart, a liaison from the CIA, sat up straighter onscreen. Dysart had to have known that he wasn't the most popular man in the brief, but his expressionless, chiseled face betrayed nothing but competence and a reasoned frown.

"We have no new information to add at this point, but we've pivoted a significant portion of our capability to focus on this." Dysart always spoke like a general counsel delivering a financial compliance report to a board of directors. "We are also trying to locate our missing officer."

"And Transvector?" Kenton again. "Are we operating under the assumption that the chemical switch and the navigation sabotage are linked?"

"We are." Beauchamp quickly fielded the question, before Craig or others could express disdain at the inanity of the query. Kenton had already decided that Transvector was innocent, Craig concluded. Must've been all those campaign donations Hallett gave to the president. "Our IT forensics team is at the Mojave site trying to hunt down the source of the bad code."

Craig looked down at his notes on the table in front of himself, mentally forcing himself to pay attention to the ensuing discussion, waiting for further questions to be directed his way. He had sat through many of these before. It was challenging to try to explain investigative procedure to people who only wanted results, and quickly. Normally, an investigation like this, even absent the grave international implications, would take months, if not years.

"What's Hallett got to say about it?" This from the image of Assistant Attorney General Simkins, a blunt fireplug in a suit who would be briefing his notoriously effete superior, a weak-link political lightweight by the name of Blomstein.

Dysart chimed back in, grave concern clearly projected in every syllable.

"Mr. Hallett has assured us that Transvector conducted their operation according to the letter of the national security finding with the NSC, the Agency, and the Mexican security ministry. They were not aware that their herbicides had been switched to the nerve agent. Hallett and the Transvector Worldwide board have been extremely candid and opened everything they have to us." He paused, panning the room. "I think it's fair to say that we're looking at an extremely serious intelligence breach here, and some very sophisticated sabotage, source-unknown at this stage."

"Thank you, Mr. Dysart." Beauchamp, not wanting to detract from the meeting's progress with muddled and perhaps intentionally misdirected theories, sought to refocus everyone's attention back to the discussion at hand. "ASAC Simms, what are the next steps you are pursuing in this investigation?"

Simms examined the expectant faces attentively, not forgetting the six heads on the teleconference screen. "Our first priority is to find CIA Officer Blair and establish his level of involvement. Additionally, we need to identify a motive behind the killing of DEA Agent Romero, and how, or if, it's connected. The third priority is to find Guy Cook and the woman going by the name of Stokes. Our fourth priority is to determine which agency or organization picked up the C-130 crew members at the Palm Springs airport. We have alerts out for all known parties at this point, including the missing crew members. These are the primary avenues of investigation at the current time, and I'm happy to go into more detail on secondary issues at this meeting, or at a later time...."

Anything else Simms might've thought of saying was cut off by Dysart, who reminded everyone not to jump to conclusions on CIA involvement, and Cassell from Homeland Security in the back stating emphatically that they did not have anything to do with picking up the remainder of the crew in California.

The images on the conference screen blinked out as the individuals presumably went to brief their superiors. Craig sagged with relief. He had survived the initial brief, and no one was pointing the finger at Simms's section for incompetence or lapses in judgment. The din in the room continued. He permitted himself a brief moment to squeeze his eyes shut in frustration. Everyone seemed to be demanding how something like this could happen, and why the usual operational security controls didn't catch it. No one was thinking like an investigator, asking why it happened, and why now.

A tap on the shoulder interrupted his reverie. It was McCray.

"Something just came in." He bent down towards Simms's ear. Craig leaned in. "El Monte PD found a Cessna single-engine under a railroad trestle next to the airport. Tail number traces back to Thermal Airport, which is about 25 miles from Palm Springs."

Craig looked at Simms, who looked up at McCray.

"Yep. Seems like Cook's in LA."

* * *

The approach to Hallett's compound was up a dark, winding road overarched by California sycamore, Valley oaks, southern magnolia, and camphor trees. Dim yellow lamps on gated driveway entrances provided occasional illumination.

Lopez sat in the front passenger seat of the black Escalade, browsing a constant stream of messages scrolling down his phone. Occasionally, he responded to one, but more often just glanced down as each new one lightly chimed. The rest of the time, he gave curt directions to the driver on his left or muttered into a radio microphone clipped to his shirt collar. A discreet earpiece fed into his left ear.

Cook doubted Lopez was his real name, but everything else about him seemed to fit with Stokes' appraisal back at the church. He acted like an intelligence agent, with a cool, assured demeanor that exuded competence and inspired confidence. He had a team of eight with him that exhibited a similar bearing, and Stokes whispered they were probably Mexican FES naval commandos or CFE special forces. Cook recognized two of them from Holman's so-called church. One drove, and another sat sideways in the middle passenger seat watching Cook to his left, and Stokes in back, a suppressed pistol in his hand resting on his lap. They all wore body armor and had suppressed HK MP5 submachine guns in satchels within easy reach. Five more rode in an identical Escalade following behind.

Cook stared out at the passing houses through a thick window of darkly tinted glass. Lopez had clearly chosen the Escalades as the least conspicuous vehicles to use on the westside of Los Angeles, and his choice seemed apt. Black chauffeured livery cars and Ubers of all sorts seemed to be emanating from or pulling into every tenth driveway along the route. No one gave them more than a passing glance.

Hallett's main residence was in one of the canyons that wound sinuously up the flanks of the eastern Santa Monica mountains near the Sepulveda Pass, part of an old Mexican land grant that encompassed Santa Monica, Brentwood and Pacific Palisades. In the 1930s, the area had been popular with movie stars and the elite of the California southland, including the head of the Douglas Aircraft Company. When he picked up the old Douglas facilities at Santa Monica airport in the seventies, Hallett had gotten the rustic canyon acreage in a side-deal from the founder's family. The nearly fifty-acre spread featured a main house surrounded by several ranch-style out-buildings, all connected by drives that looped around a couple of large water features.

Cook had been to a few parties thrown there by the old man and had wandered around when he got bored by all the Scotch-induced bluster and fabricated war stories. There were cameras covering virtually every foot of the perimeter fencing, as well as the open areas around the buildings, all monitored by a three-man armed security team in a bungalow off the main house. Then there was a driver, and another houseman who functioned as a combination secretary-valet. Both were armed and had radios. The compound was as secure as any residence Cook had seen in L.A., and it would be a hard nut to crack.

He looked over at Lopez, who was speaking softly into his lapel mike. He was probably planning on Cook's name and face to get them through the front gate. The shock value alone was likely to gain them entrance. Hallett would want to speak to him personally, to find out what he knew. Then Lopez's men could do the rest.

As they approached within a mile of Hallett's compound, Lopez's Escalade closed with a gunmetal Audi S8 in front of them. Cook guessed that this was his forward surveillance car, and that it could act as an escape vehicle if things went sideways. The fact that Lopez could so effortlessly acquire a fleet of high-end transport spoke to the size of his operation in LA. Probably has his own livery service, right under the noses of the whole federal security structure, Cook presumed. Very neat.

Lopez mumbled something to the driver, and the Escalade slowed. The Audi disappeared around the next turn.

If they made it through the front gate, the combined force would easily overwhelm Hallett's staff, although things could get messy if they had to approach via the grounds. The driveway wound up a long gradual slope to the main house, and the defenders would have the advantage firing downhill. The thought of it made Cook queasy. He had hung out with some of Hallett's guys before, and they seemed like good people. Cook hoped the assault would be overpowering and bloodless. He had no idea if Lopez shared that desire.

As far as Cook could tell from his limited understanding of the comments he heard in Spanish, the plan was for the Audi to drive slowly by the main entrance for a reconnoiter, then to reposition itself somewhere nearby. This would allow for both another line of incursion should the approach at the main gate fail, as well as keep an eye out for law enforcement.

An urgent radio call caused Lopez to hunch forward for a moment. He pressed his earpiece with his hand in an apparent attempt to hear more clearly.

"*Pasa por la finca, luego da la vuelta y prepárate. Vehículo trasero, siga.*" Lopez paused, and looked up at his men, who both had tactical earpieces and had monitored the call. He then glanced back towards Cook.

"Have you ever seen the gate open?"

Cook, sensing trouble, thought quickly. "Never."

"Change in plans. Get in back with Stokes and lay down." His tone brooked no dissent. Cook looked at his armed seatmate, who lowered the suppressed pistol's snout. Then he slid out of his seat and pivoted to the back bench opposite Stokes, who was already laying with her head to the center. Cook dropped to his side and curved his body until his head was brushing against her hair. A tart, musky odor flooded his nostrils. He could hear Lopez talking to the driver, some tension in his voice. "*Pase normalmente.*" Then, "*Vehículo siguiente, siga.*"

Lopez's operative in the middle seat reached into his satchel and removed the suppressed MP5, holding it in a low ready position. Cook twisted his neck so he could see Stokes. She was looking at him, her eyes mirroring those of a caged cat. He raised himself slightly on his forearms to peek over the edge of the window.

The bulky Escalade slowly porpoised out of a heavily treed turn before straightening on a portion of the road lined on the right by a six-foot steel fence topped with spikes and covered in mature ivy. The fence continued for another hundred yards before abruptly curving back toward two massive stone gateposts supporting substantial ornamental steel gates, which were standing wide open. The entire vehicle seemed to share a held breath.

An open gate could mean a lot of things, but to Cook, at this moment, none of them seemed particularly good. It might mean the gate was mal-functioning. It might mean recent visitors, such as the FBI or another agency. In any case, Lopez wasn't about to find out, and made a quick decision. He barked his orders rapidly into the radio, and they increased speed further up the canyon.

From the limited amount of the rapid-fire Spanish instructions Cook could interpret, Lopez was going to send the operative in the Audi straight into the compound, posing as a lost party guest, while the SUVs turned around up the road at the next intersection. A simple radio call would let them know if it was clear to approach, or if the mission was an abort. Cook didn't envy the guy running point.

In the midst of a laborious three-point turn up the canyon from Hallett's, another radio call caused Lopez to hiss for silence, and hunch over a plot of Hallett's estate on his lap, finger pressed firmly to his ear. As Cook watched, a quizzical expression grew on the man's face. He suddenly sat upright and snapped, "*¡Muévete! ¡Apaguen las luces!*"

The SUV accelerated sharply, pressing Cook and Stokes against the back of the bench seat. Lopez's man in the middle fought for handholds as the suspension rocked, attempting to keep his MP5 barrel steady. Even in the heavily insulated passenger compartment, the roar of the straining V-8 engine could be heard clearly. Cook dug a foot in and reached for Stokes, bracing against her. Within thirty seconds, their vehicle crunched up the driveway and through the gate. Cook heard another muffled thump as the trailing Escalade followed.

The vehicles swerved up the winding driveway in darkness, dim running lights providing the only illumination. Banking precariously on the turns, the sense of urgency matched their velocity. Then they braked abruptly, shuddering to a jarring halt.

The driver and the rear operative rapidly exited their doors on both sides. Lopez hissed to the back for Cook and Stokes to follow. Cook grabbed Stokes' forearm and dragged both of them into the middle seat area where they could disembark. Stokes shrugged his grip off her arm, but remained close by as they slid out. Cook peered through the darkness, trying to figure out where they were. They appeared to be in the middle of the long southern traverse up the hill below the main house.

Lopez and his men had run up the Audi, which was stopped ahead. Cook listened, but all he could hear was stealthy footfalls, the faint clinking of gun-sling D-rings, and whispered commands. He poked his head out, then beckoned Stokes with a wave of his hand.

It was almost pitch-black, only faint illumination emanating from houses and some gatepost lamps behind the trees beneath them. The Audi driver must have extinguished the headlights as soon as she stopped. The car was positioned almost diagonally across the drive, and in front of it Cook could make out a body.

Apparently, the driver of the surveillance car was a female operative, which would have reduced suspicion on the part of law enforcement, should any have been present. She crouched in a tasteful black leather jacket and flairs next to Lopez, examining the body, which was laying prone next to one of Hallett's estate golf carts. Lopez waved Cook forward as the rest of the team fanned out into a perimeter, facing uphill. Cook scurried up and took a look at the corpse. It was one of Hallett's security men, with the back of his skull blown off. Lopez shifted in his crouch, scanning the area, and leaned toward Cook. Stokes dropped into a crouch, her hands hanging at her sides, looking back at the driveway they had come up.

"What does this tell you?" Lopez kept his voice to a low whisper, pointing at the pulpy mess of the man's skull. The wound was fresh, the pulped mess steaming slightly in the night air.

Cook grimaced. "This happened recently. And we're not dealing with cops."

Lopez nodded. "And…?"

"He was either surprised or knew his attacker." Cook looked up the hill, assessing. "I'd go with the latter. Hallett's guys are all ex-special operations types – not the kind you sneak up on real easily."

Lopez regarded Cook and nodded, his pupils widely dilated in the darkness. "How many up at the house?"

"Should be four more – driver, two security and one in the house."

"Where is the main security room?"

"Bungalow north of the main house, by the tennis court." Cook didn't relish giving Lopez information that could lead to the death of Hallett's men, but a burgeoning suspicion told him that this was wasn't going to be the problem.

Lopez signaled, and they went quickly by foot toward the main residence, leaving only a driver to turn the two Escalades and the Audi around for a rapid exit. The approach took them longer than Cook anticipated. Hallett's estate was unusual in its size, even for Los Angeles. The drive wound up from the main entrance for about a third of a mile before swooping into a grand circular entry with an ornate fountain in its center.

Lopez left two of his detail from the second Escalade near the main house to cover the front. The rest of them then skirted around, remaining well away from it in the abundant foliage dispersed between towering eucalyptus and weathered oaks. Lopez's driver walked point, while the middle-seat operative and woman from the Audi screened Cook and Stokes.

They worked their way around to the two-story bungalow, which housed the security staff and the camera room. Lopez told his crew to hold and illuminated a map of the estate with a few, brief red flares from his flashlight. The plot included up-to-date information on the security system, indicating coverage zones in the video surveillance. From what Cook could glimpse, there were some gaps. Whoever had designed the system had prioritized the security of the main residence over the outbuildings, the ironic result being that the security center was a vulnerable target in its own right. Cook wondered where the hell Lopez had gotten such a current map of a secure, private residence.

They approached a line of trees at the back of the tennis court, and Lopez again signaled a pause. The sense of stillness and quiet was almost overbearing. The ranch-style lodge was the size of most single-family dwellings on its own. The bottom floor of the bungalow, where the security room was located, was dark.

Lopez called his team into a huddle, guns facing out. Cook crouched nearby. Pursing his lips, Lopez flashed the plot again, then turned to Cook.

"How many should be in the security room?"

Cook calculated. "Two. One at the monitors, and the other probably sleeping. The third one would be the guy on the road."

Lopez started to wave his team forward, then halted his arm in mid-swing, and closed his fist, obviously hearing another radio call. Cook looked over at Stokes, who favored him with a frown. Whatever was happening here was not what Lopez was expecting.

Lopez whispered a command into his lapel mike. He then crouched in stillness, waiting. After what he apparently deemed a suitable period, he signaled two nearby agents to enter the lower story of the security bungalow. They approached tactically, each covering the other as he moved, and made the door in ten seconds. There they paused, tested the door and found it unlocked. Their weapons at the ready, they entered in a classic hook-and-cross pattern. Cook could briefly see their shadows in silhouette as they momentarily illuminated the room with the flashlight attachments on their MP5s.

A moment later, they returned, the leader of the two shaking his head. He held up two fingers, then made a swiping motion across his neck, the implication of which was clear to everyone.

Lopez acknowledged the signal with a wave, and, making urgent directional gestures, launched off at a stooped lope toward the front of the big house. Herding Cook and Stokes with them, the remaining three of the team broke cover from the bushes and followed. There was a sense of exigency that hadn't been present during their cautious approach.

Mid-trot, Lopez hissed another command into his shirt collar. A faint double 'phutting' sound occurred somewhere up ahead. In defiance of every rule of tactics Cook had learned over the years, they barreled around the northeastern corner of the main residence *en masse*, without bothering to clear it.

The reason became readily apparent. A pair of dark-skinned Asians sat slumped to either side of the residence's massive oak door, each sporting a freely-bleeding wound to the forehead, the unmistakable results of the earlier suppressed fire Cook had heard. One side of the door was ajar, and a pair of Lopez's men silently braced the entrance, holding vigil for their boss.

Cook peered at the two while Lopez quietly consulted his sentinels. The dead men were in their late twenties or early thirties, and wore trendy clothes with gold neck chains and expensive shoes. One Asian one looked Filipino or Thai, the other more Vietnamese – it was hard for Cook to tell with all the blood. Cook squinted. The Asian on the left had spiky hair that reminded him of one of the crew from the silver minivan in Palm Springs. A silenced automatic pistol sat near his side. The Vietnamese-looking one had a thin mouth, a dark goatee, and wide cheekbones that looked almost Slavic. An internally-suppressed AR-15 still hung from his shoulder.

The female operative found a radio with an earpiece on the body to the left, and was in the process of extracting the earphone's cable from the man's jacket when a red LED on the transmitter chassis on the man's belt began to flicker. She snapped her fingers quietly and held the earpiece up toward Lopez. He dragged the acoustic cord from the corpse's collar, holding it up to his own ear. He then just as quickly dropped it, and hissed, "¡*Dése prisa*!" He hissed at Cook and Stokes. "Hurry!"

The two agents at the door immediately entered, their submachine guns' stocks extended, held tightly to their shoulders. They were closely followed by two more agents, then the rest of the group. Cook and Stokes were waved in by the rear guard, who remained on watch at the entry, covering the exit.

Inside, the point men moved steadily through the dim foyer into the main hall, while the second pair of agents covered openings to rooms on either side. The house was dark; the only illumination provided by dim nightlamps plugged into occasional outlets. Two more bodies lay in pools of blood on the floor. Cook peered at them, trying to see in the dim light. They looked like Hallett's guys.

A faint sound of muffled voices could be heard from the hallway leading south. Lopez was suddenly whispering at Cook's ear.

"Where's that noise coming from?"

Cook opened his mouth slightly to clear his ears, and extended his head forward, trying to pinpoint the sound. He vaguely remembered having been told by someone at a party that the floorplan was designed to resemble a smaller-scale version of the White House residential complex's first floor. Probably some patriotic gesture of Hallett's to make the president feel comfortable if he ever paid a visit, Cook mused. He concentrated. Beyond the vestibule, a transverse hall ran laterally down the axis of the house, leading to a formal dining room on the north end, and a comfortable media room on the south. Hallett would invite his cronies to watch football games in there on a giant projection screen. Straight across the hallway was a large sixties-style living and entertaining room at the rear of the house with an oval portico. There were several other rooms coming off the cross passage on either side: a library, a couple bathrooms, and Hallett's private study. The voices sounded like they were coming from there.

"The study. Double doors, second on the left."

Lopez waved his team forward with a small suppressed pistol, which Cook hadn't seen in his hand before. As the team quickly moved forward, the shooters in the rear smoothly pirouetting in the hallway to cover the back of the formation, the sounds of voices and muffled reverberations grew. The lead agent gently pressed down on the door handle, shook his head, then reached his hand to the female operative behind him and received a small charge of plastic explosive with a remote detonator already attached. A rocker switch illuminated a green LED on the charge, which he placed silently against the door's lock. Without a signal being needed, the entire group, including Cook and Stokes, pressed themselves against the walls to either side of the door.

The explosion was a deafening 'crack' accompanied by smoke as the doors violently swung inward. Lopez's lead men effected a rapid entry, followed by a second echelon of the remaining four agents. Cook heard shouts of alarm and a single loud gunshot, followed by the dull, wet 'popcorn' sound of suppressed bullets impacting flesh. In a moment, it was over. Lopez looked in, and then waved to Cook and Stokes to follow.

The air in the room was striated with sluggish strands of smoke from the door charge and gunfire, and reeked of cordite. The acrid haze made Cook's eyes water, and he squinted as he tried to distinguish figures in the dim light. Immediately in front of Stokes, to his left, was a dead Latino, a bullet hole centered on his forehead. It wasn't one of Lopez's men. His shiny blue coat, black shirt, and ash gray tie clearly separated him from the Mexican commandos. Hallett was sitting in a high-backed chair, breathing rapidly and looking pale. On the carpet to either side of him were the bodies of two more corpses, both in dark suits.

The last figure wasn't part of Lopez's team, and caused Cook to gape in disbelief.

It was Blair.

* * *

Craig slumped wearily in a reclining leather chair in the small, unoccupied office down the hall from the operations center, his tie loosened, and his eyes shut. The lights were off, but a flat glow from the ever-lit city out the window painted the ceiling a pale shade of straw. His short nap had done little to alleviate his crushing fatigue, but despite his best efforts, sleep eluded him. The extra-strong coffee hadn't helped, of course, and he couldn't keep his mind from churning over the idea that he might have missed something.

After the brief, Craig had been idled while Beauchamp, Simms and McCray huddled with the other office brass to plan strategy.

They were going to take the case from Simms, bump it up the ladder a couple of steps, and push Craig out. He knew that much, at least. Craig had been a field man too long not to understand the benefit of a home-team advantage. He was an FBI nomad from a division out of Washington, DC, and the LA Bureau was champing at the bit to keep the laurels in-house. He had laid some of the groundwork, but this was a high-profile case with international implications, and Beauchamp had a reputation for coming in on success. The size of the thing, he'd been lucky to stay on it as long as he had.

Craig couldn't blame Simms or McCray. Upper management careers had been built on a lot less. Down the road, once this thing finally got put to bed, there would be accolades and promotions galore, assuming they didn't pooch-screw it. Craig knew he'd get some sort of honorable mention for running the ball down-field, and some 'attaboys' from his colleagues in CIRG, but at this stage he was too tired to care. Answers were what he liked, and in that respect this case was proving to be a disappointment.

Self-pity, he mused. How original. He often found himself in this gloomy state when an intense operation went into idle, or once-promising leads evaporated. Colleagues had frequently joked that if he wasn't running, he was worrying. It made him an effective investigator; but also, he accepted grudgingly, a real pain in the ass as a coworker.

The intersection of the position's demands with his own obsessions had cost him a marriage, but that didn't bother him as much as it probably should have. She had been an analyst at FBI headquarters in D.C., and they had met over drinks on a blind date set up by friends not long after his training finished at Quantico. They hadn't talked much about the future, and by the time she understood his compulsion for action and constant absences weren't just a passing phase, it was over. It was a cliché to have a relationship crater within the first few years of joining the FBI, but he had been posted in the field so often that the aggregate time spent together could be counted more easily in months.

His twilit reverie was interrupted by a brief double knock on the door, followed by Simms peering into the room. "You awake?"

"Yep. What's up?"

Simms flipped on the fluorescents and cadged a seat while they pinged to life. He regarded Craig for a moment with an expression of knowing sympathy. He'd obviously given this speech before.

"You were right – Beauchamp's pulling you from the case." Simms smirked. "The man likes to feed his family first before opening the house to strangers."

Craig smiled thinly, his cheeks aching from the strain.

"Am I getting a one-way ticket back to Quantico so he can erase me from the narrative?"

Simms grinned wickedly. "Beauchamp would deny your presence if you were standing right next to him. Man has no shame. How do you think he got to be an ADIC?"

"Any developments?"

"Nothing since the brief. Mexico still hasn't made the headlines."

Craig nodded cheerlessly and rubbed his eyes. "So, what's the word?"

"Put your feet up for a while. It's stupid to dump critical resources considering the scale of this brown star cluster, and there's plenty of work to go around. Especially for someone with your background." He paused, hiding a yawn with the back of his hand. "We'll get you a tasking when more leads turn up. Work for you?"

Craig saluted, put his hands behind his head, and leaned back in his chair. "Oorah. Kill the lights when you leave."

Simms grinned at his fellow Marine and stood. "Semper Fi."

When he had left, Craig swiveled in his office chair, putting his feet up on the table in front of him and staring though the window slats out at the yellow LA nighttime sky. Thoughts fought for acknowledgment in his sleep-deprived cortex. What was Cook doing in LA, and why would he risk coming back here? Did he think he'd find help? Did he have a bolt hole in the basin somewhere? Unlikely, but not impossible. Most of the last couple of years he was up in the Lancaster area.

Bellamy's phrase 'hunt the hunters' came back to him. Was Cook hunting on the run? Bellamy said he might do that if he had help. Stokes?

Dangerous, with the feds looking for you, and your face on every police cruiser video display.

Cook's file was pretty thin on details, but Craig thought he was beginning to get a handle on the pilot's world. Peripatetic life, just like his. Operating effectively in lots of different places required flexibility and well-honed adaptation skills. And, according to Bellamy, Cook had had some extra training in that area. Intense concentration when working, and equally intense relaxation with the downtime. Lots of drinking, if Bellamy was any indicator.

What drove Cook, made him tick? There didn't seem to be a lot of self-reflection or forward planning in his movements. He just improvised with the tools available. Like getting that C-130 into Palm Springs, or the 172 into El Monte. That was a nice piece of work, considering the area was crawling with law enforcement. Quick decisions followed by instant results, something Craig was gathering was a common meme integral to the aviator psyche.

Which made it seem less and less likely that Cook would be behind any of this.

The nerve gas switch and the software sabotage were the products of a methodical, insightful mind, one instilled with the patience to develop strategy over time. That wasn't really Cook. Craig started to feel some empathy for his quarry. He had trouble sitting still too. He liked to act.

Where was Cook laagering down? Not too many friends, but the few he had were loyal to a fault. Bellamy seemed to like him, and his old boss Porter, who had brought him back in. Why had Porter done that, and what was the smuggling issue that Hallett and Veidt were dancing around back at TVA?

More unknowns. That list was stacking pretty high.

And what had happened to Cook's crew? If Homeland and the CIA were to be believed – and regarding the spooks, Craig was having serious doubts anything they said was completely truthful – someone else had just walked in and picked them up. In the middle of a room filled with feds and cops. Someone with credible identification and the right demeanor.

What kind of mind was orchestrating this? Inspired, even brilliant planning. The ability to adapt and improvise when events merited it. Case in point, kidnapping of the crew of the surviving C-130. They weren't supposed to make it, and that loose end had been cleaned up within the hour. They had intelligence and resources, pre-loaded for quick deployment.

And who was Blair? Other than the general overall impression that he was an asshole, Craig had no fix on him. Could he be the black box behind this whole pony circus? Gut instinct told him that Blair couldn't be doing this alone. He had to have some agency backing him. This had all the hallmarks of a big production.

Dysart had sworn up and down the block that the Agency wasn't involved, but it had their smell all over it. McCray believed the CIA wasn't stupid enough to be behind it, and McCray had been around the block a time or two. Who was? National Security Council? The President? Another rogue Iran-Contra-type deal?

Finally, who was Stokes? Her thread ran through the entire fabric of this case. She was with Romero in Palm Springs, and now might be with Cook, either as a kidnapper or an accomplice. Presumably, here in Los Angeles.

Static thinking was starting to give him a headache. He needed to move, to get out in the field. Fresh air, if such a thing could be found in Los Angeles, would help clarify his thoughts. Maybe he'd just close his eyes for a second. Then he'd hop to it and get going.

* * *

Blair sat dazed and bleeding in one of Hallett's walnut Baker chairs, positioned at the head of a mahogany conference table in the poshly furnished, Federal-style study. His jacketed forearms were secured by gaffer's tape to the chair's burgundy-upholstered armrests and his torso was similarly affixed to the elegantly curved back. His forehead was pale and covered with heavy beads of sweat, which occasionally dripped onto some tape covering his mouth. A dark stain emanated from a large wound in his right shoulder, but to Cook it looked as if the bleeding had slowed somewhat.

Hallett sat across the room from Blair in one of his tobacco-leather club chairs, looking haggard and unshaven in his pajamas and bathrobe. Lopez's female agent, who apparently doubled as the team medic, was attending to a deep gash on his left temple. As she hadn't done anything to stem the bleeding on Blair's shoulder, Cook could only surmise that Lopez was planning on working the wound a bit as an incentive to get Blair's cooperation.

Cook shuddered internally at that mental picture for a moment, then shrugged. Blair was a dead man, regardless if he spilled or not. If the Mexicans didn't kill him, the CIA wouldn't hesitate to cross him off their list for embarrassing them and making them look like incompetent bumblers. Whether he was doing their bidding or not. Having worked in close proximity to them for most of his adult life, Cook knew how Langley felt about botched operations. Press coverage was anathema, and sloppy work, heresy. Cook, dangling his legs over the edge of Hallett's elaborate oak partner's desk, was looking forward to the show.

When Lopez's team had breached the study doors, they had found Blair in the process of orchestrating a suicide.

Two suited goons were holding Hallett's arms out to the sides, and Blair, wearing black Nitrile gloves, was racking the slide of a .45 automatic. He had spun at the noise of the incursion and managed to get a single round off into a picture on the wall before the lead agent had disabled his shoulder with a well-aimed shot. The second agent through the door had dropped the gawking hoodlums with an efficient head shot each.

While Lopez conferred with someone on the radio, Cook tapped his heels lightly against the carved desk pillar, his eyes rimmed with exhaustion. His attention wandered between the intricately woven lattice pattern in the carpet and the activity at the other end of the room. Stokes sat at the desk behind him in Hallett's heavy leather executive chair, staring blankly at a bookshelf to her right. It was glass-fronted and looked like it was filled with richly re-covered first editions. The shiny, polished leather of their spines indicated that no one ever read them.

Cook's meandering gaze briefly settled on the corpse of the Latino he almost tripped over when he first entered. The body was dressed in a garish blue sharkskin jacket and black polyester slacks. A pistol lay on the floor near his curled right hand. Cook squinted, regarding the recumbent figure more closely. The vast pool of congealing blood beneath the corpse's shoulders seemed to indicate he'd been shot right there in the room, but earlier. At least, not within the last fifteen minutes. Probably to give Hallett something to think about while they smacked him around.

While his men finished binding Blair, Lopez had walked over and kicked the corpse lightly on the leg. Then he had crouched down, examining him closely. When Lopez rose, he had turned to Cook.

"I know this man. He worked for us in security before going over to the Acuña cartel. Good riddance." Lopez had then stepped back toward Blair.

Cook shook his head in bemused marvel. Blair had obviously gone to a lot of trouble to frame Hallett. The dead Latino was just another prop in an elaborate charade designed to make it look like a Mexican conspiracy to annihilate their rivals, and to muddle law enforcement. Cook sneered tiredly at Blair. As if any cartel had the bandwidth to pull off an operation of this caliber.

Cook looked over at Hallett, feeling a wave of tired pity for his current, and likely soon former, boss.

He looked nothing like the commanding corporate presence Cook had seen on prior occasions. With his thin pale legs sticking out of short pajama trousers beneath his bathrobe, his veiny feet clad in worn leather slippers, he mostly resembled a tired and frightened old man.

Hallett caught him staring, and returned a look of bewildered disbelief, but whether at Blair's horrific betrayal, or a former employee openly consorting with a hostile foreign intelligence service, Cook couldn't say. His own thoughts on that were mixed. He felt his cheeks flush and decided to look elsewhere.

Lopez had finished his radio conversation, and was now standing before Blair, speaking quietly to one who seemed to be his lieutenant. From behind, his posture and the tilt of his head seemed to indicate he was undecided on how to proceed next. Cook, feeling his tired anger rekindle, knew that whatever happened next, he wanted to be in on it. He slipped off the edge of the desk and joined Lopez.

Blair's head had slumped to one side, and his eyes were shut, but a faint wheezing rasped through his nose.

Cook glared at the pathetic figure tied to the chair in front of him. He barely knew the guy, had almost no acquaintance with this shitbird who had completely turned his life over, and he wanted some answers. Cook looked down at the damp black gloves the man still wore, and the now-unloaded .45 Colt M1911 nearby on the table, sitting next to a wallet and the other contents of Blair's pockets. The pistol had white ivory billets on the grip and intricate whorled engraving on the slide. It had been given to Hallett by Westmoreland or Dulles after the Vietnam conflict as a sign of appreciation for all he had done, and he never hesitated to break it out as a conversation stopper at parties. It usually lay on a velvet bed in a beautifully joined, glass-topped cherry presentation box on Hallett's desk, occupying the pride of place in his collection. Cook's fury built. This piece of whale-dung was going to kill a man with his own pistol. Cook hoped that whatever Lopez had planned for Blair, it would be a long, painful journey getting there.

Lopez, glancing over at Cook, seemed to come to a decision, and gave a curt command to his lieutenant, who picked up a decanter of amber liquor from the built-in sideboard nearby and emptied it over the wound in Blair's shoulder. The bound man's breathing increased, his head lolled forward, and a low moan emanated from behind the tape. Behind him, Cook could hear Hallett rousing and muttering something about wasting a perfectly good 21-year-old Macallan on that vulture, or something to that effect.

Lopez slapped Blair across the mouth, causing a muffled screech followed by a bout of raspy hacking and loud, whistling snorts through his nose. It took a full minute before Blair, his chin covered with bloody phlegm and drool, could dully look up at his captors. His eyes gradually focused, but Cook could see in them none of the contrived superiority and haughty disregard Blair had displayed in Guadalajara.

Lopez began.

"Mr. Blair, it is very good to see you again." He looked at his watch. "Unfortunately, our re-acquaintance is quite limited by time constraints."

Cook had forgotten for a moment that Lopez had been at the briefing, and that he had met Blair. This likely meant that Blair would not be left alive after the interrogation. Cook saw recognition of this understanding creep into Blair's eyes.

But Lopez's next comment surprised him.

"I know you want to tell us who is backing you, to prevent further unpleasantness and allow us to get you some urgent medical attention." Lopez nodded, as if agreeing with his own logic. "Let me assure you right now that if you tell us everything, we will deliver you to your employer without further injury or delay. Is that satisfactory?"

Cook could see that Blair didn't really believe Lopez, but that somewhere in his expression he held out the hope that he might live through this. Cook also knew that basic interrogation-resistance training dictated that the detainee endure some amount of physical hardship before giving up pre-arranged false information to buy time. And to his detriment, Blair looked like a by-the-book kind of guy, one who would be a real pain in the ass.

Cook saw that Lopez shared the same belief, which explained his subsequent nod to the nearby lieutenant, who went back to the sideboard and selected what looked like an expensive clear spirit in an engraved glass bottle. Hallett started muttering again from the back.

Lopez leaned closely to Blair.

"If you do not agree, I will of course get the information anyway – it will just take longer." He glanced toward his lieutenant, lifting his eyebrows. "Anything over fifty-seven percent alcohol burns quite nicely, and a strong brandy or grappa will easily melt your gloves into the skin of your hands."

Blair's already pale face grew ashen at the comment, and he swallowed audibly. He didn't look like someone who could handle a lot of physical pain. Lopez's lieutenant began to slowly pour the clear liquor over Blair's gloved hands and pant legs, paying special attention to the crotch, darkening the charcoal gabardine cloth and filling the air with the pungent scent of ethanol. The tempo of Blair's breathing through his nose increased again. Cook imagined that the appearance of a lighter or lit match at this point could elicit a sobbing confession.

The match wasn't even necessary. A loud vibrating rattle from the conference table startled everyone, including Blair. His phone, buzzing angrily, was slithering on the side table, blinking a bright LED light. The readout read 'No Caller ID'.

Everyone paused, except one of Lopez's operatives, who was in the process of attaching a cable from his tablet to the mobile. Lopez snapped his fingers and pointed at the man, who stepped back. No one reached for the phone.

Innumerable lazy Sundays spent on the couch in front of the TV watching detective dramas had taught Cook that you never, *never* answer someone else's phone if you don't know who's calling. There was always some code phrase or password designed to trip the unwary, and thus blow the ruse. What you do is call your contact at a local cell phone company and have them trace the location of the call. You should never worry about missing the call. Mobile phones lose signals all the time. They always call back.

Apparently, Lopez had watched the same movies. He snapped his fingers again hissed "*¡Rastréalo!*" at his technician, who instantly got on his own mobile, presumably getting somebody to attempt to triangulate the signal. There was a short exchange in Spanish, then the technician waited, remaining on the line.

Blair's phone had gone silent. No one made a sound, as if fearing they might stir it back to life. Even Blair was staring at it in anticipation.

Lopez broke the séance. "Mr. Blair, I know you want to tell us who is on the other end of that phone, and where they're calling from, bearing in mind our deal." He regarded the pale figure more closely. "You do, don't you?"

Blair nodded weakly; his eyes still hopeful.

Cook glared at him, hoping Lopez's promise to let him live was a feint. If he ever wanted to see someone suffer excruciating pain on the way to an untimely demise, it was this pretentious, Georgetown debutant-circuit douche-wad. Cook thought about the bodies by the front door. Must have been a real step down the social ladder to have to work with those deadbeats. Not much glory in having to rely on the local gang troll for backup. What would his tight-assed suck buddies inside the Beltway think?

Lopez returned his attention to the agent with the tablet, who had propped his own phone between his shoulder and jaw, and nodded. The technical operative plugged a multi-headed adapter cord from the tablet into Blair's mobile. He tapped a few buttons, and stared intensely at the screen while everyone, including Blair, watched with fascination. After thirty seconds, he frowned and glanced up at Lopez. "No contacts, and the call history is set to scrub. I have this phone's number."

This was in English, for the benefit of the non-team audience. Lopez hesitated. "Are you ready to trace?" he asked, also in English. The man nodded.

Lopez returned his attention to Blair.

"Mr. Blair, I need the number for the person who just called." He leaned over the bound man and rested a hand on his good shoulder, looking directly into his eyes. "Can you write with your left hand?"

Blair nodded vigorously. One of Lopez's operatives started ripping duct tape off the chair arm while the technician produced a small spiral pad and pen from his jacket. He positioned the pad against the chair arm and slid the pen in between Blair's thumb and forefinger. There was a light scraping sound as Blair's arm flopped nervelessly to the side. The technician re-centered Blair's hand on the notepad, and Blair began to awkwardly write. The numbers looked like a child's scrawl, but were legible.

Everyone leaned in and seemed to hold their breath while the technician carefully dialed the number on the mobile's keypad, each tone distinct over the external speaker. Even Blair quieted his noisy nasal exertions. There was a pause, followed by a ringing sound.

Who was running Blair? Cook felt a light hand on his shoulder, and saw that Stokes had joined the group, her eyes intently focused on the ringing phone. Lopez had cocked his head to hear better. Even Hallett seemed to stir over to the side, pushing the female medic's hand away from his head wound to listen.

The line connected with a click. A low voice emanated from the handset.

"Yep?"

Cook started, and turned pale. It was Porter's voice, unmistakably Porter.

Lopez scrutinized Cook's face, then looked over at Stokes, who bore a similarly bewildered expression. Then he glanced at his technician, who raised his index finger and swung it around, making circles. Lopez tapped Cook's shoulder and repeated the gesture.

Cook braced himself.

"Hello, Ted."

* * *

CHAPTER FOURTEEN

Porter gave a friendly-sounding chuckle. "Heard you made it, kid. Figures it would be you."

Cook's head was swimming. Nothing made sense. He was talking to a ghost. Cook held the phone for a full five seconds before he could even form words.

"What the hell, Ted?" He stammered. His voice sounded distant to himself. "Why? Why'd you do it?"

There was a pause.

"That's really not important right now, Guy. Tell the FBI I want to do a deal."

Lopez quickly shook his head, pointed at himself and made a sharp wave-off motion with both hands. Then he spun his finger around again. Cook nodded, understanding.

"I'm not sure they're in the mood."

"Convince them. And keep the phone handy – I'll let you know where you can pick up Kane and the rest of the crew."

Cook squeezed his eyes shut and clenched his jaw, stifling an urge to throw the cell phone against the wall. He then opened his eyes and snorted, recovering some composure.

"We've got Blair. He's interested in a deal, too."

"Knock yourself out. He doesn't know dick."

The line went dead.

Porter alive. Cook's head felt like it was being squeezed in a vise. The one critical factor in this whole mixed-up bag of smashed ass that he never would have thought of. His mental faculties were clicking back through the past three days, filling in gaps and completing answers to questions that he hadn't even known to ask. The routine took longer than it should have, his sluggish cortex gumming up the works. Porter… alive. He kept repeating it, as if a mantra at a Buddhist meditation retreat.

"*Claro que si. Si, claro.* Okay."

Everyone looked over at Lopez's technician, who was staring at a tablet screen and listening intently to his own phone. They all waited breathlessly, until the tech signed off with a curt "*Claro*", looked at Lopez, and shook his head.

"No GPS position – only two receivers. Signal was south and east of our position."

"Let me see." The operative stepped aside for Lopez, who tilted the device slightly so Cook could see the map. "Do you see anything that looks familiar?"

The screen displayed a typical digital map of Los Angeles overlaid with pulsing nodes presumably indicating cell tower sites. Two in the South Bay area were highlighted, generating a line of possible locations. Cook dimly remembered from a radio navigation class that they resulted from the intersection of two transmission 'hyperboloids', whatever that meant. He wasn't a radio head; he just used the damn things. The line began in the Hawaiian Gardens area, then ran south-west through the Belmont Shore neighborhood straight off the coast to the Long Beach breakwater. Certain points on the line were more likely than others, but a fleeting cell phone fix didn't offer a lot of accuracy.

Cook studied the plot, ransacking his memory for anything that seemed familiar about the area. Lopez called to Stokes, who had collapsed near Hallett in one of the leather club chairs and had her eyes closed. She walked over tiredly for a look.

The line transected the El Dorado regional parks, as well as running through Cal State Long Beach, Bixby Village, and the Alamitos Bay marina. What else was down there? He peered closer. Looked like a lot of apartments, strip malls, and some expensive condos on Naples Island. Way too much public exposure for a multiple kidnapping operation.

It was a confusing result. What mainly interested Cook was where the line didn't go. It was some distance away from Long Beach airport, the naval weapons station at Seal Beach, and the restricted California Air Guard base at Los Alamitos. Cook had landed there for work a couple of times, but couldn't for his life remember any details on the ground. As far as Cook knew, Hallett didn't have any hangars or corporate buildings down there. It was too far south from the Santa Monica facility to be of much use, and TVA had a policy of operating as much as possible away from military facilities. It was always better for the corporate cover to hide in plain sight.

Stokes leaned in. "Romero mentioned being in San Pedro a couple of times, but I wasn't with him and don't know what he was up to. Maybe he was talking about the port area."

Lopez frowned. "That's about ten thousand acres of area to search. No way will we find them in time." He paused, looking at the faces of the team surrounding him, and then settling on Blair. "Maybe we just haven't asked him the right questions."

"I think I know where he is."

The distinctive, stentorian voice rumbled up from behind them. Hallett was rising from his chair with the help of the medic on his arm, a look of determination masking what Cook assumed was a fair amount of pain. The old man was pretty tough, he reminded himself.

"We're all ears, Mr. Hallett." Lopez discreetly signaled his lieutenant, who moved slightly to position himself between Hallett and Blair.

"Give me my Colt and I'll tell you."

Lopez shook his head with what looked like a genuine expression of regret.

"I'm sorry, Mr. Hallett, but Mr. Blair is our only witness at the moment, and I'm going to need him alive for the time being." Lopez smiled slightly, opening his hands. "After we find Mr. Porter, I will be happy to consider other options."

"No deal. Porter and Blair are mine."

Lopez's look became grim, the menace barely sheathed in his formalistic patois. "Mr. Hallett, your company is responsible, either directly or indirectly, for actions that resulted in the killing of possibly thousands of my fellow countrymen. Irrespective of the fact that most of them were criminals, I'm not really of the temperament to bargain with you right now." He waved at Blair, whose eyes tracked the interchange between the two men like a spectator at a tennis match. "Tell me where you think Porter is, or I will have my men continue the information extraction process until we run through the stock of your better liqueurs."

Hallett glowered at Lopez for a long enough time that Cook began to worry for his boss' safety. Notorious for having a short fuse, especially when provoked, Hallett could be unpredictably pig-headed, and didn't always act according to his own best interests. Cook cast about for distraction. His sleep-dulled mind coughed up a thought. "Shouldn't we get out of here before anybody else shows up?"

Lopez regarded Cook balefully for a moment, then nodded. He looked back at Hallett again.

"The choice is yours, Mr. Hallett. Where are they located?"

Hallett continued to glare, but most of the venom had deserted his countenance. He glanced toward the map, squinting for focus. Cook felt a rush of relief for his boss. He really didn't want to see anything happen to him, regardless of how events played out.

"Port of Long Beach, east harbor, south side of Island Chaffee. We signed a joint contract for breaking surplus MARAD Ready Reserve ships with a firm out of Jiangsu, China." Cook glanced down at the image. He dimly remembered Bellamy mentioning something about Transvector working with US Marine Administration ships in the harbor. Hallett continued.

"We anchored them off the far side of the island to keep them out of public view. The Chinese do the internal stripping onsite and then drive them overseas."

He jerked his chin toward the tablet. "Your line goes straight through it. If Porter's working with the Asians, he'll be there. But," he added scornfully, "You'll never get near the place."

"Why not?"

"Homeland and Customs have that area sewn up tight. They check every vehicle coming into the piers and run regular boat patrols. They'd be onto you quicker than a buzzard on a meat wagon."

Lopez was perturbed, if his expression was anything to go by. "How do we get to him, then?"

Hallett gave him a thin, gallows smile. "I've got an idea, but I need some of my guys, especially Bellamy." He turned to Cook. "I'll need Guy, too. You willing to jump in on this?"

Cook smirked. "As always, boss. Just say the word."

Hallett turned back to Lopez. "Can we do a deal now?"

"Only after I've heard some specifics." Lopez didn't look like he wanted to be rushed, nor lose the hostage leverage he'd invested in Cook. He paused, his eyes calculating the options. "In any event, we need to leave. Where are we heading?"

"Santa Monica, the museum." Hallett glowered at Blair. "And we're taking that prick-headed oxygen thief with us."

Lopez canvassed the room. His people were already efficiently collecting their gear, and wiping down any traces of their presence, including picking up ejected magazines and any stray shell casings. The female medic bagged up the bloody gauze she had used on Hallett's wound and tucked it into her tactical medical bag.

Cook looked over at Stokes, who still sat in the club chair with her eyes closed, seemingly unmoved by Porter's resurrection and other recent events. Cook moved toward her. Whatever happened moving forward, she didn't really have a role to play, nor did she have the escape outlet of a friendly boss whose help Lopez presently needed. She was alone, without backup or cover, at the mercy of the gangs and Mexican security, or, in the best case, federal law enforcement. He didn't really like that situation.

Cook leaned over her chair, scrutinizing her tired face. He remembered how much it had pissed him off in Guadalajara, and then how much he had appreciated seeing it in Palm Springs at the coffee shop. He came to a decision. He would be her backup. He wouldn't let her become another piece of collateral damage from this massively twisted clown rodeo.

He tapped her shoulder lightly. She wearily opened her eyes.

"Time to go, Stokes. You're with me."

She squinted at him, searching his face for meaning. Apparently, whatever she saw there convinced her. She forced a thin smile. "I'm ready."

Cook straightened up, and focused on Lopez, who was surveying the room with expert eyes. He watched his people finish up, then turned and nodded at Hallett and Cook.

"*Alor*, let's get to the vehicles. Move!"

* * *

Craig awoke with a start in the dark room, unsure of where he was for a moment.

His back was damp against the leather chair he'd been reclining in, and his armpits were soaked with the stale smell of two-day-old shirt. He'd turned the slat shades to a more closed position at some point against the glare of the parking lot lights below, but he could see through the chinks that it was still dark. A glance at his watch showed he'd only slept a couple more hours. Because no one had woken him after Simms's visit, he groggily concluded that he was still unassigned.

It made sense. Every swinging dick in the house would be jockeying for positions, and Simms was probably straining to find enough extra taskings. He was probably giving Craig time off for good behavior, and some rest. But sleep was elusive.

Craig's mind kept turning over what made sense, and what didn't. Hallett jeopardizing his entire company to assassinate some cartel heads fit in the latter category. As did blowing up his own planes. Et cetera, et cetera.

What did they have at this point? Assemble the pieces on the board. Dead *narcos* and crashed planes. Nerve gas that could have only come from a very few places. A mixed-ethnicity Asian hit team killing a DEA agent in Palm Springs.

Thinking was getting him nowhere. Being currently unassigned, he had a luxury that few FBI field personnel ever got to enjoy – the ability to follow any lead he wanted, as long as he could wrangle permission. It didn't happen often. Sometimes an open-minded supervisor issued a *carte blanche* when every other lead had fizzled. But Craig relished the opportunity. Must be what working on cold cases was like. A promotional dead-end, but how fun would that be?

He just had to get Simms to agree to let him out.

Until then, at least he could get cleaned up. Craig found his garment bag back in the conference area where he'd first passed out, and then went hunting for a shower. The FBI SWAT room had showers and lockers for their personnel. He spent twenty minutes under the shower, letting the hot water stir some circulation back into his body.

He pulled a fresh suit, underclothes and socks from the bag, which he'd hung on the lockers, and laid it all out on the bench next to him. He dressed slowly, looking in one of the mirrors above the sinks.

McCray found him as he finished.

"I've been all over the house looking for you, asshole. You think you're at a spa, or something?"

Craig grinned. He almost felt himself again. "Been meaning to talk to management about the facilities. Where are all the masseuses?"

"Weak-ass Jarheads." McCray's sneer was Army-issue. "Simms has got something for you, sensitive detail. You sober enough for it?"

Simms was in the threat center, looking like he could use a shower himself. He nodded at Craig while Beauchamp strode around the room, looking over agents' shoulders at status screens like he understood what he was seeing, and generally annoying everyone. Simms waved Craig over to the adjacent ready room.

The ASAC looked frazzled. "Thirty years at the Bureau, and I'm playing second fiddle to this diva.

Wish he had stayed back in DC where he belongs. You rested?"

"Good to go, boss. What you got?"

"Beauchamp's got everyone in the field office out in the desert, or liaising with somebody, and I need a monitor at Hallett's place, in case Cook turns up. There's already a car on Bellamy. You okay with that?"

Craig smirked. "Gee, Gil, you sure I can handle it?"

Simms's eyes narrowed. "Don't test me, boyo. You're still here because of your subject expertise, not your glittering personality." He raised an eyebrow. "And unlike some people, I didn't get any beauty sleep."

"I'm on it, boss."

Fifteen minutes later, Craig was at the wheel of an agency pool vehicle, heading west into Brentwood. He drove at a moderate pace down Wilshire Boulevard, staying in the slow lane. Traffic was light at this hour, and a wispy marine layer that had drifted in from the coast wrapped every streetlamp with a faint orange halo.

The dispatcher on the FBI radio channel was directing a unit to a location downtown. Not likely. Why would Cook, or anyone, go there? Downtown was a ghost town at night. Cook and whatever associates were with him would stand out like sore thumbs. Craig punched the monitor button for Los Angeles' MAID-2 westside mutual aid channel to listen in on local law enforcement. It erupted with calls for some sort of gas station holdup at the 405 freeway near Westchester. He quickly turned it down, leaving it on minimum volume in case anything urgent arose.

The assignment to Hallett's residence was a sop thrown by Simms to get him out of the building. It could easily have been handled by a junior agent, or for that matter, Highway Patrol, sheriff detectives, or even local Brentwood cops. The likelihood that Hallett would confide any further useful information to Craig without his lawyer present was nil. And the odds that Cook would turn up there were even lower.

The Bureau liked it when everyone was marching to the same cadence, backing management calls and adhering to conventional investigative techniques. Craig was an outlier, a crisis-junkie. His specialty was rapid and original out-of-the-box thinking. It was the reason that Simms thought of him first when the Palm Springs residency called for help. Now that things had settled down to a relatively simple manhunt operation, Craig's brand of inventive creativity was no longer in demand.

Where are you Cook, and what are you up to? The file was pretty sparse on that line of questioning – no LA contacts, no former residences, nothing. On Stokes, there was even less. She could own several suburban homes and a downtown apartment building for all he knew. She could even be CIA, Homeland Security, or goddamned Mossad for that matter.

Mexico, CIA, DEA, DHS, Asians, heroin. Something was brewing in his deep recesses of his mind, parts assembling and reassembling themselves below the level of logical thought. It was a free-association process that he knew better than to interrupt. If you pushed it too hard, it vaporized.

It was going on one o'clock in the morning, but Craig needed to talk to Hallett again. Something about the company's Asian contacts was bothering him, something he was having trouble mentally articulating. He turned north on Bundy, heading toward Sunset. Tapping his fingers on the wheel, he weighed the expected hassle of rousing the old man from his sleep. The house staff probably wouldn't let that happen. Craig would have to wait until dawn to get his curiosity satisfied.

Craig wasn't on any kind of leash at present. In fact, he wasn't really officially attached to the investigation anymore. But something was definitely not right. And he didn't want to have to wade through the acres of cow dung that Veidt would throw at him. Maybe an early morning conversation over coffee would elicit some candor.

Coffee. Craig decided that sounded good. It wasn't like he was in a rush. He looked around for a street sign. He was in Brentwood, and it seemed like nothing would be open for hours. He slowly coasted into a driveway and turned around. He had passed a 24-hour 7-11 convenience store back on Wilshire. There was plenty of time to get to Hallett's.

* * *

Bellamy rallied pretty well for an old guy.

On the way down from the canyon house, Hallett used one of Lopez's clean cell phones in the Escalade to call Bellamy on speakerphone. He let it ring for a full minute, as there wasn't any voicemail or answering machine to interrupt. Cook recalled that Bellamy never used them – if he wasn't there, he wasn't there. The old man answered drowsily, then responded with a slurred, scathing shriek. "Who the fuck is this? Do you know what time it is, shit-for-brains?"

Cook didn't blame him for the outburst. Bellamy had one of the old Bell touch-tone Trimlines in his living room, and the ringer was loud as hell. Cook surmised it probably took the old codger half that minute to get out of bed.

Hallett replied calmly. "Is Leroy Grumman there?"

Cook smirked from the back of the SUV. Hallett was using the name of the founder of Grumman Aircraft. Must be their private code. Despite the hour, Bellamy picked up on it, nearly right away.

"Sorry." Short pause. "Grumman's in New York." Another pause, then some coughing noise, and the sound of hacked-up phlegm. Cook's grin grew wider. "He said he'll be back in one week for the airshow. He'll have a plane on static display outside the hangar." Another short pause. "Can I take a message?"

"Thanks. I'll try to get a hold of him later. Sorry for the late call."

Hallett hung up and turned to Lopez in the front seat. "Bellamy's awake, and he thinks there's a single surveillance vehicle outside."

Lopez nodded, as if expecting it, and spoke quietly into his lapel mike. Then he told the driver to proceed down Bellamy's street at a normal speed. Cook watched from the tinted back windows and saw a white GMC Yukon that looked like it might be the candidate. He told Lopez, who relayed it to the other SUV.

The FBI agent in the Tahoe had been stunned to be suddenly surrounded by armed operatives pointing submachine guns at him, and quickly raised his arms in surrender. Stakeouts were seldom stimulating, especially on old geezers completely peripheral to the investigation, and he had apparently been half-asleep. Lopez's men made sure the FBI agent kept his hands in view and didn't have a chance to key his radio's emergency button or touch his cell phone. They then bound and gagged him and stuffed him in the back of the Tahoe. Cook whistled up to Bellamy's balcony with the 'all clear'.

Bellamy carefully negotiated the complex's stairway from the second floor. He stared at Lopez and his men for a moment, but seemed relieved to see Hallett in the Escalade. "What's the deal, Hugh?"

"We've got a short-fuse situation. I'll fill you in on the way."

Ten minutes later, the SUVs pulled into a lot in front of the Pacific Aviation Museum at the Santa Monica Airport, where Cook had had his dinner with Bellamy only four days before.

* * *

As soon as Craig saw the open entrance to Hallett's estate, he knew something was wrong.

The drive up the canyon had been quiet and uneventful, a world removed from the sea of streetlamps and car headlights in the basin below. At this time of night, the chirps of crickets and the buzz of an occasional high-voltage transformer on a transmission pole were the only sounds. Through his door's open window, the sweet-honey odor of blue Jacaranda blossoms was subdued in the cool nighttime air. Houses appeared suddenly to either side, and just as quickly vanished.

As Craig had approached the estate's entrance, his antennae rose. Gate open, no lights. There was no gravel shoulder to pull off on, so he simply stopped in the middle of the street, thinking. For a moment, he thought it might be intentional, that Hallett had instructed his men to darken the property to allow Cook to sneak in. Craig quickly abandoned the idea as nonsense. The fence line ran along Mandeville for about a quarter of a mile. Cook could jump over it at any point.

Craig unholstered his compact Glock 19 pistol and set it on the passenger seat. Then he reached for the radio microphone. He waited for a pause in the FBI radio traffic.

"LA Dispatch, Agent Craig, 51453, at 2998 Mandeville Canyon."

"Go ahead, Craig."

"I've got an open gate here, with no lights. Requesting LEO backup." Craig used the generic term for law enforcement officer. He didn't know if Brentwood cops would be available, or if they'd send someone else.

Upon acknowledgement, Craig released the brake and proceeded slowly up the driveway and through the gate.

Around the first corner, his headlights illuminated the golf cart on the side of the road, with what was obviously a corpse in the driving seat. He doused the lights and turned off the car. The silence was deafening. He turned the radio speaker down and rasped into the handset.

"Dispatch, Craig with an update. I've got a dead body at my location, approximately 200 yards up from the gate. Need immediate backup – Code-2 plus – and medical. I'll stay in position."

'Code-2 plus' wasn't an official term. It basically meant 'come as fast as you can without lights or sirens'. It was discouraged by higher-ups because of the danger to the public, and the potential liability. But Craig didn't want anyone at the house to know that law enforcement had arrived. The dispatcher was crisply efficient.

"Copy. Dispatching LAPD Code-2 ASAP. All FBI traffic switch to Green. Do you want tone?"

'Tone' meant a chirp on the frequency that indicated to anyone listening on the channel that an emergency was underway, and they should not break in.

"Negative. I'll be out of the vehicle on a handheld. Advise PD there's an armed federal agent on scene."

Craig dropped the car handset and activated the handheld radio on his belt. He wiggled the earpiece into his ear and broke squelch to make sure the battery was working. He reached for his pistol and quietly slid out his vehicle, approaching the golf cart on foot.

The security guard was cold to the touch, and stiff with rigor mortis, his shirt plastered to his skin with dried blood. To Craig, it looked like the body was in an unnatural position, with one of his arms stuck stiffly down his side. His pistol was still in his holster. Must've been moved, Craig decided. He pulled out his flashlight and waved the beam on the asphalt around the cart. A large pool of sticky blood lay up the road a few feet, with drag marks emanating from it and multiple tire imprints running through it.

So that's where he bled out. Craig faced the slope above, scanning the dark undergrowth over the barrel of his Glock. He strained his ears. There was nothing besides the crickets, and a faint background noise of traffic from the 405 freeway to the east. The sound of high-revving engines could be heard in the canyon below.

Los Angeles city proper has about four million inhabitants, served by nearly ten thousand police officers. Craig knew from past experience with the LA Police Department that, at any given time, there are about thirty patrol cruisers on LAPD West Bureau city streets. He hoped the vehicles he heard were some of them.

Craig followed the engine noises with his ears as they wound up the canyon, intermittently muffled by overhanging trees, the noise shouldering aside the peaceful stillness. He set his pistol on the trunk, stood with his hands raised, and maintained his position as two police cruisers crashed up the driveway entrance, their engines roaring and headlights blinding him. Craig waved at them with his open hands, his badge wallet clipped to his belt and conspicuously in view. The lead cruiser crunched to a halt, the driver's side door slamming open, while the second unit skidded to a stop behind. Please don't shoot me, Craig thought. He felt his body armor clutching his torso – at least I remembered to bring it, he thought. Jumpy cops sometimes made rash decisions in the dark.

In the glaring light, he could barely make out a figure crouching behind the open door. There was a muted shout.

"LAPD! Identify yourself!"

"Craig, FBI. I called it in. Kill your lights," Craig barked hoarsely.

The pair of headlights were extinguished. Booted feet jogged toward him, with the sounds of gear clinking on duty belts. Two heavy figures silhouetted against the dim amber running lights of the lead vehicle, and approached Craig, dropping into crouches. The leader had his pistol out, the second officer covering the slope above with an AR-15 carbine.

"Corporal Heck, LAPD West," the senior office hissed. "What's the situation?"

"I've got a dead security guard in a golf cart in front of me," Craig curtly indicated with his left hand. "He was shot in the head. The main house is above. We're probably going to need a SWAT team to sweep this place further."

Heck nodded. "I'll update dispatch. Midkiff here is SWAT," he nodded at the other officer, "but we'll have enough cover units here for a sweep in about ten to fifteen minutes. Good enough?"

"Affirmative. Let's keep the backup Code-2, and tell your partner to suit up." Craig peered around. "This place is pretty damn big. Can you get a map of this location on your terminal?"

"Yeah, I'll show you what I've got."

"Copy that."

* * *

The trussed ceiling of the unlit museum hangar glowed dimly in the light emanating from the two-story interior office stack at the rear of the cavernous space.

The pilot's briefing lounge on the ground floor of the hangar's administrative suite was crowded. Most of Lopez's team stood by the windows looking out on the hangered aircraft while Hallett, Bellamy, Cook, Stokes, Lopez and his lieutenant stood in a loose semi-circle around a central table, examining an aviation chart that lay spread before them. On the other side of the table were a couple of TVA corporate pilots that lived within quick commuting distance from Santa Monica and were on-call to the company Gulfstream on a 24-hour basis. When they heard what had happened to Hallett, they were willing converts to the cause.

The four-man security detail from Transvector headquarters had decamped across the street when Hallett summoned them, after sealing their building. Word of the killing of the protection team at Mandeville had infuriated them, and they were hot for Porter's hide. They had stationed themselves in the lobby and the parking lot with two of Lopez's operatives, to provide advance warning of any law enforcement approach.

Hallett hadn't dared call the TVA operations center in Mojave, recognizing the likelihood that the FBI was monitoring all incoming calls. And he didn't want to waste time bringing the feds in on the rescue. Hallett seemed to think that Porter would already be trying to move, and that time was of the essence.

It was 1:45 am in the morning.

Between bites of a three-day-old sandwich out of one of the vending machines in the break room, Cook watched as Bellamy tapped his finger on a satellite image of the MARAD surplus ships off Island Chaffee, which was laying on top of the terminal area aviation chart for Los Angeles.

"If they've got any kind of security there, which I'm sure they do, we'll be easy pickings when we come in. The place is wide open."

Cook leaned closer. Chaffee was one of four THUMS artificial islands in the bay, built in the '60s to camouflage the oil derricks tapping the Wilmington oil field under the shallow seabed. The 'THUMS' acronym came from the first letter of the names of the parent companies that formed the pumping consortium. The three reserve-fleet ships were moored side-by-side about a hundred yards south of the island, surrounded by a ring of containment booms positioned to catch any pollution from the ship-breaking operations. At the southeast end of the row rested two dock barges with office containers for the demolition operators, as well as several covered dumpsters for the stripped interior garbage. As Bellamy had noted, there didn't seem to be a lot of cover once you arrived, and they didn't even know where Kane and the others were being held.

Stokes interjected. "Are you sure he's there? He couldn't be anywhere else in the port?"

Hallett shook his head. "We don't have any facilities down there, just the ships and the barges. And there aren't any other China-related buildings along Lopez's phone trace line. Their structures are all over on the container terminals."

Bellamy ran a hand over his sparse hair. "It's pretty exposed. We'll get noticed."

Hallett bit his lower lip and nodded, gazing at another large printout showing the overall layout of the harbor. The satellite pictures had been printed up from sources straight off the internet, but if Cook hadn't known any better, he might have been looking at military-quality imagery at a real operational briefing. It's amazing what you can find online these days, he mused.

Hallett pointed at a structure across from the old Navy mole on Terminal Island, where Sea Launch docked their space-launch vessels. "How much time will we have before Harbor Patrol gets in on the action?"

Lopez jumped in, pointing at the Port of Los Angeles' West Basin, the furthest part of the port from the island. "We can create a diversion to draw them off. I can have a dock fire started in thirty minutes if needed. Perhaps one of these container cranes. But that still doesn't answer Mr. Bellamy's point." He indicated the mooring barges off the demolition ships. "Any boarding party landing here will be cut to pieces."

"What about smoke?"

Everyone turned to look at Cook, except Bellamy, who grinned at the satellite plot. "Spoken like a true airshow jockey. That could do it."

Lopez raised his eyebrows. "Perhaps you could enlighten the rest of us, Mr. Cook."

"All of these warbirds are equipped with smoke generators for airshows and film work, so the planes can make it look like they've taken a critical hit in aerial combat." He glanced at Bellamy for confirmation, receiving an encouraging nod. "All we'd have to do is max out the oil flow rheostat and run some passes over the boats."

"We'd have to make continuous runs," Bellamy added. "That way we don't get the wind drifting it clear."

Hallett grunted. "Sounds doable." He surveyed the other two pilots around the table, who were nodding agreement. "How long to get us up and running?"

Bellamy squeezed his eyes in fatigue, then popped them open. "We can open the hangar in forty minutes if we hump some butt. But we need some more sticks."

"I've called everyone I can think of nearby. We can scale up depending on who shows." Hallett turned to Lopez. "Do we have a deal, Mr. Lopez?"

Lopez surveyed his crew, then turned back to Hallett. "We do. But I want Porter alive."

Cook watched the pair's exchange with a growing uneasiness, like a couple of snarling lions squaring off to see who got to lead the pride. The two seemed more interested in taking Porter down than rescuing the hostage crewman. He interjected.

"We're focusing on getting Kane, Hendricks, and Barowicz out first, right?"

Hallett turned from Lopez, regarded Bellamy's stooped figure for a moment, then stared at Cook. Bellamy's sleep-drained eyes looked up from his charts.

"Do you even have to ask?"

* * *

What a mess.

Surveying the carnage at Hallett's mansion, Craig was overcome with the sensation that he was always going to be about five steps behind whatever was going on here. It wasn't something that comported well with his competitive nature. He really wanted to get in front of this thing, at the very least to keep the body count from growing.

The transverse hall running the length of the house was filled with bunny-suited FBI and LAPD crime scene technicians collecting evidence, while LA fire department paramedics rolled corpses out on gurneys for the trip to the coroner's office. The rest of the crowd was law enforcement: LAPD, sheriff's office, LA district attorney investigators and the county coroner. Seemed like everyone wanted to sign in on the action, or just have a look around.

McCray was with the first Bureau agents on scene, and he had assumed overall command upon arrival. As soon as Craig had called in the dead security guard, Simms had the threat center shift its attention to the Mandeville estate. One of McCray's first priorities was to control access to the crime scene. There were already too many agencies involved, and the FBI wanted to keep the confusion to a minimum.

Craig slid between two CSI technicians dusting for prints and made his way to the north end dining room, where McCray had established his command post. He was briefing a pair of agents, giving them colorful instructions on where to go next.

"Any sign of Hallett?"

McCray looked up with a harried scowl, then nodded when he saw it was Craig. "Nothing yet. We're getting some K-9 units up here ASAP to sniff the grounds." He arched his back, kneading his lower oblique muscles with his hands and grimacing. "You can sure cough up a real furball when you want to. I thought Simms gave you light duty."

"Yeah, no rest for the wicked. Where's Hallett's wife?"

"No body, and looks like some toiletries missing from their bathroom. Empty spaces in the closet too, so maybe on vacation – or she left him." Either option seemed plausible to McCray. "We're still trying to track her down." His back ministrations ceased, and McCray rolled his head on his shoulders, his neck cracking audibly. "They didn't seem to miss much else, though. Techs found a couple dead dogs out back."

Craig shook his head. "Assholes."

"Real steaming pile of squat."

"I just happened to step in it. What's your read?"

McCray, both his hands propping himself up on the table, snorted. "Beats the fuck out of me. Two dead Asian bangers, two dead Caucasian suits, and one Latino with really bad taste in clothing. All three of Hallett's security, plus the driver. Evidence of at least one body tied to a chair – we're typing the bloodstains there for Hallett and getting DNA as soon as possible. And it looks like a bunch of other people were here and left."

"So, same as when we came in. Any prints come back yet?"

"No, but we're sending them as we lift them." McCray yawned. "Any fresh ideas?"

"One." Craig paused. "The two dead suits in the study. Send pictures to Riverside sheriff. They might be the guys who picked up the rest of the TVA crew."

McCray nodded. "Good thinking. Oh, and by the way, Simms called in. He wants to talk to you."

Craig stepped out of the room, and dialed. When it connected, Craig could hear boisterous noise from the threat center, with Beauchamp yelling at someone in the background.

"You're a one-man wrecking crew, Craig. You were supposed to go there to catch some Z-time on Hallett's couch."

Craig snickered. "Yeah, didn't work out that way, Gil. Any leads on your end?"

"Nothing. Did Cook do this?"

Craig paused, listening to the background hubbub.

"No way. At least, not alone." Craig surveyed the hallway. "This was professional, all the way down the line. Clean head shots. Neighbors heard nothing, so they definitely used suppressors."

Simms didn't respond for a moment. Craig could hear him talking to someone in the background. Then he came back on the line.

"Got any ideas?"

"Just gave McCray my latest and greatest. Need me for anything here?"

"Hell no. McCray says its overstaffed as it is. What are you thinking?"

"I'd pull Bellamy in." Craig chewed his lip. "If someone's doing a cleanup, they might go after him too."

"Okay, standby." Craig could hear Simms hollering to a dispatcher in the center. "Get me the SOG unit on Bellamy in Mar Vista."

Craig waited. SOG, or the Surveillance Operations Group, was a unit usually staffed by farmed-out agents near retirement or those who had consistently low performance reviews. There was an extended pause, then a sub-audible reply. Simms barked, "Get some units down there, pronto!"

Craig felt tension fill his gut. There was more yelling in the background from Beauchamp. Simms came back on the line.

"No response from the surveillance unit. Can you head down there to cover that while I get LAPD rolling?"

"On it."

Craig ran toward the door.

* * *

CHAPTER FIFTEEN

At twenty minutes to three, Bellamy gave a raspy growl to gather the troops in front of the hangar door for a final pep talk.

Cook, who had just finished rigging a drop tank on a Douglas Skyraider with another pilot, wiped grease off his hand on the trailing edge of a flap as he ducked under the wing to go forward. He instantly regretted it. Bellamy might have been old and tired, but he had eyes like a hawk.

"Cook! Goddammit! Wipe that filth on your dungarees, not my goddamned bird!" Bellamy was clearly excited that his museum collection would see some action, but apparently that didn't mean he was willing to let his unusually high standards slide, even for a minute. Stokes threw him a smirk from her position by the door. Cook wondered how the old coot was going to handle his precious aircraft getting shot all to hell.

The last forty-five minutes had been filled with frenetic activity, getting the planes prepped for an anticipated combat rescue. Tanks and tires were topped off, and batteries checked for a full charge. Smoke generator oil reservoirs had been filled to capacity and recalibrated to produce as heavy a smoke plume as possible.

Hallett had put his vintage aircraft collection under Bellamy's sole authority, and Bellamy had one rule: everything flies. Each aircraft, no matter what its age, was a superbly maintained specimen of its kind. Two of the planes, which were experimental prototypes never put into full production, had even been built from scratch off the original plans. They were the only models in existence, flying or static. Cook knew from extensive experience that there was not a finer collection in existence.

No company member present had questioned the rational of the plan, such was the level of their loyalty to Hallett and Bellamy. Three additional pilots had made it in, propelled to the museum on the strength of a phone call from their boss. One was the chief museum pilot, Weir, who Cook knew from past TVA airshows. Once inside, he had taken over supervision of the aircraft prep from Bellamy. Two more off-duty security officers had been drafted without complaint to protect Hallett personally, once the situation had been explained. Cook felt the burgeoning surge of morale inspired by being a part of an outfit that had its act together.

Because they were expecting armed opposition, Bellamy had taken Cook, Stokes and one of the night-shift security personnel in a flatbed golf cart down to the vault to collect whatever could be useful. They had returned bearing a veritable armory of historical weaponry. Olive-colored steel ammunition boxes shared the cart bed with an Italian MG 42/59 light machine gun, a Sten submachine gun, a Vietnam-era belt-fed M60, and sundry other items that weren't too big to fit in an airplane. Cook had bagged the Swedish K sub-gun and a Belgian Hi-Power for his personal use, while Bellamy sported a pair of Colt M1911 .45s in an antiquated shoulder rig. Stokes and the security guard were draped with clacking assemblies of slung M4 carbines from the upstairs armory, as well as a satchel bulging with spare magazines.

The assembled crew sat or kneeled in front of Bellamy and Hallett, loading cartridges into magazines as they listened to the final brief. Lopez stood with his personnel in a group slightly to the rear, after having refilled their ammunition expended at Hallett's estate.

Bellamy led off.

"In ten minutes, we're going to cut the hanger lights and open the doors. After that it's flashlights only and use them sparingly. I want tow bars on everything we can't push out manually. We are going to be as stealthy as possible until I give the start command to avoid attracting attention from the airport police. Mr. Lopez," he nodded in his direction, "has arranged for a series of diversions both here in Santa Monica and in the back-harbor area to keep law enforcement busy while we make our run."

Bellamy, old pro that he was, had set up a white board on an easel and had drawn a rough diagram of the west of Los Angeles and San Pedro Bay in black with the target vessels outlined in red. He uncapped a green felt pen and referred to the board.

"We're taking five aircraft on this mission: two amphibs, two cover birds and the Huey. I'll be in the

Catalina with Swann, callsign 'Dumbo'. Hugh will be flying the Albatross with Kohl, callsign 'Goat'. Cook and Lehman are in the Huey, callsign 'Dust Off'. Weir in the Skyraider and Hanks in the TBM are 'Sandy' and 'Turkey' respectively. The flight's name is 'Angel', and the people on the ships are 'Boarding Party', to keep things simple. The Huey will depart first with Lopez and six of his team to get a head start and provide overwatch and reconnaissance. The rest of us will get airborne as soon as we're warmed up."

He drew a curved green line on the board running from Santa Monica around the Palos Verdes peninsula to the target island.

"We'll do a gaggle takeoff, with the light planes in front, off runway 21 and head due southwest for the coastline. Stay low – we'll be going right under the LAX departure after we bank south. We'll hook out and around Palos Verdes and do a low orbit counter-clockwise around the bay, and line up on the boats for the first smoke pass. Use the southeastern container terminal and the entrance to Alamitos Bay," Bellamy gestured, "for orientation. The helicopter will loiter by Island Chaffee and approach the barges after the first pass." He looked over at Lehman. "Do an immediate dust-off with one of our shooters to provide air cover. Orbit south of the island and wait for their call. Keep an eye out for boat patrols."

Bellamy pointed at the red ship outlines on the board. "We're designating the three ships 'Alpha', 'Bravo' and 'Charlie', with 'Alpha' being the clos-est to the barge docks. We don't know where Kane and the others are located, so Cook and Lopez," he pointed at each man, "your crew will have to clear them one-by-one, starting at the structures on the docks."

Cook glanced up at Lopez and received a curt nod in return. Stokes was staring forward from her cross-legged position on the floor, clicking 5.56mm rounds into the M4 magazines. Cook wondered which team she felt she belonged to. He hoped it was his. Bellamy continued.

"After the second pass, the four aircraft will come around for another run, but the Albatross and Catalina will break off and land on the water, and step-taxi toward the south side of the ships. There will be one gunner on each."

"Stokes," he grinned, "you and Byrd are with me." He nodded at another security man. "Chenoweth, you're on the Albatross. We will do continuous step-taxi runs past the ships to draw fire and keep the attention off the chopper. The Skyraider and TBM will carry on making smoke passes and after that third pass flash their gas guns to keep the opposition's heads down. Any questions so far?"

There were none. To Cook, everyone seemed to be steeling themselves for combat, their eyes focused somewhere just in front of Bellamy and their hands reflexively checking their weapons. He had experienced it himself a few times. The mind was absorbing the details of the operation, but the grimness of the impending action blanketed one's perception with a slight haze. It always cleared once you got into the thick of it.

Bellamy looked at Hallett, who nodded for him to proceed.

"You're going to have about twenty minutes on site before we have to bug out. Thirty max. Coast Guard, Harbor Patrol and LAPD are going to notice our activity pretty fast, so move quickly once you're there. Island Chaffee will have some security too, but we expect they won't intervene. Hopefully, law enforcement will be as confused as the targets on the boats. Do not engage them under any circumstances – if you get stopped, surrender immediately, and we'll take care of you afterwards."

"Once we acquire Kane and others, or," he scowled, "find out they're dead, we extract via the Huey or call in the amphibians on the radio and we'll get you by the barge docks. If anyone goes overboard, swim for the nearest land and stay behind cover. Keep communications to a minimum unless you need help, and be specific. After Cook makes the call that they've cleared the docks, Weir and Hanks will do a final pass for cover."

Bellamy gave a thin smile. "I was thinking of putting Blair in the TBM's torpedo bay and dropping him as a special parting gift, but Langley probably wants him alive, so we're going to leave him on the docks for the spooks to deal with. Hopefully, he'll get shot in the crossfire. Hugh."

Bellamy stepped to the side and Hallett looked over the assembled grouping.

"Ted Porter broke the sacred trust, and decided, at some point, to kill our friends and try to destroy this company." He paused for a moment, looking toward the ceiling, his face taut with anger. He then composed himself, returning his gaze to the cluster of waiting faces. "I don't know why he did this, and I don't care. He has three of our people hostage. They are our first and only priority. I know some of you would like to put a bullet in Porter's head, and I'm right there in line with you, but," he paused again for emphasis, his eyes settling on Cook, "we get our people out first. Is that understood?"

Cook and all the TVA personnel nodded their assent immediately, but Lopez just stared at Hallett for a moment before finally giving a peremptory nod. He didn't look happy to Cook, but if he wanted to get extracted from the ship barges, he was going to have to play ball.

"Good. We open the doors in three minutes. If you haven't finished loading up, do it on board. Mr. Lopez, we could use those distractions you have planned right about now."

* * *

The night sky above San Pedro Bay was a soft grey blanket of high marine layer, scattered stars peeking through the occasional thin spots like glitter seen through a cotton quilt. The swoosh-suck of the calm dark water against ship hulls was complemented by the creaking of mooring lines and the tinkle of chains as the tide gently caressed the rusty steel sides. A faint odor of seaweed, oil and decay was buffeted by a light wind from seaward.

Porter leaned on the rail of the *SS Strathcona*, looking over the flurry of activity on the barge docks below, and decided that this relatively peaceful prospect was the last he would see for a while. He would have to run, that much he knew, and fast. And find a deep hole. He was more worried about the Agency than the FBI. The CIA had a long reach and would backcomb every region they had contacts in to find him. He would have to completely drop off the grid.

Off in the distance, he heard a helicopter passing over the port, heading south.

He could do it. The group he worked with would exfiltrate him out of Los Angeles, probably later today on a plane out of Orange County. They wouldn't be happy to hear how their mission had ostensibly imploded, if they didn't know already, but he had proved his worth in the past, and wasn't worried about becoming operational collateral.

Porter had always considered himself more CIA than TVA, not that there was a tremendous distinction between the two. And he thought of his current employer as the 'real CIA', unlike the group in Langley that had become a toothless, worldwide social welfare agency. He had never been given a name for it. They had contacted him through known and trusted CIA associates. Their operations seemed to be largely funded offshore, and they deniably conducted the crucial intelligence and direct-action operations that their feeble parent institution couldn't handle any longer.

They had provided the binary nerve agent precursors, the most difficult aspect of the whole operation, from some unknown offshore stockpile. Probably Syria. After that, it was easy. One tank of chemicals looks a lot like another, and the handling protocols were virtually identical.

He fingered a cell phone in his windbreaker's pocket and wondered if he should call Blair's mobile again. He was pretty sure the FBI couldn't have tracked his signal during his brief conversation with Cook, and in any case the odds of them figuring out the seaborne location were close to nil. They would spend a lot of time running around the harbor area, scoping out warehouses and other likely venues. He wasn't actually interested in any kind of deal with the feds. He just wanted to stall them long enough to high-tail it out of town. Kane and his crew were almost useless as bargaining chips. He was fairly confident the U.S. government would scorch the earth to try to take him down.

They had almost gotten lucky blowing it open on the DEA side. Porter had caught Romero sniffing around TVA's fences months before and had decided to muddy the waters to bring the opposition in for a close-up. Romero had sucked up all of Porter's 'leaked' chicken-feed information through Massey, convinced that the TVA narcotics window-dressing was the real thing, and had walked himself into a bear trap. Had Porter let him live, Romero would have been forever discredited for the off-the-books foray, and probably shit-canned.

He pulled the flip phone from his pocket and stared at it. It was a new phone, completely clean and even primitive in its lack of a GPS. Mr. Hu, his appropriately and vaguely-named triad contact, had given him a half dozen for this deal. As he turned it over in his hands, he speculated whether Cook would answer again if he called.

Cook. What a worthless deadbeat. The washout piece of crap had nearly scuppered the entire god-damned operation, besides giving him a migraine and an endless amount of hassle for the last three days. As if the low-altitude parachute jump from Strongman One and subsequent hike out of the area hadn't been trouble enough. His right ankle still ached from turning it on a boulder during the pitch-black landing. Porter had hardly slept trying to keep all the loose ends tied together. Romero had to be taken care of, Kane and the others picked up. But Cook, that cagey wrench-monkey, kept slipping the noose.

How the lucky bastard had managed to crash land his Hercules was beyond Porter. The plan to lawn-dart the birds into a mountainside was foolproof, even inspired. Blair had followed his role perfectly, inserting the bad code into the navigation program under the guise of a system test. But how did Cook, that simple, crop-dusting sap, foul up his endgame? Just goes to show you can't take anything for granted. Should have left him in that jerkwater dust-hole where I found him. If he hadn't been so short on qualified spec-ops pilots due to the company's numerous foreign taskings, Porter wouldn't have bothered.

And somehow, they had gotten Blair. Another sorry excuse for an operator. Porter had used his overseas Chinese contacts to flip the greenhorn CIA agent in Hong Kong when he was sniffing around for sources. It hadn't taken much. He had fallen into a honey trap with a slim piece of Wan Chai tail, and hadn't wanted to come out again. He also liked gambling, thinking his Georgetown-honed math skills gave him an edge.

The bookies were more than happy to take his markers. When Porter's group had dropped the net on him, they had sweetened-the-sour with a fat payout. He was in their pocket ever since. They had made sure he had gotten promotion track assignments and positioned him perfectly for a job like this.

Not that everything had gone perfectly to plan. Fucking Blair. Now just another checkbox on the 'to-do' list, which seemed to keep getting longer.

A clanging sound came from below, causing Porter to look down. The triad-hired crews were about half finished transferring their cargo onto a quartet of fishing trawlers tied to the south side of the barge dock. They had been loading the fat-hulled boats non-stop for the last hour, ever since Porter had sent up the rocket following Cook's phone call. It took a long time to pack nearly five metric tons of liquid fentanyl, heroin, pills, and methamphetamine. As soon as they finished, the ships were going to head out to sea on preplanned routes and drop the loads overboard *en route*. Each of the watertight containers had a sensor package attached to the top that would trigger a flotation bladder on receipt of the proper signal. Then they'd be able to collect the contraband at their convenience.

Selling the operation to the Vancouver triads had been breathtaking in its simplicity. The expense of partially financing the operation had been measured against the temporary elimination of the Mexican competition and the expected supply-chain domination of the western US narcotics markets for at least the next year. There would be reprisals, of course, vicious ones, but those anticipated costs had also been factored in. Eventually, everyone would have to recognize the stunning *fait accompli*. But, in order for the plan to have the greatest chance of success, the anonymity of the principal actors was required.

Cook had thrown a wrench in some pretty finely tuned machinery, denting it beyond repair.

Over the last three days, Porter's triad contacts had expressed ever-increasing disapproval with the progression of events. Not aggressively, but in the calm and reserved manner that was far more menacing. They would kill him without hesitation or remorse if he couldn't contain this in time. After all, he had personally been promised five million USD from them for consulting services on this operation, half upfront. And they paid for competence and discretion.

At this point, Porter was hoping that their age-old reverence for the verbal contract would still buy him enough time for a quiet exit of the area.

Otherwise, he was roadkill.

* * *

Craig skidded to a halt near the LAPD cruiser's flashing strobes just as one of the officers was smashing the front driver side's window with his collapsible baton. He ran toward the white Yukon as the officer reached through the broken glass to unlock the doors. A junior officer, whose startled expression betrayed his trainee-status, moved to intercept Craig with his left arm forward and his right on his firearm. "Hold it! Stay where you are!"

"Craig, FBI!" Craig snarled as he continued striding. "Where is he?" This was directed at the senior officer by the window.

"In the back."

Craig reached the vehicle and ran his flashlight over the tinted glass. "Is he alive?"

"He's kicking."

"I'll get the tailgate." Craig pivoted around the rear quarter panel and yanked the black glass hatch open. The FBI agent duct-taped eyes and mouth turned toward him, his face contorting. "Wells, SA Craig, you're safe."

The agent let out a muffled moan of relief. Craig dropped the tailgate and reached in to start tearing the tape off the man's face. "Brace yourself."

Wells nodded. Craig ripped quickly, and Wells blinked and took several deep breaths before rattling out his information.

"There were at least eight of them. Hispanic males, maybe a female – well-dressed – Glocks and suppressed MP5s. Very professional. Have you got some water?"

The LAPD sergeant, who'd been listening intently, nodded and hustled to the trunk of his cruiser, returning with a plastic bottle. Craig dragged the agent halfway on to the tailgate to rip off the tape binding his hands, then cracked the cap on the water bottle. Wells stiffly pushed himself to a sitting position, his arms obviously numb with a lack of circulation. He accepted the bottle with trembling hands and drank deeply. Craig took the bottle from him gently. "Easy. Short sips."

Wells nodded and continued. "They came to pick up Bellamy – I think they got him. They had at least two vehicles, an SUV and maybe a sedan, both dark-colored. They left about an hour ago. That's all I got."

Craig nodded while working the tape off of Wells' legs hanging over the tailgate. "Any sign of Hallett, Cook or Stokes?"

"Negative."

"Did you hear them say anything, like where they were heading?"

"Nope. I was already in the back. I could hear some voices, but I couldn't make anything out. They were gone in less than a minute."

Craig patted him lightly on the arm. "Don't feel bad about it. They sound like a tight crew, and they move very fast. Hold on while I call this in."

Craig got FBI dispatch on his radio and relayed the essential details. As he finished, an ambulance bus arrived, strobes blazing. Two paramedics hopped out and rushed over. Craig put his hand on Wells' shoulder. "I've got to make some calls. You get yourself checked out by these guys, and then head back in to report. Have LAPD give you a ride if you need it, ok?"

Wells nodded his assent as he kept drinking, and Craig walked back to his car. He leaned against the side and cleared the fatigue from his mind to run through the progression. A crew of sharp-looking, professional Hispanics had shown up at the stakeout. They had taken Bellamy, and probably had Hallett as well. How did they fit in with the Asians at Mandeville? Was the dead Latino one of theirs?

He dialed Simms.

"Simms, Craig. Wells is ok, but a very professional Hispanic crew took Bellamy. We might have some kind of high-level Mexican-Asian gang war going on."

"What's your thinking?"

"The crew in Palm Springs was all Asian, and there were a couple more at Hallett's. I don't know how this figures against the TVA thing, but maybe the Asians had some involvement."

"Where do you think they're going?"

Craig fought against his mental haze. "No clue. But this is really starting to look like a tiger kidnapping, or something similar. They might try to fly them out. I'd have your team call county dispatch and see if there's any activity around the local airports. And maybe get the Homeland liaison to contact the FAA air traffic center – see if they have any charters with flight plans scheduled to leave this morning that fit the profile."

"I'll get them on it. You coming back in?"

Craig was getting discouraged by still being so many steps behind his unknown quarry. "Yep. There's nothing more to do here."

* * *

Cook buckled on his harness and looked back in the rear of the Bell UH-1D Iroquois to make sure everyone was aboard. In the gloom, he felt more than saw Lopez give a thumbs-up in response. Off in the distance, on the southwest corner of the airport, Cook could see a pair of emergency strobes flashing off the hangar rows, presumably where Lopez had set his distraction for the Santa Monica airport police. He hoped they kept it up long enough for the other aircraft to launch.

Commonly dubbed a 'Huey', the museum's UH-1D was, like all of Bellamy's aircraft, in pristine condition, and sported a paint job straight out of an air cavalry regiment in Vietnam. The rear cabin could seat up to thirteen, but with Lopez and his eight-person team there was plenty of space. One of the TVA security men sat in a 'pocket' behind the main cabin, manning a belt-fed M60 machine gun from Bellamy's private collection hanging on a bungee from the roof. He was to provide air cover if needed while the rest of the team was on the ships.

Blair was a duct-taped bundle laying in the athwart-ship aisle between the forward and rear facing seats, providing a convenient footrest for Lopez's crew.

Cook was flying left seat, with Lehman as pilot-in-command on the right. Seating positions on helicopters were the reverse of fixed-wing planes. Cook was riding co-pilot because he would be exiting with Lopez's assault team, something he had occasionally experienced in the past but had never gotten wholly accustomed to. Jumping out of a helicopter in a Nicaraguan jungle to drag someone on board was a lot different than being left behind to fight with the ground forces. He felt a fleeting stab of envy for Stokes. At least she got to stay on the Albatross and shoot from cover. Cook glanced over at Lehman as he stowed a submachine gun next to his seat. He looked competent enough. Bastard better come back pronto when they called, Cook griped to himself.

The radio on Cook's lap crackled with Bellamy's call. "Dust Off, fire up."

Lehman hit the master switch, illuminating the 'Christmas tree' of lights on the center console. The low whines of gyros and turbines spinning up could be heard as Lehman then hit the engine start rocker, followed by the ignition. Overhead, the massive pair of blades began to slowly rotate, gradually increasing in tempo.

Cook turned the helicopter's radio on, listening for any airport traffic. As could be expected at this hour, it was silent. Cook rapidly went through the checklist, leaving the navigation lights off. No sense in drawing attention while they were still on the ground.

Behind him, even through the deadening effect of his Clark headset, Cook could hear the belching roar of the other aircraft firing up their massive radial engines. Bellamy clearly wasn't waiting for the local cops to investigate an unscheduled, late-night departure. He was going to get everyone off the tarmac as soon as possible. The tower at Santa Monica was continuously attended, and the on-duty controllers couldn't miss the noise of five radial-engined aircraft departing, even without lights.

When the rotor disc had wound up to full potential, Lehman pulled up the collective and lifted the Huey into a smooth hover. He loitered for a moment, then tilted the nose and drifted forward into a smooth ground effect takeoff. Cook instantly felt better. Lehman clearly knew his stuff. The helicopter coasted down the taxiway at a height of about eight feet for a few hundred yards, and then sharply transitioned into a gut-dropping climb into the night sky.

Cook concentrated on scanning the sky around them as they proceeded at a height of one hundred feet. The residential and streetlamps of the bright cityscape below provided plenty of background light, but that fell off suddenly into darkness as they crossed the Pacific coastline. Cook keyed his handheld radio with a 'Dust Off, feet wet' call while Lehman pulled a set of night optics down over his eyes and made an abrupt dive to about thirty feet over the water. They would maintain this altitude until they reached the harbor.

Lehman had clearly done some time in military helicopters. His comfort with the night vision headset told Cook that much. Lehman's movements were smooth and practiced, with no visible hesitation. Cook stopped worrying about whether he would be there for the pickup.

A couple of minutes later, the radio crackled again. "Angel flight, legs up." Bellamy was announcing that the warbirds had made it into the air. Cook checked the time. The two single-pilot aircraft had a significant speed advantage over the Huey, while the Albatross and the Catalina both cruised at roughly the same velocity. The faster planes would have to hold back to allow the formation to stay together, but after their arrival they'd be able to make multiple runs of obscuring smoke before the vulnerable amphibians hit the water. And Cook knew Hallett and Bellamy would be pouring on the coals to stay up with the timetable.

Bellamy had estimated the total flight time from Santa Monica down to San Pedro Bay would be about twenty minutes, and the scattered lights of millionaire horse-ranch properties on the Palos Verdes peninsula on his left indicated to Cook that they were a little more than halfway there. He keyed his handheld to give a position update.

"Dust Off at Limbo," he enunciated carefully, giving the VOR intersection and speaking slowly so his call could be heard clearly in the other aircrafts' noisy cockpits. They were using handheld radios tuned to encrypted commercial frequencies to keep the traffic off the aviation bands, but the downside was a drop in signal strength due to the short, rubber-duck antennas inside the aircraft.

Bellamy replied instantaneously. "Dust Off, Angel flight. We're about five behind you. Step on the gas."

"Roger."

Lehman dipped the rotor disc slightly and pulled more collective to increase their forward speed as much as possible. Faint reflected light off the rolling Pacific swells streaked below. Cook adjusted himself to a more upright sitting position, and noted Lehman doing the same thing. The bright glare of the Los Angeles harbor haloed the top of the peninsular ridge in front of them. Another couple minutes and they'd see the bay.

"Put on psywar op, make it loud," Cook muttered into the intercom, parroting Lt. Colonel Kilgore in *Apocalypse Now*. Under his night-optics, Lehman grinned his assent, nodding.

* * *

CHAPTER SIXTEEN

The yawning darkness of the Pacific Aviation Museum's hangar loomed above Craig. He played his flashlight over the vast space. There were several aircraft parked at the back of the hangar, but most of the glossy, gray-painted floor surface was empty, except for the odd stain of oil and what looked like recent tire marks. He walked towards the massive bifold door, which was closed, and felt something under his shoe. Craig shone the beam on a ratchet socket and some nuts that lay on the floor. They were out of place on an otherwise pristine and uncluttered floor.

Funny, Craig thought. This hangar seemed to be a museum space, not the kind of place Transvector would keep a corporate jet. And it looked like a good portion of the collection was missing. What the hell was going on?

He turned to the TVA security officer who had followed him to the hangar in a golf cart and opened the facility's side door. "Shouldn't there be more planes in here?"

The guard looked uncomfortable. "Yes sir. It's usually full."

"What kind of aircraft does the company keep in here?"

"Old World War II stuff. Mostly." The guard looked nervous, his phrasing clipped. "Look, uh…I just do the night shift here at the parking lot part-time. I'm in college."

Decades of experience told Craig that the guard, who was shifting his weight from one foot to the other, not sure how to stand, was not telling him everything. "Do you know where they are?"

The guard closed his eyes, exhaling. "I…was in the booth, asleep. I don't know what happened to them."

Craig looked hard at the man, who averted his eyes.

"You're telling me that several large World War II planes were taken from the hangar, and you didn't see or hear anything?" He snorted. "Are you aware that making false statements to a federal agent is punishable by up to five years in prison?"

The security guard blanched. "No sir."

"Then tell me what you do know."

"I checked a bunch of cars into the lot at about 2 o'clock. Mr. Bellamy was in the first car. He told me that there was a late-night company party and to let everybody in."

"How many cars were there?"

"Two at first, and more showed up later."

Maybe he really had been asleep, Craig thought. The guy looks scared piss-less. And not too bright. And Bellamy had been here.

On the short drive back to Wilshire from Bellamy's apartment, Simms had called back to tell him that the Santa Monica police were in the process of arresting a gang of Hispanic juveniles who had jumped the south fence and were breaking into planes. The police had also taken calls from a number of residents that had complained about loud aircraft departing at low altitude from Santa Monica. The DHS liaison was working to confirm that with the FAA, but the aviation controllers hadn't received any radar returns on their screens, and if any aircraft had been flying in that area, they were running without transponders.

Craig had instantly diverted from his route, heading toward Santa Monica.

A SMPD airport supervisor's car drove up as Craig was walking back to his vehicle. He rolled down his window. "You Craig?"

"Yep. You see anything here?"

"Negative. We were checking out an alarm trip at one of the FBOs on the south side. About a dozen kids had jumped the fence and were breaking into planes. We caught a few of 'em, the rest bailed. We're booking them down at the station."

"You see any aircraft take off?"

"Naw, was chasing those bangers. Fast little pricks. Heard some engine noise, though."

Craig closed his eyes tiredly. "You didn't think that was worth checking out?"

The supervisor's eyes narrowed. "Planes take off and land here all night. We get a lot of nighttime lifeguard helo ops here too, so I didn't really get too worked up about it. Too busy hooking up those punks to rubberneck."

"You didn't get an FAA advisory about aircraft activity?"

"Not yet."

Craig pressed his thumbs against his eyelids, and slowly counted to ten.

The supervisor seemed to sense Craig's fatigue. He leisurely got out of his vehicle, hitched his belt over his ample gut, and walked over. He gave the security guard a nod. "What are you here for anyway?"

"Bunch of aircraft are missing from this hangar."

The supervisor waved at the TVA museum. "Those hangar doors are alarmed. Rings down at the Olympic station. And I would've gotten a call. Whoever opened the doors knew the codes, or knew how to get 'em open without trippin' 'em."

Craig pointed at the hangar door. "You know how many aircraft are usually in there?"

"Not my specialty, agent." The supervisor shook his head. "A dozen? I've been to a couple airshow open houses here. How many are missing?"

"No idea."

The supervisor shrugged and looked at the security guard. "Guess I'll get some paper started on this, then."

As the supervisor reached into his open door, Craig stifled an urge to kick him in his ample ass. "Yeah, maybe you should do that." He stalked back to his car, his fists balled, and leaned against the fender while he dialed Simms.

"What'd you find?"

"They're in the air somewhere. And the weird thing is, Bellamy was with them, and they took a bunch of antique aircraft, at least three or four. Doesn't make any sense. Can you get me a chopper?"

"The Bureau's bird is Palm Springs. A WMD detail went out to supervise the airport quarantine operation."

Craig pounded the roof of the car in frustration. "Get me LAPD, Coast Guard or the fucking Forest Service if you have to! I need some air, Gil. I can't look for these guys from the ground."

"Hold your piss, Denny." Simms growled. "You're not the only agent on this. We're burning both ends here."

Craig sighed, nodding to the phone. "Sorry, Gil. Getting frustrated from all the dropped balls."

"Hang tight. I'll see what I can scare up."

* * *

"We are extremely disappointed with the outcome of your operation, Mr. Porter," said the voice calmly, enunciating each word with a careful Asian inflection. "The crucial element of secrecy you promised our organization has not been realized, and forces us to utilize extraordinary countermeasures to preserve our cargo. According to the terms of our agreement, we cannot release the balance of your fee to you."

Porter leaned with his back to the deck rail, arms crossed, and regarded the pair of triads facing him. The senior of the two, doing all the speaking, called himself 'Mr. Hu', apparently believing the enigmatic alias would protect his identity. Porter knew better. His real name was Hung Hsi-kuan, and he served as the 'Straw Sandal' messenger of the Shan Gu Bang Triad out of east Vancouver. He was Fujian-born *hongman* of the old school who had a reputation for genteel ruthlessness. Hu also was known to be affiliated with the People's Liberation Army intelligence organs, helping their military and commercial espionage branches obtain useful information. In return, they let him traffic opioids and heroin from mainland China to Canadian ports.

The younger man, ropily-built and tall for a Chinese, was a Shan Gu enforcer. Both triads wore white hardhats and navy-blue belted coveralls as part of their corporate cover, the muscle wearing a short navy jacket to cover his weapons. Hu, being management, wore a tie.

Porter had first encountered Hu under a different name as an official observer during some clandestine anti-drug operations near the China-Laos border where TVA was a logistics contractor. He had run into him again in the Shan states in Myanmar, where Hu had pulled some favors to allow TVA to operate in Chinese airspace. He was an unusually talented fixer with broad and deep connections. In his dual role as poacher and gamekeeper, Hu seemed mainly interested in eliminating competing opium growers and ensuring his group's product made it to market.

The Shan Gu Bang was an offshoot of the Four Lotus Triad out of Guangdong and cooperated with drug traffickers of other ethnicities to distribute their narcotics in the US, including certain Mexican cartels. Their partners had gotten greedy, and started a turf-war to gain market share. The triad had suffered some losses in their Los Angeles operations, and were keen to send a message. Porter had heard about their problems through his special CIA group contacts and had provided the Shan Gu the opportunity to bootstrap onto the TVA mission.

The agreement Hu referred to was Porter's consulting fee for his services.

Now those arrangements were in jeopardy, and he had gotten only half of the five million in advance. The presence of the triad foot soldier incited Porter to think quickly – he was pretty sure that guy was supposed to shoot him. He needed to stall for time to figure out an escape route.

"Secrecy was only important at the outset, and that was achieved. You will still have your product available at short notice – that was a contingency I arranged, by the way." Porter paused to catch his breath, and smiled. "The feds will be chasing dead ends for months."

Hu shook his head slowly. "No, Mr. Porter, I fear they will come to the logical conclusion only too soon. Your attempt to eliminate Mr. Hallett failed, and my sources inform me that he is nowhere to be found."

"Right, I heard that too." Porter nodded sympathetically, and looked right toward the fishing trawlers, meditatively scratching at his chin stubble with his left hand. He then quickly pulled a suppressed Walther .22 from its concealment in his left armpit and shot the bodyguard in the neck. Hu, who had been in the process of making a hand signal to his accomplice, froze in shock. Porter shot Hu once in each eye socket, and then quickly moved forward to catch his body. He dragged the upright figure into the shadow of a stairwell and let it slump against the bulkhead. He went back and dragged the still burbling assassin by the heels. Once behind cover, Porter put another round through the man's forehead, mainly to shut him up, and took his pistol. He then strode casually along the rail toward the bow of the vessel.

Fuck, he thought, when he had reached the comparative darkness of the bow stem. He had to get off these ships before someone noticed the bodies. Hijacking one of the trawlers was out. There were a dozen armed goons on the barges supervising the loading work. The triad's helicopter wouldn't come in until the last container had left, and it would be heavily protected.

He changed magazines in the Walther, and then checked the suppressed Glock, which he had pulled off the back of the bodyguard's belt. The magazine was full, topped off with subsonic hollow points. Porter sneered. They were probably planning to eliminate him the whole time. So much for honor among thieves.

The faint blade-slap of another helicopter could be heard in the distance. Porter knew it wasn't the triad's copter by the rotor noise. Probably a USMC AH-1 Cobra on a night training mission, heading back to Camp Pendleton, although it sounded like the older, twin-blade model. He still had some time, he ruminated, as he racked his brain for options. There were a couple maintenance boats moored at the other end of the row of ships. They were accessed by an aluminum gangway and used for work around the waterlines and on the buoyed retention barrier. He was pretty sure they were both unguarded, relatively speaking.

Where to go? Asia was out for the time being. South America, maybe? He had good contacts down there, and he could lie low until he had figured something else out. The Bombardier jet out of Orange County airport had long legs, and shouldn't have to refuel until Colombia at the earliest. Argentina, Ecuador and Bolivia all had ambivalent feelings towards the US, and extradition could be delayed for years. Paraguay, maybe? Nicaragua and Venezuela weren't out of the question, but he'd have to sell his soul for the protection. But, first things first.

Porter started moving aft toward the trussed span that linked the *Strathcona* to its next-door neighbor the *USNS Grundy*, then paused. The sound of the helicopter approaching from the southwest was getting louder, and its blade signature was distinctive. Funny, now it sounded more like a Huey.

* * *

Cook's Huey rounded Point Fermin and arced out across the San Pedro breakwater, climbing from just above sea level to an altitude of eighty feet. To the left was the dark maw of the main channel of the Port of Los Angeles, flanked by the Signal Street pier and the Terminal Island Coast Guard base. Rushing toward him were the myriad moles, wharfs and container terminals of the giant west coast port complex, their lit surfaces resembling glowing fingers reaching out into the dark Pacific.

Even though the tower derricks on the THUMS islands were brightly lit, Cook couldn't make out the ships yet. But he knew from their heading that they lay just a few miles ahead.

Further inland, to the north, near a basin called the Northwest Slip, Lopez had arranged a diversion for the port's law enforcement. Cook didn't know the exact details, but the Mexican had made it sound like his gang contacts would light some pallets on fire and do some general mayhem. Just the thing to get port security in action, and out of their way. Cook glanced left but saw nothing unusual; there were too many obstructions in the way. But he hoped it would be big, and buy them enough time for the rescue.

He guessed that the Coast Guard would scramble their HH-60 Jayhawk helicopter within five or ten minutes of the beginning of the smoke run, but he was more worried about their maritime security teams, and their rapid-response Defender SAFE boats. Small and speedy, they carried a complement of highly trained security specialists and a couple of belt-fed 7.62mm general-purpose machine guns in addition to a .50 caliber heavy machine gun. They were part of the combined ports' 24-hour Homeland Security anti-terrorist coverage, along with whatever the port police forces could throw at them. While the Coast Guard chopper would likely stand off and observe until they could figure out what the hell was going on, their boat crews might try to board the barges or surplus ships and intervene. It was also possible the harbor cops might try the same thing. They would have to move fast once onboard.

Lehman, still wearing his infrared headset, pointed out the ships, which, at their anchorage near the island, were only dimly lit. "Target acquired. Twenty seconds to flyover."

Cook and Lopez's team all turned to the port-side windows as they passed overhead in a slight left bank. The barge decks were brightly illuminated, with the same cranes and container layout they had seen in the overhead image. The surplus ships were shrouded in darkness, with a few signal beacons to warn off passing traffic. Figures could be seen moving on the barges, along with a couple of forklifts apparently carrying barrels on pallets, but whatever they were doing wasn't immediately discernible. What looked like four fishing trawlers were butted stern-first against the barge sidings. There were no signs of the hostages.

Cook shook himself. What had he expected – a billboard? They would have to do this the hard way, searching door-to-door. He keyed the radio.

"Angel flight, Dust Off. Approximately ten to fifteen personnel on the docks, light activity, no visible sign of targets. Wind is light, about two knots at two-five-zero degrees. Moving to ready position."

Bellamy's voice rasped over the handset.

"Roger, commencing first run."

* * *

Craig squinted against the flying dust and debris as he ducked toward the LAPD A-Star, which had just landed on the tarmac near Transvector's museum hangars. The co-pilot hopped out, slid open the rear door, and waved Craig onboard with the rotor still running at near full power. Inside, Craig grabbed a headset off a hook behind his seat.

"Thanks for the lift."

Craig saw the pilot's helmet nod. "We were doing some training over South Central, and are on-call to county for backup, so no problemo."

"Appreciate it. Can we head west, and then circle around the westside area counterclockwise?"

"Roger. We'll have to fly low by the beaches to stay under the LAX departure corridor. What are you looking for?"

"Three or four vintage aircraft took off from here about twenty minutes ago, heading west." Craig's conversation with the tower controllers had been brief. They had heard the noise and felt the glass shake, but saw nothing. "I'm trying to figure out where they are heading."

As they spiraled back up over the city, Craig sagged against his seat, and with the dull drone of the rotors as a backdrop, let his mind go blank. He felt like a hunter who had gone still while stalking his quarry, pausing to see if his prey would betray its position. But he didn't even know if it was nearby, or over the next ridge. Craig mentally kicked himself for not getting enough rest. There hadn't been time, but his ability to think coherently was suffering. He closed his eyes, risking sleep in his overly fatigued state, knowing the flight crew would alert him if a message came through.

So, go over it again, until the pieces fall into place. Somebody, actually a number of 'somebodies', had cracked the hangar at TVA and yanked out a bunch of planes: Bellamy probably, some Mexicans, and likely Cook, Hallett and Stokes. If they were running, why take so many aircraft? And where did they plan on running to? It wasn't like they could just cross the border into Mexico or Canada – they had a helicopter, for Christ's sake, which was slow and limited on range.

They weren't running, he decided dopily. And they probably weren't hostages. If the team at Mandeville was six to eight people, they would have all been able to fit on a medium sized business jet. So, what were they up to, and why take old planes?

And what altitude were they flying at? SoCal TRACON hadn't picked them up, nor had LA Center. Other than the excessive noise complaints, they had completely vanished.

A thought popped into his head. He keyed the mike. "Can you check with LAPD dispatch, find out if there have been any aircraft noise complaints outside of the Santa Monica area?"

"Standby." Craig stared out the Plexiglas window at the endless rows of streetlamps and uncountable headlights below. The pilot came back on. "Nothing from LAPD. Want me to check county?"

"Yeah, thanks."

They were flying under radar, so someone had to have heard them. And they were loud. And people in Los Angeles, especially the nicer parts, didn't seem to be real shy about calling in noise complaints. He let his eyes close again. The drone of the rotor above him was hypnotic, bathing him in white noise. God, when was the last time he'd slept?

He must have drifted off, because the pilot had to call his name twice, and had turned around to look at him. "Agent Craig? Is your headset working?"

"Sorry. What've you got?"

"LA Sheriff got an aviation noise call in Rancho Palos Verdes, down by Portugese Bend."

"Where is that?"

"On the peninsula southwest of us, right on the ocean."

"Take me there."

* * *

"Dust Off, Angel flight. We're laying down smoke."

"Roger Angel, I see good smoke. Correct left two degrees for drift." Lehman had taken the Huey south to hover at a position tangent to the apex of the warbirds' turn, and was now following behind, the helicopter's slightly elevated position giving them a perspective on the pale smoke's distribution. Cook was especially concerned to get them an accurate heading adjustment. Once onboard, the puffy white trail would be their only cover.

"Copy Dust Off. Angel flight, bank two degrees left."

Cook checked his time, adjusting his watch's bezel: quarter after three. Port police and Coast Guard boats could be there within fifteen minutes; sooner if they weren't all tied up with Lopez's diversion. Add about ten more minutes for them to assess the situation and decide to take action. Twenty-five minutes max. That was about all they'd have to search the ships and make the rescue. Maybe enough time for one ship, Cook guessed. After that, it would be a crap shoot.

Copious white smoke spilled prolifically from the tails of the four aircraft, like a quartet of fast-moving brides with heavily laced trains running toward an altar. This is what the Guadalajara run must have looked like from above, Cook reflected. The formation rumbled over the ships, dousing them in a thick fog, before climbing in a slow left bank.

The helicopter plunged into the band of smoke, which was slowly descending upon the twin barges, already forming rounded topographies over the stacked office containers and the docked trawlers. The windscreen went completely white. Cook stiffened and covered Lehman on the collective and the cyclic. "Do we go around?"

"Negative." Lehman still had his night optics on and could see thermal imagery through the haze. "We're good. Ten seconds."

Cook keyed the intercom. "Touchdown in ten seconds." He shifted around in his seat, and Lopez shot him another thumbs up.

They felt the barge before they saw it. Suddenly, Lehman was flaring the Iroquois with a tooth-rattling shudder, and the skids were scraping along the gritty, non-slip deck coating. Cook ripped off his headset as the side doors slammed open and heard the boot thuds of Lopez's departing team over cries of alarm further in the distance. He twisted his harness' quick-release, slung the Swedish-K's shoulder strap, and dropped out of his door to a low crouch on the barge's surface. Two of Lopez's team were waiting for him, kneeling, facing outward from the helicopter in a protective arc, one of them kneeling on Blair's writhing, prostrate form; they had obviously tossed him out like a garbage sack. The rest had already disappeared into the thick haze.

Lopez. His abrupt vanishing act told Cook he was going after Porter.

Cook rose and slammed the door hatch, giving Lehman the lift signal. The Huey's turbine whine spun up to a high scream, and Cook was pushed down by rotor wash as the helicopter slipped into a reverse hover and disappeared backwards. The murky smoke churned furiously in its wake, dissipating somewhat and exposing the row of containers nearby. Cook edged forward, then looked pitilessly down at Blair and met his wild, darting eyes.

Not a good idea to leave him behind us, where he could break free and cause all kinds of trouble. Cook kicked him savagely in the jaw and saw the lights go out. One of his Mexican escorts grinned.

Cook waved the two team members toward the first cargo container.

Distant shouts in Chinese, and the clatter of metal from the direction of the fishing trawlers suggested that the loading crews were regrouping from their shock and preparing for action. Cook knew from experience that explosive movement was a lot more confusing and harder to target than a cautiously moving group, so he sprinted past the members of his squad and led a running charge to the side of the containers without attracting a single round. As they slammed noisily against the corrugated steel wall, Cook heard the thundering growl of approaching radial engines, and motioned for the team to hunker down.

The clamor resulting from the low pass was tremendous. Every nearby metal surface translated the giant throb of pistons into a resonant harmonic, producing a momentarily deafening feedback. The smoke density increased to almost choking proportions.

Perfect time to move, Cook decided. He slapped the shoulder of Lopez's squad leader next to him and ran toward what he thought were the office containers.

*   *   *

CHAPTER SEVENTEEN

Craig could scarcely believe what he was seeing. From his vantage point eight hundred feet above the bay, he watched with an open jaw as a formation of World War II planes dumped a dense plume of white smoke on a trio of ships nearby, then faded into the darkness in some kind of complicated breaking maneuver. If he hadn't have known any better, he might have suspected a movie shoot was in progress.

The co-pilot confirmed that impression. "They filming down there?"

Craig shook his head, more for emphasis than communication, since the pilots couldn't see him. "Negative. That's our objective." He scanned the cabin bulkhead in front of him, looking for a radio selector near the intercom jack. "Can you get me Coast Guard or port police back here?"

"Roger, standby." The co-pilot leaned down and fiddled with the communications panel.

During their sweep over the Palos Verdes peninsula, in the area where the noise complaint had been called in, Craig had caught a faint glimpse of some rapidly moving objects over the San Pedro bay to the south, and had asked the crew to head in that direction. Since the aircraft were running without lights, he hadn't seen them again until they started spewing smoke down by the Queen Mary docks.

He slid one of the headset's earmuffs off and dialed Simms.

"Craig! Talk loud, I can barely hear you! Where are you?"

"Over the port. I think I found them!" Craig shouted. "There's some planes flying over one of the oil islands by Long Beach, and they're covering it with smoke!"

"Say again?" Simms sounded confused. Craig didn't blame him. "Did you say they were covering the islands with...smoke?"

"Affirmative!" Craig shouted. "They have no lights, and we don't have them on radio!"

"Any idea why?"

"Negative! I'm going in closer for a look!"

The co-pilot interrupted on the intercom. "You've got Coast Guard on channel one, and Long Beach port police on two."

Craig nodded. "Gotta go! Call me on the LAPD air channel!"

Craig tossed his phone on the bench seat and punched the first button, guessing that Coast Guard had primary anti-terrorism jurisdiction for the ports. The frequency crashed to life with a flurry of confused traffic. To Craig, it sounded like the harried, on-duty dispatcher was simultaneously acknowledging reports from Coast Guard and law enforcement and directing all related traffic to a side tactical channel. Craig pounced on a rare moment of quiet.

"Break, break, break – information."

It took him a couple of tries. "Go ahead, break."

"FBI agent with information. Who's your incident commander?"

"Lieutenant Derris on Tac One. Callsign Lima Two."

"Copy." The co-pilot nodded and bent forward again. After a moment, he held up three fingers. Craig punched the third button on the panel.

"…looks like two, check that, three fires burning by the Mormon Island tank farm, and one more off Smith Island. Stingray Two called in a fire at Pier Alpha and there might be one at the Northwest Slip terminal…we're checking that out…."

"Break, break, break – FBI for Lima Two." It took another attempt to get through.

"FBI, Lima Two. Confirm your identity."

"FBI Special Agent Craig, 51453, in LAPD helicopter with information."

There was a brief pause. "Confirm FBI has information on the port fires?"

"That's affirmative – they are not, repeat, not a terrorist attack. They are a diversion. You've got an active aerial assault in progress by one of your oil islands with possibly a dozen or more armed suspects. How many boats do you have deployed?"

"One response boat, and we're scrambling the other one right now. LA Fire is on its way with fireboats Two and Five. LA Port Police has two boats *en route*."

Craig paused for a moment to consider. "Lima Two, I advise you call out every boat you can spare to the islands. Can LA fire and the harbor police handle the pier fires?"

"Affirmative. Are you positive this is a diversion?"

"Affirmative." Craig tapped the co-pilot's shoulder and made an orbit motion with his finger. "I'd recommend throwing everything you've got into a perimeter, but stand off until we can get a handle on this situation. Is your Jayhawk available?"

"The Jayhawk and Dolphin are at the air station at LAX on a 'ready twenty' status."

"You'll want them up for this." The co-pilot waved to get Craig's attention. "Standby."

The co-pilot cut through on the intercom. "NORAD must've gotten an airspace warning from the ports. They've scrambled an Air Guard F-15 from the 144th at March Air Force Base and an Army reserve helicopter out of Los Alamitos. The F-15 will be here in a few."

Then the pilot waved his hand, and pointed at the fuel gauge. "We're getting thirsty. Nearest fuel for us is Zamperini in Torrance."

Craig nodded. "Copy that." He switched back to radio. "Lima Two, we're headed to Torrance to fuel up. Be advised NORAD has an F-15 fighter and an Army chopper inbound. I'll monitor Tac One, and let you know when we're back in the air."

* * *

Cook pressed himself as close to the forklift's front wheel as he could and peered around it toward the container office's door. He was greeted by banging flashes and the staccato tattoo of automatic rounds impacting the hulking machine's steel skin. He slid back and leaned against the tire, his arm still stinging from a graze he had gotten earlier. The shooters in the office had him well bracketed, and he was trapped for the moment. Cook tried not to think what would happen if they ignited the diesel tank. They didn't need a forklift fire making things any more exciting.

The first container had been a bust, an administrative space filled with desks and cabinets, but otherwise empty. The next one in the row had been a different story. The point man of Lopez's squad escorting Cook had been leading the way down the alley between them when he caught a round in the head, and was lying near the doorway in a pool of dark blood. There were at least two Asian shooters in the second container, and they were well dug in, with overlapping diagonal fields of fire covering both ends of the alley.

Cook had a fragmentation grenade, but didn't dare throw it in. If Kane and the others were being held inside, the shrapnel could shred them or the over-pressure from the explosion could blow out their eardrums. He had to find a less lethal way to shut down the shooters.

Another staccato burst erupted and one of Lopez's men called 'Chuy' skidded to a crouch behind the battered lift truck. "Need any help?" he gasped, breathing heavily.

"Got a gas grenade?"

"Flashbang." He held up a perforated concussion unit.

"Good enough. I'll cover you." Chuy pulled the pin, but held the release lever. Cook leaned out and stitched an 'X' pattern at the doorway with his submachine gun while Chuy skipped the black canister over the door sill. A blinding white flash burned an image of a doorway into Cook's dilated pupils. He had forgotten to close his eyes. "Damnit!"

Chuy was already at the door delivering coup-de-grace shots when Cook stumbled up, a large green vertical rectangle floating at the center of his vision. He stepped over the triad corpses as he entered behind his Lopez's man. A hasty search revealed no further occupants. Cook grabbed what looked like a 9mm pistol from one of the gang members' waistbands, while Chuy called in his report, in English for the benefit of non-Spanish speakers. "Containers are clear, one casualty."

"Copy." Lopez's acknowledgement sounded strained. "We're on the main deck of the first ship. We're taking fire from the bridge superstructure and the stairways."

Bellamy's voice broke in. "Alpha boarding party, Dumbo. We're coming around the back to give you some cover. Sandy and Turkey are making another pass."

Cook smacked Chuy's arm. "Let's use that to get up there!"

"*¡Alora! ¡Vamanos hombres!*" Chuy waved his two remaining men forward, then motioned for Cook to go. Because of his attentive demeanor and the risks he had taken during the rescue a few moments before, Cook surmised that Chuy had a special brief from Lopez to keep him alive and upright. They scuttled after the others and, in a widely stretched trapezoid, with weapons ready at the shoulder, made the bottom of the scaffolded stairway that led up to the first ship's aft quarter without any resistance.

As they rounded the first landing, the Skyraider and the TBM made another smoke-laying pass, their gas guns banging loudly overhead. Cook didn't know if the pounding bursts of the simulated fifty-caliber cannons above had any effect on the Asian triads, but the thunderous noise rattled the staircase and masked their approach. In addition, the southwestern breeze had died down to almost nothing, and the white fog was starting to limit their visibility to a few feet.

A growing rumble from the stern indicated the arrival of Bellamy's Catalina. Cook heard Stokes voice for the first time since the airport. "Alpha party, Dumbo. I can only make out the aft rail. Where do you want it?"

Cook felt a warm surge that helped propel him upward.

"Anywhere above that point, Dumbo. Alpha party's on the main deck." Cook could hear Lopez in the distance issuing sharp commands in Spanish off the air.

A muffled ripping sound of light machinegun fire broke out from between the oil island and the first ship's tail. Bellamy had had Stokes open the PBY's nose hatch and brace up the Beretta MG 42/59's forearm against the hatch's rim. She sent burst after burst of .30 caliber rounds sparking and ricocheting around the upper decks, which only became visible through the smoke by the tracer bullets' bright impacts. Another of Hallett's men assisted her by feeding the linked ammo belt as she fired.

Cook and Chuy's men used the distraction to cross the perforated aluminum planks leading from the stair scaffolding to the ship's gunwale without mishap, keeping their heads low to avoid Stokes enthusiastic broadsides. Lopez chirped on the radio that he had taken the starboard stairwell and was proceeding below decks. Chuy hissed at Cook to follow him to the port stairwell.

They paused at the top. It was a mess. Bodies sprawled haphazardly across the rusting steel deck, and blood and body spatter coated paint-scraped bulkheads. Only one of the bodies was visibly Latino – the rest were all Asian. Lopez had clearly encountered heavy resistance at the access point from the docks, and Cook expected nothing different from the gangways to the other ships. As he cautiously descended after Chuy down the ladder to the next deck, he really hoped Kane and the others weren't on the last ship of the row.

They might not ever make it that far.

* * *

Through a gap in the dense haze, Porter watched from his crouch behind the port gunwale of the *Grundy*, the second hulk in the line, as Gallardo directed his men down the aft starboard ladder of the *Strathcona*. He knew the CNI officer was hunting him personally, and could care less about the hostage aircrew. Porter figured that if he stayed ahead of the Mexicans long enough to get to the far end of the row, he might yet make it out alive.

When Porter heard the first pass of the Transvector museum formation and saw the trailing cloud of smoke blanket the ships, he had been elated. Prior to that moment, his best escape option had been to try to finesse his way past the triad sentries to the tenders at the west end of the stack, and otherwise shoot anyone who got in his way. The dense smoke had rendered stealthy movement almost superfluous, and the shooting kept all eyes focused on the rescue party. To avoid getting caught, he just had to keep moving away from the fighting, and not attract any undue attention. That, and not catch any stray rounds from the wild machine-gunning occurring back at the stern.

Bellamy must be in on this, Porter concluded. The planning was outstanding, and the execution first-rate. He wouldn't have changed a thing. He wondered what aircraft the old geezer was piloting.

He moved forward cautiously. The bows, facing seaward, were the darkest part of the ships, with only a forward warning beacon providing illumination. With the thick smoky layer laid down by the warbirds, it didn't amount to much light. From the little he could make out of the waters to the south, there were no lights at all. He could hear some helicopters circling, including the distinctive thrumming of the TVA Huey, but vision skyward was as restricted as it was laterally. He glanced quickly back at the wheelhouse. Smoke obscured most detail, but he could hear a lot of shooting and shouting, and occasionally make out muzzle flashes.

For a moment, the shooting paused, and all Porter could hear above the roar of aircraft engines was the rhythmic screeching of the giant rubber Yokohama fenders keeping the boats from scraping against each other. He sagged against the bow gunwale, breathing deeply and gathering his strength. One last gangway, and he'd make it to the last hulk, the SS *Thomas Kolinsky.*

After he shot Hu and his henchman, Porter had felt strangely adrift, as if he was now in charge of a failed operation and a crew of thirty murderous triad foot soldiers. Of course, they wouldn't take his orders, considering him a shifty *gwailou* mercenary and a necessary evil for their scheme. Which was his idea to begin with.

And the operation wasn't really a failure. The real objective, as described by Porter's obscure employer, was to penetrate the upper ranks of the overseas Chinese triad network in Canada in order to find PLA-connected operatives that they could turn against China. This objective had been accomplished, with a few individuals identified and marked for further exploitation.

The tasking had been a reward for previous work done, with the consulting fee a sort of retirement bonus. Even though Porter hadn't received the full five million, with the half he did have he could live comfortably for years in any number of tropical, extradition-free locations. He also recognized that another side benefit of this whole fiasco was that this triad was going to lose a lot of its narcotics inventory in the US, and probably be blamed for the Mexico debacle.

But when this was all over, the Shang Gu Bang was going to demand accountability, and call in their Chinese intelligence helpers to start looking for scalps.

The TVA incursion solved all his problems. He could get in contact with the triad and tell them that Gallardo and the Mexicans had spiked the deal, that they had taken out Hu along with the rest of their members, and he had been helpless to intervene. Of course, he would do that from a safe distance, using a cutout so they wouldn't know he was still alive. His organization had myriad ways to accomplish that. TVA and the Mexicans made the perfect foil.

Porter snorted as he crept forward past the *Grundy*'s bow capstan, slowly creeping toward the starboard rail. Gallardo was such a worthless shit-pony, taking the whole thing personally as if he really cared about Mexico, or any of its inhabitants. Though he had adopted the cover name 'Lopez' for his participation in the TVA spray mission, his real name was Gallardo Aparza, and he was a trust-fund baby from one of the Distrito Federal's richest families, an aristocratic wannabe playing all grown-up. He gleefully carried water for any administration that would support his family's interests, even though the current socialist regime wasn't exactly friendly. Porter wished he had the time and bandwidth to deal with him, but escape had to be his priority. Plenty of time later for the luxury problems.

He ducked quickly as he heard the hull wake and twin engines of the Albatross speed by the bows, providing yet another distraction for the overwhelmed triad personnel. Bellamy was such an artist at operational planning, even in his dotage. Porter was going to miss him.

A few moments later, the airborne planes made another thundering pass, their fake wing guns sputtering sharp, propane bangs. The smoke shifted sluggishly in their wake, and Porter could make out the railed truss leading to the *Kolinsky*. One more deck and he was free.

* * *

CHAPTER EIGHTEEN

The *SS Strathcona* was a large, break bulk cargo freighter decommissioned from the US MARAD reserve fleet, and was being made just seaworthy enough to make its final journey overseas for demolition. Crews had obviously spent months preparing it, ripping out toxic asbestos paneling and scraping off lead paint. Everything of possible salvage value had been stripped, leaving rusty bolts and brackets sticking out everywhere to snag the unwary.

At just over six hundred feet, the vessel was a common size for a late 1960s general cargo hauler, with two hatch-covered holds forward and one aft of the superstructure. It was built before the use of containers became standard, and was intended to carry crates, barrels, drums and other loads on pallets. At the stern was a crane derrick and a raised awning deck with a helipad, near the stairway where Cook and his team had come aboard.

Lopez had cleared the stern area before Cook and Chuy's team had made it aboard, so the targeted search areas were the holds, the superstructure, and the forecastle at the bow.

Cook had been in a few fire fights before, covering men retreating to a helicopter or extraction plane. But those had all been at airfields, with lots of wide-open space and things you could get behind for cover. This was different.

The passageways on the ship were narrow and broken every so many yards by bulkhead door openings, which provided excellent cover for retreating shooters. Every time gunfire erupted, bullets ricocheted freely off the gray-painted steel bulkheads. One of the Mexican commandos on Cook's squad was struck in the neck by a round that had careened off a passageway bracing. Arterial blood spray spatter covered surfaces all around him as he spiraled onto the deck, splashing against Cook's jeans and boots. Chuy had called in the body-count to Lopez, stripped the corpse of weapons and ammunition, and put their squad's sole remaining operative on point.

Cook quietly shuffled forward, bringing up the rear behind Chuy and constantly glancing backwards to make sure they weren't being flanked. The tense search was exhausting, and Cook was breathing heavily in addition to being soaked with sweat despite the cold damp interior. The passages reeked of mildew. Every so often they would pass an open cabin with berths, the bare cotton mattresses speckled with mold. The dim yellow passageway lights gave the drab bulkheads a sickly complexion. At least they'd left them on, Cook mused. He hated to think of doing this with flashlights in the dark.

They checked every compartment they passed, both for the hostages and to clear them of hostiles. It was gruelingly slow work, and Cook fervently hoped they wouldn't have to go through the exercise twice more.

The occasional panicked shout in Chinese metallically echoed below decks between gun bursts, but it was nothing compared to what they'd heard earlier topside. As Cook edged through yet another open hatch, he wondered how many triad shooters could be left. Counting the two from the barge office container, he had seen at least ten other triad corpses. Bellamy had originally put the crew estimate at about twenty-five, but of course that had been just a guess.

The point man suddenly raised his fist, indicating they should freeze and crouch. Cook could make out muffled whispers coming from around the corner ahead. They were just forward of what should have been the aft cargo hold. Chuy's sole remaining squad member silently edged up to the corner and peered around.

Gunfire exploded, and the point man slumped and fell slackly forward, obviously mortally hit. Chuy sprayed the area with his submachine gun as he retreated, pushing Cook back towards a passageway frame. He then bounced another flash-bang grenade off the port bulkhead, causing its path to deflect around the corner. An alarmed cry was cut off by an ear-popping blast that Cook actually managed to get his eyes closed for this time. In the ringing silence and potassium nitrate-smelling haze that followed, Chuy surged forward to clean up while Cook covered the approaches toward the bow.

The radio on Cook's belt squawked. It was Lopez, sounding even more strained. "We're pinned inside the engine room, on the upper level. Can you assist?"

Cook felt a stab of panic. Lopez was clearly drawing most of the fire, and he'd already lost at least four men, fully half his force. There could be another ten to fifteen triad foot soldiers still operating. "Where are the shooters?"

"Two floors down in from this level, and they've got all the stairways covered."

"We're on our way."

Chuy pushed past Cook and rushed down the passageway, pivoting right into the next transverse passage forward. Cook hurried to keep up.

It was a charnel house, with blood marking every surface, even the ceiling. Splatters marked where triads had been shot against the wall, with red streaks leading down to the folded corpses, and crimson stains indicated where a bleeding casualty had dragged themselves along a bulkhead or a deck. Twice, they had to step over triad corpses that had fallen on top of each other. One of the bodies was still burbling, and Chuy spat on him as he shuffled past.

Just ahead of them was an open door that looked like it led to the engine room. The edges were covered with fresh bloody hand marks, and there were some blackened chipped areas in the primer where bullets had clearly impacted. Chuy edged carefully to the door, quickly peeked in, and waved for Cook to dash to the other side. His heart racing, Cook slipped past the opening, a quick glance revealing what looked like a control room. Other than bloodstains covering the deck, it was empty.

Chuy keyed his radio. "We are in the engine control room."

"Follow the blood. We are two rooms in."

Cook trailed Chuy as he cautiously worked his way through a couple of workshops. The last door was partially open and riddled with bullet holes. Chuy shouted hoarsely. "*Somos aqui.*"

Lopez responded faintly. "Come through. We are by the stairs."

At the top of the companionway ladder leading down to the engine compartment, Lopez was propped against a bulkhead covered with pipes, his face pale. His right thigh was stained with dark blood. The female medic was twisting an Israeli combat tourniquet around the upper leg, to stanch the blood flow to the wound while another provided cover. She then covered the exposed area with a hemostatic dressing. To Cook, the quality of the field medical equipment was revealing. These guys must see a lot of action.

Lopez regarded Cook; his face tight with pain. "We think the hostages are below, but there's no cover on the stairway down. They are dug in behind the engine. I got one before I was shot, but it sounded like there are at least four more gunmen down there."

Cook examined the workroom, biting his upper lip. Engine rooms were bad news, filled with all kinds of places to hide. There was only one ladder heading below, and no other options to get in or out. No way to shoot down on them from above without exposing oneself and endangering the hostages. He tried to think creatively, but in his fatigued and slow-witted state, he realized it was useless.

And Lopez wasn't even sure that Kane and the other captives were being held there. He glanced at his watch for the first time since coming aboard the docks: fifteen minutes. Time was running out. Even Lopez's diversions weren't going to hold off the Coast Guard and others for long.

As if to reinforce the last thought, a call chirped on the radio, the hashed signal barely audible through the steel hull. It was Bellamy. "Boarding party, Angel, what's your status?"

Cook looked at Lopez, who shook his head. "Still on Alpha, no sighting of hostages with," he calculated quickly, "four casualties."

"Copy. Be advised we're starting to get some surface activity out here."

"Roger, out."

They had to be here. The first ship was the only logical place to keep cargo and the hostages; the other ships were too inaccessible if you had to move things quickly. And the trawlers were all lined up right next door.

When Cook had been in Honduras, in his late teens, he had met a former Green Beret sergeant working as a contract employee for the CIA. Cook had once asked him how he and his team had gotten out of a Sandinista ambush the previous day, while outnumbered two-to-one. The man had simply replied, "Extreme aggression. They expected us to run, and we counterattacked, very aggressively. Dropped their fudge right and left."

When you can't do something smart, he reasoned muddily, do something stupid, but do it so stupidly and with such ferocious resolve that it throws your enemy off-balance, and forces them to do something stupid. He turned to Chuy. "What do you have for grenades?"

"Three smoke, one tear gas, one flash bang."

"Ok, this is what I think we should do."

* * *

Craig watched a Coast Guard SAFE boat pass beneath him, red and blue strobes pulsing brightly as it streaked across the black bay toward its sister-ship, already on station near the oil island. From his vantage aloft, he could see other law enforcement beacons snaking their way from the Los Angeles inner harbor toward the anchored ships. There wasn't much of a perimeter at this point, but more assets were becoming available every passing minute, and with the helicopter he could cover more area than any boat.

The LAPD helicopter was on its way back from Torrance's Zamperini Field where the crew had refueled in an expedited fashion. Scanning the sky around the bay, Craig could see a couple other helicopters, but had no idea who they belonged to. He really hoped they weren't press. "Lima Two, Craig on Tac One."

"Lima Two, go ahead."

"Do you have any units airborne?"

"Negative, not yet. ETA on the Dolphin is about one-zero minutes. The Jayhawk is down on a maintenance issue. Traffic could be the Air Guard helo out of Los Alamitos."

'Ready twenty' my ass, thought Craig. "Copy. How many boats are deployed?"

"Romeo Bravo One is on site, I'm *en route,* and two more are being called up. LA and Long Beach

408

port police are sending boats, as well as Long Beach harbor patrol."

"Roger. I'm back on station, monitoring."

The LAPD co-pilot cut back in on the intercom, waving a small pair of binoculars. "One of those helicopters is an old Huey D-model. And they're not coming up on civilian frequencies."

Craig reached for a pair of binoculars clipped to the back of the co-pilot's seat and peered through them at the ships below, then hunted for the Huey. He found it slowly orbiting over the smoke-covered ships, its rotor wash swirling smoke out and upward as it nosed around the ship structures. This did look like a film scene, Craig thought. He focused on the cabin through the open side doors. It looked like there was a man in back, but he couldn't make him out clearly, nor see what he was doing.

"Craig, Lima Two. Be advised that the F-15 from March is overhead."

"Copy. Craig out."

What the California Air Guard thought they could do with a fighter-interceptor jet in this situation was beyond Craig. He considered trying to find out if he could get on a common frequency with the jet, but then demurred. If NORAD wanted a fighter up to keep an eye on things and protect the LA airspace, it was not really his business. He just hoped they stayed well above his altitude.

With the binoculars, he could make out some detail of the ships' masts and superstructures through the smoke, but very little of the decks. The docks which were moored against the easternmost hulk were also densely covered, but he could make out the shapes of the trawlers tied to the south side. Four fishing smacks on a work site seemed out-of-place to Craig.

The radio crackled. "Lima Two, Romeo Bravo One...possible sounds of automatic weapons fire."

"Copy, Romeo Bravo One. Maintain position and do not engage."

The response boat acknowledged and went silent. Craig watched as the slowly flying warbirds lumbered over in yet another pass, their wing guns flickering long tongues of flame. He felt completely helpless watching them. There was absolutely nothing he could do to stop them, short of forcing a mid-air collision. He leaned forward. "Any way you can find out what frequency they're using?"

The co-pilot shook his head. "We've got all the aviation, marine, and public safety bands, and I don't hear them coming up on any of them. Must be using some other mode."

Great, Craig thought. He panned from one end of the row to the other. He stiffened. What looked like a couple of flashes had just emanated on the starboard side of the westernmost ship, near a stairway attached to the hull. There also seemed to be a couple small barges or tenders docked alongside below. Craig keyed the radio.

"Lima Two, Craig. I've sighted what might be muzzle flashes. Do you have anyone on the west side of the ships?"

"Negative, my boat is to the south. Long Beach Harbor Patrol is heading to that side."

"Can you call them to check that area out? It looks like there are a couple small boats there, and somebody might be trying to get off."

"Roger that. Keep us posted if you see anything else."

Craig kept his glasses aimed at the western side of the row of ships. There was another muzzle flash, and then it was dark. In the faint reflection of light from the oil island on the water, he struggled to make out any details.

The co-pilot interrupted. "There's what looks like a couple of flying boats taxiing around the ships."

He looked in the water around the ships and found a lumbering amphibian from the frothy wake streaming from its nose. It was taxiing on the water in a counterclockwise circle, and it looked like a person was sitting on the nose of the plane, but it was hard to tell. Another amphibian rounded the westmost ship as he watched, and it followed the same path.

As if the rest of this wasn't enough of a circus. What in God's name are they doing? Craig wondered. Why would the Transvector museum flight crew hook up with a gang of Mexicans to assault a bunch of anchored hulks? Did it have something to do with the oil islands? Craig used his glasses to scan the lit perimeter of Island Chaffee nearest the ships. A couple security vehicles with flashing strobes were parked on the south side near the ships, but other than that there was nothing unusual. Maybe one of the other islands? He looked at the one further toward shore, Island White.

A bizarre montage leapt back at him. At night, the condo-tower cover for the oil derrick and the tall, marquee-like screens shielding the oil operations from beachside viewers were illuminated in bold red and purple colors, looking more like something out of Las Vegas or Disneyland than Exxon. Along with the graceful palm trees and even a waterfall, it almost seemed like it would be a nice place to stay. All it needs is a golf course, and some lounge chairs. And less crude oil. Craig dropped the binoculars for a moment to clear his haphazard thinking, then refocused. More strobes from security forces, but no other activity.

Would they try to bomb the islands, maybe blow up the oil tanks? It didn't seem likely, because if that was their intention, they would have already done it. While he was trying to figure out how the pieces might fit in this particular puzzle, Derris called.

"Craig, Lima Two, on site south of the ships. Do you know what's going on here?"

"Negative. Not a clue. They're not attacking the oil islands, just focusing on the ships."

"I'm open to ideas. Should we attempt intervention on this?"

"Standby." Intervene how? Craig thought. Shoot them down? They weren't threatening national security, just a row of ships that had seen better days. And whoever was in the Huey just seemed to be watching the whole thing, and maybe filming it. Eventually, they'd run out of gas and ammo, and have to set down somewhere. Then Craig would think about intervening.

Maybe start small? Take some baby steps? The fishing trawlers docked at the barges were almost as out-of-place as the antique aircraft blazing away over the top. Almost.

"Can you get a boat in closer to the barge by the trawlers, see if they can see what's going on there?"

"Roger. Romeo Bravo One, Lima Two. Move in towards the trawlers on the barge. Use extreme caution."

* * *

Porter fiddled in the dark to get the boat key in the ignition.

He had waited for the Catalina to run its taxi circuit around the west side before clattering down the accommodation ladder to the work boats tied to the small dock at its base. Then he had spent about half a minute ransacking the steering console for a key. He had finally found it in the usual place, wedged above the sun visor like it would have been in a car.

The last ten yards to the top of the gangway had been the hardest. The thick haze from the constant passes overhead reduced vision down to a few feet. Porter had felt his way from capstan to bollard across the weather deck in front of the raised forecastle at the ship's bow until he found a hatch coaming. He peered around through the smoky air and found 'Number Three Cargo Hold' stenciled on the side. He followed its line west and rounded its corner to the north, trying to estimate where on the *Kolinsky* the accommodation ladder was located. Before long he had heard the triad sentries talking.

The voices had been nervous, speaking in clipped phrases, and even without being able to understand Cantonese he could tell they were discussing whether to bail out on one of the boats. Needing to act fast,

Porter had picked up a stray piece of steel plating from the litter on the deck and threw it like a Frisbee high against the nearby boom derrick mast. The loud clanging sound prompted the stirred guards to loose off a string of automatic fire, giving away their positions by their muzzle flashes. Porter simply waited for the noise cover from the next pass of the warbirds and stalked forward, shooting both of them at point-blank range.

Porter checked the throttle was in neutral and turned the ignition key. The motor quietly grumbled to life, a good indicator that the tenders were well-maintained. He untied the dock lines from their cleats on the boat further inboard, and gently pushed himself out. Now, where to go, he wondered. The Albatross was going to come around on its circuit soon, and he really didn't want whoever was piloting that aircraft to see him. Head inland, then cut down the coast? The jet was waiting for him in Orange County, about eighteen miles south. Seemed like a good option, but that's where everyone was looking. Maybe straight out to sea for a bit, then head east? He cautiously nosed the boat out at three knots, Island Chaffee's lights to his rear, keeping his wake to a minimum to avoid being seen.

He headed for a large gap in the strobes of the patrol boats to the southwest.

Suddenly, he was silhouetted by a small searchlight from a craft whose flashers he had missed against the illuminated harbor landscape. He threw up his left arm, to block the light. A voice boomed over a PA system. "Long Beach Harbor Patrol! Turn off your motor and keep your hands where I can see them!"

Porter reached down and turned off the ignition, discreetly setting the pistol he had liberated from Hu's triad henchman in a compartment on the console below the engine gauges. He had expected an interdiction, from the number of public safety strobes he could see from the top of the accommodation ladder. But he had hoped to get a bit further away from the ships before being intercepted. He raised his hands and shouted with a quaver in his voice. "Don't shoot! I'm a hostage! Please don't shoot!"

"Stay where you are and don't move. We will come to you." The speaker sounded nervous to Porter. Apparently, the harbor cops didn't get a lot of aircraft-heavy, wild west shootout calls. The next comment reinforced that. "Keep your hands up!"

"Please help me! Get me out of here!" Porter tried to add some extra anguish to his voice as he watched the vessel's spotlight approach, its beam trained on his face to blind him. He kept his forearm in front of his eyes, calculating the distance of the boat from the growing warm spot on his arm. A sudden growl of reverse thrust on the engine, a slight bump to the tender's hull, and a heavy dip toward the water on the starboard side indicated that a harbor police officer had boarded his watercraft. Behind his forearm, Porter could see the beam of a flashlight playing around.

"Kneel and face the stern, and put your hands together behind your back, palms facing outward and thumbs up."

The person controlling the security vessel kept the light on while his colleague snapped handcuffs on Porter's wrists, and hastily patted him down. "He's clean."

The spotlight snapped off, replaced by a flashlight beam. "Get him on board fast, before that amphibian comes around again. It's still too hot to be this close."

"Roger."

Porter felt the patrol officer grip his elbow, assisting him toward the patrol vessel which had adjusted its position to present its side rail. The officer steadied him, then counted to three. "Move!"

They both jumped the narrow gap and lurched to a halt just aft of the helm. The lifeguard at the helm quickly ground the transmission into gear, lifting the bow as he accelerated away from the drifting tender. Both Porter and the other officer staggered aft with the movement, slumping to their knees on the small open deck. Porter rolled to a sitting position, bracing his back against the port gunwale. The detaining officer recovered with both of his hands on the deck. "Easy, Ray!"

"We need to get out of here! Hang on!" The bow of the rescue boat dipped as the hull started planing. Porter watched as they rapidly sped from the area, well away from the TVA Albatross, which was just then rounding the stern of the *Kolinsky* in a slow taxi, a ponderous giant from the water's surface.

Porter watched the backs of the two patrol officers carefully, satisfactorily observing that they were more focused on events on the ships than their detainee. He didn't blame them. Porter's frantic flight across the deck of the last cargo ship had left black grease stains all over his clothes and face. He was a mess, and probably looked like an escaped hostage. The search by the cuffing officer had been perfunctory at best, performed more in the interest of speed than efficacy. He hadn't, for instance, thoroughly checked Porter's beltline, which is where Porter was currently fishing behind his back for the handcuff key he had secreted there. The officer also had simply run a quick hand up each pant leg, missing the compact Walther and its suppressor stuffed into Porter's groin.

The officer who was driving the boat pointed the radio. "Call it in to Lima Two. One hostage detained and on board." His fellow officer peered back at Porter briefly, but clearly couldn't make much out in the dim light. "Copy."

As he started to make the call, Porter inserted the key into the lock of the handcuffs and turned it, noting to his satisfaction that the secondary locks hadn't been engaged. He freed one wrist and surreptitiously began to work on the other. The lifeguard on the radio was having trouble breaking through the radio traffic and was waiting for a gap. His superior on at the wheel was still looking outboard, watching the spray kicked up in the Albatross' wake.

Porter carefully reached into his waistband and drew out his .22 Walther. He didn't bother with the silencer. He braced his legs and shot the officer on the radio twice, then the boat's skipper. They both cried out in surprise before slumping to the deck.

Porter looked back at the ships. No one seemed to have noticed the interception, or at least no strobes were headed his direction. He then crawled against the boat's momentum to the helm console and throttled the boat down. No sense in leaving a big, visible trail. Finding the switches for the navigation lights and strobe beacons, he extinguished them. The launch was completely dark.

He stripped the bodies of their radios and weapons, and, still moving at a crawl, heaved each of them overboard. They disappeared into the black, salty brine. Porter stood breathing heavily for a moment, his legs accustoming themselves to the gentle rocking of a light swell.

Then he slowly steered toward the signal light at the east end of the San Pedro breakwater.

* * *

CHAPTER NINETEEN

Engine rooms on modern container ships are large affairs, but relatively small compared to the typical thousand-foot plus overall length of the ship. Besides the main control room and a suite of workshops above, the cavernous powerplant compartment houses a towering, four-story low-RPM diesel engine with a massive drive shaft attached at the bottom. A small office complex on land would have the equivalent amount of room.

Even though the *SS Strathcona* was less than half the length of the largest container ship classes, its engine room was nearly as cavernous, utilizing an obsolete steam turbine engine with dual high-capacity boilers. Uncountable pipes and machinery were fixed to every surface, and ladders with landings connected the decks. That meant lots of good cover for shooters.

Cook knew the ladder leading down was a killing field. But he also knew that in order to kill someone with a gun, you had to see what you're shooting at. Otherwise, it was just spray and pray. Cook decided to even the odds somewhat. Slinging his Swedish K, he pulled the pin on their last flashbang grenade, but held the lever so it didn't activate.

"Drop the smoke."

Chuy and Lopez's three remaining operatives tossed the last three smoke grenades down the ladder. He could clearly hear the containers clanging on landings and pipes as they worked their way into the compartment. The triads' response was predictable. What sounded like four shooters opened up on the ladder at the same time, thinking the assault force would storm down. Cook waited another five seconds before signaling Chuy to throw the CS gas grenade. It clattered off a few rails before emitting a muffled bang.

Ventilation hatches in older cargo ships are extremely simple, completely mechanical affairs. While modern vessels have fan ducts and HEPA filters in their engine ventilation systems, Cook figured that an old scow like this would sport nothing more complicated than fans and louvered hatches. And with no engine running, the fans wouldn't be going either.

The now-sporadic shooting halted, replaced by dry, hacking coughs and panicked, hoarse shouts in Chinese.

Last one, Cook thought. He tossed the flash-bang into the opaque white smoke that had filled the compartment and clapped Chuy on the shoulder. "Wait for it."

With the thunderous whump of the flashbang igniting, there was a moment of silence, followed by the isolated crack of a single shot.

Chuy lead the way down the stairs, a pair of infrared goggles strapped to his head, a triangular bandage from the medical kit covering his mouth. Cook followed behind, his left hand on Chuy's shoulder. He kept his submachine gun slung, since he couldn't see his hand in front of his face. Cook was completely blinded by the smoke, and started to cough lightly as he inhaled the riot-control agent. The three surviving members of Lopez's team, also wearing night vision, brought up the rear. In the voluminous but enclosed engine space, Cook hoped the smoke and the flashbang's concussion effect had provided enough disorientation. One tear gas grenade would irritate the occupants' eyes and throats, but it wasn't enough to fill the giant room.

At the bottom of the main ladder, Chuy gently, and without a word, pushed Cook against the wall and stalked away. Cook could feel the other two agents quickly brush past him. Then he was alone. He could hear more coughing coming from somewhere in the distance.

He was starting to reconsider his decision. Cook had come down to help with the hostage extraction, if they turned out to be in the room. But without sight, he wasn't going to be of much assistance. Maybe I should have stayed up with Lopez, he mused.

Cook heard a suppressed shot and a cry, then the sound of a body slumping. He tried to be as silent as possible, but to his alarm he felt a cough coming on. He tried to swallow it and breath through his nose, but that just made it worse. He bent over double and hacked loudly a few times.

He felt more than heard a shuffling nearby. He hissed quietly. "Chuy?"

There was a rush of movement, and a hand clawed his face. He fumbled for his gun, and felt a forearm slam him against the bulkhead. The cold steel of a pistol barrel pressed at his temple.

The Chinese-accented voice was hushed and tremulous, and sounded to Cook more scared than he was. "Drop your gun now."

Cook whispered back. "It's on a sling."

He felt a hand grasp the Swedish K's action, and the sound of a sling clip being removed. The sling slid off his shoulder and Cook felt the gun being taken away. The high-pitched and wavering voice continued.

"Now you gonna get me out of here, bra."

Strictly an amateur, Cook realized. No professional ever holds a firearm against someone's body, primarily because it tells the victim where the weapon is. It was something this guy had clearly learned from watching too many Chinese 'gun-fu' movies. Since the average human requires three-quarters of a second to become aware of a stimulus, and another half-second to react, Cook had more than a second to work with. Plenty of time under normal circumstance, but it didn't seem like a lot with a gun pointed at his head.

To distract the man, he whispered something absolutely true. "I can't see anything."

He explosively arced his right hand up, using the webbing between his thumb and forefinger as a lever to push the pistol away from his face. The gun fired as the triad drew back, something Cook had cringingly anticipated, so it had little effect on the thrust of his left fist into the general area of the man's throat. It was a weak strike from his off-hand, thrown somewhat wildly, but it connected with a satisfyingly wet-sounding crunch.

Cook's grip on the man's gun hand followed the Asian to the ground as he collapsed in a coughing pile. Cook wrenched the pistol away from his unseen assailant and kicked hard into something soft. His assailant's coughing loudened. Then he sucked in a desperately needed breath and started hacking himself, dropping to his knees. He tried to hold the pistol at low ready as he scrambled back against the bulkhead with a clang.

A sustained burst of fire laced the air above him, the muted muzzle flash only yards away from his position. Bullets ricocheted wildly off the steel surfaces. He pointed at the flash and pulled the trigger. Nothing. The gun was empty.

The firing paused. The opaque air reeked of flashbangs and cordite, with the bite of the tear gas' cyanocarbon making it almost unbreathable. He started coughing uncontrollably.

The sound brought another string of fire, but it was still above his crouched position, and seemed to be coming from only a single source. He felt a sting on his scalp as one of the bounced bullets glanced off his skull. He started thrashing around blindly on the deck for his submachine gun.

The firing abruptly ceased as the gun's bolt locked open on an empty chamber. A couple of seconds later, Cook heard an alarmed shriek cut short by a wet, coughing sound. The sound of a body slapping the floor came next.

"Cook?"

It was Chuy. Cook exhaled with relief.

"On the deck," he grunted.

Cook thought he could hear a smirk. "Yeah, I can see that. It's over. We have your men with us."

"There's a guy still alive on the deck here somewhere."

There was a pause and a phutting 'splat' sound. "Not any more."

Cook scrambled to his feet and felt for Chuy's hand. He was led to the ladder back toward the control room. Cook grabbed the rails and climbed slowly, his breath still raspy. He could hear others shuffling and coughing below him.

The first thing he saw when he emerged from the thick smoke was Chuy wiping fresh arterial blood off the blade of his knife. Chuy had clearly used it to open the last man's throat while he was shooting at Cook. He nodded his wordless thanks to the operative and received one in return.

Lopez was still sitting up against the bulkhead, his face pale.

"Any sign of Porter?"

Cook squatted down next to him. "Couldn't see a damn thing. You're better off asking your men. Any word from the topside?"

"*Nada*."

At that moment, the female operative climbed up out of the smoky gloom, followed by Kane latched onto her shoulders, with Hendricks and Barowicz holding on similarly behind. The two flight technicians collapsed to the floor, heaving. But Kane, a flap of duct tape still hanging from the side of his face, stood wavering, his hands spread for balance. His streaming eyes, blinking in the clear air, settled on Cook.

"What kind of circle jerk rescue was that? I almost suffocated down there."

"Good to see you too, meathead." Cook felt a warmth flush his cheeks. "You okay?"

Kane scowled and hawked up a mouthful of phlegm, which he turned and spit to the side. "You didn't need the CS gas." He leaned against a bulkhead, wheezing. "Those triad clowns loaded their shorts when you threw in the smoke."

Cook grinned and grabbed his friend, hugging him tightly. "Everyone's a critic."

Kane gripped him back for a few moments, then pushed back, still coughing lightly.

"Ok, ok…good to see you too. Who do we have to thank for this?"

"Our new Mexican friends here. Airlift and smoke cover courtesy of Hallett and Bellamy."

Kane whistled. "No kiddin'. You brought the big leagues." He paused to spit again, regarding his buddy. "You might've enjoyed that a little too much, Guy."

"If you love your job, it isn't really work, right?"

"You get Porter?"

Cook's face darkened. "Negative. We didn't see him."

Kane glowered, glancing at Hendricks and Barowicz still on the floor.

"If we do find him, he's mine."

"Get in line, Mr. Kane." Lopez's voice issued weakly from the bulkhead. "But I don't think he's here any longer."

Cook frowned in agreement. "Yeah, I wouldn't have stuck around either." He looked down at Lopez. "Should we call for an extraction?"

Lopez shook his head. "I do not think that we will be flying out of here. We've been in this ship too long. Your FBI and military are probably waiting for us outside."

Kane stared at Lopez for a moment, then placed him. "He was at the mission brief. Who's your friend, Guy?"

"Kane, Lopez. Lopez, Kane."

"No," Lopez replied. "My name is Gallardo. My friends call me Luis."

He extended his hand. Kane shook it, holding it for a long moment. "Thank you."

Cook reached for the radio still clipped to his belt. He pressed the transmit button. "Angel flight, Alpha party. We got them. Repeat, the hostages are safe."

The radio hashed to life with Bellamy's rasp. "Bring 'em out. We've got a lot of company out here, the friendly kind. We'll see you by the barges. I'm sending the cover birds home."

"Roger that."

* * *

From the helicopter above, Craig watched as both amphibians ceased their revolutions and taxied to a spot south of the barges, cutting their engines back to idle and drifting on the light swells. One of the Coast Guard response boats approached the position, but held off at safe distance to observe, its .50 caliber main gun covering the pair. The Skyraider and the Grumman

TBM made a final formation pass without producing smoke, then broke off for the west, activating their navigation lights like normal air traffic. For a moment, Craig considered calling Derris to see if he could have the Dolphin shadow the departing aircraft, but he was beaten to it by the thunderous sound of the descending Air Guard F-15, which followed at what must have been its slowest pursuit speed.

Well, whatever the hell that was, it looks like it's over, Craig thought. Of all the bizarre and pointless-looking things he'd seen people do in his career, this had to take the cake, just by sheer volume of effort and expense alone.

The radio pinged. "Craig, Lima Two. The pilot of one of the amphibians wants FBI to come up on aviation band 135.95."

The co-pilot up front nodded, turned a radio knob, and then held up four fingers. Craig punched the fourth button on his console.

"This is Special Agent Craig. Who am I speaking to?"

"Let's keep names off the air for now. You recognize my voice, Agent Craig?" Hallett's distinctive tones were clearly identifiable through the flattened VHF transmission.

"Roger. What can I do for you?"

"We've achieved our objective – our people are safe and sound. But your people are going to have a lot of cleanup work on the ground here. And my birds are running low on fuel. What do you say we work this all out back at the home field?"

Craig stared down at the docks as the Huey came in for a landing, swirling what was left of the smoke on that end. He saw figures stumbling, limping, or being carried toward it. As more smoke dissipated, Craig could see there were other bodies that they just left lying there.

Clean up was right. This was going to be a messy one.

He wanted to get in there right now, but logistically speaking, there was no room to put the helicopter down anywhere. And it would take at least twenty minutes before he could find somewhere to land, get on a boat, and motor out to the scene. With that amount of time, a person with bad intentions could mess with a lot of critical evidence.

He could think of a dozen good reasons to deny the request – loss of forensic data, chain of custody, the importance of maintaining the crime scene. But lengthy experience in national security work and sensitive contingency operations told him this one wasn't going to go by the book, or at least any book he was familiar with. And the head of TVA was making the request, personally. He clearly wasn't going anywhere soon.

Craig pursed his lips. What could he ask for – Hallett's word?

"That's a lot to ask for."

"You've got my word on it."

"Roger that. We'll see you back at the hangar." Craig decided he would make a gesture. Then he'd see what Hallett's word was worth. "We'll be escorting you back."

"Copy. We have wounded. Can you have some medics meet us there?"

Craig smirked. "That's an affirmative."

The whole world was going to be meeting them back at Santa Monica airport.

* * *

"We have instructions to let you board the helicopter, but you're going to have to put all your weapons down here. Understood?"

The Coast Guard MSST petty officer stared at Cook steadily over his M4 assault rifle, the barrel slightly declined to allow Cook to clearly see his eyes though the clear combat goggles. Cook nodded slowly, supporting Kane's arm over his shoulder. The Maritime Enforcement Specialist 1st Class wore dark combat coveralls and helmet, a flotation rig, and a load-bearing vest containing multiple rifle magazines. Cook knew that some of the MSST members trained with the SEAL teams, which meant he would be all business.

Fine with me, Cook reasoned. Hallett had clearly cut a deal with someone, and they were getting a temporary immunity holiday. Cook unslung his Swedish K and, together with the Glock he had stripped from one of the triads and Bellamy's Hi-Power, dropped the guns on the growing pile near the Iroquois.

Behind him, Chuy and one of his surviving team members brought Lopez out in a fireman's carry, looking very pale but still conscious. They brushed past Cook and Kane and deposited Lopez on the Huey's deck. A Coast Guard medic, armored and goggled like his comrade and bearing a medical kit and IV bag, moved forward to render assistance.

More boats docked, and disgorged law enforcement personnel of various stripes, who proceeded to fan out, weapons at the ready, flashlights probing.

Cook sat with Kane on webbed seats next to the portside gunner's pocket while Hendricks and Barowicz made their way aboard. Kane shifted uncomfortably and kept massaging his wrists. Cook watched his friend sympathetically.

"Sorry I got you into this, Ron."

Kane looked at him blankly, then shook his head. "You've got nothing to be sorry for. You didn't do this. It was Porter, all the way through."

"Did he say anything to you?"

Kane coughed and spat. "He came down once, after they brought us to the ship. Didn't say a word – just looked at us like we were a smear of dogshit on his shoe."

"What the hell was this all about?"

Kane grimaced. His wrists were clearly hurting. "Drugs. Had to be. Those Chinese were moving a lot of taped plastic bundles up from the engine room. Place was loaded with them. Goddamned scary Tong racket or something."

"What a waste."

Kane nodded. "What happened while I was out of the action?"

"Oh, nothing much." Cook smiled. "We found out the company nerve-gassed a bunch of Mexican *narcos* and we had to save Hallett from getting shot by Blair. Oh, and I stole a plane."

Kane pursed his mouth. "Glad you signed back on?"

"I did miss the action a bit. But not this much." Cook shook his head absently, staring at the submersion barrels lining the edge of the barge that hadn't yet made it on the trawlers. "Think those are the drugs?"

"Likely." Kane turned. "You ever see him? Porter?"

"Talked on the phone." Cook snorted. "Asked him why. Got nothing. Seems like he thought he could cut a deal with the feds, though. Said he'd tell us where you were."

Kane peered at the medics treating the wound in Gallardo's leg. "You believe him?"

Cook shrugged. "Maybe if he hadn't tried to turn us into barbeque first." He paused to sip a bottle of water that had been brought by someone.

"Think they're going to find him?"

"Negative." Cook snorted again, more derisively, as he scanned the area. "Only the feds could lose someone on a bunch of ships."

Some of the triad bodies in the dock area still seemed to be alive, as various agents combing the area called out. Cook watched with a detached curiosity, not really caring whether they made it or not. Presumably one of those sprawled figures was in charge of this whole thing. Or maybe these were just the low-level stooges who were unlucky enough to grab the short stick.

As the airshow smoke dissipated, one of the Coast Guard MSSTs found Blair, who had evidently regained consciousness and wormed his way behind a forklift. Cook and Kane impassively watched as the officer sat him up and ripped the duct tape off his mouth, eliciting a hacking cough which dislodged a chunk of congealed blood from his red-stained teeth.

Kane leaned over. "Is that Blair?"

"Yep. Hold on a second." Cook hopped down from his perch on the helicopter and shuffled over to the officer, who regarded him warily. "You're going to want to give that one special handling. He's a spook, and his fingerprints are all over this thing." The MSST nodded acknowledgement. Cook scowled at Blair. "And don't listen to a goddamned word he says."

Admonition delivered, Cook trudged back to the Huey and dumped himself next to Kane. They shared a moment of congenial silence.

"What happened with that DEA gal?" Kane asked wearily. "You get to have any fun with her?"

"Yeah," Cook smirked, "Real treat. Almost shot me a couple times. What were Porter's phony feds like?"

Kane nodded. "Good. I didn't know anything was up until they put hoods on us."

Both men sat quietly for a moment, peaceful in the knowledge that their part was over. Kane broke the silence.

"You think we still got jobs?"

* * *

CHAPTER TWENTY

As Cook had anticipated, the cover-up was as massive as it was predictable, awkward both for those promoting it, as well as the press and public expected to digest it. He was neither invited to participate, nor was his input requested by the federal authorities. He didn't have a problem with that. He really just wanted to be left alone.

Upon the Transvector flight's return to Santa Monica airport, they found a veritable sea of law enforcement and emergency vehicles from every agency imaginable, all running strobes and blaring their radio calls on PA systems. Lopez – Gallardo, Cook corrected himself – was whisked away on an ambulance with what was left of his team, both preceded and followed by FBI agents and LAPD motor units. Cook imagined that Gallardo and his agents were in for some lengthy interrogation sessions, but he figured they'd probably come out okay considering their country was basically attacked by the U.S.

Getting an officer attached to this was the big time, the real red carpet. Any group that could find an excuse to participate, no matter how peripheral the jurisdiction, tried to get a foot in the door: FAA, Cal Forestry, MARAD, the district attorney's office, etc. To their credit, the FBI built a ring of fire around the whole affair, creating a protective cordon against the most enthusiastic interlopers.

Homeland Security fought hard to get a major role, but they were politely told to fuck off. The Palm Springs abduction incident was still too fresh, and nobody thought they'd overly distinguished themselves with their harbor response. Had Gallardo's diversions been real attacks on the Port of Los Angeles' oil infrastructure, the American west would have been low on gasoline for weeks. DHS reached up the ladder in Washington for some help, but desperation makes a foul-smelling cologne, and their benefactors received the polite brushoff. They were told they'd get a seat in the peanut gallery and receive a copy of the findings, just like the rest of the unwashed. The CIA barely fared better, but since TVA was their delinquent stepchild, they had to be shown some minimal courtesy.

With Veidt at his side, Hallett got down to the crucial business of negotiating with the Justice Department and the FBI. The CIA was invited for their input and advice, but treated like a virtual co-conspirator. The facts on the ground did not stand in their favor. The main actors, Porter and Blair, seemed to be working directly for the Agency, and most of their denials were condemned as outright lies or manifest displays of institutional incompetence. The spray mission in Mexico alone had resulted in over eight hundred deaths, not to mention the extensive forest fire damage that occurred as a collateral effect of the drug traffickers' anti-aircraft response. Compared to that, the narrative of a covert and aggressive attack on a friendly sovereign nation's territory was considered hardly worth mentioning, except in terms of the size of financial reparations.

At the request of the US government, Canadian authorities were rolling up every known triad organization in British Columbia on even the flimsiest of pretexts. Institutional self-examination was the order of the day. Their country's role in refined opium distribution and money laundering for criminal organizations on the U.S. west coast forced some introspection at the highest levels of the Canadian intelligence hierarchy.

What did trend in Transvector's favor was that the real story was far too combustible for public consumption, especially the part about how a shadowy, foreign criminal consortium managed to hijack a domestic intelligence contractor. TVA was a valued provider of discreet, but necessary services that the federal government often required. Such a revelation would bring down the entire company, and nobody was looking forward to trying to rebuild that capability from scratch.

The intelligence community and Justice ended up forging a compromise that no one liked. The whole debacle was divided into two discrete tranches, neither to be related to each other by verbal testimony or written record. The massive body count of the spray mission was attributed to an abnormally toxic experimental herbicide that had accidently ended up in TVA's tanks. DEA and USDA issued a joint statement expressing regret that their miscalculation had cost lives. The U.S. president offered a publicly heartfelt apology to his Mexican counterpart, which made for suitably dramatic television viewing.

For the second piece, the TVA aircraft crashes and subsequent wildfires were deemed by the FAA and NTSB to be the result of a malfunction in a new kind of navigation system that Transvector was testing for the government. The public service and human cost was tallied up and further regrets were issued. As opposed to the international implications of the herbicide spray scandal, this tranche fell more into the category of corporate liability, and gargantuan civil penalties were proposed.

Televised congressional hearings were a given, with the usual contingent of white-haired, ex-hippy leftists angrily venting outrage, complete with shaking fingers, flushed faces and trembling, spittle-flecked self-righteousness. Happy to have what they considered yet another example of America's heavy-handed, imperialist oppression of traditionally subjugated peoples, the liberals enlisted their mainstream journalistic fellow-travelers into a monthlong media circus.

If later polls were any indicator, the general public couldn't have cared less. The majority of those following the story were secretly thrilled that hundreds of extremely violent drug pushers had been gassed and suffocated to death. And then maybe burned. It was the kind of ironic, karma-laden street justice that brings smiles to the faces of sensible folk.

Cook learned most of this from his extensive debriefing with Craig, who seemed only too happy to share sensitive details, if for no other reason than to have someone other than himself know the whole story, which was likely to be deeply buried in some archive. It took place at Transvector headquarters rather than the federal building, in a nod to the still deeply sensitive nature of the information should anything leak. As Cook lead Craig through the entire sequence of events, he got the impression that the FBI man was impressed by his actions, that he might have done similar things in the same situation.

Cook knew that some heads would have to roll, and Hallett offered himself up as the first casualty, mainly to save his company. He sat through all the congressional hearings, his demeanor one of abject apology, his long, lined visage expressing deep regret for what had been done in his company's name. His legislative and government allies managed to help him avoid jail time, but he had to officially step down from running his own corporation. Hallett resigned at a press conference, and became an *ex officio* outside consultant to TVA's board, which Cook guessed really meant that he was still actually running everything.

By equitably apportioning the blame and giving each of the involved parties their respective fifteen minutes in the barrel, out of public view, the matter ran its course. DHS finally got to participate in the coverup, but likely not in any way they anticipated. The ship assault in San Pedro Bay was depicted as a joint film-shoot and exigent Homeland Security training exercise developed to assess port security readiness in the LA area. The assessment, published later online, was unduly mild over perceived lapses in performance. The oil tank-farm fires were described as harmless blazes, some of which exceeded their carefully defined boundaries due to unexpected wind gusts. Cook avidly watched every painful moment of public coverage, wickedly enjoying seeing various intelligence community officials jinking-and-juking through tortuous explanations that left their politician and media questioners nonplussed.

The Chinese were never mentioned, except as overseas owners of the decommissioned MARAD ships. The massive seizure of metric tons of heroin, methamphetamine, and sundry other narcotics was never publicized, much to the chagrin of a DEA ever eager for large drug-bust propaganda. They quickly tamped down their enthusiasm when the FBI later reminded them that this entire stockpile had been assembled undetected under their watch, and that they had ignored all of Romero's calls to investigate.

Gallardo Aparza was left out of the media proffer entirely, his name only occurring a few times in closed congressional intelligence committee testimony as a Mexican government liaison. The scale and capabilities of the CNI's Los Angeles area intelligence network were probably something of a shock to both the CIA and FBI, the exposure of which undoubtedly cost Gallardo some credit back home. But Cook was happy that he'd made it, along with Chuy and a couple others. They had done quickly what the feds would have taken weeks to accomplish, if ever, and were ruthlessly efficient in their dispatch of the opposition. They had also spared the U.S. a boatload of embarrassing gang, narcotics and espionage trials. As far as Cook was concerned, they all deserved medals. Of course, they would never get any.

One part missing from the entire post-incident equation was what to do with Cook himself.

* * *

EPILOGUE

Something caught Cook's attention on the horizon, briefly flashing white below an almost painfully cerulean-blue sky before disappearing.

Cook idly scanned the sea through his dark, polarized sunglasses, but he couldn't find it again. No matter. Probably a Bermuda-rigged cutter or ketch beating to windward, the change in heading causing the sails to occasionally vanish from view. He had seen a few of them at a distance, but one had never come near.

Cook shifted his legs to a more comfortable brace on the forward strut that ran from the Catalina's fuselage to the underside of the wing, and adjusted the position of his rod. No bites yet, and it had been a while. Might have to switch to a different bait if we're going to get something by lunch, he reflected.

From his perch under the Catalina PBY's main wing, Cook gazed upon the tiny, palm-covered cay that served as the flying boat's anchorage. A grey inflatable was pulled up on the pristine white beach, with footprints leading up to an umbrella shading a slim figure on top of a yellow beach towel. Cook's eyes lingered on the long, tanned body, and he smiled. Stokes seemed to be adapting to her new situation pretty well.

For Cook, Stokes was the best thing to come out of the whole affair, and, as unaccustomed as he was in his life to extended good fortune in relationships, there had been no shortage of accruing benefits. He grinned. Frequently repeated and ongoing accruing benefits. A sudden tug at his rod almost caused him to drop it in the water. He looked down. Something had hit his bait, but changed its mind.

After things had hushed down somewhat, it seemed like, in equal parts, everyone wanted to both reward Cook and have him quietly disappear. He had accepted the former willingly, and rejected the latter, conditionally.

When asked by Transvector's counsel what his plans were, he realized the extent of his leverage. He knew things that could never get out, and that was worth something. He had told Veidt he wanted to keep flying, preferably for TVA. Veidt's expression had telegraphed skepticism. Management had collectively frowned.

He couldn't fly again for the company's transport arm; that was clearly out of the question. Cook's temporary experience as a wanted federal suspect and the concomitant public exposure had precluded all that. And as a result of the whole Mexican operation, TVA's clandestine arm was being restructured to allow greater intelligence community oversight. Its operational headquarters was being rebranded and moved to northern Virginia, so the Beltway boys could keep a closer eye on them. There really wasn't a place for a pilot with a face that had been featured on the FBI's

Most Wanted website in such a publicity-sensitive organization. Cook tried, even pushed a bit, but they were adamant.

He went with his next best proposition.

Bellamy was retiring. He considered the ship action as a suitable climax to a long, event-filled service, and was pulling up stakes to move to a quiet airpark in New Mexico with Hallett's somber blessing. The Santa Monica corporate complex was being refitted as a hardened data center, with the museum closing its facility and the collection going to a repurposed hangar at the Mojave spaceport.

They would need someone to look after the warbird collection there, and Cook lobbied to go with it. The intensity of Veidt's swift approval was only exceeded by his obvious relief, and he had happily signed off on it. But Cook needed some vacation first. And one of the aircraft. And he needed some company.

Stokes was still a wildcard in the whole affair. Her pending charges of impersonating a federal officer and working for a Mexican drug-trafficking organization had been dropped, swept cleanly from the table. In exchange for her free and far-ranging testimony in front of a joint FBI-CIA-DEA task force, she had been given total immunity from prosecution, as well as a new identity. Gallardo had assured her that there would be no further contact or reprisals from his people, but that he couldn't guarantee the same from her former trafficking pals, and she should probably avoid spending time in Southern California for a while.

Stokes had been utterly free to go anywhere, and Cook didn't have any kind of claim on her. But she had shown up one day during the move at Santa Monica, and he had suggested a little out-of-town R & R. He had tried not to look too pleased when she accepted. With a few extra fuel bladders on board, the Catalina's range made a lot of places accessible for a visit, and the South Pacific seemed nice this time of year. The no-name coral cay was somewhere between the Marquesas and Kiribati. They had been eating off stored food from the plane's lockers and fishing for the last week.

* * *

Savoring the cool, humid shade under the wing, the air boat's wing pylon making a comfortably warm backrest, Cook gazed ardently over Stokes' recumbent bikinied body and pondered the last two undefined variables of the equation.

There had been no visible reaction by the Shang Gu Bang or any of the other known triad organizations in the event's aftermath. The Chinese ship-breaking subsidiary that claimed ownership of the hulks had simply waited for the cessation of the investigation, and then moved them overseas. Since relations with the Chinese government were not strong in the current political climate, it seemed like no one wanted to break the civility with crassly worded accusations. Cook had initially expected some kind of reprisal, but since he was only peripherally related to the exposure and seizure of the Shang Gu's massive drug hoard, no one seemed all that interested in him. They were probably spending the bulk of their capital trying to find Porter.

In some fashion, and nobody quite knew how, Porter had slipped the net and disappeared. A Long Beach Harbor Patrol vessel had been found drifting near Newport Beach, and the corpses of two harbor officers had drifted into Long Beach's Pier J, both shot in the back. The usual all-points-bulletin had been put out immediately and updated regularly in the following weeks, but if they had caught up with Porter, Cook hadn't heard about it.

As he reclined in his state of content repose, Cook assessed his feelings toward his old boss. Porter had broken every oath and vow he had ever made and had tried to have Cook killed on multiple occasions. By all rights, he should hate the man's guts. But somehow Cook only felt a sort of melancholy loss, the kind that overtakes you when your best buddy sleeps with your girlfriend or never returns the money you loaned him. Porter had been a surrogate father to Cook, a figure of outsized proportions in his prime, and the man's actions had forever tarnished him and scarred everyone he worked with. If Cook ever saw him again, he would probably kill him on sight. But still, he couldn't quite absent himself from the feeling that he'd lost a family member somehow.

Cook blinked away the train of thought as he saw some movement under the umbrella on the spit of powdery strand. For the last week since they began their voyage, Stokes' appetites had operated like clockwork: swimming before breakfast, tanning on the beach, drinks at sunset, dinner sitting on the plane, and intense lovemaking at night, waves slapping against the fuselage in counterpoint. He shifted the fishing rod in his hand as he replayed the previous evening's session and exhaled slowly. Last night, dropping caution in a spell of post-coital lassitude, she had told him her real name was Valerie, and that she felt safe with him. He grinned through his week-long's growth of stubble. He decided he would always call her Stokes, regardless of what her new papers said. TVA had given him no restrictions on the length of the vacation time – hell, he didn't really even have a contract yet. They could conceivably keep this thing going for a while.

Cook watched as Stokes stood and stretched, her languorous curves provoking a reaction in Cook's groin. Damn, he thought. I better get some food on the hook soon, or it's another freeze-dried dinner for tonight. Valerie, Riggs, Stokes…whoever she was had smiled naughtily the other night and made it clear that mai-tais with fresh sashimi made her particularly passionate.

Time to get busy on that. At least there was plenty of rum.

THE END

•

Made in the USA
Las Vegas, NV
25 March 2021

20200660R00268